SYDNEY HUNT

CURSEBREAKER

Chronicles of The Deep Book 1

1

CURSEBREAKER

WELCOME TO BANNON

I am so delighted to share Gwenna's story with you!

Before reading, I want to take a moment and acknowledge that this is a Young Adult fantasy. Cursebreaker contains themes of violence and minimal swearing. Infant death is mentioned in passing at the very end of Chapter Twenty-Nine.

To anyone who has ever felt less than beautiful.

To C, S, and S,
You are magic.
Never lose sight of that.

PRONUNCIATION GUIDE

Gwenna - Gwehn-uh (rhymes with henna)

Bannon - Buh-nohn

Catriona - Cat-ree-oh-nuh

Orlaith - Or-la

Domhnall - Doe-nall (rhymes with tonal)

Marrock - Mar-rock

Joanya - Joan-yah

Irrywellium - Ear-ee-well-ee-um

Maeve - May-vuh

Reiluisa - Ray-loo-see-uh

Liatira - Lee-uh-tier-uh

Treasa - Trees-uh

Curran - Cur-uhn

PART I

CHAPTER I

THE NIGHT BEFORE

The King was on his deathbed. So, naturally, Princess Gwenna planned a royal ball.

It was absolutely her idea, but no one outside the family could ever know. No, for everything to go according to plan, Gwenna needed to uphold her mousy, bookish, and altogether wallflower-like reputation.

The ballroom at Thornvale Keep was circular, with a grand domed ceiling and thick marble pillars bearing the balcony's weight. Torches blazed in their brackets along the wall, and the glass-paneled doors were thrown open at the far end of the room to invite in a springtime breeze and better display the sweeping views of the canopy of Braewood Forest. The musicians were seated along the balustrade, letting their symphonies echo off the dome and rain down on the heads of the guests waltzing below. The gilded ceiling naturally drew attention, causing the true decadence of the room, in Gwenna's opinion, to lay largely unnoticed.

Commissioned by her grandfather, King Domhnall, tiles of every shade of blue, turquoise, and purple were inlaid on the marble floor. Together, they created a magnificent mosaic showcasing a misty waterfall cascading into a darkened moonlit lake. It was the princess' favorite piece of art in the Keep, but no one else seemed to care for it as she did. Everyone else was too busy dancing and gossiping.

But tonight, Gwenna counted on the oblivious nature of the nobility. Her entire plan hinged on it.

Movement from the corner of her eye sent Gwenna scurrying back behind a marble column and out of sight. Duke Byrne prowled closer. His flabby hands rested comfortably against his paunch. Those calculating eyes took in the high-arched windows with the navy drapes. He paused in his circuit of the room, staring at the velvet curtains for just a moment too long, most likely planning how he would redecorate. He chuckled, the loose skin of his neck wobbling, before helping himself to another goblet of wine from a passing tray. He downed the goblet and continued his strut towards the glass-paneled doors thrown open to the terrace beyond.

Gwenna remained out of view as he passed, and she smiled at his retreat. The more the council members drank and celebrated their new regime, the more fun it would be to see the look on their faces when their coup ended before it began.

If everything went according to plan, the history books would have no reason to mention the name of Gwenna Lorne. The schemings and plottings would be just as invisible as she. They'd just see two young, attractive nobles in love. Everyone wanted a good love story. Especially one on a public stage. That's what the Lorne family would give them.

They just needed the Kaldonna family to arrive on time.

Restless, Gwenna felt like an oversized, ruffled cuckoo clock. It took conscious effort to resist poking out from behind the column to check the gilded double doors on the other side of the room again. She had spent every ball, and most banquets, behind this column. It was her favorite spot in the room- present but out of the way and largely unnoticed by guests and her mother and grandfather sitting on their thrones on the other side.

But tonight, the column felt too small. Or perhaps Gwenna was too broad. The new trends with layers and layers of petticoats did nothing to compliment her already larger-than-average frame. Royal sewers had worked tirelessly to try and find a fashionable way to conceal how large she was. Gauzy pale blue sleeves came to her forearms to hide her thick arms, and the lace-trimmed neckline of her gown was considerably high. Her dark blue dress was studded with tiny diamonds and was loose, flowing, and forgiving over her stomach, hips, and thighs.

It wasn't until pain pricked her finger that she realized she was biting her nails. Again. A blood sphere swelled on her thumbnail, and she clasped her hands behind her back to stop fidgeting.

A trio of council members stood beneath a sconce a few feet away, loudly reminiscing on the parties of their youth. Each was stooped and balding now, but they had been quite the womanizers in their day. They had a complete and utter lack of respect for women, as they were actively plotting to remove the Lorne family from power when King Domhnall passed. So it should have come as no surprise that they had engaged in all forms of debauchery, mistreating and humiliating many young ladies of their day.

Unfortunately, these men had the most money in the kingdom and, therefore, the most power.

Listening to these old lechers laugh so openly about their conquests would have roiled her stomach if she hadn't already been nauseous. These men did not deserve more power, nor did they deserve to sit on the throne the ancestors had built, and her grandfather had preserved.

Gwenna's neck twinged with the beginnings of a tension headache. Food would help, but the stew from lunch threatened to make a reappearance. She had purposefully positioned herself as far away from the banquet table as she could to avoid the smell of the roast. Still, it left her within direct sight of the dessert table.

The torches blazing in their brackets along the walls caused the candied fruits to sparkle like jewels. Her eyes flicked across the circular ballroom to her favorite indulgence, a soft sponge piled high with strawberries and cream. Despite her upset stomach, the delicacy called to her. It sat atop a gilded platter, untouched by the guests but taunting her nonetheless. The courtiers would let the food go to waste. They nibbled at tiny pieces but wouldn't eat more than a few bites throughout the evening. No one had even pretended to be interested in the cake, which felt inherently criminal. The fruit platter was the only dish that looked like somebody had touched it.

She pushed her shoulders down from where they kept creeping up near her ears.

The song ended. Gwenna sidestepped around the column, looking for her elder sister over the heads of the dancers. Catriona had danced six waltzes in a row, so now she would excuse herself. Each dance had been with a different man; Cat certainly couldn't afford to be seen favoring someone.

Gwenna spotted her sister on the north end of the dance floor as she demurely curtsied and giggled at something her latest partner said. She was too far away for Gwenna to read her lips, but right on schedule, she turned her back on the dancing to visit with the guests along the side of the room.

Catriona was the very image of what a princess, and heir to the throne, should be. Her bodice was pure white with a sweetheart neckline and off-the-shoulder gauzy sleeves. The full skirts bled into deeper shades of blue until the hem of her long train appeared black as midnight. Her golden hair had been braided elegantly atop her head and adorned with glittering blue sapphires, the largest of which was shaped like a teardrop and hung low on her forehead.

The eldest princess was animated as she greeted guests. She graciously worked the crowd, pausing to spend a few extra moments with Lord Whyte. He appeared the picture of innocence tonight as he smiled widely. Cat signaled a servant to bring Lord Whyte another goblet of wine, appearing very interested in whatever he said. No one but Gwenna noticed that Cat's smile didn't reach her eyes.

An olive-skinned man in a burnt orange waistcoat stumbled from the dance floor, almost crashing into Gwenna.

"Are you all right?" she asked, quickly moving out of the way.

He appeared in his early twenties, hardly older than Cat, but clearly too foolhardy to handle his wine. Gwenna instantly recognized him at once as a visiting nephew of one of the earls but didn't know his name. She made a quick mental note to find out. He steadied himself with a laugh, looking up to see who spoke.

They locked eyes, and instantly, his face shifted to a lip-curling sneer of disgust as he recognized her. He pressed his nose to the inside of his wrist, where a woman may have dabbed perfume, and inhaled deeply.

"Cursed One," he muttered darkly before darting back into the crowd.

It was the fifth time tonight someone had prayed for protection from her, and usually, that was her limit at court events. But tonight, Gwenna couldn't escape back to her chambers and the books stashed beneath her bed. She moved further into the shadows behind the column, out of sight of the dance floor. That guest wouldn't get the satisfaction of pointing out the cursed princess to his friends.

She released her exhale slowly, feeling the heat slowly leave her cheeks.

Gwenna's curse was going to lose the family the crown if Catriona didn't get engaged tonight.

It should have been her mother, High Princess Orlaith, next in line for the throne, not Catriona. But the law decreed that no unwed woman be allowed to rule. Orlaith refused to remarry after ruby fever had claimed her husband. Gwenna had been a surprise; the last gift Prince Curran had left, Orlaith always said. He died nine months before Gwenna was born.

The council members campaigned for Duke Byrne to take the throne, claiming that the Lorne family was unworthy to rule once the

King died. It was nothing new. They were not the first royal family to face a coup when their patriarch died, and they would not be the last. A family with no men at the helm was not fit to lead a kingdom. It was disgustingly archaic, but that was the way of the world.

And so, Gwenna hatched her plot to get her beautiful sister engaged to be married *before* the King died. A public proposal, in full sight of the court, and no one would dare question Catriona's right to be queen. They just needed the groom, Lord Tristan Kaldonna, to arrive and get down on one knee before the night ended. The council claimed that the Lornes were unfit to continue ruling because they were unmarried. Well, Gwenna could solve that problem.

The actual problem, the one the council wisely didn't want to voice too loudly, was that they were afraid of Gwenna getting too close to the throne. As it stood, she stood third in the line of succession. But that was much too close for someone cursed like her.

Getting Catriona and Tristan married would not break Gwenna's curse. But it did get one step closer for Cat to provide heirs, all of whom would have a stronger claim to the throne than Gwenna. She couldn't break her curse or change how she looked, but she could prove to the council that she had no interest in ever ruling.

But Catriona, the Beauty of Bannon, made up for what Gwenna lacked. Cat was always gracious, never self-centered or cruel. True, she could be a little naive and always insisted on seeing the best in people. But she had a kind heart, which Gwenna felt truly grateful for. There was no rivalry between the sisters and never had been.

Gwenna was the harmony to Catriona's melody: they were always better together.

But tonight, they were two solo acts.

Gwenna glanced at the double doors leading to the entrance hall once again. A familiar weight settled on her chest. She silently prayed to The Deep, begging for any sign of the Kaldonnas or a handsome man to show up and save her.

Them. Gwenna corrected herself with a slight shake.

Save them, plural—the Lorne family as a whole.

With a sigh, she permitted herself to abandon her post for a moment in the name of a slice of cake with strawberries and cream. She needed sugary reinforcements if the secret guest of honor took any longer.

As she approached the door to the servant's entrance, it opened just a crack. A young man wearing the red livery of the Kaldonnas casually slid inside the ballroom.

Gwenna gasped so loudly she startled two men passing by arm in arm. They jumped in surprise, nearly knocking over an elderly countess.

It was a servant who worked for the Kaldonna family. They had arrived.

Gwenna couldn't hold back her smile as she turned expectantly to face the double doors. The current waltz finished with a flourish, and she waited for the herald to signal the conductor to halt the next song. It had taken longer than anticipated, but things were finally falling into place.

One moment of suspended silence hung over the guests.

The viola in the balcony took up the opening notes to a reel. Several younger courtiers cheered, excited by a faster-paced song, and the dancing continued.

Mind reeling, Gwenna glanced up to the balcony. The conductor was facing her direction, crooked teeth poking through his wide grin. He had excellent eyesight and had no excuse for missing the signal to stop the music.

Milton, the royal herald, stood at attention at the doors. Age had begun to stoop his shoulders, but he refused High Princess Orlaith's gentle hints at retirement. If there were a guest who needed to be announced, he would not hesitate.

Where was Lord Tristan?

Swallowing roughly, Gwenna did a double take and glanced at the servant wearing red one more time. His tunic had the Kaldonna flame embroidered over his heart, meaning he personally attended to the young lord.

Over half the men in this room would kill for the opportunity to marry Cat, even if she didn't come with a crown. All Tristan had to do was show up, and they would basically hand him the throne. Was it too much to ask that he also be prompt?

Several decidedly un-proper phrases ran through Gwenna's mind as she gnawed on her fingernails, trying not to outright stare at the servant boy. Just because Tristan was the oldest son didn't guarantee he was the sharpest sword in the armory.

The Kaldonnas oversaw the southernmost tip of the kingdom, cut off from the rest of the domain by one of the largest fjords. Small and relatively powerless, they didn't have much of a foothold in court. They weren't a big name politically but weren't aligned with the Byrnes or the rest of the council.

Orlaith was very good friends with Lady Sorcha Kaldonnna. Both women were widowed at a young age, so Orlaith began taking her girls to visit a few times a year. The families were close friends, and the mother had whispered for years about getting Sorcha's boys to marry Orlaith's girls.

When it became necessary to arrange a marriage, the Kaldonna family was the clear option. But Tristan Kaldonna did not have enough reputation for sending someone to propose in his place. He couldn't possibly think he could send a servant to propose to a princess. Even Tristan wasn't that stupid.

Gwenna quirked an eyebrow at the thought, doubting it the moment she thought it. If anyone was that stupid, it was definitely Tristan.

Tristan was friendly enough as children, but Cat and Gwenna quickly learned they didn't want him on their team in any game. Not if they wanted to win. He was kind, charming, and always able to make anyone laugh. But if there was any kind of strategy needed, Tristan was useless.

"And he's our best choice for King…." Gwenna grumbled under her breath, glancing towards the dancing at the center of the ballroom to catch her sister's eye.

Maybe Cat would know what to do. If nothing else, she needed to be warned that her future husband had sent someone else to get down on one knee in his place. That wasn't something Gwenna wanted her sister blindsided by.

But trying to catch Cat's eye was hopeless. She wasn't due to check in again for another thirty minutes, so her attention remained entirely on the dance, precisely as Gwenna had instructed. It was just as well. Catriona's patience could grate on Gwenna's nerves like nothing else sometimes. She'd probably have something insufferably kind to say. Perhaps Lord Tristan simply needed to relieve himself after such a long journey.

Gwenna had half a mind to check every last chamberpot in the Keep. She'd drag him to his proposal by his ear if necessary. Too much time and effort had gone into setting this plan in motion. One idiot's bowels were not going to get in the way.

Miraculously, the guests hadn't noticed the Kaldonna servant. To the members of the nobility, one servant was, sadly, interchangeable with the next. But regardless of how many drained wine casks there were, someone was bound to notice the violent red of the man's tunic at some point when all of the Thornvale staff wore sky blue. If Duke Byrne or the other members of the council saw the man before Tristan arrived, it could spoil the element of surprise and ruin everything.

Gwenna poked around the column to see where the Duke had gone. He still stood out on the terrace overlooking Braewood Forest,

regaling a group of young ladies with some story he no doubt found
fascinating.

Gwenna bit down hard on her thumbnail as she considered her
choices. Unfortunately, there weren't many. She needed answers, but
her mother sat on her throne on the other side of the room, and Cat
was occupying the guests. They immediately attracted an entourage
wherever they went; they couldn't confront the Kaldonna servant for
answers without drawing attention. Gwenna wasn't exactly invisible,
but people naturally paid less attention to her. Years of melting into
the background had paid off for her.

But now, she would have to be the one to step forward and
make things happen rather than wait for her sister to do it. The thought
of stepping out from behind her beautiful, sturdy column made her
legs shaky. Not for the first time, she wished a Mage would appear to
give her a Weaving of Invisibility. She exhaled slowly and tried to rein
in her racing pulse, allowing for one tentative peek to ensure the coast
was mostly clear. Everyone nearby faced the center of the ballroom
floor, their backs to her. No one looked at her.

Chin held high, she stepped out of the shadows and kept
moving. She kept a very restrained pace, with one foot in front of the
other. She could only imagine the rumors swirling if someone saw her
scurrying like a rat from one shadow to another.

The Kaldonna man stood only a few feet away, but he may as
well have been on the other side of the Keep. His bronzed skin
gleamed beneath the torchlight as she approached. The loose-fitting
tunic gave the impression that he was drowning in his livery. A
cracked leather belt cinched the too-large scarlet tunic around his
narrow waist. He wore a flat cap with a feather sticking out of one
side. Its floppy nature made the sides droop down over his ears. There
was something oddly whimsical about it, vintage and out of place in
this room full of the high-fashioned elite. He was handsome but not
intimidating, with a crooked grin as he took in the ballroom.

"Has Lord Kaldonna arrived?" Gwenna whispered, voice hoarse from hours of disuse, drawing up alongside the servant.

He flinched at her sudden appearance but pivoted to face her and dropped into a deep bow.

As he straightened, Gwenna sucked in her stomach out of habit and willed herself to appear smaller, all too conscious that she was twice as wide as him. She waited for the shock of recognition and a glimmer of fear or hatred to coat his features.

But it never did.

He stared, but not out of disgust. Silence stretched between them for a moment too long, and panic clawed at her throat. She should never have approached him.

"Your Highness, I am Kellen, Lord Kaldonna's steward, and valet." He dropped his gaze from the small tiara on her head and smiled softly. "Lord Kaldonna will arrive shortly. He apologized and sent me ahead to notify you of our arrival. He should only be another moment or so."

The heavy sigh was completely undignified, but Gwenna couldn't help it. All the stress rushed out of her body. It was miraculous she remained upright instead of ending up in an emotional puddle on the marble floor.

Tristan had made it after all.

The servant, Kellen, grinned a little wider, seeing her noticeable relief. She drew herself up to full regal height. This was a moment for a leader. She could play the part, at least for a moment.

"Thank you. Welcome to Thornvale Keep. Please, enjoy the celebration," she said regally, bobbing a polite curtsy before turning away quickly.

She had only gotten a few steps away from the steward when she stopped abruptly. This was her chance to retreat to her chambers. She had done what she set out to do, and now it was time to retire for the evening. But a small voice inside her head fought against the idea. Why shouldn't she witness everything finally coming together?

Gwenna realized with a sudden start that, for the first time, she didn't want to retreat. She wanted to stand her ground.

Excitement fizzed through her veins like bubbles in champagne as she glanced towards the gilded doors again. Gwenna always felt a little extra giddy anytime the Kaldonna brothers were around.

Aidan Kaldonna, the younger brother, was one of her closest friends. However, she couldn't let anyone, least of all him, know that. She didn't know how he would describe their relationship, but she didn't want to find out. It was better never to ask and stay content with the small kindnesses he showed. That was what endeared him to her: his kindness. He didn't run away, laughing and making jokes at her expense. Instead, he sat down across the chessboard and taught her the game.

That became their tradition, chess. Aidan would talk, and she would listen. Over the years, he started listening more as he became more interested in what Gwenna knew about different girls at court. But he never asked about Catriona. In fact, he rarely spent any time with her. Their relationship sounded like a friendship to her. But he was so popular and well-liked, she knew he'd never admit it. Sorcha began visiting the capital for whole summers when the boys were teenagers. Aidan loved all the balls and parties. But a friendship with Gwenna wouldn't endear him to the other girls at court. It didn't bother her, though. She loved any chance to see him.

Gwenna reflected on the letters received from the Kaldonnas as they had planned this proposal. None had ever specifically said Tristan was the *only* son coming. Butterflies erupted in her stomach at the thought that perhaps it wouldn't just be Tristan walking through the door. Maybe she and Aidan could celebrate the engagement with a chess game after the guests left.

"Did both Kaldonna brothers make the journey?" Gwenna asked delicately, moving back to stand by the steward. She restrained herself from glancing in the steward's direction as though it was a mere passing whim unworthy of her full attention, the epitome of casualness.

Out of the corner of her eye, she watched him stiffen. His eyes widened at the question, and he almost looked like he searched for the right words. Now he had her full attention.

"His brother was... He had to remain at the family home. I assure you, my lord will explain everything," Kellen said awkwardly.

The herald blew his trumpet in fanfare before she had a chance to ask for further clarification. Hopefully, Aidan was alright.

The crowd turned in unison to the double doors, gloved hands obscuring faces as they speculated on who would have the audacity to arrive so late to a royal ball. Unable to keep the triumphant smile off her face any longer, Gwenna surged forward, with the Kaldonna's steward matching her step for step. She rose on tiptoes to look over the sea of heads in the opposite direction, towards the terrace.

Where was Duke Byrne? She wanted to see the look on his smug face when he realized he'd lost.

"Presenting, his grace, Lord Aidan of House Kaldonna!"

CHAPTER 2

G wenna almost laughed out loud. Still scanning the crowd for any sign of the Duke, she waited for the herald to correct himself and announce the correct Kaldonna brother.

But the heavy double doors opened. No correction was offered.

A chill washed over Gwenna that had nothing to do with the sudden stream of fresh air pouring in from the entrance hall. All thoughts of Duke Byrne disappeared as she slowly swiveled toward the guest of honor.

The only boy she had ever loved, Aidan Kaldonna, strode confidently through the court.

It had been over three years since she had last seen him. He was nearly nineteen years old, no longer a child at all. Gone was the playful charm of the boy Gwenna had known. Aidan was a confident young lord of a small but thriving province.

The image she had held in her heart all this time was woefully inadequate for who he was now. His finger-length jet-black hair contrasted nicely with his olive complexion. A strong jaw offset by lips that appeared impossibly soft. He wore a well-fitted scarlet tunic over a billowy white shirt, a belt encircling his trim waist, and a scabbard hanging near his hip. He had tucked his tailored dark pants into shiny black boots.

Those boots clicked across the tiles as he approached the dais, like the foreboding rat-a-tat-tat of drums at the gallows. Gwenna felt a noose tightening around her neck with each step he took. Her heartbeat thundered in her ears, and her mouth was dry.

Aidan was the younger brother. If both Kaldonna brothers had arrived, court procedure was to announce the eldest first.

She couldn't breathe, but for the first time in over a decade, it had nothing to do with how impossibly handsome he was. He wasn't supposed to be here, not like this.

This was not her plan.

"Wh-where is Tristan?" She jerked her head towards the steward. "Where is the elder Lord Kaldonna?"

The valet blinked, shaking his head slowly as though he didn't understand. "It's only Lord Aidan...."

She was moving through the crowd before she realized it. Guests grumbled as she stepped before them, but etiquette was the last thing on her mind. She needed to pull Cat aside to reassess. Nothing had to happen tonight. They had time to adjust and adapt.

Aidan dropped to his knees before the dais as Gwenna pushed to the front of the crowd. The picture of humility, he bowed low to pay respect to King Domhnall, who looked like a shell of his former self. With dark veins visible through paper-thin skin, Gwenna's grandfather looked positively dwarfed by his ornate gold throne.

The formal introductions hardly reached her ears as Gwenna scanned the crowd desperately to find Cat. It wouldn't be very polite, but if Gwenna moved quickly enough, perhaps she could pull Catriona aside before anyone noticed.

"Rise, my boy." The King's warbly voice was not nearly powerful enough to echo off the domed ceiling. However, his breathy words still captivated his audience.

Gwenna finally spotted Catriona less than ten feet away. But there may as well have been an ocean between them. There was no way to get to her through the crowd.

"King Domhnall, I apologize for my late arrival." Aidan's familiar timbre made Gwenna immediately turn to face him, heart oddly fluttery. "On behalf of the House of Kaldonna, we thank you for your kind invitation. My brother apologizes for his absence but feels he could not leave his new bride at this time."

Tristan was already married.

Gwenna's knees felt dangerously weak, and she swallowed roughly. There was nothing more for her to do, no way to scramble to save anything. She already knew how this would end.

There was only one reason Aidan would spend three weeks at sea to come all this way, and it wasn't to personally deliver the message that his brother had already been married.

Gwenna wanted to scream in frustration. No one wanted her grandfather's legacy to continue more than she did. If Aidan didn't propose to Catriona, her family would lose everything.

But if he did propose, Gwenna would lose one of the only hopes she had ever kept for herself. She would have to stand aside and watch the life she wanted play out before her eyes. Cat could have any man in the five kingdoms except for Aidan.

"We wish your brother every happiness." Gwenna's mother smiled. There was no crack in her veneer, nothing to indicate she had ever referred to Tristan as her future son-in-law in the privacy of their family chambers. She remained a perfect lady—a perfect queen.

"Thank you, High Princess Orlaith." Aidan inclined his head respectfully.

"Lord Aidan, you remember my eldest granddaughter, Catriona?" The King waved a liver-spotted hand in Cat's direction.

A smile of pure joy spread across Aidan's chiseled features as he saw Catriona. Gwenna's heart twisted in on itself.

Maybe it wasn't joy. Maybe Aidan was being polite, playing a part in a grand charade.

Every boy or young man who had spoken with Gwenna always turned the conversation around to Cat. They wanted to know her interests, habits, and any other useful information that would gain them favor with her. But not Aidan.

He had never once asked about Cat. She was intended for Tristan, and both families knew it, which left Gwenna entirely available to fall in love with Aidan Kaldonna with no fear of ever betraying Cat.

She had planted that seed deep in her heart, tending to it and watering it with the greatest care. It was a fragile thing and very embarrassing. More like a wish than a crush. It wouldn't come true if she spoke about it to anyone, even Cat, it wouldn't come true. It was something that needed to be nurtured in private. That's how it was with true love: something sacred, personal, and stronger than anything else. Why else would so many of her favorite books be written about it?

"You remember my second-born granddaughter, Princess Gwenna?"

The sound of her name just about knocked the breath from her lungs and reminded her where she was.

Gwenna dropped into a curtsy, head bowed before anyone saw the shock on her face.

True love. The idea of it sent a new hope blossoming in her chest. If Aidan only looked into her eyes, he would see the truth. He would see her. Aidan would know, and he would recognize that he felt the same. Then he could stop pretending to be thrilled to marry Cat and finally admit that Gwenna made him happy. Together, with the power of their true love, they could find a way to make everything else right.

Every storybook romance hiding under her bed flashed through Gwenna's mind. All of those 'happily ever afters.' All of those joyous weddings and true love kisses. Catriona never cared for reading or put any stock in those tales, even when they were little girls. But Gwenna did.

She was being ridiculous. It was silly and childish. But this was all she had to cling to: the hope that some magic was left in the world.

If true love held any power, surely this would be the time for it to manifest itself.

Aidan's strong hand appeared before her. She took it lightly as she rose from her curtsy, conscious not to crush his fingers. Gwenna took a steadying breath and looked deep into his emerald eyes, letting everything she felt swim to the surface for him to see.

His gorgeous eyes widened as he caught sight of her face. His nostrils flared like he smelled something repulsive, and his lip twitched into a smirk. He dropped her hand quickly as if burned.

"Ah, yes," he said shortly. "Of course."

"It's a pleasure–" she began.

Aidan pressed his wrist to his nose, inhaling deeply as he locked eyes with her. He maintained eye contact for a beat, praying for protection from her.

From the Cursed Princess.

Then, acting as though he was merely scratching his nose, Aidan turned away from her and back to the dais as though nothing had happened.

Any greeting Gwenna had shriveled in her throat. Her face flamed as she stared at the strong lines of his back. She fell back a few steps, a rushing sound in her ears. The crowd of courtiers instantly surged forward to fill the space, desperate to be closer to the moment's drama.

"King Domhnall, I have traveled many weeks to be present tonight because I have a question for your eldest granddaughter." Aidan's voice was the epitome of confidence, completely unaware that he and his stupid brother had ruined everything.

Gasps swept through the crowd. Apparently, some guests didn't understand why the Kaldonnas had arrived with so much fanfare. In another life, with Tristan here instead of Aidan, Gwenna would have laughed. But not tonight.

There was no humor in this ballroom tonight.

She kept moving through the crowd until she bumped against one of the marble columns. It wasn't her favorite one, but it would do. Leaning against the column for stability, the world pitched dangerously beneath her feet. Tears pricked her eyes, and she wiped them away with the back of her hand before anyone could see. She wished she could dissolve into nothingness on the spot.

Whether it was an act or not, Aidan would never look at her the way he looked at Cat. He would never feel for Gwenna what she felt for him. The weight of that truth ground itself into Gwenna's bones.

Aidan was on one knee, holding both of Cat's delicate hands in one of his.

Gwenna's balled hands curled into fists, nails stabbing into her palms. The physical pain grounded her.

"Princess Catriona Lorne of Bannon, would you do me the unparalleled honor of becoming my wife?" Aidan asked.

Gwenna rolled up on her tiptoes, ready for Cat to look to her for approval. Catriona would only accept after checking in with her sister. This was Gwenna's plan, after all. Cat was just executing it.

"I would love nothing more, Lord Aidan." The joy in Cat's voice was unmistakable. "Yes- yes, of course!"

The room erupted in cheers. Thunderous applause echoed off the high ceiling, solidifying the court's approval.

Something within Gwenna shattered.

Maybe Cat was also playing a part. Perhaps both she and Aidan were fantastic actors. Or perhaps Gwenna had drastically miscalculated.

Maybe she wasn't the only one harboring secret feelings.

"A waltz! For my bride!" Aidan cried, springing to his feet again.

The music swelled as he led the beautiful princess to the center of the room for a dance. Their portraits would fit beautifully in any storybook: two attractive people in love. Duke Byrne would never gain traction to try for the throne now. In an instant, the entire court was enamored with them and their love story.

"They make such a handsome couple," Countess Parcell remarked to her wife as they hobbled past Gwenna's hiding spot and headed for a servant holding a tray of wine goblets.

Gwenna wrapped her arms around herself tightly, sure that the strength of her arms was the only thing binding the pieces of herself together. The Parcell women paused outside the servants' entrance, grabbing their goblets of wine from a maid. As soon as they moved, Gwenna would make her exit; she was in no mood to deal with either of the busybodies tonight.

Instead, she moved further around the pillar, out of their sight but close enough to escape at the first opportunity.

"You, boy, must be with the happy groom. Welcome to Thornvale. Have a drink with us!" the other Lady Parcell announced, seizing the arm of Aidan's steward as he walked by. The two middle-aged women were hopelessly in love with one another. Still, they always enjoyed finding a young man or two to flirt with at these events.

"I'm Kellen, steward to Lord Aidan." He smiled hesitantly but didn't refuse the goblet of wine.

"What do you think of your master's new bride?" Countess Parcell waggled her eyebrows wickedly, winking at him over the rim of her cup. A short and squat woman, she barely came up to Kellen's chin.

"Is it true the Fairies Blessed her with Beauty?" he asked in a low whisper.

"Of course! It's a Bannon tradition- all the royal women receive a Blessing of Beauty when they're born," the Countess replied loudly.

Lady Parcell looked down her hooked nose and leaned over her wife to grab Kellen's arm. "The King tried to get the same Blessing when the other princess was born. But the Fairy said no. And none of those Fairies have been seen since. Something's wrong with that girl; mark my words. She's cursed. You'd do well to keep your distance from her."

Jaw clenched, Gwenna watched Countess Parcell take her lady's arm, and the two waddled away. The steward stood before the servant's entrance, but she couldn't find the energy to care.

He straightened as he saw Gwenna step out of the shadows of the pillar, realizing she'd overheard everything. She averted her gaze and brushed past him without a word, heading for her chambers before the tears could fall.

For the first time in her life, Gwenna truly felt cursed.

CHAPTER 3

THE MORNING OF

Sharp staccato footsteps in the stairwell shattered the silence of the cistern. Gwenna kept focused on the book in her hands, refusing to give her mother the satisfaction of interrupting her.

Deep below Thornvale Keep, the shadows of the royal cisterns were the best place for a moment alone. A series of interconnected stone arches wove together to create a maze of crisscrossing beams throughout the fading frescoed ceiling. Thick stone support beams plunged into the depths of the water reserves. Cavernous, a singular skylight in the middle of the room let in one column of light. Particles of dust shone like glitter in the morning light.

Gwenna sat on a circular pedestal directly below the skylight, a stone peninsula stretching out from the base of the spiral staircase where once servants drew water for the castle. Now they enjoyed the convenience of pipes and spigots, leaving the cistern abandoned. It still held the Keep's water reserves, but no one ever went down there anymore. Some of the newer staff members didn't even know it existed.

With her navy skirts fanned out around her and a stack of books in the wicker basket beside her, Gwenna intended to spend the day right there. Still puffy-eyed after a sleepless night, she was in no mood to deal with anyone.

High Princess Orlaith waited in the arched doorway, hands clasped behind her. She wore a high-necked purple gown and dark hair swept up in a neat chignon.

"I've already eaten," Gwenna announced, not looking up from her reading. "Aldessa will bring me a tray for the afternoon meal."

With any luck, her mother would take that as a sufficient answer and go back the way she came. But if the events of the past twelve hours had proven anything, Gwenna had no luck.

Orlaith waited, unruffled by her daughter's curt greeting.

But even her mother's silent presence was too much. There was a serenity and peace to this place that Gwenna craved. It was her private cathedral, and somehow the presence of another person spoiled it.

"If I ask what you want, will you tell me and then go away?" Gwenna grumbled, admitting defeat and looking up to give her mother her full attention.

"Your sister has invited you to go riding," Orlaith spoke softly, full of patience.

"Oh? I thought she would be too busy today." It was an effort to keep the bitterness out of Gwenna's voice.

She had laid awake all night, torturing herself with every possibility and rehearsing every potential encounter with Aidan so that her heart scabbed over by daybreak. It hadn't worked; everything still felt so raw and tender. It was all she could do to pray that her emotional calluses formed quickly.

"Catriona wanted to show Aidan the lake," Orlaith continued.

Gwenna winced. Hours of work were ripped away just at the sound of his name. She felt that familiar wound begin to ache again, but she didn't know how to staunch this before she bled out. For now, avoidance was her only solution.

She glanced up towards her mother to see if she suspected anything, but Orlaith's face was expressionless. If she suspected what was happening with her youngest daughter, she did nothing to vocalize it.

"They are a new couple, not yet married. They need a chaperone," her mother continued, not unkindly, as she began to approach cautiously.

"Send one of the maids."

"She asked for you."

Of course, she did. Gwenna grimaced.

Malicious, that was the word for it. It felt so incredibly malicious for Cat to do this to her.

Gwenna massaged her temples, reminding herself there was no mean bone in her beautiful sister's body, even if sometimes it didn't feel that way. Everything Cat did was rooted in good, albeit occasionally naive, intentions. Cat wasn't inviting her along to rub Gwenna's nose in her joy or to flaunt that she had what Gwenna wanted. This was Cat's attempt at being a good sister and friend to ensure Gwenna didn't feel left out or forgotten. Cat was kind-hearted like that.

"Tell her I'm unavailable," Gwenna mumbled.

"It will be good for you to get out of the Keep. You've worked so hard the last few weeks, and last night was an obvious success." Reaching down, Orlaith gently closed her daughter's book. "Go get some sun."

Gwenna tipped her head back, eyes closed, and arms outstretched above her head as she gestured to the cool air billowing through the skylight directly overhead—a silent argument for why she didn't need to go anywhere to get sun.

Lady Orlaith brought a hand down on Gwenna's shoulder, deftly plucking the book off her lap. "Enjoy yourself this afternoon. You can come back to your books later. Once Cat is crowned, she'll have more responsibilities. Take this time together while you can."

"I can't."

"Give me one good reason why not," Orlaith challenged.

Gwenna opened her mouth to defend herself smartly and slowly closed it again. Part of her preparations last night had been to rehearse every possible variation of this exact conversation.

There was no way to say anything about her feelings for Aidan now. It was too late. The only thing worse than no one knowing of her feelings for Aidan was if everyone knew. If Catriona knew and still went through with the wedding… Gwenna didn't think she could survive that. And after Aidan's reaction to her last night, she'd go to the grave instead of letting him find out how she felt.

No, it was easiest for Gwenna to silently move on, and that's what she intended. Her first plan was to hide from Aidan and Catriona for as long as possible. That had worked for precisely ninety minutes, and now here was her mother, wanting to know why she couldn't spend time with the happy couple.

"I… I guess I don't have a reason…." Gwenna said weakly.

"Excellent. You'll meet them at the stables." Her mother grinned triumphantly, grabbing the basket of extra books before Gwenna could change her mind.

The sky was overcast with thick, puffy clouds as Gwenna stepped outside for the first time in days. But they weren't dark enough to be storm clouds, sadly. Rain wouldn't save her from her fate. She pulled her cloak around herself more tightly, a nip in the spring morning air.

An expansive cobblestoned courtyard separated the large stone castle from the outbuildings where some staff lived, the dogs were kenneled, and the blacksmiths worked. The royal stables were nestled at the base of the western wall, directly across from the entrance hall to the Keep.

Gwenna paused at the base of the steps, breathing in the pine-scented air. The tall mountain peaks were barely visible over the castle walls. Built at the top of a rocky outcropping, Thornvale Keep loomed high over the wide fjord. The surrounding slopes were far too steep for any wagon team to cross. This left Thornvale nestled in a very private valley at the spot where the fjord met the open sea. A town had sprouted up by the harbor; otherwise, it was quite a remote spot. The Keep was built on an outcropping, only connected to the rest of the mainland by a white stone bridge.

Standing in the courtyard and staring at nothing but the wide expanse of sky overhead felt humbling. Gwenna had been born at the height of the world. This was her home. She glanced towards the southern turret, not surprised to find the curtains drawn over the scalloped windows. A silent prayer to The Deep was all she could offer her grandfather today. He wasn't allowing visitors this morning, saying he needed to recover from the excitement of last night.

Last night. Catriona and Aidan. She could forget about them for a few blissful moments, but there was no escaping this new reality.

Spine straight, Gwenna steadied herself and marched across the courtyard with purpose, her cloak fanning out behind her.

In the moments it took for her eyes to adjust to the darkness of the stables, Gwenna could hear Cat's voice. It sounded like Catriona was observing the horses in their stalls around the corner from the entrance. Gwenna hurried towards the sound of her sister's voice and was about to round the corner to join them when she heard her name. She flattened herself against the wall, listening closely.

"— I felt a little nervous about riding, but by the time I worked up the nerve to try, Gwenna had been riding for over a week. She really is wonderful on horseback. You should see how she can shoot while riding!" Cat's voice burst with pride.

Warmth spread through Gwenna's chest. She grinned at Cat's kind words but leaned in closer to hear what Aidan would say in response.

It shouldn't matter. Gwenna knew that. But she still held her breath, waiting to see if he was impressed.

"She shoots?"

It took a moment for her to recognize the male voice as the steward, Kellen. Gwenna hadn't anticipated him joining the ride. She wasn't looking forward to an afternoon with him after the pitying looks he had given her last night. But he at least sounded impressed about her archery.

"Oh yes! She's an excellent shot on foot, but she's not half bad when she's riding either," Cat said warmly. "But, if we go out riding, you'll be hard-pressed to beat her. It's like she and her mount are of the same mind."

"Not to mention the same face." Aidan chuckled.

Gwenna flinched like someone had slapped her. Whatever warmth she had felt instantly went cold. Around the corner, the trio went silent and allowed Aidan's words to hang in the air.

Kellen cleared his throat. "The weather is colder in Bannon than I anticipated, Princess. Is that common—?"

"Tell me I'm wrong!" Aidan's voice rose as he got defensive. "I'm sure she's very talented for a woman. But there's not a chance she could beat me. She certainly could never ride any Kaldonna stallions. They're susceptible, and she would just unsettle them."

"Because she's a woman?" Cat asked, a warning tone in her voice.

"No, no, nothing like that. But, well, The Deep has marked her, hasn't it? Our stallions can sense unnatural things like that...." Aidan hesitated momentarily, but when no one else spoke, he continued. "But really, I dare you. Tell me I'm wrong and that the girl isn't a tad bit... well, *horse-faced.* I can't quite put my finger on it, but it might be something about her teeth."

Aidan trailed off, laughing to himself.

Gwenna clapped a hand over her mouth and her teeth. She tried to guard her heart against the words, but she could already feel the roots of a new insecurity burrowing down inside her. For a moment, she thought she would cry. But she pressed the heels of her hands into her eyes and forbade herself from shedding one more tear over the boy.

Aidan was an ass.

He had been kind to Gwenna for years, never showing this side of him. The only thing that had changed was his chance to win over and marry Cat. But she couldn't follow his logic. Trying to distance himself from Gwenna, she could understand. But why would he say such cruel things about her *to* Cat? He knew their dynamic; the sisters were best friends. Cat would never tolerate it from anyone, especially not from the man she was supposed to marry.

Gwenna leaned in closer, more than ready to hear her fiercely protective older sister put Aidan in his place. Today would be fun, after all.

There was a moment's hesitation as Cat considered what Aidan had said.

Then Catriona giggled, laughing louder and harder as the amusement swelled within her.

Face burning, Gwenna turned away. With Kellen in attendance, there was a chaperone for the happy couple. She didn't need to endure this any longer.

"Good morning, Princess Gwenna!" a voice called from behind. Gwenna turned to see a young stablehand holding the reins of her dappled mare in his outstretched hand. "Your sister told me to prepare your mount!"

"Oh, that won't be neces–" Gwenna said quickly, trying to wave him away before the others found her.

"Gwenna!" Cat's voice sounded a bit more shrill than usual. Her face was flushed, words tumbling out of her mouth in a panic. "Oh, my, you look wonderful. Is that a new gown?"

Gwenna glanced down at the simple blue gown that had been hanging in her wardrobe for years. Cat wore a pink one cut in the same style.

"You were there when I got it," Gwenna said coolly, silently daring her sister to meet her gaze. Cat refused, looking anywhere else, guilt written all over her face. "Thank you for the invitation, but I must decline. You enjoy your ride."

She started to turn away when Aidan stepped forward.

He looked less formal than he had at the ball, dressed in a simple white tunic with a scarlet doublet and dusty gray trousers.

"What a pity. I looked forward to beating you in a race," he said, a familiar spark in his eye. He shrugged casually. "But if you're not up for it, I understand."

It was subtle, but the challenge in his voice was unmistakable. Gwenna immediately hated him for it. Through years of chess matches, she had taught him how to challenge her and get under her skin. She was too competitive for her own good, and he knew it.

How could he, in less than a minute, go from insulting her behind her back to trying to coax her into playing along with his stupid games?

She narrowed her eyes at him, trying to ignore the look of complete innocence he gave in response. Gwenna allowed herself to imagine how good it would feel to slap him across the face and tell him exactly what she thought of him.

But that may tip her hand too far. She certainly didn't want to be seen showing Aidan too much attention so that everyone knew how she felt. But she also couldn't be a blushing fool constantly hiding from him. That could be equally as telling. And for some infuriating reason, anger with a boy was often misinterpreted as flirting. Running away might cause too much suspicion, but so would giving him a tongue-lashing.

"If we race, you won't win," Gwenna hissed through gritted teeth.

"We'll see." Aidan flashed his perfect smile.

The urge to slap him intensified as he smirked, confident in his ability to charm and manipulate her. If both retreat and violence weren't an option, perhaps humiliating him in front of Cat would have to be enough.

"You'll come with us?" Cat cried, and Gwenna nodded wearily. Cat cheered and threw her arms around her sister, which Gwenna immediately shrugged away from.

"Our horses should be ready by this point. I'll go get them, sir," Kellen murmured.

He was dressed similarly to Aidan, with the white tunic and dusty gray trousers. His doublet was a dark maroon with the sigil of House Kaldonna over his heart. Kellen tipped his floppy, feathered cap in Gwenna's direction before hurrying away.

Already regretting her decision to stay, Gwenna took the reins from the stablehand. "Can you please bring me my bow and a quiver of arrows from the armory?"

She led the mare into the courtyard, silently chastising herself for allowing Aidan so much power over her and her emotions.

"Your sister was telling us what a remarkable rider you are," Aidan said casually, following behind her.

"How kind of her," Gwenna said, hoisting herself into the saddle and trying to give him as little attention as possible

"I can't help but notice you aren't riding sidesaddle," Aidan called as he mounted a large black stallion.

"You have excellent eyesight," Gwenna said dryly.

"Catriona is riding sidesaddle."

"Once again, I commend your eyesight."

"It makes me curious about your customs here in the capital." Aidan continued, ignoring her glib tone as he checked the sword at his waist. "Is it common for a woman—especially a woman of high birth —to ride like a man?"

Gwenna looked up to see him smirking at her. "I may be many things, your lordship. But common is not one of them."

Cat, carefully perched sidesaddle, moved her mare forward and purposefully positioned herself between Aidan and her sister.

"Aidan and I have discussed riding down to Braewood Mists," Catriona said, head held high as she tried to diplomatically diffuse the tension. "We've packed a picnic, and we'll be able to spend the whole afternoon together at the lake."

"How wonderful," Gwenna muttered, rubbing the mare's neck.

Aidan's eyes narrowed at her tone as his steward rode up on a dusty mare. "Kellen, will you accompany Princess Catriona? I would like to see Princess Gwenna's horsemanship for myself."

Gwenna shook her head, chuckling wryly. "This is a mistake. You don't know the way. You'll be at a disadvantage."

"Your sister told me of the route. I'm sure I'll be able to manage." He smirked again. "I don't want to intimidate you, Princess. But if we are to be family, I would like to see how you can handle a horse."

"Then I would be honored," Gwenna responded sweetly, not breaking eye contact. "Cat, dear, will you count us off?"

"This might not be a good idea. Why spoil the day with competition?" Cat said, her voice a little more high-pitched than usual.

"Who said anything about spoiling the day? This is just good fun between friends!" Aidan's tone was jovial, but his eye had a competitive spark.

"Absolutely." Gwenna let her voice drip with all the feminine honey she could muster.

"Well..." Cat wavered.

"Please, Catriona?" Aidan turned to her, flashing his dazzling smile. Cat's cheeks flushed even more, and Gwenna couldn't stop rolling her eyes.

It seemed neither sister was immune to that smile.

CHAPTER 4

I t was an honor and a privilege to humble the future king. For a moment, Gwenna considered holding back and allowing Aidan to pull ahead as they raced out of the courtyard.

But he already lagged behind when she turned west onto the dirt-packed road leading into Braewood Forest. He had plenty in his life to boost his ego. She refused to hold back or diminish herself so a man would feel better about himself.

Half a league into the race, Gwenna glanced over her shoulder to see that Aidan had fallen back to ride at a leisurely trot beside Catriona. Apparently, he quit when things got complicated. Not a great look for the future king.

She rolled her eyes, refusing to dwell on how disappointing her choice in boys had been, and spurred her mare on. Arriving at the lake well before the others, Gwenna felt grateful for the solitude and secured her mare to a nearby tree so she could graze.

Braewood Mist Lake lived up to its name today, a low fog clinging to the tops of the tall trees. The lake was an oblong shape, much too wide to be able to swim across. Thick tree trunks butted right up to the waterside to the north and south, but the eastern shore where she now stood had a vast expanse of gravelly beach.

No amount of fog could dilute the green expanse of Braewood Forest. She had learned so much about color theory from trying to recreate the forest on canvas. But she could never do justice to capture the many hues and shades of life present in Braewood. There were at least a hundred lichen-covered trees, each with its own nuance and detail regarding color variation.

Gwenna, with her paint, could never create as many shades of green that The Deep so naturally breathed into life in Braewood. It felt almost sacrilegious to try.

Charcoal, on the other hand, was appropriate for her mortal hands. Black and white were two stark contrasts offering a million subtle shading variations. That was where she excelled.

Years of sketching both her face and Catriona's had provided natural lessons on symmetry. Beauty was all symmetry.

As much as the court liked to pretend Gwenna was hideous and vile, she wasn't disfigured or misformed. If she had been born into any other family, no one would even spare a second glance at her. But Bannon royal women were supposed to be perfect.

She was just average, when the standard was perfection.

Her eyes were perpetually a little bug-eyed, with the right a little higher than the other, yet her left eyelid seemed to droop more. Her nose was a bit too wide and flat for her face. She had the same round face as her mother and sister, but she looked doughier while they appeared delicate, smooth, and curved. Gwenna had broad shoulders, thick arms, wide-set hips, and a stomach that never was flat. Her cheeks were always an angry splotchy red regardless of what she ate. She had the same black curls as Mother, but hers refused to be tamed or softened into a graceful updo.

Plain, perhaps, but still feminine. Gwenna loved to sketch, embroider and could play the harp well enough. Those things came far more naturally to her than they did to Cat. She was an excellent dancer and light on her feet but had never been asked to dance. Even without heeled shoes, Gwenna would have been as tall or taller than her dance partners.

Archery was one arena where she felt particularly grateful for the Strength of her arms. Even if they weren't beautiful, they were useful.

About a year ago, some of the new recruits to her grandfather's guards had hung five archery targets from different tree branches over the water. She and Cat jumped from those same branches into the water as children, giggling furiously. Now, she nocked her arrow and carefully took aim before firing.

She missed the first target completely.

Cursing under her breath, she immediately restrung and shot again, hitting both the first and second targets slightly off center. Her next two shots came even closer to perfect, but it was the fifth and farthest target where she finally got a bullseye.

Any one of those would have been a deadly shot.

With a small smile of satisfaction, Gwenna relaxed her bow arm and breathed in the crisp air of the morning. Eventually, she'd have to shimmy up each tree to retrieve the arrows, but that could wait until Aidan had seen her marksmanship. She'd already humbled him in riding. It'd be pure joy to do it with archery as well.

The deep gray water reflected the overcast sky but was still as glass. Absently, Gwenna ran her hand over her thick braid hanging over one shoulder. A chill breeze rustled the leaves on the nearby trees, and Gwenna was grateful for the heavy fabrics of her gown. It wasn't the most fashionable, but it kept the early spring chill out.

She nearly jumped out of her skin as a voice spoke directly behind her.

"Well-shot." A man's voice, but far too low a tone to be Aidan.

Gwenna whirled around, restringing her bow and aiming it perfectly at the head of the intruder.

"Who are you?" she demanded. Adrenaline coursed through her veins, but her shooting arm was steady, the arrow pointed directly between his eyes. Anyone sneaking up on a young woman alone was a threat until proven otherwise.

It was a young man, a few years older than her by the look of him, but his voice was deceptively deep. His white blonde hair fell in waves past his shoulders, but the scruff along his jawline and bushy eyebrows were black as pitch. He wore a faded blue shirt, tight brown breeches just above his ankles, and no shoes. Keeping her arrow trained on him, Gwenna realized that he was at least two heads taller than she. He was abnormally tall for this area, though he was too pale to be from the southern kingdom. His eyes were the same cold gray as the lake, and instantly she wished she hadn't noticed. It would make it so much harder to kill him now that she knew what color his eyes were.

"I didn't mean to startle you." He raised his hands in surrender.

"That wasn't my question." She didn't lower the bow an inch, staring him down unblinkingly.

"You're not a bad shot." He nodded toward the targets behind her, but she didn't take her eyes off him.

Something about him made her stomach twist into knots. The lake at her back, he stood between her and her horse. She was fast, but with his long legs and her heavy skirts, she knew she wouldn't be fast enough to outrun him.

"You're about to find out how good a shot I am if you don't tell me who you are and what you're doing here," Gwenna hissed.

"I'm from the village," he said simply.

"Liar."

Thornvale, the town outside the Keep, was a decent-sized harbor town. While she didn't know every resident by name, she was certain she had never seen him. And the nearest village was a three-day ride in the opposite direction.

An insect landed on his face, and he flinched back, shooing it away. His long hair moved, revealing two pointed ears.

43

The hair on the back of her neck stood up. Story after story swirled through Gwenna's mind about creatures of the night with their pointed ears. None ended well for the humans that faced them. There was no clue as to what he was, whether a Mage, Shifter or something far darker. But he certainly wasn't human.

"*What* are you?" Gwenna breathed, refusing to let her hands tremble now.

"How is your grandfather fairing?" He grinned, hands still raised high. "Your King?"

She tightened her grip on the bow. The stranger knew she was royal.

"He's your King too."

"Oh no, he hasn't been my king. Not for many years now...." He chuckled darkly.

"If he's not your king, you have no claim to these woods. Be gone from here!" she cried, more bravely than she felt. "I will not ask you again."

"If you're here for a day at the lake, he must still be alive." His eyes sparkled with something she couldn't identify. "Not for long, I would imagine..."

"Hey! Get away from her!" A voice bellowed across the foggy grounds, catching them by surprise.

The stranger whipped around, turning his back on her, and they both stared. Aidan charged towards them on his stallion, sword raised high as he broke through the treeline.

"Get out of here!" Aidan yelled again.

The stranger stumbled backward past Gwenna and into the shallow water to put distance between himself and the horse, conspicuously using her as a human shield.

Gwenna realized she was aiming her bow at Aidan now and quickly lowered it.

Suddenly, she was yanked backward by her braid. She stumbled, feet scrambling to find purchase over the gravel as she was dragged back into the lake, cold water soaking the hem of her gown. The stranger knocked the bow out of her hands, breaking the strap on her quiver and throwing that away as well.

Gwenna still had one arrow in her hand, which she immediately buried in the folds of her skirt.

Aidan leaped from his horse, stumbling to a halt at the water's edge, sword still drawn.

One thick forearm wrapped around Gwenna's waist, pulling her against the stranger's broad chest as he dragged her further back into the lake. "Don't move, or the maid dies."

"You know I'm the princess," Gwenna said softly, the lie coming to her instantly. "I have a column of men that will be arriving any moment. Leave while you still can."

"The last two in your party just arrived," he said, hot breath hitting her ear. "Don't lie to me."

Kellen and Catriona rode out of the tree line, horses trotting leisurely. The princess was laughing at something the steward said when she glanced in Gwenna's direction.

Catriona's eyes widened. *"You."*

Gwenna read the word clearly on her sister's lips, even hundreds of feet away. A chill ran down Gwenna's spine at the look of undeniable recognition in Cat's eyes as she stared at the pale stranger.

Kellen leaped off his horse and raced to Aidan's side, hand reaching for the hilt of his sword. He tried maneuvering himself before the man he served, but Aidan shouldered him away.

"Let the Princess go. You and I can handle this without the women present," Aidan said confidently as he bounced slightly on the balls of his feet. He almost looked excited.

"*Two* princesses…" the stranger mused. "What an interesting development…"

Gwenna glanced at Cat, and her stomach churned.

"I said *let her go,*" Aidan called again.

Gwenna spoke softly, just loud enough for the stranger holding her hostage to hear. "Get out of here before you make a mistake and do something you regret."

"Who says I'm making a mistake?" There was a smug tone in his voice now.

"You're either making a mistake or a complete fool," she snapped. "I gave you the benefit of the doubt."

"I won't tell you again!" Aidan yelled, oblivious to the fact that his threats were going unnoticed.

"Trust me, Princess." The bandit tightened his grip around her waist, yanking her closer. Gwenna's head slammed against his collarbone, and she could feel the muscles in his arm pinning her in place. "I'm no fool."

"Neither am I."

Gwenna plunged the arrow she was holding into the fleshy part of his thigh.

He screamed in pain and dropped the dagger, shoving Gwenna into the shallow water. She went under, head slamming against a rock hidden beneath the surface.

Pain radiated through her body. The water wasn't deep, but she couldn't get her legs under her, trapped in the layers of petticoats and skirts. Hands grabbed at her, yanking her to her feet.

Gwenna gasped for air. Someone was yelling. Splashing as though running through water.

"You're ok." Kellen dragged her out of the water and onto the rocky beach before twisting back around to the action. "Aidan!"

"Stay with the girls!" Aidan yelled. "I'll handle this!"

Aidan charged through the shallow water after the stranger. They were both running for the far treeline. The stranger was tall enough that the water didn't hinder him, but he ran with a pronounced limp and favoring the leg with an arrow protruding from it. Aidan quickly gained on him.

Kellen draped his cloak over Gwenna's shoulders before scooping down and picking up her bow that had floated to the beach. He mumbled something about the girls returning to the Keep, absently reaching up for the brim of his hat and pulling it down farther on his head. The steward took a few steps in Aidan's direction, knuckles whitening as he watched Aidan close in on the stranger.

Cat appeared beside Gwenna, clinging to her arm. She tried to pull Gwenna back towards the horses. "We need to go, Gwenna. Now."

"Who is that?" Gwenna demanded, rounding on her sister. "Have you seen him before?"

A loud yell from Aidan caused both girls to turn back as Aidan leaped and tackled the pale man to the ground.

The stranger flipped onto his back as he fell and pulled his knees to his chest, kicking Aidan in the stomach and launching him off. Aidan fell, tumbling and rolling a few times before coming to a halt.

Gwenna shrugged off the cloak, rushing forward like she had some idea how to help, but Kelle stuck out an arm to keep her behind him.

Aidan quickly leaped to his feet, sword in hand. The stranger stayed down, completely vulnerable, lying on his back on the rocky beach.

Catriona whimpered. A chill washed over Gwenna that had nothing to do with her soaked gown. She covered her mouth with her hands as Aidan raised his sword overhead. The steward gently touched her shoulder as if to brace her for what came next. She'd never seen a man killed before but wouldn't look away now.

A flash of sudden pure white light blinded her for just a moment.

When the light cleared, the pale stranger was gone. Standing in his place was a giant black wolf, except for a shock of white hair on the top of his head.

Kellen sucked in a gasp, and Cat muttered a prayer under her breath. It took Gwenna a moment to catch up with what her eyes were seeing.

The stranger who had put a knife to her neck was a Shifter.
Her stomach lurched.

"My lord!" Kellen warned, clenching his jaw. "Watch out!"

"Stay out of this! That's an order!" Aidan refused to tear his eyes away from the creature.

To Aidan's credit, he didn't falter. He screamed a battle cry as he swung his sword at the wolf. The beast quickly swerved out of the way and put distance between himself and the blade before suddenly doubling back and swiping at Aidan.

Aidan cried out as the sword was knocked from his hand and fell back a few steps. The sleeve of his green tunic was shredded, three bloody stripes visible across his forearm.

With a chilling growl, the wolf positioned himself between Aidan and the blade lying a few feet away.

Aidan froze, standing defenseless before the Shifter. The creature stared him down, hackles rising.

An arrow drifting in the water caught Gwenna's attention. It was as though it had been sent by The Deep itself. She slowly stooped to pick it up, careful that her movement didn't attract Kellen's attention. She had one chance to catch him off-guard.

To catch all three men off-guard.

She suddenly leaped forward and wrenched her bow out of Kellen's hands. She ran past him, stringing the bow as she went, stumbling as her drenched skirts clung to her legs.

"Gwenna, no!" Kellen chased her, trying to hold her back. "The lord said not to intervene!"

"He's not *my* lord!" she snapped, pulling out of his grasp.

Kellen cursed under his breath but faltered momentarily, allowing her to line up her shot.

She aimed for a few paces east of the beast, far enough away that she knew she wasn't in danger of hitting Aidan or the Shifter. She needed their attention, not their blood.

Gwenna silently prayed to The Deep that neither man would be harmed when she released the arrow. Her aim wasn't perfect, and the arrow landed a bit further north than expected, but it was still close enough to startle Aidan and the Shifter.

Kellen immediately grabbed her wrist to prevent her from interfering further.

Aidan and the Shifter flinched in surprise, swiveling to see Gwenna struggling to fight against Kellen's ironclad grasp.

"Kellen, get her out of here!" Aidan yelled over his shoulder, not wanting to turn his back on the Shifter entirely.

Kellen looped an arm around her waist, lifting her clean off her feet like a small child. Gwenna shrieked loudly as she struggled and fought against him, kicking, thrashing, and making more of a scene than necessary to distract the wolf.

It seemed to be working.

"Leave!" she screamed at the Shifter, staring directly into his gray eyes. "Leave him alone and get out of here!"

Thinking fast, she wrapped her leg around the back of Kellen's, landing a solid kick at the back of his knee. His knee buckled, and they both fell into the water with a loud splash.

Sitting up quickly, she turned, sputtering, to see the Shifter's lips curled back, revealing a smirk across his canine snout.

The wolf *laughed* at her.

The Shifter dipped his head in almost a nod of understanding before turning and running directly into the woods. As he disappeared into the treeline, a broken arrow shaft stuck out of his hind leg. The sight gave her a slight feeling of satisfaction amid everything else.

Once the wolf was out of sight, the fight instantly left Gwenna. She stopped struggling against Kellen, breathing heavily.

"Would you really have shot that… thing?" Kellen asked her quietly, loosening his grasp on her.

"If I needed to," she panted. "It wasn't my first choice."

"Wow."

There was an odd tone to his voice that made Gwenna turn to look up at him.

His dark eyes were so intense, staring at her like he saw her for the first time, that she couldn't look away. She was vaguely aware his hat had gotten knocked off at some point in the chaos, a mop of wet curls clinging to his cheeks. They framed his face nicely.

"Are you hurt?" Kellen asked suddenly. "You're shaking!"

Gwenna shook her head as they both climbed to their feet. She peeled her soaking wet skirts away from her legs as Kellen ducked down and grabbed his hat. He shoved his back over his pointed ears before Gwenna or anyone else on the beach noticed.

When Gwenna glanced up, her attention snagged on his white tunic. It was almost completely transparent, clinging to the muscled outlines of his abdomen.

She quickly averted her gaze, cheeks warming as she remembered what it felt like for him to lift her off her feet. The steward looked slender but certainly not weak. She could see the proof of that for herself. He had actively held her back, and he wasn't even winded.

Watching closely in case she slipped, Kellen followed her out of the shallow water and back up the rocky beach. He took his cloak from Cat's outstretched hands and draped it over Gwenna's shoulders again. She wrapped her arms around herself beneath the cloak, trying to catch her breath.

She couldn't stop trembling. The shock of the situation was setting in. She glanced back towards the woods. A Shifter had threatened her life. She could have been killed. Any of them could have been killed.

"Gwenna, it's over," Kellen ducked his head to catch her gaze. He straightened as she looked up at him, flashing a small smile. "He's gone."

She offered him a weak smile, trying and failing to avert her gaze from his chest. Hopefully, he would assume her cheeks were red from the chill.

"Is the Princess hurt?" Aidan barked, coming up behind Kellen. The steward turned away from Gwenna, ready to answer, but Aidan pushed past him and hurried to Catriona's side.

Gwenna cleared her throat. "I'm fine."

But she may as well have been invisible.

Aidan's green tunic was damp along the hem and had come untucked from his dark trousers, a bit of gravel clinging to it. But besides his mussed hair, he looked like he did back at the castle this morning. Whereas she and Kellen looked half-drowned.

"Did I not give strict instructions not to intervene?" Aidan asked sharply as he turned to his steward, lips tight with anger.

"You did, sir." Kellen was formal, his voice measured. "I'm sorry, I didn't expect the Princess to–"

"She's a *girl*!" Aidan spat. "If you can't handle a hysterical woman, perhaps I need to rethink your application to the guard."

"You selfish, pompous–" Gwenna hissed, inhaling sharply to fuel her rage.

"Thank The Deep you're safe," Cat murmured against her betrothed's chest, clinging to him tightly and capturing his attention. "I don't know what Gwenna would have done without you. We are forever in your debt!"

Aidan closed his eyes, momentarily stroking Cat's golden hair as he reveled in her praise. The smug look on his face made Gwenna nauseous.

"I was perfectly safe. If Aidan hadn't come in screaming his head off with his sword out, things would have never escalated to that point," Gwenna grumbled, hiking up her wet skirts and stalking away into the tall grass. She wanted to mount up and return to the Keep as soon as possible.

"He would have torn your throat out and had your corpse for his breakfast," Aidan called after her. "You're lucky I showed up when I did."

"Lucky?" she repeated, eyes widening as she rounded on him. "You almost got me killed!"

"Don't be an idiot. Shifters hate all royals. Once they've gotten a taste of royal blood, they're insatiable. I saved your life!" Aidan shot back.

Cat shot her a pleading look, begging Gwenna to stay silent and stop arguing.

"You scared him! He could have been looking for something to eat. But we'll never know now because *you* jumped in sword first!" Gwenna snapped. She clearly remembered the strong arms wrapped around her waist. The Shifter certainly wasn't starving, but Aidan didn't need to know the details. "I wasn't in any danger until you showed up!"

It wasn't a solid stance, considering she had a bow trained on the Shifter when Aidan rode up. But he also hadn't pulled a weapon or threatened her until Aidan interfered.

"All the more reason you should have listened to the men and moved to safety the moment that *thing* was clear." Aidan shook his head with disappointment.

"He would have skinned you alive if it wasn't for me!" Gwenna balled her hands into fists, unable to believe his condescension.

"You missed your shot!"

"I missed on purpose!" she shrieked, voice rising.

"Just because you know the basics of using a bow does not mean that you're any good with one," he said scathingly, wrapping his arm around Cat's waist and allowing her to lead him toward the horses.

"I could say the same about you and your swordsmanship," Gwenna muttered under her breath.

He whipped around to face her, eyebrows raised. "What was that?"

"You were disarmed by an animal. An overgrown dog," she said coolly, crossing her arms. "He had no weapon. A real swordsman would have had a clear advantage."

"Under the circumstances, I really must suggest that we ride back to the Keep," Kellen interjected, casually moving between her and Aidan.

"Yes, I think that's wise," Cat said, coming up behind her betrothed and placing a gentle but meaningful hand on his shoulder. "We can always picnic another time."

"I refuse to listen to a woman's opinion on swordplay." Aidan narrowed his eyes at Gwenna.

"Tell me, my lord: is it my womanhood that disgusts you so?" Gwenna asked lightly. "Or, perhaps, is your fragile ego aching now that this horse-faced woman bested you in riding, shooting, *and* saved your royal hide, all before lunch?"

The color drained from Aidan's face, mouth falling open as he gaped at her. Kellen shifted uncomfortably, face flushing.

"I-I didn't know you were there…" Aidan's eyes searched hers and, for the first time, seemed thoroughly lost for words. "I didn't know you heard…"

"I know," Gwenna said coldly, shoving past them to prepare her horse.

CHAPTER 5

Gwenna hardly paid attention to the trail back to the castle. She was trying to remember everything she'd ever heard about Shifters. Everything she'd ever read came from children's storybooks. The Shifters were always the villain, opposite whole casts of beautiful damsels in distress, magic-wielding Mages, and heroic princes.

Her grandfather loved reading the scary stories to the girls, warning them not to stray into the woods or a big, bad, Shifter would come along to eat them. The girls had laughed and laughed, never for a moment thinking there was any literal danger hiding in the trees. Braewood Forest was their playground. There was nothing ever written about Shifters to make them seem real.

But that man at the lake– the wolf– was all too real. What did it mean that the stories of her childhood now appeared to be coming true?

In the stories, a handsome man always came along to save the beautiful girl from a grisly end at the hands, or claws, of Shifters. After the morning's events, that irony was not lost on Gwenna. But long before the handsome prince saved the day, the Shifter in the stories would always try to befriend the beautiful girl. He wasn't initially violent or scary.

The look in Catriona's eyes when she saw the white-haired man was seared into Gwenna's memory. It wasn't one of fear.

Catriona knew the Shifter.

Gwenna was willing to stake her life on the fact that the wolf had tried to befriend Catriona. The only question was *why*.

"Care for some company?" Kellen's voice broke through Gwenna's bitter musing as he reined his horse alongside hers.

"Certainly." She smiled tightly.

Her insides were twisted into knots, tightening further as she worried about what secrets Catriona might be hiding. But now wasn't the time for that conversation, not if she wanted Cat to be honest. Her sister would never open up with Aidan around. A discussion with Kellen would be a welcome distraction.

Plus, his tunic had started drying, so she wouldn't be *too* distracted.

"They seemed like they needed a moment alone," Kellen explained, eyes sweeping back and forth to inspect the overgrown trees on either side of the muddy trail.

Gwenna glanced over her shoulder. Cat and Aidan rode side-by-side, completely engrossed in conversation with one another. The chaperones, Gwenna and Kellen, were still within eyesight yet far enough ahead to afford the newly engaged couple a measure of perceived privacy.

"That's kind of you," Gwenna said softly, a small smile blooming as she watched her sister.

Had Cat ever laughed that hard with Tristan?

"Marrying the one intended for your sibling can't be easy." Kellen shrugged. "I'm sure there's much they need to discuss."

Gwenna straightened in surprise, heart hammering. Were her feelings for Aidan so obvious? Everything she had done, especially coming on this stupid picnic, had been to avoid this very situation. Her face warmed, trying to find something to say to deflect and deny his statement.

But Kellen continued on before she could say something. "Aidan was caught pretty off-guard when he realized he'd be the one to marry Catriona. I can't imagine feeling so... *replaceable*. Like one brother is interchangeable with the other."

Something inside Gwenna twinged with guilt. She hadn't considered how Aidan must have felt. Catriona was beautiful, so Gwenna had assumed surely he must have been elated. Not to mention he would be next in line for the throne of Bannon. This was a perfect arrangement for him. Wasn't it?

Could that be why he was acting so cruel to her? Aidan was so privileged he had no room to argue or complain. But that didn't mean it was easy for him. Perhaps he couldn't express his true feelings and needed some outlet to blow off steam.

A governess once told her that children behave the worst with the one they care the most about. Gwenna never entirely understood it. But the governess explained that it was something about the child knowing that they were safe.

Maybe that's what Gwenna was for Aidan: someone he could be himself with, even if it was ugly. Perhaps his unkindness was really rooted in a good place. Maybe it indicated something more valuable about their friendship, and she could come to terms with that.

It didn't excuse everything about him. She was still furious about everything he had said at the lake.

"About Lord Tristan's marriage...." Gwenna said carefully, ready to change the subject off of Aidan.

A wry smile twisted across Kellen's freckled face. "It's not really my place to say anything.."

"I completely understand," she said immediately.

"...but let's just say we anticipate his wife to produce an heir before the summer solstice."

Gwenna paused for a moment, trying to calculate the timing. "But... when were they wed?"

"Just before we set sail." Kellen was actively avoiding her eyes, smiling like he was trying to keep from laughing. "Less than a month ago."

A laugh burst out, and she clapped her hand over her mouth, realizing how callous it sounded. But Kellen laughed too.

"Really, this is the best match possible for Tristan. All's well that ended well. His wife is the daughter of some duke. They've been sweet on each other since they were children," he assured her quickly.

Gwenna nodded, processing the information. That could explain why Tristan never seemed merely polite to Cat whenever they visited. His heart was already taken by another.

She snuck another look back at the couple riding behind her.

Had Aidan left someone behind in the South? He had always been popular and knew how to charm the ladies. Firstborn children, like Catriona or Tristan, always had a duty to uphold. They were the pawns of the family, positioned appropriately and used to advance their cause. Second-borns weren't even on the game board. Aidan could have had a whole life planned out for him that was ripped away from him without a moment's notice. Perhaps moving to the capital and proposing was a much bigger sacrifice than anyone suspected.

"I wish them every happiness," Gwenna heard herself say, eyes lingering a moment too long on Aidan.

"May I ask you a question now, your Highness?" Kellen asked.

"Of course," she said, quickly turning around in her saddle. "But please, call me Gwenna."

"Gwenna." He nodded once. "Are Shifters common around here?"

She shook her head. "No, not at all. I didn't think they existed. Why? Are they common in the South?"

"No, I've never seen one, but my Ma used to tell me stories. She claimed all the magic folk, like Shifters and Fairies, drew their power from The Deep in your religion," Kellen said.

"My religion?" Her eyebrows shot up in surprise. "Do you not worship The Deep?"

As soon as the words left her mouth, Gwenna invoked the sign of The Deep by pressing her wrist to her nose. She wanted to avoid even the tiniest hint of offending Her.

Another small smile played at the edge of Kellen's mouth. "Not like you Northerners do. Are you going to condemn me for being a heretic?"

She shook her head quickly. "Not at all."

Faith was a messy thing in the best of times. She'd never met someone with a different faith but knew that not everyone recognized The Deep. The other kingdoms had different names for their deities and different things they held sacred. It was interesting to see what others believed. Still, Gwenna couldn't judge anyone else for believing or not believing. Most days, she wasn't sure where she stood in her faith.

"Are those the Marshora Mountains?" Kellen asked, changing the conversation as he pointed to the tall granite peaks looming overhead.

"They are." Gwenna nodded. "They say The Deep can be found somewhere in those peaks. Nothing has ever been found, though people have searched hundreds of times. But if that's where the faith originated, it would make sense why you in the South wouldn't necessarily claim Her."

An unreadable shadow crossed Kellen's face. "Ma told me about the Marshora. I didn't ever expect to see them for myself. They're... humbling."

Gwenna held her tongue, not wanting to disturb whatever moment this was for Kellen. She didn't dare speak when he intently stared at the granite majesty. All of the peaks were tall, but one in particular reached higher than the others. It was the one the villagers referred to as The Mother. She knew some claimed to have a religious experience just by standing before the Marshora. But they were mountains to her.

"If I may..." Kellen was the one to break the silence this time, and Gwenna eagerly looked over at him. The more he spoke, the less she could dwell on Catriona and mysterious Shifters. "What is the meaning of that gesture you did just now? I reason it has something to do with your people's reverence for The Deep, but...."

Twisting in his saddle to face her, he slowly and hesitantly invoked the sign of The Deep while observing her for a response.

"Think of it like a silent prayer," Gwenna offered, surprised at how awkward it felt to explain beliefs that felt so innate. "My Grandfather says that when he was young, peddlers would come to market carrying tiny vials that they swore contained the essence of The Deep. He says people were encouraged to anoint their wrists daily to carry The Deep's protection with them at all times. Then people began smelling and 'breathing in' the essence during times of stress. It was a sign of asking for even more protection."

"So it's a prayer... for safety?" Kellen clarified.

Gwenna nodded. "Now it's considered blasphemous for anyone to try and profit off of The Deep. Those vials haven't been sold for years. But that act of breathing in the essence remains. I guess it's a little strange, now that I say it out loud..."

He nodded in understanding, but his long nose was scrunched in confusion.

"You may have seen our guests invoking the sign of The Deep in my presence last night," she said, trying to remain casual. "And yes, they're asking The Deep for protection from me."

"Protection? I didn't realize your reputation as a superior archer was well-known at court." Kellen forced a grin, trying a little too hard for humor. But she appreciated the effort.

She inhaled sharply and let everything come out immediately, willing everything into the open. "You may also have heard that while Cat is the Beauty of Bannon, I am the Curse."

Kellen flinched, opening his mouth to say something, but she continued.

"I suppose that if you do not have Shifters or The Deep in the south, then you also don't practice Fairy Blessings for your infant girls?" Gwenna guessed, laughing a little despite herself.

Kellen shook his head.

"By The Deep, what *do* you have in the south?"

"A lot of fish?" he offered in a strangled voice, scratching the nape of his neck.

Gwenna threw back her head in a laugh, his timing catching her off-guard.

"From what I have heard, and please correct me if I offend, your sister's Fairy provided her a Blessing of Beauty. And when your grandfather asked for the same for you, the request was denied?" Kellen asked hesitantly.

Gwenna nodded. "For years, all infant girls in Bannon were given a Blessing from a Fairy. It was tradition for centuries for a princess to be Blessed with Beauty. Still, in the villages, the Fairies followed the wishes of the babe's guardian. Fairy Maeve gave Cat Beauty but said no to Grandfather when he asked for the same for me."

"Wait, it was the *same* Fairy?" Kellen's jaw dropped. "For both of you?"

"Yep."

"And it was the only request from a guardian ever denied?" he pressed.

"According to all the ledgers." Gwenna shrugged. "Blessings are well-documented, and trust me, I've done a lot of research on the topic."

"What about since then? Since your Blessing?"

Gwenna hesitated. It was one thing for her to be the first child ever denied a requested Blessing. But admitting the next part would be enough for the steward to agree she was cursed.

"That was the last time a Fairy has ever been seen in Bannon."

Kellen's eyes widened, but he said nothing. Something rustled in the bushes along the path, and he turned away quickly, scanning the forest for signs of hidden threats as he tried to regain composure.

A moment ago, they were laughing and talking. Now things were awkward. It shouldn't have come as any surprise to her, but it still hurt. Shame sank down to the pit of Gwenna's stomach like a stone. Feeling such guilt over something she couldn't even remember was strange.

Only hours old, but she had forever altered Bannon. And not in the way that anyone wanted to be remembered.

"Look, I know I'm a southern heretic that doesn't understand your beliefs." Kellen broke the silence again.

Gwenna flinched and nervously glanced in his direction.

He was facing her again, leveling her with a solemn gaze. "But I don't think you're cursed."

A small ray of warmth erupted within her under his gaze. Gwenna flashed a shy smile before ducking her head so he wouldn't see the tears pricking at the corners of her eyes.

No one had ever said that to her before.

Except for her mother. But mothers didn't count in situations like this.

Suddenly, they both heard the unmistakable sound of the pounding hooves of horses at a hard gallop. They were approaching a blind curve in the road, unable to see who was riding towards them.

Gwenna looked up in alarm. Kellen spurred his horse forward, motioning with his arm that she should slow down. She pulled her mare to a stop as Aidan and Cat arrived wide-eyed beside her.

"What is it?" Cat whispered.

Gwenna shrugged, images of the white-haired Shifter charging them on horseback flooding her mind. Although this time, it didn't sound like he was alone. She instinctively reached behind her for an arrow, forgetting that the strap on her quiver had been broken and her arrows thrown in the lake.

Aidan nudged his horse forward, both he and Kellen drawing their swords as the sound of horses drew nearer.

Three horses came galloping around the corner, each bearing a knight in full plate carrying the banners of Thornvale Keep. Seeing the group on the road, the knights reigned hard to avoid collisions.

"Your Highnesses!" one of the knights called. "You must return to the Keep. It's the King!"

CHAPTER 6

RIGHT BEFORE

A s if there was doubt about who was the superior rider, Gwenna beat Aidan and all three of the knights back to the Keep. She would take the time to soak in her victory any other time, but not now. She didn't even wait to change her gown, just ran, still damp, to the King's chambers.

Orlaith stood in the hall, deep in conversation with Lord Whyt from the council, as Gwenna ran around the corner. Her mother sighed, visible relief washing over her lined face. Orlaith waved Lord Whyt away and turned to her daughter.

"I'm so glad you made it in time," she said, arms outstretched for an embrace. "He's been asking for you. Where's your sister?"

"She'll be along in a moment," Gwenna assured her, wrapping her arms around her mother half-heartedly, careful to not hug too tightly. "Sorry, I don't want to get you wet."

"What happened to you?" Orlatith's brow furrowed, taking in what remained of her daughter's braid. Most of Gwenna's dark curls now clung to her neck and shoulders, and her dark skirts were heavy with moisture.

Gwenna glanced anxiously at the closed door to her grandfather's chambers. Her mother needed to know of a Shifter in the lands. But...

"You're right," Orlaith said quickly, understanding the hesitancy. She escorted Gwenna to the door and gestured to the guard to allow her entrance. "Tell me later. He's been asking for you. Take your time."

Light flooded through the tall arching windows opposite her grandfather's bed, the floor-length curtains tied back and illuminated where he lay in his four-poster. His face was almost as white as the pillows he reclined against. Whatever color he had at the ball last night was gone. The fire blazing in the hearth provided a welcome wave of heat as Gwenna crossed the embroidered carpet to stand at his bedside. His eyes were closed, but his chest still rose and fell steadily.

"Grandfather?" she asked quietly.

His eyes fluttered open, looking wildly around the room as though disoriented until he finally saw her. A weak smile quirked at the edge of his mouth.

"Treasa?" he croaked.

"Gwenna," she corrected gently.

He nodded, patting the edge of the bed and indicating that she should sit. Gwenna kicked off her slippers, not wanting to get mud on his thick blankets, and eased herself onto the tall mattress. She sat near his feet, so she could face him.

"You look so much like your grandmother." He took her hands. Gwenna forced herself not to flinch at how cold his touch was, despite the roaring heat of the room. "Have I ever told you that?"

"Only every time you see me." Gwenna smiled.

"She was a beauty, my Treasa," the King said softly, eyes fluttering closed. "And you look just like her."

"Tell me about her," Gwenna said quickly, and his eyes opened again. She'd say anything to keep him talking a little longer.

"Her cheeks were rosy like yours," he wheezed. "And she loved to... to draw. You must get that from her."

"I must," she agreed, running her thumb gently over the back of his hand. It was liver-spotted and papery thin, trembling slightly in her grasp.

"Her hair... curly... and thick..." His blue eyes slid out of focus.

"What else?"

His eyes fluttered closed again, his breaths coming deeper now. Gwenna glanced nervously towards the door for help.

"Grandfather?" She spoke louder now, leaning slightly towards him.

The King snapped upright. Every muscle tensed, spine erect.

She flinched away, but his hand seized Gwenna's, gripping it so tightly that his nails dug into her skin. She tried to pull away, but he was no longer a frail, sick old man on his deathbed.

This was something else. It was wrong.

The fire in the hearth guttered out. Light still streamed through the tall windows, but it somehow couldn't touch the four-poster bed. Gwenna and her grandfather were swathed in shadows.

"Cursed." The word was exhaled with a rattling breath. The King stared straight ahead, past Gwenna, eyes unseeing.

"Grandfather?" Gwenna tried to break his grip but couldn't. He was inhumanely strong.

Using her free hand, she tried to gently push him back down on the pillows. She had to break whatever kind of trance this was. Her pulse echoed in her ears.

He snatched her wrist, holding both of her hands captive in his.

"Lay down. Please," she begged, looking towards the closed door for help.

With a wheezing gasp of pain, the King arched his back and pressed his frail sternum against her palms.

That's when her hands began to glow.

Faintly at first but quickly growing in power, the plum-colored light became the main light source in the room. Her hands appeared almost transparent, with unnatural light radiating from them.

They burned where her hands touched her grandfather's bare skin beneath his nightgown. *She* burned. Pain seared through her palms, searing the flesh right off of them.

Gwenna screamed, but no sound came out. Her voice was choked off and silenced.

Her grandfather shook under her grip, seizing like a leaf about to snap off the vine. He made no noise. But his face was contorted in pain, eyes rolled to the back of his head.

She was on her knees now, hovering over him. Whether he pulled her in or she pushed him down, she couldn't tell.

But neither one could pull themselves apart.

Small drops of water plinked onto Gwenna's forearms. She was sobbing.

The door banged open behind her. She twisted over her shoulder to see her mother standing in the doorway.

Gwenna immediately knew how awful it looked: leaning over the King, pushing power into his chest, or drawing it out. She didn't know which was worse.

But she couldn't stop whatever this was.

"Mother! Help me!" Gwenna choked out.

But it was like the violet light pouring from her hands absorbed all of the sound in the room and the light.

Orlaith ran forward, rounding the far side of the bed and clambering up on the other side of her father.

"Let go!" Orlaith gripped Gwenna's forearms, trying to pull her off of the King. Her voice was muffled too.

"I can't!" Gwenna shook her head.

"The curse!" King Domhnall's head tilted upwards now, only the whites of his eyes visible. He screamed hoarsely before slumping back onto the pillows, severing whatever connection Gwenna had with him.

Light and sound flooded back into the room. The hearth reignited instantly as though nothing had ever happened.

Gwenna scrambled backward off the bed, shaking violently. She massaged her hands, sure there would be nothing but charred, shriveled flesh.

Looking down, her palms were faintly pink. That was it.

"Gwenna?" A voice behind her breathed her name.

She turned to see Catriona, wide-eyed and pale, take a few steps towards her. Aidan gently grasped her elbow, pulling her back where he could shield her with his body.

Cat's face was one of concern. But Aidan's was nothing but horror and disgust.

Shrinking away, Gwenna turned hesitantly towards her grandfather's bed, where Orlaith pulled the blankets over his shoulders once more.

"Father... come back to us," the High Princess begged.

Cat appeared behind her mother, invoking the sign of The Deep as her shoulders shook with quiet sobs. Aidan laid a reassuring hand on his princess's shoulder, but his eyes darted toward Gwenna.

"Orlaith, my child," he said hoarsely.

"What's wrong, Father? What's happening?" Orlaith asked, searching his face for some sign of distress.

"I am ready to rest with The Deep. Your mother, my dear, she calls me..."

Orlaith wiped her eyes quickly. "Tell her that I love her."

The King's eyes drifted past Orlaith to where Cat stood, Aidan still at her shoulder. King Domhnall paused for a moment, drinking in the sight of his heirs, before slowly turning his head to look at his other granddaughter on the opposite side of the bed.

"Grandfather?" Gwenna whispered.

He held her gaze for a heartbeat, a look of unmistakable sadness in his blue eyes. She leaned forward as he opened his mouth to say something.

King Domhnall took a wheezing breath.

"Cursed."

He breathed out one final time, eyes closed, and his thin lips twisted in a frown.

Cat let out a wail, collapsing onto her knees and burying her face in the bed skirt as she sobbed. Mother sat motionless next to the King's body, tears streaming.

Gwenna's vision blurred, chest constricted. What had she done to her grandfather? Her insides felt twisted and wrung out, shredded with guilt. He had loved her his entire life, never mentioning her failed Blessing. Only seeing the good in her, he constantly told her how much he reminded her of his late wife, his sweetheart.

But in these last moments of his life...

What had overcome her? She glanced down at her trembling hands, terrified to see any hint of light. Whatever power that had been, it had never manifested itself before. She had no idea how to control or stop it from happening again.

Was this her curse: to kill the King?

A deep rumbling sounded somewhere in the distance.

At first, it sounded like the pounding of hooves. But this was too continuous. Too strong. And it was growing louder.

"Wh-what is that?" Cat spoke first, eyes puffy as she looked around.

Gwenna pushed away from the far wall, moving around the foot of the bed to stand at the windows overlooking the town of Thornvale. Aidan was at her side. He looked out the window, emitting a crude curse under his breath.

A thick, heavy storm wall filled the horizon. It started in the open ocean but raced into the canyon of the fjord and towards Thornvale, gathering speed as it approached. It was a strange murky brown color, too light to be a rainstorm, yet ominously dark.

Dry lightning cracked across the sky.

The roaring wind tore at the banners and flags in the courtyard of the Keep. Several broke off, tumbling away. The evergreen treetops of Braewood bent low beneath the fierce power of the incoming storm.

"By The Deep…" Mother whispered, appearing behind Aidan.

Gwenna stood, frozen to the spot as the dark cloud moved closer and closer, obscuring everything in its path. Shouts from the courtyard were faintly audible as stablehands and servants ran for cover.

As the storm wall overtook the town of Thornvale, hiding it from view, the roaring swelled so loud Gwenna covered her ears. It was so loud that the whole Keep was shaking beneath her.

Aidan grabbed Gwenna's shoulders, wrenching her away from the window so he could glare at her.

"What in the name of all the gods did you do?" he yelled over the storm's fury. "Are you a witch?"

Gwenna shook her head, eyes wide. She glanced back at the window just in time to see the storm wall slam into the castle.

The sun was snuffed out like a candle. Tiny particles of gravel, dirt, and sand scraped against the glass, grating at Gwenna's ears. She fell back a few steps as the wind infiltrated every crevice, crack, or imperfection in the glass-paned window it could find. Something began pouring through the seams and onto the carpet at her feet.

"Is this… sand?" Gwenna reached for it, but her mother pulled her back.

"Close the curtains."

The door to the chamber flew open, two knights in full plate in the doorway.

"You need to come with us. Now!" Captain Draven yelled over the noise. "We need to get you to shelter!"

CHAPTER 7

DURING

Glass shattered underfoot. Knights formed a tight circle around the royals as they ran. Terrified nobles flooded the corridors. Captain Draven yelled something inaudible as he shouldered past, forging a path for the royal family.

Desperate hands grabbed at Orlaith as she passed, begging for answers. The knights shoved the crowd back.

"Where are we going?" Aidan shouted over the noise of the storm.

"We have to get to the dungeon!" Draven yelled over his shoulder. "It's windowless and most secure."

"I want everyone within these walls taking shelter down there, regardless of status," Orlaith commanded.

"Your Highness–" Draven began.

"*Everyone*, Captain."

Gwenna hung towards the back of their little group, trembling as she hurried down the main staircase to the entrance hall. She didn't dare make eye contact with anyone in case her hands started glowing and she hurt someone else.

Rounding the landing, the storm was suddenly much louder.

The ornate stained glass masterpiece on the wall now had a huge gaping hole where King Domhnall's head once was. Sand and grime rained down through the opening.

A knight met them at the bottom of the stairs, tearing a tablecloth into handkerchief-sized pieces.

"Thank you, Davy. Cover your faces!" Draven shouted as the linen pieces were handed around, "Don't breathe this stuff in."

"Where do we go?" Countess Parcell shrieked as she approached the captain of the guard. She already had a piece of her own skirt covering her mouth and nose.

"Through there," Orlaith spoke loudly but gently as she took the woman by the arm and led her to the small unmarked wooden door off the side of the entrance hall. "Captain, can you or one of your men help the Countess and her lady down the stairs?"

The knight, Davy, pulled the dungeon door open, another escorting the elderly Parcells down the spiral staircase. Other nobles began filing down the stairs behind them.

"I'll see to the staff and the rest of the guests," Draven announced before he and the rest of his men darted off.

"Aidan, take the girls downstairs," Orlaith shouted. "I'll be behind you momentarily."

Aidan shook his head firmly, a hard glint in his eyes. "You take the girls. I'll ensure the Keep is clear and all the staff are safe."

Orlaith and Aidan stared at each other, silently sizing one another up as the wind whipped and tore at them. Two monarchs, wordlessly negotiating a new chain of command.

It was Orlaith who deferred, dropping her gaze.

"Thank you."

He nodded. " Is this the only entrance to the dungeons?"

"Yes. Grandfather had the other passageways sealed up. He felt it was more secure that way," Gwenna yelled over the wind.

"Stay out of this," Aidan barked, steely-eyed at the sight of her. A vein throbbed in his forehead. He turned back to Orlaith, the edge in his voice immediately gone. "I'll be down soon. Stay together and take note of any missing staff members."

"The mouth coverings were a good idea. If you need more, use anything you can find. Tablecloths, bedsheets, whatever you need. Just... be safe."

Aidan took off in a run, heading back up the marble staircase the way they came, taking the steps two at a time.

"Come on, girls." Orlaith turned away.

"Mother, I'd like to help too–" Gwenna began.

"Absolutely not," Orlaith said shortly. She grabbed her daughter's hand and towed her down the stairs behind her. Cat followed right behind.

As soon as the heavy door slammed shut behind them, the sudden quiet was suddenly unnerving. The storm still howled outside but was dampened to a low roar.

Orlaith grabbed a torch from its bracket on the wall, and the three hurried down the spiral staircase, ragged breathing echoing off of the dark stone. Around and around they went, skirts dragging on the worn steps as they headed down into the dark depths of Thornvale Keep.

"Thankfully, most nobles left last night or early this morning. The council members have all gone to their estates in the village. We only have about a dozen court members and then the staff," Orlaith whispered to her girls. "We should have plenty of room for everyone."

"Your Highness?" a nervous voice called as the royals finally reached the bottom of the stairs.

A group of six maids stood at the base of the steps, a few young pages from the Hall of Records standing behind them. All were wide-eyed and covered in grime. Catriona's trio of maids, Kaylyn, Makayla, and Amaya, swarmed their princess instantly to fuss over her.

"We'll take refuge here until the storm passes. It won't be long now," Orlaith spoke loudly but calmly, emitting confidence that Gwenna knew she didn't possess at that moment. "Lord Aidan will fetch the others on staff to join us here. Please, Aymer, can you light the torches? A bit of light would do us all well."

Orlaith passed the torch off to Aymer, a boy with dark corkscrew curls wearing a pages' tunic. He bowed low and ran off to do as commanded. The crowd of nervous staff parted, and Orlaith glided to a wooden bench against the far wall where the nobles had congregated, a contented smile on her face.

The dungeon in Thornvale Keep had never been utilized, so there was nothing to fear down here. No ominous stains or chains hanging from the thick oak beams. Once Aymer and the other pages had all the torches lit, it seemed like an expansive stone room that radiated warmth and safety. A row of cells lined one wall, each large enough to fit one prisoner with a little room to pace.

Maids moved to drag the benches and lumpy mattresses out of the cells, creating a seating area for the nobility near where Orlaith had settled. Gwenna numbly settled down on the bench beside her mother, mind still racing. The two knights stood at attention at the bottom of the staircase. Slowly more and more servants stumbled down the steps and into the torchlights' glow, almost all with remnants of miscellaneous tablecloths pressed to their faces.

The kitchen staff were some of the last to join the group below, several in tears.

"Chrisalyn, are you hurt?" Orlaith stood, eyes wide with alarm.

A tanned girl with long brown hair shook her head quickly. "No, your Highness. We are safe. We were trying to block the larder doors against the wind, but… it was too strong…." Regretful tears flooded the girl's eyes again. "I'm not sure what we will be able to recover."

Gwenna felt a heavy stone plummet to the pit of her stomach. She resisted burying her head in her hands.

"There's a cold storeroom down here with some cured meats and cheeses." A redheaded maid dipped a low curtsy at Orlaith's feet.

"I'd be happy to bring some out for Her Royal Highness and the princesses."

Orlaith nodded wearily. "Please, bring enough for everyone to have their fill." She smiled at the girl's look of surprise. "What good is a full storeroom for later when there are empty bellies now? Thank you, Joni."

"Ladies, please go help," Cat instructed wearily, sending her three maids off.

"How long do you think we've been down here?" Gwenna whispered to her mother as they left, leaning her head against her shoulder.

"A few hours."

"Aidan should have been back by now," Cat murmured from where she sat on Orlaith's other side.

"The boy can take care of himself," Orlaith sighed. "He'll have to, now that…."

Silence fell heavy between them. No announcement was made that King Domhnall had been claimed by The Deep. But his conspicuous absence from the stone dungeon spoke volumes. Snatches of whispers had floated to Gwenna, but she had tried to ignore them.

Selfishly, she was grateful that all attention seemed to be on the open secret of her grandfather's death. It didn't leave anyone time to question the origins of the storm. That she potentially caused with her glowing purple hands…

No one had said anything about it thus far, but it was only a matter of time. The look on Aidan's face told her that she wouldn't escape unscathed.

"You could take the throne, you know," Gwenna spoke the treacherous words softly, ensuring only her mother could hear.

Orlaith stiffened, subtly adjusting so her daughter was no longer leaning against her. Then she leveled a hard look at Gwenna.

"After all we went through to ensure we had a man to pass Grandfather's crown to, you dare suggest we violate the sworn oaths of Bannon?" Orlaith asked coldly.

"You know these people–"

"As does your sister!" her mother hissed sharply. "She will make a fine queen at Aidan's side. Hold your tongue lest you anger The Deep further."

"Further?"

"I don't know what happened in Grandfather's chambers, but–" Orlaith dropped her voice barely above a whisper.

"It's not what it looked like," Gwenna insisted, panic clawing up her throat. "I would never do anything to hurt him."

"I know that. I do." Orlaith laid a comforting hand on her daughter's knee, squeezing gently. "But… Gwenna, what *happened?* Did you say something? Did he?"

She tried to remember, shaking her head frantically. "No, not really… He was speaking about Grandmother."

"What else?"

"Nothing," she said honestly, staring calmly back into her mother's unblinking eyes. "He mentioned Grandmother's name and then started convulsing and…."

Gwenna glanced down at her hands, hardly pink in the low torchlight. Orlaith followed her gaze.

"Gwenna, I am your mother first and a queen second. I love you with everything that I am. And I know that you would never do anything on purpose to hurt anyone, least of all Grandfather. But if something happened, if you did something, you have to tell me," Orlaith said urgently, holding Gwenna's forearm tightly. "I can protect you. If word should get out–"

Gwenna wrenched her arm free of her grasp.

"I didn't do anything," she snapped, pushing to her feet.

She picked her way through the crowd, stepping carefully to avoid treading on any fingertips of people huddled on the bare stone floor. There was nowhere to go, but she couldn't sit and try to answer her mother's questions. Not now.

Not when she was too busy with questions of her own.

Finding a small, unoccupied cell in the corner, Gwenna opened the iron door and let herself in. She was still in full view of the rest of the Keep's residents, but at least she had space alone from the mass of bodies.

If she had caused that purple light, did that mean she killed the King? Had she caused this storm or plague or whatever it was?

Gwenna didn't know the cause of anything. Which also meant she didn't know how to control it. And she certainly didn't know how to prevent it from happening again.

Keeping to herself was the safest option for everyone.

Pressing her back against the cool stone, Gwenna slid down to sit roughly on the floor, letting her legs splay in front of her. Very unladylike.

But killing someone was unladylike. Especially if that person happened to be your grandfather. And most especially if he was the King.

If she thought about it, she could almost still feel the palms of her hands burning against her grandfather's chest. She had never felt anything similar to that level of pain. Never before had she seen that ethereal purple light, let alone have any part of her body glow.

Gwenna knew there was something wrong with her. Something that made a Fairy deny her and then disappear. She had made peace with the rumors and whispers, understanding that she would never be considered a great beauty. If that was her curse, she could bear it.

But what if her curse was something far worse? Something that now wasn't just affecting her, but spreading to kill and destroy those around her?

The heavy oak door slammed somewhere above.

"Water! We need water!" Aidan's raw and raspy voice echoed down the stairwell, instantly stirring the dungeon into a panic.

One of the knights posted at the base of the stairs hurried to meet Aidan halfway up the stairwell.

Cat ran to the base of the stairs, carrying a heavy bucket of water with a wooden ladle, eyes wide with worry. Gwenna remained frozen in place. She had a front-row seat as Aidan and the knight came stumbling down the steps, a young woman's unconscious body in Aidan's arms.

Gwenna's pulse thudded in her ears, nausea roiling. She recognized the maid's uniform, tanned skin, and mass of dark curls beneath the cream kerchief. It was Aldessa, one of her personal maids.

Everyone surged forward, obscuring Aidan and Aldessa from view. Gwenna curled into herself, wrapping her arms around her legs, and tried to steady her breathing. She could vaguely hear whispered tones, but she hardly noticed.

Gwenna pressed her wrist to her nose, inhaling as her lips moved noiselessly. She begged The Deep to not claim Aldessa. She couldn't have another soul on her conscience.

"She's awake!" Aidan yelled. "Give her some space!"

They weren't happy about it, but the crowd parted and drifted back to their groups and huddles, casting anxious glances over their shoulders.

Gwenna crept to the bars of her cell to get a better look.

Aldessa was half-reclined on the stone floor, Aidan supporting her weight. Cat hovered, ensuring that she was getting enough to drink. Aldessa's simple frock and bodice were covered in grime, with sand matted in her hair and clinging to any exposed skin. Aidan, however, was surprisingly clean.

"I was helping get the horses stabled," Aldessa explained quietly, touching her temple gingerly as she looked up at Catriona.

"One of the beams was falling, and I went to steady it, but it must have caught me in the head…."

"I was also assisting in the stables," Aidan interjected quickly. "I was able to rescue her from any further harm."

"Lucky you were there, then." Cat's eyes flickered to Aidan, giving him a warm smile. "I don't know what we would have done without you, Aldessa." She hugged the maid tightly,

"Thank you, your Grace," Aldessa murmured. "It is a pleasure to serve your family. You've always been so kind to me and to my family. I cannot express my gratitude enough."

"Now it's time for us to return the favor. You rest. I'll send your brother over in a moment. He was very worried about you. I need to finish laying out the food but sit down, and I'll bring you something to eat." Cat squeezed Aldessa's hand affectionately before handing her a spare blanket.

It wasn't particularly cold, but something about a blanket was comforting.

The crown princess straightened, brushing her hands on her gown before picking up her water pail and heading back toward her mother.

Aidan watched her go, eyes full of tenderness.

"You are a lucky man, my lord, if I may say so," Aldessa murmured, climbing to her feet and wrapping the blanket around her shoulders. "Princess Catriona is without equal."

"I'd have to agree with that assessment," Aidan replied softly, staring at Catriona's retreating back.

Aymer called out his sister's name, and Aldessa hurried to join him on the other side of the room, leaving Aidan alone for a moment.

His shoulders sagged, weariness seeming to hit him all at once. Aidan let his head droop as he ran his fingers through his hair and attempted to stifle a yawn.

Gwenna couldn't take her eyes off of him. Had he really gone out into the storm to assist in the stables? This wasn't his home or his people. But he had risked himself for them. He would make a good king.

"That was brave of you." Gwenna heard the words tumble out of her mouth, giving away her hiding place in the shadows. Too late, she clapped a hand over her mouth.

Aidan's head whipped around to follow the sound of her voice, and she flinched as he laid eyes on her. Slowly, he moved towards the door of the cell. Bracing himself in the doorway, he sighed and looked down at where Gwenna huddled on the floor.

"So… the witch speaks," he sighed.

"Forget it," Gwenna muttered, shifting uncomfortably. "I was about to compliment you, but then you quickly reminded me why it's a waste of my breath."

"Me?" Aidan repeated, eyebrows shooting up his forehead. "Big words coming from a literal walking plague. Do you see all of these people here? They're here because of *you*. Because of what you did."

"Oh?" Gwenna rose to her feet, face burning with rage as he gave voice to all the cruelty already trapped inside her own mind. "And what exactly did I do?"

"Tell me you didn't cause this," he said, leaning toward her.

His hot breath hit her cheek as he exhaled, staring her down. They stood toe to toe in the doorway, glaring at each other. His eyes narrowed as he studied her.

Above, the door to the dungeon swung shut again. Aidan and Gwenna froze, both looking toward the sound of scuffling footsteps as the knights gripped the hilts of their swords. All the staff and guests were accounted for, but someone quickly moved down the stairs.

Kellen emerged, every square inch of him coated in dust. Gwenna's jaw dropped, falling back a step as he approached. His nose and mouth were covered with cloth, tied at the back of his head over his shaggy curls, and he pulled it down as he approached, revealing a noticeably cleaner lower face.

"Where have you been?" Aidan barked.

"Securing the gates," Kellen panted, adjusting his floppy feathered cap. "I was on my way back when I heard the stable collapse. Thank you for meeting me at the entrance hall to assist with the maid."

"I thought Lord Kaldonna was assisting in the stables," Gwenna said innocently, watching with glee as Aidan's face burned with humiliation.

"What? No, only the maid and a few stablehands." Kellen was still trying to catch his breath, looking between Gwenna and Aidan in confusion. "Is she alright?"

"She's fine," Gwenna said quickly, trying to fight back laughter at the look on Aidan's face. "Where was our dear future king in all of this, then?"

"Waiting in the dining hall. He was taking cover under the high table and waiting for my report when I brought the girl in," Kellen explained absently, craning his neck to see what food was being passed out. "I beg your apologies; I need water to clear my throat...."

"Of course," Gwenna said quickly, and he hurried off.

Aidan's knuckles turned white as he gripped the bars of the cell. "He's not yours to dismiss."

"Just yours to command into danger while you cower," she snorted.

"He volunteered," he muttered through gritted teeth.

"Did he also volunteer for you to take credit?" Gwenna snapped. "Catriona thinks you risked life and limb to rescue my maid. I saw the way Cat looked at you. Don't you think she deserves the truth?"

"I am the future king. I have people at my disposal for a reason," he said coldly. "In light of everything that happened, your people can't afford for me to get hurt. The princess understands that."

"Does she?"

"She knows the roles we all play. I am the future king, and she will be my queen," Aidan said coolly. "But what about you, Gwenna? What role do you play here? What are you? What's *wrong* with you?"

She inhaled slowly, smiling gently at him as she moved closer to where he loomed in the doorway.

"I hope you lay awake at night thinking of me," Gwenna whispered. "I hope I haunt your every waking thought, and you go mad trying to puzzle me out. I am a mystery no one can solve, least of all you. You're pathetic."

"Pathetic?" he repeated darkly. "You cursed this land, this people! *Your* people! And then you dare to hide down here as if you're one of them? As though you didn't cause this?"

His words landed like a blow to the chest, despite her attempts to steel herself against them. She flinched, looking away as his barbs broke through the internal dam she had constructed to keep out the shame. Guilt flooded through her, the current so strong it took her breath away.

Gwenna fell back a few steps, staring guiltily at the masses of huddled people on the floor.

"I don't know what you are or what unnatural powers you possess. Right now, I can only guess. But I saw you with the King. I don't know what happened to him or what caused this storm. Should I find out that you are responsible, I will have no choice but to recommend you be executed for treason," Aidan said quietly. "It is only out of respect for your sister that I don't turn you over to the council right now."

Her eyes stung with tears. She wrapped her arms around her chest and wanted to push away from the accusations he hurled at her. She wanted to deny everything he said… but she couldn't.

Gwenna looked back to Aidan, trying to breathe through her panic, only to be met with a smug smile of satisfaction.

He saw her drowning.

And he smirked as it pulled her under.

CHAPTER 8

THE MORNING AFTER

G wenna lay awake over half the night, listening to the faint howling of the wind outside.

When she did drift into sleep, she was met with visions of violet light streaming from her hands. Screams of pain echoed around her in her dreams. Sometimes they were from herself, but usually from her mother or Catriona. Even Aidan, once.

Their bodies thrashed, eyes rolling back in their head, shaking like rag dolls as Gwenna's hands glowed and burned. Her screams drowned out theirs. Apologies, so many apologies. Prayers to The Deep that went unanswered. No way to control it or to banish the light.

She shook violently. They were yelling at her now. Yelling her name…

"Gwenna!"

She bolted upright, wiping sweat or tears from her eyes. The dungeon had seemed sheltered from the elements last night, but already she felt sand clinging to her cheeks. Kellen crouched over her, hand on her shoulder and eyes wide with concern.

Looking around, the dungeon was almost empty. A few stragglers remained, including stablehands returning the benches to the other cells and maids cleaning up the remnants of last night's meal. No sight of Cat and Aidan. Or Orlaith.

"It's daybreak," Kellen said quietly. "The wind died down a few hours ago."

It was the news she had waited for all night. But something about how he spoke told her he wasn't delivering good news.

He extended a calloused hand to help her to her feet. Gwenna reached to take his outstretched hand but then hesitated. She wasn't as lithe as her sister.

"Come on." He smiled encouragingly, and she took his hand. He lifted her to her feet as though she weighed nothing at all. "How did you sleep?"

Gwenna opened her mouth to answer but closed it again. The nightmares left her feeling more worn out than when she had first laid down.

"You were shivering over here all by yourself." Kellen stooped down to pick up his cloak from the ground.

"Oh." Gwenna stared, her mind taking a moment to catch up with what she was seeing. "Th-that was very thoughtful of you. Thank you. How are you feeling?"

He grinned, nodding at her to follow him up the staircase. "A hot meal and a warm bath, and I'll be right as rain. Your mother gave the staff the morning off to tend to their families. I expect most of the day will be spent in clean-up efforts."

Together, they climbed the stairs to the entrance hall.

Gwenna's slippered feet sank ankle-deep into hot sand as she stepped across the threshold to the entrance hall. She gasped aloud, unable to see the slate floor at all. The frame holding the stained glass window was completely empty now, showcasing a cloudless blue sky. Gwenna held her skirts a little higher, determined to step carefully to avoid stepping on any glass shards hidden in the grime.

Footprints ran every which way, most either up the marble staircase to the rest of the Keep or out the large double doors to the courtyard. Kellen and Gwenna exchanged dubious looks before picking their way across the sandy floor toward the double doors leading to the courtyard.

Stepping out onto the marble entry steps, a blast of overpowering heat almost knocked them back. Gwenna had stood directly in front of the large ovens in the kitchens and felt less warmth. Sweat instantly beaded across her forehead.

Kellen dropped his heavy winter cloak on the ground, rolling up his shirt sleeves. Gwenna hiked her skirts up even higher. If a man could show his elbows in this heat, a glimpse of her ankle wouldn't make anyone faint.

The sand was even deeper in the open-air courtyard. Knights were up on the Keep walls, pacing the parapets and shouting at one another. As Kellen had reported, one end of the stable's roof had collapsed entirely. Stablehands were already hard at work digging out the doors to the stable.

"Any injuries?" Gwenna called to a stablehand.

"Not that we've been able to see. All the livestock were accounted for after the roof collapsed. Once we can open the doors, we'll see who survived the night," a dark-haired young man called back.

"Do you need any help?" Kellen asked.

The stablehand shook his head. "We've got enough manpower here. They may need help in the village, though. The princess and her betrothed went to check with a few knights. Last night before the storm, some saw a bear near the village, so be careful."

Kellen swore under his breath, and Gwenna shared the feeling. This area of Bannon hadn't had any big game in years, and suddenly both a wolf and a bear were sighted? Odds were, the bear was another Shifter sniffing around the castle. The thought made her stomach twist.

Gwenna shielded her eyes from the sun as she turned and inspected the rest of the Keep. From where she stood, no other windows had been shattered by the storm, thank The Deep, and no damage seemed to have been done to the stone walls.

"Let's go find your sister and Aidan," Kellen said. "See if we can be of some use."

He moved woodenly down the Keep steps and under the portcullis. Gwenna quickly followed him over the marble bridge that spanned the river and connected the Keep to the mainland.

Kellen suddenly halted, swearing again under his breath. He moved to look over the railing, and, curious, she followed.

There was no river.

Gwenna stumbled forward a few steps, blinking rapidly with disbelief. Peering over the side of the grimy marble railing, she kept leaning out farther and farther, sure that she'd see water far below if she kept looking.

Kellen's tight grip on her arm pulled her back before she leaned out too far.

"The river's gone," he said hoarsely. "It's all... *gone*."

Gwenna straightened up, following his gaze out past the dry, sandy riverbed towards the fjord... or what used to be the Safyra Fjord.

Her stomach twisted, nausea drying out her mouth as she stared at the vast expanse of sand dunes that stretched to the horizon. Everywhere the sea had once been was now sand.

The mountains still reached the heavens but were blanched and stripped of color. All those colors Gwenna loved so dearly, those wide expanses of vivid greens in every shade that breathed life into this kingdom, were all gone. Replaced overnight with browns. Parched and withering. Leaves were gone, with only bare branches and stripped trunks remaining. Braewood Forest was completely unrecognizable now, almost like a wildfire had torn through it.

"How did this happen?" Gwenna whispered.

"That storm wasn't natural," Kellen muttered.

She cleared her throat, moving away quickly and praying he didn't start questioning the source of the unnatural storm. "We need to check the town. See if they need help."

Gwenna made it to the end of the bridge before Kellen caught up with his long legs. The dirt road leading down the mountain to Thornvale Town was usually thick with mud. Now, wide, jagged cracks ran through it.

"It's so dry the dirt itself has split...." Kellen muttered, stooping to run his hand through the dirt. He looked up at her, sifting the earth in his hand. "There's no moisture here. Where are your fields? For the crops?"

"Around the bend," she said faintly, nodding to where the road turned sharply out of sight.

Gwenna broke into a run. Something inside of her already knew what she was going to see. But she couldn't believe it until she saw it with her own eyes. As she came barreling around the corner, she had to pull up short to avoid crashing into Aidan and Cat.

Dumbstruck, they turned to look at her.

"It's all gone..." Cat said blankly.

Gwenna's chest constricted as she looked out on the barren fields. Thornvale's farmers wandered listlessly up, and down the rows, shoulders slumped. One woman, grimy kerchief holding back her hair, fell to her knees and wailed.

"How could this happen?" Kellen asked, arriving behind her.

Gwenna felt the weight of Aidan's suspicious gaze land on her, but she said nothing.

"We need to get back to the Keep," Aidan said quietly. "Take stock of the food stores there. If there's no harvest this year, we must be prepared."

"No harvest?" Cat grabbed at his arm, eyes wide with fear. "It's still early in the year. Surely we can plant again."

"Even if the soil isn't ruined by the sand, how would your farmers water the crops?" Kellen said quietly.

Cat gasped as the realization hit her, and Aidan wrapped a comforting arm around her. Gwenna closed her eyes, wanting to surrender the weight she felt pressing down on her.

"No harvest. And no water," Cat whispered. "We're all going to starve…."

"We will not starve," Gwenna hissed emphatically.

She opened her eyes to see all three gaping at her. Whatever had happened, it was her responsibility to fix it. Her kingdom should not be punished because of her curse. She could find a way to fix it. She had to. There would be no more death on her hands.

"Let's return to the Keep and have this conversation behind closed doors," Kellen suggested quietly, staring at the nearby farmers. "We wouldn't want to incite a panic."

Aidan nodded resignedly and turned to head back to the Keep. Cat turned to follow but paused, looking at her sister.

"Gwenna? Are you coming?" she asked wearily.

"Soon. I just need a moment alone…" Gwenna sighed.

Cat nodded, squeezing Gwenna's hand gently before following Aidan. Kellen hesitated for a moment but reluctantly followed in Aidan's footsteps.

Once they were out of sight, Gwenna collapsed under the weight of her guilt and fell onto her hands and knees in the dust. Her fingers dug through the dirt, lips silently muttering prayer after prayer to The Deep. If all of this destruction happened in one night, surely it could be undone in the same amount of time.

"Please, if I am a curse or have done something to displease Her, I beg forgiveness. Punish *me*, not my people. If I have caused this, show me the way to fix it. Whatever it takes, I'll do it," Gwenna whispered.

The hairs on the back of her neck stood on end.

Someone was watching her.

Looking up and sitting back on her feet, Gwenna searched the wide expanses of barren, parched fields. The farmers were retreating towards the town. It seemed she was completely alone.

Gwenna watched and waited, knowing that the solitude was only an illusion. After a moment, movement at the field's far edge caught her eye.

A large, shaggy black wolf with a crown of pure white stared at her unblinkingly. She could see his haunting silver eyes.

Slowly, Gwenna rose to her feet, never breaking eye contact with the beast. He never moved, just watched her.

"What do you want?" Gwenna called, taking a step towards him. "Did you do this?"

His lips curled up, a wolfish approximation of a smile. His head shook back and forth. No, he didn't cause this.

She sucked in a breath, afraid to ask this next question. "Do you know why this happened? How do I fix it?"

The wolf turned his back to her, taking a few steps towards the treeline he had come from. He looked over his shoulder, piercing her with his silver eyes. Slowly, deliberately, he nodded towards the trees, inviting her to join him.

Her pulse thundered in her ears. Every Shifter story she had ever heard began this way: a girl lured into the woods by a beast who feigned friendship.

"What do you want with me?" she whispered.

Gwenna risked a look over her shoulder towards the road to see if anyone was watching. She and the Shifter were utterly alone. Turning back to face him, he was smiling again.

His sharp canine teeth seemed to glisten in the harsh sunlight. He was a wolf, after all. She didn't expect any friendliness from him. But how much was man, and how much was beast?

He jerked his head towards the treeline again, and she took a hesitant step forward. It couldn't be a coincidence that he revealed himself before the storm. He must have known something.

A sudden look of hunger glinted in the wolf's eyes. Gwenna halted in her tracks, suddenly chilled despite the blazing heat.

Yes, he was feral and animalistic. She knew he was no friend. But this was something more.

Something deep within begged Gwenna not to go with him. The wolf's eyes narrowed as he watched her take another step back.

"I can't," she whispered, almost apologetically.

The panic in her chest let up for a moment, confirming she was making the right decision. Gwenna took another step back, eyes never leaving the wolf.

Now that she wasn't following obediently, would he attack?

The wolf huffed out a breath, clearly irritated. One final time, he nodded towards the treeline and invited her to join him.

Logically, she knew going with him made sense. Surely, if he had any answers to save her people, it would be worth the risk.

But she couldn't shake that inner voice. Primal and terror-stricken, it *screamed* at her not to trust him.

Gwenna shook her head firmly, stepping back towards the road and the Keep. "I can't."

The wolf watched for an agonizingly long moment. She tensed, ready for him to leap toward her. How far could she get before he caught her with those claws and teeth?

But instead, the wolf bowed his head once. He deferred to her and her decision before turning and running back into the darkness of the trees.

CHAPTER 9

Gwenna marched up to Catriona in the doorway of the Keep and grabbed her by the elbow.

Cat flinched at her touch, so deep in conversation with Aidan that she hadn't noticed her sister come up behind her.

"We need to talk. Now," Gwenna said in a deadly quiet tone.

Aidan immediately inserted himself between the girls, grabbing Gwenna by the wrist and wrenching her arm violently away from Cat. "I'll thank you for not laying a hand on my bride."

"Take your hands off me," Gwenna spat.

"Don't touch Catriona," Aidan warned softly. "I meant what I said last night. I'll go to the council."

"Aidan." Cat laid a gentle hand on his bicep, pulling his attention away from threatening her sister. "It's alright. I'll speak with her."

Gwenna resisted the urge to roll her eyes. Cat made it sound like she was doing Gwenna a favor by permitting her a moment of her time.

Aidan released his grip on her roughly, and Gwenna immediately massaged her wrist. "I'll go check on the clean-up efforts. If we get the courtyard swept out in time, we can light the pyre there this evening," Aidan announced.

"What pyre?" Gwenna asked, watching his retreating back.

"Grandfather's," Cat said softly, quiet weariness radiating off her. "There's no way to sail his body away, and the ground is too hard for burial. It will have to be a funeral pyre." She inhaled sharply, throwing back her shoulders and straightening as she cleared her throat. "You wanted to speak with me?"

"Yes, but not here." Gwenna glanced up, noting the many servants bustling in one door and out the other as they hurried to clean up from the storm. "Follow me."

Catriona had never been down to the cisterns as far as Gwenna knew but followed along without question. Cat was always pleasant that way. She would be a benevolent and patient queen, willing to listen to all sides before deciding.

Gwenna's stomach curdled with dread when she stepped inside the narrow staircase leading down to the cisterns. There was no sign of trouble, but Gwenna could feel the wrongness in the air. She dashed down the stairs, leaving Cat behind.

Yesterday, Gwenna had felt like an island here, surrounded by water reserves on all sides. She had expected some of the sand and grit from the storm to have fallen through the skylight, but that could easily be scooped out of the water. This place was so well-fortified and secure that one little dust storm could not have touched it.

Catriona sucked in a breath as she stepped over the threshold, eyes wide as she took in the vast emptiness of the space.

The thick square pillars supporting the arched ceilings were tall, stretching easily twice as tall as Gwenna. But she had never been able to clearly understand how deep the cistern went, unable to see to the bottom with such low light. Now it was all too obvious.

The cistern's floor had been hollowed out nearly thirty feet below where Gwenna and Catriona now stood. Yesterday, all of that space was filled with water reserves.

Now it stood almost empty, the water maybe three feet deep where it had been thirty yesterday. Sand coated the walkways, but the water that remained seemed miraculously clean. The Deep had given them one small mercy, it seemed.

"It's all gone," Cat whispered. "No food, no water… We'll starve."

"We have plenty of food stores. We'll run out of water long before we starve to death," Gwenna said bitterly, sinking onto her knees.

"How long do we have?" Cat asked, coming up behind her sister.

"These cisterns were built specifically for this purpose. We should have been able to last for months if not years…" Gwenna recalled seeing the architect's sketches in the Hall of Ledgers. This place had been carefully designed, with so much consideration to ensure the Keep never ran out of water.

"How long?" Cat repeated.

"With the remaining ball guests and the town… I'd guess less than two months," Gwenna said quietly.

Her sister made some odd choking sound, and Gwenna looked up to see Catriona dissolve into tears. She gasped as Cat sank down beside her and buried her face in Gwenna's shoulder.

Gwenna wrapped her arms around her sister, unsure of what else to do besides hold Cat for as long as it took.

"We're going to be ok," Gwenna murmured, rubbing Cat's back. It was a blatant lie, but she didn't know what else to say.

"I can't do this, Gwenna," Cat whispered.

"Can't do what?"

"How am I going to be the queen of… *this*?" Cat sniffled, sitting back on her heels and wiping at her eyes. "People are going to look to me to lead, to be brave, and get us out of this. I studied, and I studied, and I learned everything about court politics and foreign treaties… But this was never something I prepared for. What am I going to do?"

Gwenna squeezed her shoulder to comfort her. "First, you'll stop acting like you're in this alone. You have Mother and I. We'll be here to help you. Besides, you're technically not even queen yet."

Cat nodded. "That's what Aidan said too."

Gwenna swallowed the unladylike words that came to mind when she heard his name.

"I need to ask you about the wolf...." Gwenna said quietly.

Cat froze, slowly looking up at her with wide eyes. "What wolf?"

"You know exactly what wolf I'm talking about," Gwenna snapped. "You know him, Cat. Admit it!"

"I don't know what you're talking about." Cat climbed to her feet, focusing on smoothing her skirts.

"Don't do that. Don't lie to me," Gwenna hissed, climbing to her feet. "I saw your face at the lake. I know you recognized him."

"Again, I don't know what you're talking about. You probably misread what you thought you saw. I was a little caught off-guard by seeing a *dagger* at your neck," Cat seethed, face splotched pink with emotion. "Honestly, Gwenna, what were you thinking? You shouldn't have ridden off by yourself. If we hadn't arrived when we did, I shudder to think what would have happened. I need to go. I don't have any more time to waste. I need to help Mother plan the funeral."

Gathering her skirts, Cat turned her back on her sister and rushed towards the stairwell.

"He told me he's talked to you," Gwenna called, and Cat froze. "What did you two talk about? I can't imagine a princess and a wolf having anything in common."

It was a bold lie but effective. Cat's beautiful face was pale with terror as she turned back around to stare at her sister. Gwenna noted how Cat looked nervously over her shoulder to ensure they weren't being overheard.

"What did he say to you?" Gwenna asked quietly.

"What did he tell you?" Cat asked in a strangled voice.

"I asked you first."

"I-It doesn't matter. It doesn't mean anything," Cat stammered, wringing her hands. "It was only a handful of stolen kisses, but I didn't know what he was."

"What?"

"Please don't say anything. It was way before Aidan got here. I swear to you, Gwenna, it meant nothing. He means nothing to me now. I ended things as soon as you told me your plan for the Kaldonnas to come to the ball." Catriona's blue eyes were full of tears.

"Cat…" Gwenna was at a complete loss for words.

She didn't know what to expect when she questioned Cat about the wolf, but certainly not this. One question answered, sort of, but now a million more were on the tip of her tongue.

"Promise me you won't say anything to Aidan," Cat begged, lip trembling. "I really like him, Gwenna. Tristan was always kind to me, but… I don't know. I never felt that *spark* with him. You always got to spend so much time with Aidan, who always made you laugh. I guess I was jealous. But I ignored it and focused on Tristan. It was always supposed to be me and him. But then Aidan walked through the door at the ball and…." She sighed, blushing slightly. "It all felt so *right*. Like the perfect fairytale ending."

Gwenna swallowed roughly, trying to pretend her sister's words didn't feel like a blow to the chest. She didn't know how she felt about Aidan anymore. It felt like two different Aidans were in her mind: one she loved with childlike hope and one she hated. But she didn't have time to unknot that particular tangle of emotions in light of everything else.

"Please don't think poorly of me, but I don't think I ever would have let that boy kiss me if I knew Aidan was going to be the one to propose…." Cat admitted, panicking a little in the silence. "It shouldn't matter, and I know that. I knew it could never lead anywhere. But stupid Jane Byrne was always talking on and on about all the boys she kissed… I felt like an old maid, sitting in a tower waiting to be married off to someone convenient. But it meant nothing to me, Gwenna. I swear to you. I didn't know who he was– *what* he was– until the lake yesterday."

"You never noticed his ears?" Gwenna snorted.

"What's wrong with his ears?" Cat asked blankly.

Gwenna rolled her eyes. She loved her sister, but Cat could be naive, to say the least.

"Never mind," Gwenna sighed. "When did all of this happen?"

"The harvest last fall. It only lasted a few months."

"Mother made me go to the lake with you yesterday to make sure nothing happened to your virtue," Gwenna said scathingly. "If she ever finds out–"

"Nothing like that happened!" Cat said immediately, and Gwenna arched a skeptical eyebrow. "Just a few kisses. I swear to The Deep, Gwenna. I didn't let it go further. I couldn't."

Of course. Nothing more scandalous than the eldest princess losing her virtue before she could be auctioned off to the highest bidder like a broodmare. It was almost ironic. Had things played out slightly differently, both Tristan *and* Catriona would have been unable to go through with the engagement.

It would have been Gwenna and Aidan, after all.

Gwenna banished the thought immediately. He was marrying her sister.

"Please, Gwenna," Cat said softly. "You have to believe me."

"I do," she said wearily, head starting to pound. "I won't say anything to Aidan. You have my word."

Cat wrapped her arms around her sister and squeezed tightly. "Thank you. I don't know how I'll ever repay you."

"You can repay me by never seeing that wolf again," Gwenna muttered.

"Of course," Cat said, straightening up and staring into her sister's eyes. "Before the lake, I hadn't seen him since the winter solstice when I ended things."

Gwenna nodded, considering. "Did he ever… ask anything of you?"

"He asked me to run away with him," Cat admitted. "At the time, it seemed terribly romantic. But he kept… pushing the subject? Almost *insisting* that I go away with him. He said some really odd things at the end…."

"What kind of things?" Gwenna demanded.

"He had the answers I needed… I could restore Bannon to its former glory, but only by standing by his side…." Cat trailed off. "At the time, I didn't really pay attention, I guess. I thought he wanted what Mother says all boys want. And that was his way of trying to persuade me…."

Goosebumps erupted over Gwenna's arms, even though she was still sweating from the stifling heat. She nodded absently, mind going faster than her mouth could.

"Thank you for telling me. You're right; we should go help Mother," she said quietly.

Numb, she drifted along in Cat's wake as they headed back upstairs. Aidan hurried Cat away immediately, wanting her to rest after such an eventful morning. Her mother was off preparing for her grandfather's funeral, and Gwenna was alone in the entrance hall.

Numb, she headed outside to the courtyard, where she found a spare broom and set to work helping to sweep out the yard. The monotony of the work was comforting and allowed her plenty of time to get lost in her thoughts.

The wolf had tried to romance Catriona; that much was certain. Perhaps his intentions were pure. He might have had no idea who she was. Maybe he was just a lovestruck boy wanting to run away with the girl of his dreams.

But he had mentioned restoring Bannon to its former glory. Gwenna had no idea what kind of glory that would be, but she doubted he went around talking about that with every farmgirl. No, that kind of talk seemed reserved specifically for a princess.

The wolf absolutely knew who Catriona was. He pursued her for a purpose. But then she ended things, so he… went after her younger sister?

Gwenna reflected on everything he had said at the lake. It wasn't remotely romantic. Granted, she had a bow aimed at his head at the time. But that hadn't softened him at all. He'd been cryptic, and almost threatening.

She considered that perhaps she was reading too much into things. Maybe the wolf she saw in the field was a completely different wolf altogether. But no, the white tufts of fur on his head were very specific to him. It wasn't regular coloring for a wolf.

That was the Shifter in the fields this morning. He had asked Gwenna to go with him. He'd asked Cat too, but pretended it was out of love and a dying need to be together. That approach didn't work on Cat, but he was making the same offer now to Gwenna.

Why?

The questions tumbled around and around in Gwenna's mind, but she couldn't answer. So she swept. Swept and worried about what a wolf could mean for herself and for her sister.

CHAPTER 10

THE EVENING AFTER

T he funeral for the King was supposed to be held at sunset, according to tradition. But Orlaith did not signal to light the pyres until the moon was almost at its peak. She kept delaying, waiting for the heat to subside, before finally acknowledging the night would be just as broiling hot as the day had been.

Townspeople and courtiers stood shoulder to shoulder in the courtyard for hours, waiting patiently. But now that the pyre was lit, no one spoke. Almost every heart was unified in prayer.

For help.

For mercy.

For an end to this stifling heat and a few hours of cool night air. They prayed for answers, for clarity. Some prayed for rain and for their crops to be restored.

The stagnant air was punishing, but standing before open flames seemed especially cruel. Waves of heat slapped across already sweaty faces. Several flinched as the temperature spiked, but no one said a word.

It was supposed to be joyous when someone returned to The Deep. Funerals were a time for laughing and remembering. Bittersweet, but perhaps more sweet than bitter. Not tonight. The only sound was the occasional sniffle, but even that was few and far between.

Gwenna stood at the front of the crowd, closest to the pyre. But it wasn't enough. She didn't realize she was slowly moving closer and closer to the flames until her maid gently laid a hand on her arm to restrain her.

"You're going to catch fire yourself," Aldessa whispered.

It felt wrong to stop moving. Gwenna's sunburned face was so tender that standing even this close was punishing. But it wasn't enough. Gwenna needed the fire to snuff out any of the curse still remaining inside her. If The Deep could plant this inside her, she needed the flames to find it and scorch everything until nothing was left.

Perhaps that would end this curse.

Tears flowed freely down her cheeks, mixing with the beads of sweat that left her perpetually damp. The hair clinging to her neck made her feel claustrophobic, and it felt like every layer of clothing she had was soaked through. She kept waiting for the slightest breeze, any wind at all, but there was nothing.

Gwenna kept one eye on the entrance to the courtyard, the portcullis fully open so the townspeople could come and go as needed. Every so often, she scanned the high parapets of the castle wall where the guards patrolled. She scanned faces, looking for any hint of silver eyes.

Whatever the wolf knew, he was smart enough not to appear.

It could have been minutes or hours that Gwenna stood before the funeral pyre, hoping to atone for her curse. Someone whispered her name softly and brought her out of her stupor.

"I apologize, milady." Aldessa bobbed a curtsy, frowning. "I've already turned down your bed chamber but must return home for the night. My sister has fallen ill, and Mama needs my help."

Gwenna glanced around and saw that only a handful of people remained in the courtyard. Aldessa and her young brother Aymer stood before her.

"Of course," Gwenna said immediately, shaking her head slightly to clear her thoughts. "Are you sure you're feeling alright? Did you ever let the court physician look at that bump on your head?"

"I'll be fine," Aldessa assured her.

"Is your house safe for you to sleep in?" Gwenna asked.

Aymer nodded, bronzed face glistening with sweat. "Our roof held up. We swept it out this morning, and aside from a few broken dishes, everything's alright."

"And your sister? Was she injured in the storm?" These were all answers that she should have gotten this morning. But she had been too wrapped up in herself to remember that not everyone's homes were fortified with layers and layers of heavy stone.

"She had a mild fever when we left. And a cough," Aldessa said quietly. It was the same symptoms many of the other villagers were showing after the storm. So far, the physician had no idea what could have caused it or what would cure it. "Mama wanted to come to pay her respects; she loved your grandfather so much. But she felt staying home and letting Isabeau rest was better."

"The court physician has provided some courtiers a tonic to help with their cough. If she's not feeling better by tomorrow, please let me know, and I'll send him to call on her personally," Gwenna said.

Aldessa's dark eyes went wide. "That's very kind of you, your Grace. If there is anything we can do to repay you, please let us know."

"Aymer, do you still work in the Hall of Records?" Gwenna asked suddenly.

The twelve-year-old straightened up importantly. "I do."

Royal scholars always hired a group of young men, called pages, to do the manual labor associated with referencing dozens of different heavy books. The older pages were assistants to the scholars in the royal library, while younger pages were in charge of keeping the dusty Hall of Records organized in case a scholar needed anything.

"Come find me the moment you arrive tomorrow. I have something I need to research… and I think you could be quite helpful," Gwenna said, an idea sparking.

Aymer saluted, and Gwenna laughed, completely caught off-guard. No one had ever saluted her before. His sister rolled her eyes, mussing his hair affectionately.

"Thank you, your Grace. He will," Aldessa said. "We will see you first thing in the morning."

Gwenna watched the pair safely to the road before turning and heading to the Keep.

Thanks to the cold stone walls, the temperature was a little colder inside, but it was still brutally warm. Every window was thrown open to try and lure in some nonexistent breeze. No torches were lit, the heat not worth the light. The full moon coated the Keep in its light but cast eerie shadows in the corners.

Gwenna didn't see a single soul as she hurried up the stairs toward her mother's chambers. Many of the servants who usually slept in the Keep, like Aldessa, had decided to spend the night in town to help their families. The Keep had been cleaned out, and the nobility cared for, but the village was still struggling. They needed as many hands as possible, and Orlaith hadn't hesitated in allowing any staff to return to their families. Any of the Keep's guests, like courtiers who had not made it home before the storm hit, had retired for the night. The silence was almost liberating.

It was past time to tell Orlaith about the Shifter at the lake. Gwenna was determined to keep Catriona's name out of it, but her mother needed to know everything. If creatures from children's stories were roaming through the woods making veiled threats against royalty, Orlaith needed to know.

Gwenna rounded the final corner and saw that the door to the King's study was ajar, golden light spilling out into the hallway. She reached out a hand to knock.

"We are all going to starve."

Orlaith's voice had an edge to her words that had Gwenna instantly flattening herself against the wall, out of sight but still within earshot.

"I took inventory of what food remains," Aidan said quietly. "If we ration the court and the town, we can stretch our resources a month. Maybe two"

A long pause hung heavy in the air.

"Two months?" Orlaith whispered. "That's all we have?"

"If all we needed was food, yes," Aidan said hesitantly. "The Keep's cisterns have dried up too. We have six weeks of water if we're lucky."

Gwenna's pulse echoed in her ears, suddenly aware of how dry her mouth was.

"We need to send word to our allies. Call for aid." Orlaith's voice was rising, a feverish pitch to her words. Parchment rustled, and Gwenna could imagine her mother searching for a quill. "We don't know how big that storm was. Maybe only Thornvale was hit."

"Maybe," Aidan said, clearly doubtful. "I have riders ready to be dispatched at first light. Some will go over the Marshora to try and reach the other villages. And some will attempt to cross the sea."

"The sea that's full of sand, you mean?" Orlaith hissed. "We have no waterways, and we're completely cut off from everyone. And we have no idea if anyone else survived!"

"I've found men willing to ride out across the sand to find help. It's the best we can do until we learn more about what's out there." Aidan sighed. A chair creaked, and Gwenna pictured him lowering himself into one of her grandfather's favorite wooden chairs. "My lands are three weeks away by ship, and I'm sending men that direction over land. There's good reason to suspect that the South was unaffected by the storm and could send us supplies. It all just comes down to whether they get back in time...."

Silence fell in the study once more.

"I suppose we should plan your wedding. And coronation..." Orlaith sighed, voice muffled as though she was burying her face in her hands.

"With all due respect, your Grace, you are High Princess. Your people love and trust you. While you may not qualify for the crown without a husband, perhaps it would be better for you to continue to lead for the time being," Aidan said. "I am in no rush. It seems silly to plan a wedding, given the circumstances."

"You will be a wise king," Orlaith said, pride bleeding into her voice. "How many messengers are you deploying?"

"Two dozen."

"Find me another dozen. I'll send word to our noble houses. Perhaps they were safe from the storm. They were here two nights ago, eating our food. Now it's time for them to return the favor," Orlaith said wearily.

"I will."

"Is there anything else you require this evening?"

Aidan paused before answering. "About the Princess...."

"Catriona will understand if we postpone the wedding," Orlaith said quickly. "I'll speak with her myself."

"About *Gwenna*."

For the second time in as many days, Gwenna found herself hiding in the shadows with her heart in her throat as Aidan discussed her. She steeled herself for whatever he said next.

Orlaith sat in silence for a moment before she spoke. "What about Gwenna?"

"You saw with King Domhnall–"

"I did."

"Are you not at all concerned?" Aidan pressed. "Or suspicious?"

Orlaith inhaled sharply. Gwenna felt a knife turn in her gut.

"I need you to hear me clearly and not misunderstand. Yes, I saw all that you did, and yes, I have had all those same thoughts that you undoubtedly have had. But Gwenna is my daughter," Orlaith began. Aidan huffed a disgruntled sigh, but Orlaith continued. "I need you to trust me when I say that she is *not* the one causing these things."

"You can't possibly know that!" Aidan hissed.

"No, but Aidan... I *feel* it. There is something more happening here. I do not deny Gwenna may be involved, but I will stake my life on the fact that she is not the cause of it all," Orlaith said firmly. "She is not cursed."

Gwenna had heard enough. She hurried up to her chambers. Her mother's words replayed over and over in Gwenna's mind. Orlaith knew of Gwenna's innocence even when she wasn't sure herself.

That had to count for something.

Once alone in her chambers, Gwenna looked out on the remnants of Braewood Forest before she climbed into bed.

A dark shape moved through the spindly trees. Gwenna grabbed the windowsill, heart pounding in her ears. It was too far away to say for certain, but it was something large and furry.

Like a wolf.

The moon drifted out from behind a cloud, illuminating the mountains. It wasn't a wolf, but a huge black bear ambling through the trees.

There wasn't anything wrong about the bear itself, but Gwenna felt certain that it shouldn't be this close to Thornvale. It was an omen, just like the wolf. They were probably friends.

Whatever happened here, it *felt* wrong. Something deep within the marrow of the kingdom had shattered. Whether or not Gwenna was responsible for the shattering was irrelevant. She needed to mend it.

Fast.

CHAPTER II

ONE DAY AFTER

Gwenna woke up with no real plan other than to learn as much as she could about the Fairies. Her chambers already felt boiling hot, but she didn't dare waste any water bathing. She piled her hair on top of her head, dressed in the thinnest gown, and met Aymer outside her chambers.

"How is your sister feeling?" Gwenna asked immediately.

"Still feverish, but her cough seems better," the boy responded. "What can I help you with, Princess?"

Gwenna glanced up and down the corridor. It appeared empty, but she couldn't count on that. She nodded for Aymer to follow and led the way to the Hall of Records. A little privacy would be helpful until she had anything to share.

"I want you to bring me every book or ledger the Hall has on curses," Gwenna said as soon as Aymer closed the thick wooden door behind them. She'd never heard of anything like this happening before, but maybe she'd get lucky.

"The only thing written about a curse is in the record of one baby's Blessing," Aymer said slowly. "Yours…"

Gwenna sank into a wooden chair, holding her face in her hands. "That's what I was afraid of."

"I can still bring you the ledger if you'd like?"

"Yes, please."

"Right away."

Soon, Gwenna was skimming the faded parchment, browsing the text lazily. Her mother had told her the story of her Blessing many times, but to see it recorded as history was something else entirely.

"Fairy Maeve." Gwenna ran her fingers over the scrawling script. The last one ever seen.

The only one who dared to defy a King. Was it displeasure with the King? Or displeasure with Gwenna?

"Aymer, are there any records of the Fairies?" Gwenna asked suddenly, looking up as an idea hit her.

He popped his head out of the tall row of shelves nearby, a puzzled look twisting his face as he thought about it.

"I don't know if they kept any ledgers... Aren't they tiny? How would they hold a quill?" he asked, one eyebrow raised.

She fought back a laugh. "I meant, have any of our historians chronicled interactions with Fairies? I don't need *their* version of records."

"But our records with them!" he finished her thought with glee, scurrying away to begin the search.

Smiling at his enthusiasm, Gwenna turned back to the ledger. All of the other pages after her Blessing were blank. She was the last infant to be Blessed. Over a century of Blessings for thousands of girls in Bannon, but it all ended with her.

"Secondborn granddaughter Blessed with Strength," Gwenna read aloud, propping her chin on her hand.

Her Blessing didn't infuriate her anymore. She'd begged her mother for years to undo it or reverse it. But Fairy magic could never be altered. It was the only brand of magic with that weight of finality. The Mages in books could set Weavings, but those were full of loopholes.

Only a Fairy could do something permanent.

Aymer hefted three large leather-bound books with gilded edges onto the table. "These are the only mention of Fairies. They appear to be more records of Blessings, but you're welcome to search through them."

"There's nothing else?" Gwenna asked, peeking inside the first book. Like he had said, more Blessings were detailed. Nothing more. "Did Fairies only appear for Blessings? Nothing else?"

Aymer shrugged. "I've been cataloging the historical records, with all the charters and treatises. I haven't found anything with Fairies, but I can let you know if I find anything."

"Yes, please," Gwenna murmured, mind racing. "There's nothing else? No other record of them living in Bannon?"

"Just what's written in children's stories." Aymer frowned. "Would you like me to bring those to you? I'd be happy to run up to the library to collect them."

Gwenna nodded, feeling more hopeless by the minute. "Yes, please."

It wasn't until she began flipping idly through the pages of the tenth or eleventh storybook that she recognized the pattern. Of the nearly thirty books that Aymer had found, they all had different authors yet contained almost identical depictions of the Fairies themselves.

Fairies were always depicted as hardly bigger than a man's palm, fluttering and floating through the air. Each Fairy was feminine and seemed to have its own color, appearing like an orb of light with a tiny creature at the very center. They were reclusive creatures, living in a tree hidden far away from any peasants.

Every story was consistent: they were peaceful creatures who bestowed Blessings on children out of love, not obligation. They had no interest in politics but wanted everyone to live in peace and comfort. And every single illustration showed them living in small colonies near the water's edge.

"Not just any water." Aymer nodded solemnly, interrupting Gwenna talking aloud to herself and looking over her shoulder at one of the illustrations. "That's The Deep itself. That's where they live."

"The Deep?" Gwenna repeated. "But The Deep isn't a real place...."

He shrugged. "That's what my Mama always told me. Fairies, Shifters, and Mages all come from the shores of The Deep. That's where their power comes from."

"They live... *together*?" Gwenna stared down at the illustration.

"That's what she always told me." Aymer nodded.

Gwenna pushed to her feet, causing the boy to flinch with the sudden movement. She mumbled an apology and raced out of the room.

As she raced through the Keep, the sun was already sinking low behind the mountains. Shifters and Fairies lived together. She pictured the black wolf with the white tufts of hair on his head, nodding for her to join him.

If she went with him... maybe she could find the Fairies.

Rounding a corner quickly, she bumped into someone and knocked them to the ground.

"Oh, I'm so sorry!" Gwenna cried, seeing Kellen splayed on the floor.

He grabbed his floppy hat and pulled it on again. "Don't worry about me, your Highness. I'm fine." He grinned and bounded to his feet. "I actually was worried you'd fallen ill. I didn't see you at any of the meals today..."

"I'm fine, thank you. I have been lost in my studies, and the day got away from me," she explained.

"Studies?" Aidan repeated, coming up behind her with a scowl. "Your people are starving, and you're busy reading?"

Gwenna imagined the snide remark like an arrow missing its mark, falling harmlessly to the floor without injuring her. It would be worth it if she found something that would break the curse. But she wasn't willing to tip her hand and reveal what she found before she was ready.

Especially since running off with a Shifter was categorically insane. The Fairies were the only ones to grant Blessings and, therefore, *must* know why she was cursed as a baby. They also would know how to break whatever curse she had put on the kingdom.

If the Shifters lived near the Fairies, getting herself captured and taken to their homeland seemed like the best way to find them. The last thing she needed now was to have her mother put her under lock and key.

"I was heading down to the kitchens to get a small bite to eat." Gwenna ignored Aidan, addressing Kellen instead. "Have you seen my sister?"

"She's retired for the evening. Your mother is insisting on taking her riding at daybreak," Aidan answered, folding his arms across his broad chest.

"You'll be accompanying them, I assume?" Gwenna asked immediately, the image of a black wolf with white hair on his head springing to mind.

"I was told this was something just for Catriona and her mother. Some kind of tradition Lady Orlaith wishes to maintain. She went riding with her mother after she was betrothed, and she'd like to do the same with Catriona," Aidan explained with a yawn.

"They need to take guards with them," Gwenna insisted. "You'll see to it?"

"They wanted to be on their own. Probably talk about… womanly things," Aidan grimaced at the thought. "I can't in good conscience send any men to standby and have to listen to that."

Blowing out an angry sigh, Gwenna marched forward and stabbed a finger into Aidan's chest. "A Shifter appeared in our lands days ago, threatening a royal family member. You *will* send guards with them to see to their protection. That's not a question. It's an order!"

Aidan scrambled backward from her advance until his back pressed against the wall. "I don't think you underst—"

"I understand perfectly fine," Gwenna said through gritted teeth, poking him in the chest again. "Catriona needs protection. It's not safe for her out there."

"You're hurt that you weren't invited," Aidan said coolly, pushing her hand away and rubbing at the tender spot in his chest that would surely be bruised by morning. "Don't tell me how to command the men. I'm the future king here, not you."

"I'm telling you to protect your future wife," Gwenna snapped. "If you let anything happen to her–"

"You'll what? Cast a spell on me, too?" Aidan scoffed, pushing past her without a backward glance. "I'll send three men. I can't spare more."

Kellen flashed her an apologetic smile before following in Aidan's wake. Gwenna turned on her heel and stormed down to the kitchens to get a bite to eat before returning to the Hall of Records.

She couldn't sleep now, not knowing that she was finally onto something. If she worked through the night, she could have answers and a plan to present to her mother in the morning.

They only had six weeks of drinking water. Every day counted.

Aymer was straightening up the Hall when she returned, having swallowed down a crust of bread and a few bites of stew. She assured him that she would lock up and sent him home. There was no need for anyone else to lose sleep over this.

Not when she could fix it herself.

Gwenna settled back at the table, now illuminated by moonlight pouring through the window high in the wall. Aymer had left out the storybooks for her, and she picked up right where she left off.

There was no record of any dispute or fight with the Fairies. So why did they leave? Why did they disappear?

What about her, her Blessing, caused them to flee?

She had gone over the names of guests at her Blessing repeatedly. Many she had known her entire life, the others since returned to The Deep. But no name stuck out as someone who would have any answers to explain away the Fairies' behavior.

That meant she had to go to the Fairies themselves.

She didn't know where the Fairies were but knew where at least one Shifter was. The wolf might know exactly what she needed, after all. He had said as much to Catriona.

But could she trust him?

Gwenna leaned back in her chair, staring out at the cloudless night sky as she considered what she knew about Shifters.

Shifters were always opposed to humans. Always. But the Mages seemed to side with the Shifters in any conflict. Fairies never involved themselves in the conflict between Shifters and mankind but tried to assist women where possible.

By the time the sky began to lighten, Gwenna was still sitting with the same conclusion she had the night before. She had fought against it, trying to find any other avenue to explore. Thoroughly combing through any and all storybooks she could see was her way of looking for any other possible action to take. But it was no use.

She needed to find the Fairies and talk to Fairy Maeve.

To do that, Gwenna needed to go with the Shifter.

CHAPTER 12

THE MORNING, TWO DAYS AFTER

A quiet knock at the door, and then Cat timidly poked her head inside.

"Aidan's steward told me I could find you here." Catriona took in Gwenna's bloodshot eyes and stack of books on the table and paused. She glanced around the Hall of Records, but it was empty other than the pair of them. "Have you been here all night?"

"I lost track of time. I needed to research a few things…." Gwenna yawned, leaning back in her chair and stretching her arms above her head.

Catriona's blonde hair was intricately braided and fell down the middle of her back. She wore a simple dress and riding cloak. "I came to see if you wanted to go riding with us."

"I can't." Gwenna shook her head adamantly. "You and Mother should enjoy yourselves."

"I'd love it if you joined us." Cat moved closer, standing across the table. "I miss you, Gwenna."

"I haven't gone anywhere."

"You haven't been hiding?" Cat arched a skeptical eyebrow, and Gwenna's face burned. Catriona sank down in the opposite chair, reaching across the table to take her sister's hand. "None of this is your fault, Gwenna."

"You don't know that," Gwenna mumbled, tears pricking her eyes. She tried to pull her hand away, but Cat hung onto it.

"I do," Catriona said firmly. "So trust me, even if you doubt yourself. I know you, Gwenna. You'd never harm anyone."

Gwenna exhaled shakily, scrubbing the back of her hand across her eyes. "You're just being kind because you took my boots."

"If you come with us, I'll give them back to you so you can wear them," Cat teased, squeezing her hand gently.

Gwenna shook her head. "You and Mother enjoy yourselves. It'll be good to have some normalcy for a while."

"You deserve normalcy, too," Cat said softly. "It's not good to hide away from the world."

"I'm not hiding—" she started to protest.

"You think that if you hide yourself away, you can't hurt anyone else," Cat folded her arms smugly. Gwenna faltered, feeling exposed under her sister's knowing look. "This *isn't* your fault, Gwenna."

"I think I know how to fix it," Gwenna whispered. She hadn't expected to tell anyone this soon but needed someone to know what she was working on.

Cat tensed, studying her sister's face intently. "You do?"

Gwenna nodded. "That's what I've been working on. I'll explain everything when you and Mother get back. But yes... I have a plan. I think I can break this curse, or whatever it is."

Catriona leaped from her chair and almost tackled Gwenna in a hug. "I know you can."

"Don't mention anything to Mother. I don't want to worry her," Gwenna sighed, and Cat nodded in understanding.

"Get some sleep," Cat teased, letting her go and slowly heading towards the closed door. "You can awe us with your genius after you've rested. We should only be gone an hour or two at most."

"Be safe," Gwenna called, settling back in her chair. "Aldessa was saying they've seen that bear lingering in the woods near the village. Take some guards with you!"

Cat laughed but didn't say anything else before she sailed out the door and let it fall shut behind her.

Gwenna flipped through picture after picture of Fairies, steeling her resolve. Catriona was the heir. She had commitments to the crown. The Shifter seemed to have wanted her initially, but he would settle for Gwenna. He wouldn't have a choice. Gwenna was the princess who could be spared.

It just meant she would have to knowingly walk into a trap. Her days lurking behind columns in the ballroom were far behind her. This was something only she could do. Gwenna was the last to have a Blessing from a Fairy, so she should be the one to find the Fairies and bring them back.

She never intended to fall asleep. Her head felt heavy, so she propped her chin against her hand. Her eyelids fluttered open and closed, chin bobbing as she tried to stay awake. Eventually, cheek pressed to the table, she surrendered to sleep.

CHAPTER 13

EARLY AFTERNOON, TWO DAYS AFTER

R aised voices out in the hallway dragged Gwenna's consciousness to the surface. She bolted upright and wiped the drool from her chin, blinked rapidly, and tried to get her bearings.

Her dreams had all been about Aidan. It had been the pair of them dancing, he was laughing at something she said. Gwenna wore a beautiful gossamer gown with pearls studded in her bodice, a long white veil trailing behind her. Aidan had just been leaning in for a kiss when she was so rudely awoken.

Sunlight was streaming through the window beside her. She must have been asleep for a few hours.

Aymer poked his head out of the nearby aisle of books, head tilting to the side as he gave the closed oak door a quizzical look.

"What is that?" Gwenna asked him as the voices got louder.

Someone was approaching the Hall. And they were angry.

"I'll go look…" The boy hurried for the door. "I hope you're not upset I didn't wake you."

The oak door was thrown open with a loud bang before Aymer could get there.

Aidan stood at the door, rage clearly written all over his face as he cast his eyes around the room until they landed on Gwenna at the desk. For a moment, she was terrified he knew what she had been dreaming about. But then she saw Kellen visible in the doorway behind him, flanked by other knights wearing chainmail.

Aymer silently drifted out of sight and back between the tall shelves.

"Where did Catriona go riding?" Aidan demanded.

"She didn't tell me where they were headed..." Gwenna began. Aidan turned, giving Kellen a knowing look that she couldn't decipher. "What is it? What's wrong?"

The future king turned back, inhaling sharply. As he met her eyes, she realized that it wasn't anger she saw pooled there. It was fear.

Ice poured through Gwenna's veins. She rose to her feet.

"What's wrong?" she repeated, taking in his pale face.

"Your sister and mother have not returned. One of their horses returned alone a few moments ago." Aidan said shortly, turning around abruptly to command the men standing at attention behind him. "Prepare the horses. I want every armed man we've got. If something's happened to them ..."

"Prepare mine as well!" Gwenna called before the knights could disperse.

"Yes, your Highness," Captain Draven nodded before dashing after his men.

Aidan paused in his retreat, turning back to her. "You're not coming."

"It's not up to you," Gwenna said shortly, turning to see Aymer's dark eyes peeking around the corner of the nearest shelf. "Leave my things on the table. I'll be back for them."

"Gwenna–" Aidan said quietly, a warning tone in his voice. She vaguely recognized that it was the gentlest he'd spoken to her since his arrival, but it was the wrong time for him to try and coddle her.

"You do not have time to debate this with me!" Gwenna snapped, pushing through the doorway past him and stalking down the hall to the courtyard. "I'll simply follow you if you try to leave me behind."

119

Knights dressed in Bannonite livery rushed back and forth between the armory and their horses in the packed stableyard. It was pure chaos.

Near the portcullis, a stablehand held the reins to a saddled horse. Captain Draven saw Gwenna standing at the steps to the entrance hall and gestured to the mount, indicating it was waiting for her.

She nodded appreciation, heading down the steps in that direction as Draven returned to a conversation with a knight wearing plate.

"Gwenna!" A hand caught her arm, holding her back. She turned to see Aidan standing on the step above, concern etched across his features. "You need to stay here."

"There's not a chance I'm staying behind," she said flatly, pulling out of his grip.

Aidan opened his mouth to argue but was interrupted by Kellen.

"Here you go, Gwenna." The steward handed her a bow and quiver of arrows. "I figured you'd want these."

"Thanks." She flashed a quick smile, turning to go mount up.

Aidan grabbed her arm again, slightly more gently this time. Irritation rising, she swiveled back to face him.

"They've been gone for hours," Aidan said in a low voice. "There's a good possibility that they could be in danger."

"Good thing I'm armed then." Gwenna rattled the quiver of arrows at him and again turned to mount her horse.

"You don't know what's out there!" Aidan called, stomping across the cobblestones behind her.

"Neither do you!" she shot back, not breaking stride. She wanted to keep arguing, to point out that she knew a hell of a lot more than he did. But she also didn't want to incriminate herself.

"It's not safe for a wom–"

"I'm going to *strongly* recommend you don't finish that sentence," Gwenna snapped, planting her foot in the stirrups and easily swinging into the saddle. She took the reins from the groom, and he hurried to help someone else. "If you're so concerned about safety, you should have sent them with guards like I suggested."

"I did!" He hissed. "Gwenna, you can't do this–"

"I don't know what happened, but neither do you. If my sister is involved, I'm going. Don't try to stop me."

"I-I-I … I *forbid* it!" Aidan sputtered, face bright red.

Now it was Gwenna's turn to be surprised.

"I beg your pardon?" she said in an icy tone.

"I forbid you to accompany us," he repeated, confidence returning.

Gwenna stared down at him for a moment. He glared, but haughty superiority wafted off him like a foul stench. She looked to the sky to compose herself, huffing out a laugh of disbelief before looking him right in the eyes.

"You're not the king yet," Gwenna said coldly, snapping the reins and spurring the mare to join Draven at the head of the column.

She forced herself to keep riding and not look back. But she still heard Kellen's low whistle of approval.

The search party consisted of nearly sixty riders by the time they left. Gwenna wanted to ride at the head of the column, but Draven insisted she move to the middle to be better surrounded by guards in case of an ambush. Reluctantly, she complied.

The look of pure outrage on Aidan's face almost made it worth it when he watched her obediently take orders from the captain without objection.

The group rode hard across the narrow stone bridge connecting the Keep to the hillside over the fjord. The path took them straight through Thornvale Town, horses thundering down the main road. The dry, cracked ground beneath the hooves sent up a massive cloud of dust in their wake. The few villagers Gwenna saw were already covered in so much dirt she felt bad at how much the horses churned up.

But they couldn't afford to slow down.

Cat and Orlaith were missing, along with three knights hand-selected by Captain Draven.

On the far side of town, the search party turned northwest and headed inland. The towering pine trees were needleless and barren, standing sentinel as they pounded by.

The smug satisfaction of defying the future king was enough to keep Gwenna's growing anxiety at bay for at least the first bit of the journey. She couldn't help but notice how intentionally he avoided looking at her. He was *so* furious that she had defied him. In any other circumstance, it would be laughable. But now it felt petty and juvenile.

They took a mountain trail and had gone a few leagues when one of Draven's rangers came racing back. He conferred with Aidan for a moment.

Aidan suddenly called a dozen knights to his side and raced up the trail. Gwenna heard Kellen yell something over his shoulder to Draven before following his lord.

Draven rode back to Gwenna to explain.

"Our rangers found something," Draven explained over the noise of the hooves. "It's not your mother or sister, but… you should prepare yourself."

Gwenna inhaled shakily, refusing to let her emotions break through any more than that. Clearing her throat, she worked up the courage to ask.

"It's your men, isn't it?"

Draven nodded.

"Show me." The words came out before she could stop them.

The captain of the guard, old enough to be her father, gave her a stern look but didn't comment on whether or not it would be appropriate for a woman's eyes. Instead, he pulled his horse around, and they rode hard after Aidan, with the rest of the column pounding through the dirt after her.

The treeline broke, revealing a broad meadow that, at some point, was probably full of lush grass. It had a beautiful view of the sand dunes of the fjord, a wide space in the middle cleared of debris, and covered with what appeared to be a picnic blanket.

But it was the three bodies lying in the parched grass that Gwenna couldn't look away from. Someone had pulled blankets from a saddlebag and covered the corpses. But there was no mistaking the three pairs of boots sticking out the bottom of the shrouds.

A group of knights were congregated around their fallen comrades, some on their knees to pay respect to the dead. Aidan and his forward guard had dismounted, stalking the edges of the meadow for some sign of Orlaith or Cat.

Gwenna climbed off her horse, wordlessly passing the reins to a nearby knight. He murmured something about watering the horses and brushing them down, but she didn't process it.

"Don't get too close, Gwenna." Kellen hurried back towards her. "You won't want to see."

She nodded, hardly able to speak over the lump in her throat. "Was it the wolf?"

Kellen hesitated. "There's really no way to say…"

"Did an animal do this?" she insisted. "Tell me, Kellen. Please."

"Something with claws, yes," he admitted.

A few dishes were strewn about the large blanket, but whatever food was left had been picked off by animals. There was no sign of her mother or Cat, but this proved they were on the right track. If that wolf had done anything to them…

Gwenna wrapped her arms around herself as she silently prayed, somehow chilled with fear despite the mounting heat. A warm breeze blew against her like a blaze from a hearth. There was no grass or leaves to rustle. The silence was unnatural.

It was only her stubborn pride that kept her from breaking down into tears. Aidan would not see her cry after she had fought so hard to come.

But three armed men had been taken down by a beast. Now her mother and sister were nowhere to be found. Gwenna *knew* the Shifter wanted a princess to go with him. Why hadn't she said something? Why hadn't she stopped Cat from leaving the Keep?

Standing in the middle of the meadow, the vulnerability was almost tangible. She was a wide-eyed doe waiting to be slaughtered. An eerie prickling sensation caused the hair to rise on the back of her neck. Someone, or something, was watching her. She could feel it. If it was that Shifter again…

"I'm sure they're fine, by the way," Kellen said, but she wasn't listening. "I probably should have said that earlier. But I'm sure they're ok. Probably a horse slipped a shoe or something simple like that."

"Thank you," Gwenna said distractedly, searching the tree line for the gleam of silver eyes watching her.

"Your Majesty. We found tracks on the other side of the meadow." The ranger approached Aidan directly. Kellen and Gwenna exchanged looks, hurrying to join the conversation.

"The princess?"

"No, sir. These appear to be the tracks of… another."

"What other?" Aidan snapped.

"A dog. A large one," the ranger explained quietly.

Gwenna's breath hitched. "A large dog? Or a wolf?"

"Did it attack?" Aidan asked sharply, talking over her.

"It pursued two horses from the royal stable, which we assume to be the mounts of the High Princess and her daughter," the ranger explained. "We've lost the trail for a moment, but we're looking for it now."

Aidan's eyes turned steely.

Covering her mouth with her hand, Gwenna fell back a step. A stone formed in the pit of her stomach.

"We found their trail!" Another ranger yelled from the eastern end of the meadow.

"Mount up!" Captain Draven yelled to the group, and everyone returned to the waiting horses.

Gwenna didn't let the Bannonite captain get ahead of her this time. She snapped her reins and galloped after the ranger, forcing even Aidan to ride behind her. Draven pulled up alongside her, and they rode directly behind the rangers together, the rest of the column stretched out behind.

Her lungs couldn't bring in enough air, breaths were ragged and shaky.

Draven suddenly reigned up hard, and Gwenna followed suit. The ground suddenly fell away to reveal a steep ravine, and her stomach leaped into her throat.

Swearing, Gwenna slid off her tall horse. The dirt was thick, wolf tracks clear even to her untrained eyes. Numbly, she followed the tracks. Boot tracks stopped about where Draven did. But the horse tracks didn't. The horses kept going...

"Gwenna- don't!" someone called from behind, but her feet kept moving. Forward. Towards the edge of the ravine.

Where the horse tracks... disappeared.

The sun-baked dirt burned through the thin soles of her slippers. She could feel each tiny pebble. But she kept going, kept moving towards the edge of that ravine.

She stopped at the edge and willed herself to look down. Tears blurred her vision. But she already knew. She could feel it.

Gwenna had to see it for herself.

About twenty-five feet down, the horse's unblinking eyes stared up at her, knocking the air from her lungs. Its hindquarters were shredded and mutilated by claw and teeth marks, limbs splayed.

Her mother lay motionless beside the dead horse, head at an odd angle and unbound hair covering her face. Gwenna's vision snagged on her hands, almost gray. Her mother was wearing Gwenna's favorite gown, which reminded Gwenna of a pool of refined gold.

She fell back a step, swallowing back a sob.

Aidan swam into view, grabbing her by the shoulders and looking into her eyes, searching for answers.

"Catriona?" he asked, face pale.

Gwenna shook her head. "I-It's Mother."

His face closed off as he released her roughly and turned back to his men, shouting an order.

Catriona.

She wasn't there. They hadn't found her. It would have been her horse that made it back to the castle. Maybe there was a chance she was still alive.

Aidan's men swarmed the ravine, yelling Catriona's name as they searched.

Gwenna wiped her eyes and nose on her sleeve, heading back to the bootprints. Tracking wasn't something she had any experience with, but something had to indicate where Cat went.

Her eyes combed through the landscape, trying to distinguish any patterns at all. Whatever evidence was left behind had been destroyed as the search party arrived at the scene. Any flicker of hope within her began to be smothered by the returning wave of panic when Gwenna finally was able to make one individual paw print.

It was large and certainly canine.

It was heading eastward, running parallel to the ravine, and she followed it, heart pounding in her ears. The gorge suddenly jutted east, wolf tracks continuing parallel. Gwenna wound out of sight of Aidan and the others, adrenaline coursing through her veins.

Something inside of her screamed that she was on the right path.

She was so focused on the wolf tracks that she didn't see the large slab of stone that jutted out of the ground and tripped her. The skin scraped off her palms as Gwenna caught herself moments before her face hit the ground. She lifted her head, seeing only red beneath her.

Confused, Gwenna pushed to her hands and knees, realizing that she had landed on a large, fresh bloodstain.

She shrieked, standing up quickly. Men in chainmail ran to her side.

"Milady!" A guard cried. "You're injured!"

"It's not my blood!" Gwenna's voice broke, pushing him away. The blood clung to the front of her gown and hands. She could feel it on her neck.

Whatever had happened here, it was recent.

Gwenna stepped around the guards, looking at the pool of blood on the rock. There was a strange outline, with blood pooled on either side. Like something had been in the middle of the rock, bleeding out around it.

The rock stretched like a shelf over the ravine, and the blood ran directly off it, dripping into the gorge below.

She stumbled forward, following the path of the blood, and looked over the ravine's edge.

The corpse was face down, but Gwenna saw the golden blonde hair and the boots that had been borrowed that morning.

Strong hands pulled her away from the edge of the ravine as a primal scream tore from Gwenna's throat.

CHAPTER 14

THE EVENING, TWO DAYS AFTER

Three funeral pyres were lit within twenty-four hours. Gwenna was the last member of the Lorne family. Someone spoke, but nothing registered.

Gwenna had no energy left for heavy sobs, but the tears were neverending. They streamed down her face like rivers rushing out to sea, a steady current keeping them flowing. How could one body contain so much moisture? She felt like the dried reeds covering the pyre, withered and almost hollow. A passing breeze would disintegrate her until nothing was left but dust.

Still, the tears continued.

She stood there, rooted to the spot, listening to the crackle and snap of the wood long into the night. The heat was more oppressive than the night of her grandfather's pyre. But she could barely feel it.

It was all varying shades of pain.

The moon was beginning to set when a soft hand touched her elbow.

"You need to get some rest," Draven said softly. "It will be dawn soon."

Looking around, Gwenna realized she was the only one left in the courtyard. The crowd had dissipated silently, or perhaps she didn't want to hear them.

She nodded blankly, slowly heading inside. Draven stayed at her side, carefully observing her from the corner of his eye to see if he needed to steady her. Gwenna noted his concern but felt like she sat at the bottom of a well of grief. She would eventually find the strength to pull herself out, and then she could thank him. But not tonight.

"You need to see the council," Kellen said quietly, meeting her inside the entrance hall. "They called a meeting a few minutes ago. Aidan is in with them now."

"The council?" she repeated blankly. "Did they ask for me?"

"No... But you should be there." Kellen glanced around nervously before leaning in close and dropping his voice to a whisper. "If you want to keep the throne, you must go to them. Now."

Adrenaline coursed through her body, and she nodded in understanding. Not everyone was weighed down by grief. The vultures were primed to attack, and she was the last one able to fend them off.

Kellen led her to a small wood-paneled room on the first floor of the Keep where the council regularly met. Every seat at the large rectangular table dominating the space was occupied. Duke Byrne sat at the head of the table, fingers steepled. A scowl creased his drooping jowls as he saw her darkening the doorstep of his clandestine mutinous meeting.

Aidan grabbed her wrist and drew her into the room before she could open her mouth to say anything. He nodded a quiet thanks to Kellen before shutting the door, positioning himself just behind Gwenna to stare down the council. She glanced over her shoulder at him, noting his tensed jaw and a spark of anger behind his eyes. He was restrained but furious.

"Good morning, Princess." Duke Byrne was formal but not unkind. "Were you able to sleep well?"

"I haven't yet been to my chambers," Gwenna said, eyes taking each face in turn. "I was too busy paying my respects to the dead to rest or scheme. Though scheming seems to be something you have no problem engaging in before the funeral pyre flames have been snuffed out. What is this? What's going on?"

"Please, have a seat." The Duke waved his leathery hand towards the chair opposite him, but Gwenna didn't move. He sighed before continuing. "The royal constitution signifies that should a sitting monarch pass away before a new one can be crowned, a council of the highest ranking noblemen should convene to ensure a peaceful transition of power."

Gwenna glanced behind at Aidan, who was conspicuously clenching his jaw.

"I appreciate your dedication to our constitution, gentlemen. But I believe the future king is standing before you, rendering this council obsolete," she said, trying to be as commanding and regal as possible.

Aidan's eyes darted to her, eyebrows quirked upward in clear surprise. She didn't like him very much at the moment, but he was still the heir that her grandfather had approved. Gwenna's respect for her late grandfather outweighed her personal feelings for the youngest Kaldonna brother. She was not about to allow this council of power-hungry men destroy her family's legacy.

"We agree." Lord Whyte cleared his throat. He sat closest to Byrne, beady eyes darting nervously towards the Duke. "Prince Aidan is to be crowned as soon as possible."

Gwenna heard Aidan exhale softly, relieved that his claim to the crown was secure. Her own suspicion heightened, a knot forming in her stomach. The council was being far too eager to play nice.

"I'm glad we all agree," she said, narrowing her eyes at Duke Byrne once. "What else can we address for the council?"

The other men at the table averted their gaze, not looking at her or Aidan directly. Duke Byne took a deep breath, composing himself.

"Our kingdoms require us to continue to do our duty despite... the circumstances." Byrne hesitated, swallowing roughly.

The first ray of sunlight shone through the window behind the Duke, hitting Gwenna between the eyes. She blinked, raising her hand to shade herself.

"The council called an emergency session to discuss this matter, and we've come to a decision…" the Duke continued.

The suddenly bright sunlight caused a headache to throb in her temple, and Gwenna could feel that her eyes were swollen from the tears.

"We agree that Aidan Kaldonna received the late King Domhnall's blessing to take the throne upon the condition of his marriage to Princess Catriona," Duke Byrne recounted. "Given current circumstances, the council still desires to honor the late King's request for his successor, but the conditions must be upheld. The heir to the throne must marry a Bannonite princess."

Gwenna stiffened, the air rushing out of her lungs.

"This is absurd!" Aidan hissed coldly.

"My sister just passed. This is barbaric," Gwenna whispered, shaking her head furiously.

"The constitution is clear," Lord Whyt said weakly, still not meeting their eyes.

"We understand that there may be some… discomfort," Byrne said delicately. "Which is why we decided to discuss this as men before we were interrupted, Princess. Let's remain level-headed as we decide what is best for Bannon. I understand and share your concerns. Which is why I humbly present an alternative."

"What alternative?" Aidan scoffed.

"My daughter, Jeyne, is of noble birth and marrying age. Our family is next in line for the throne anyways, and–"

"Absolutely not," Gwenna interrupted. "What you're suggesting is treason, Duke Byrne, and as the last remaining member of the Lorne family, I command you to be silent. There will be no coup, no changing of the guard, not while I am here, ready and able to maintain the Lorne family's proud legacy. The Deep granted us the right to rule, and I am willing to defend that title with my life."

Silence fell in the room, all eyes on Gwenna. She could feel their scrutiny like a thousand tiny needles digging into her skin, but she refused to show them her discomfort. Let them stare.

She was Queen now.

Gwenna turned to Lord Whyt, blatantly ignoring Duke Byrne now. "Arrange the wedding and the coronation. This meeting is over."

"Don't I get a say in this?" Aidan stormed forward, slamming his fist into the heavy table. His face was red with anger. "This is my life you're talking about."

"Your life, but also a throne, your Grace," one council member suggested with a reassuring smile.

"Sacrifice is a key component of leadership," Lord Whyt chimed in.

"Aren't you going to say anything to me?"

The question lingered in the air, and it took a moment before Gwenna realized Aidan was addressing her.

She looked up, realizing he was glaring at her.

"I'm sorry if you were expecting more romance, but I will not get down on one knee and beg for you, Lord Aidan. The council is right: at least you get a crown out of this 'sacrifice,'" Gwenna said snidely. "I refuse to sit here and let some archaic rules give this council the right to steal the throne out from under me. The idea that the small thing hanging between your legs gives you more of a right to rule is disgusting and barbaric. I am the acting queen of Bannon."

Uncomfortable coughs and disapproving mutters echoed through the room. Aidan's face turned crimson, practically vibrating with rage.

"Plan the wedding for whenever you want," Gwenna said, turning on her heel and shoving the door open. "I'll be ready."

CHAPTER 15

THREE DAYS AFTER

"I'm sorry to disturb you, milady, but Lord Aidan is here to see you," Aldessa said quietly, opening the door to Gwenna's chambers. "I told him you required rest, but he insisted. You missed today's rations allotment, but I'll have it sent up shortly."

Wordlessly, Gwenna rose from her bed and padded to the small sitting room off of her chambers. Aidan stood with his elbow propped on the mantle, no hint of a smile anywhere on his face.

"What are you doing in bed in the middle of the day?" he demanded. "Are you ill?"

"I think I must be," Gwenna said, flopping onto the settee. "I dreamt that I lost the two women I loved most in the world and didn't even have a full day to mourn them before I was sold off as a consolation prize to a boy who wanted a throne. I certainly must be feverish!"

He narrowed his eyes. "I mourn her too, Gwenna."

"Do you?" she demanded. Fury rose up inside her, which was almost comforting. She was impenetrable as long as she kept this anger around her like a quilt. The suffocating guilt couldn't reach her.

A heavy silence hung in the air.

Aidan's face was pale and expressionless as he sank into an armchair. He held his head in his hands.

"Are you going to say something?" Gwenna finally asked softly.

"I bet this is probably the best day of your life," Aidan said in a low voice, not looking up.

"*Excuse me?*"

"Your lot in life went way up. From a witch to a queen," he scoffed. "Pretty sure my nursemaid read me a fairytale about that."

"How dare you!"

"You have to admit, it's a good deal for you," Aidan finally sat up, staring at her coolly.

"My mother and sister are *dead*." Gwenna stared at him. "So is my grandfather. I'm the only member of my family left."

"Trust me, I know."

Another heavy silence.

Aidan got to his feet and crossed to the window along the back wall, staring at the courtyard below.

"Did you love her?" Gwenna asked.

"What?"

"My sister." She fought to keep her voice quiet and calm. "She loved you. She never said it in those words, but I could see it in her eyes. What about you? Did you love her?"

Aidan blew out a shaky breath, leaning into the window's alcove and pressing his forehead against the cool glass.

"We're children," he muttered. "What do we know about love?"

"You're not a *child*, for one thing. You're a grown man and a future king. For another, I believe it's common to shed a tear when someone you love dies," Gwenna said coldly. He looked up in surprise. "You haven't shed a tear. Not when we found their bodies. Not at the pyre. Not once."

"And because I didn't cry, what? Does that make me some kind of a monster?"

"Maybe."

"Well then, maybe this is a good match after all! A monster for a monster!" Aidan jeered. She didn't respond. "Oh, come on, Gwenna. You know deep down you're thrilled. Who else would've married you?"

"Is that what this is all about, Aidan?"

"What?"

"That I'm too ugly for you?" She let out a wry chuckle as she rose to her feet. "I suppose I shouldn't be surprised or expect anything more from you."

"You're being ridiculous," Aidan grumbled. But he wasn't denying any of it.

"Is beauty your only requirement for a wife?" Gwenna asked softly.

That brought his head up quickly. "What?"

"Is that all you're looking for?"

There was a long silence between the two. The ticking clock on the mantle was the only sound in the room.

Gwenna folded her arms. She would wait as long as it took. Silence was not something she feared.

Aidan's face grew more and more red. He wouldn't meet her gaze, but also couldn't stay still. The future king fidgeted uncomfortably. Glancing out the window, then over to the hearth, and back again, Aidan looked for any assistance.

None was coming for him.

Gwenna bit back a smirk. Watching Aidan squirm in discomfort was almost satisfying.

"Perhaps you didn't hear my question," she said, rounding the settee and moving closer to him. "Is beauty the only thing you require in a wife?"

Gwenna stared up at him with one eyebrow raised in expectation.

Aidan shoved to his feet, looming over her so close that their chests almost touched.

"Why else would I get married?" Aidan ground his teeth together.

She smirked, feeling pity for him for the first time in her life. He wasn't worthy of the position he was being given. Catriona was too good for him. And he knew it. She could see the hint of fear in his eyes.

"You're pathetic," she chuckled.

"And you're plain," Aidan shot back.

"By The Deep–" Gwenna threw her hands up in disgust, starting to turn away.

"I'm not finished," he snapped, grabbing her arm and pulling her back before she could retreat. "You're plain. But that's the least troubling thing about you. There's something *wrong* with you. I don't know what you did to your grandfather. But if I ever find out you hurt Catriona in order to take her place–"

Gwenna trembled as white-hot fury coursed through her veins.

"Don't you dare…." She stared up at the hard planes of his face, frozen in place.

"You weren't jealous of her?" Aidan lowered his voice, leaning in even closer to taunt her. "This wasn't everything you ever wanted?"

"Get out." She seethed, wrenching her hand from his grasp.

"Do you deny it?" he asked coldly. "I know you have feelings for me. It would be understandable for you to feel jealous, Gwenna. But dabbling in some kind of evil arts to remove your sister–"

"Get out!"

Gwenna's fist cocked back as the door to the sitting room opened.

Kellen dropped the tray of food he was holding as Gwenna's fists collided with Aidan's face in a satisfying one-two punch.

Aidan's head snapped back, nose bleeding immediately.

Wide-eyed and stammering, Kellen hurried across the room to check on Aidan.

"Get him to the court physician as quickly as you can. His nose is broken," Gwenna said coldly, sweeping past both of them without a backwards glance.

CHAPTER 16

Four days after

G wenna had spent years dreaming about being Aidan's wife. Now it was a nightmare playing out before her eyes. The irony was so thick she could choke on it.

Had he always been this cruel? Had she been blinded by his mesmerizing eyes and easy charm? Or had she brought out this side of him, her curse pulling the worst out of everyone and everything?

The council refused to disband, and their presence in the Keep had Aidan's full attention. The only thing worse than having to marry an ugly woman to gain power was the threat of that power being taken away. On the one hand, Gwenna was spared most of Aidan's wrath because he was so furious over the council supervising him. But on the other, her days researching in the Hall of Records were over.

"That's what you're wearing to court?" Aidan demanded, pushing himself off the wall as she stepped out of her chambers.

His nose was red and slightly crooked, but the court physician had done the best he could. But the future king was also sporting a huge black eye. Apparently nothing could be done about that.

It filled Gwenna with a sense of satisfaction to know that her handiwork would be admired by the entire court at.

Gwenna rolled her eyes as Aidan questioned her fashion choices. "Yes...?"

"You wore that yesterday!"

"We're in a drought, Aidan. I'm not about to send this out to be washed," she snapped.

"No other lady in court is re-wearing gowns," he hissed. "You have to go change!"

"That's your concern right now?" Gwenna stared at him. "We're about to debate restricting everyone to half rations, and you're concerned about court fashion?"

"We have to set a precedent for the others! With the council watching–"

"I will sit beside you on the dais because of the stupid council, but enough is enough. Either you walk in there and forbid these ridiculous women from wasting our drinking water by washing their clothes, or I will," Gwenna snapped, trying to push past him, but he stuck his arm out to halt her progress.

"Prove to me that you haven't caused this drought, and then you can say whatever you want in court," he said, narrowing his eyes. "Until then, you hold your tongue before you curse us again."

She glared at him. "I didn't do this!"

"Prove it!" Aidan hissed.

"I don't know how." She hastily wiped her hand under her eyes, hating herself for showing any sign of weakness in front of him.

"I know." He grimaced before holding out his arm stiffly for her. "Take my arm. The least you can do is appear to be delighted to be my wife."

Gwenna took his arm. She wanted to make some snide comment that he should appear delighted for their marriage, but she didn't have the energy. Aidan conspicuously held his arm further away from his body than necessary, determined to limit contact with her.

She had claimed her throne to the council, but now she needed to do the same with the court. Today was all about appearances. All she had to do was sit there and listen to the debates. She wouldn't even have to say anything.

The newly-engaged couple was announced, and, together, they made their way through the ballroom to the dais. Gwenna kept her eyes focused on a far spot on the wall, trying to avoid seeing the many courtiers invoking the sign of The Deep as she passed. Her future husband was not alone in his suspicions of her. Not by a long shot. It was all she could do to block out the rumors swirling.

"I bet she killed her sister to get him...." Jeyne Byrne sneered as they passed. Aidan tensed, but they kept moving.

She had been so focused on guarding herself against the cruelty of the court that she had forgotten entirely about the thrones until she was standing before them. This was her grandfather's throne. Gwenna had never approached it without being summoned, let alone sat in it before.

Aidan dropped her arm at the top of the dais completely unceremoniously. He sat down on the King's throne without hesitation.

Gwenna froze, blinking as she tried to process what she was seeing.

Aidan stared up at her from the throne– her grandfather's throne, *her* throne. Discreetly, he nodded towards the smaller of the two thrones, which her late grandmother and then mother had occupied. The throne of the consort.

Whispers swirled even louder behind her. Aidan's eyes widened, almost imperceptibly, silently, begging her to just sit down and not make a scene. Gwenna sank down onto her mother's throne, heart hammering in her ears.

This was something she intended to fight for. But not with an audience of gossips present.

No sooner had Gwenna smoothed her skirts than Duke Byrne immediately approached, bowing low before the two young people on the thrones. Musicians played in the balcony, and the court carried on with idle conversation.

"Good afternoon, Duke Byrne." Aidan forced a smile.

Gwenna stared at the Duke, unwilling to smile and unable to find the words to say anything to the man.

"The council wanted to inform you that your wedding is planned for the month's end." Byrne's eyes twinkled as he took in both shocked faces.

"So soon?" Aidan asked tightly.

"The sooner the marriage, the sooner we can arrange a coronation, my lord," the Duke said grandly. "Although…"

"Yes?"

"There has been discussion of delaying the coronation until the birth of an heir," Duke Byrne said with forced casualness.

Aidan inhaled sharply. "I beg your pardon?"

"The council feels it may be best to delay coronation until the line of succession has been secured. Begging your pardon, your Highness, but we feel that it would not be in Bannon's best interest should an heir be born with your particular… ailment," Byrne said lightly, eyes falling on Gwenna for the first time, a malicious spark to them.

Her face burned. She hadn't given any thought to producing heirs when she had claimed the throne and consequently claimed Aidan. If there was any indication that her children were also cursed, Duke Byrne would not hesitate to take the throne from her.

But no babies received Blessings anymore. The Fairies were gone. Her daughters, if she had any, wouldn't be Blessed with Beauty either. Did that mean the council would automatically call them cursed as well?

"You wouldn't dare," Aidan said in a low voice. Gwenna shot him an appreciative glance.

"Please don't misunderstand, Lord Aidan. If the Lorne bloodline is not considered stable enough to continue ruling, you would be given a choice to remarry. Your position would not be compromised, of course," Duke Byrne said smoothly.

Aidan nodded, shoulders falling away from his ears as his fears were alleviated.

Nausea climbed up her throat. It wasn't enough to blackmail someone into marrying her so she could keep her family's title. No, now the title of queen would be held hostage until she produced an heir. And not any heir, a suitable and un-cursed heir. Whatever that meant, in this world with no Fairy Blessings.

"I need some air," Gwenna said suddenly, rising to her feet.

Aidan shot her a furious glare, but she spun on her heel and strode from the hall.

Her racing feet took her out of the Keep and across the courtyard. Gwenna raced up the narrow staircase leading to the parapet atop the walls of the Keep, slamming the door at the top behind her. Silence and solitude in a place where not even her future husband could find her.

The sun was caressing the top of the Marshora Mountains as it sank behind the peaks, golden light bathing the sand-covered valley. Gwenna leaned against the low stone wall, looking out at the dunes. The riders that had been sent out across the dunes, set on finding out how far this new desert lasted and where the sea was, had yet to return.

Her lips tasted salt, and she realized she was crying. Again. She let the tears fall, bowing her head against the stones as sobs wracked her body.

Part of her, a large part, embraced the guilt pressing against her chest like a millstone. She deserved it. She had dreamt and fantasized about being Aidan's wife for years. Even after he proposed to Cat, Gwenna had dreamt about it. She fell asleep the morning of Cat's murder and dreamed about marrying Aidan.

As her sister was being brutally murdered, Gwenna was busy dreaming about kissing Aidan. Perhaps she deserved this pain.

But no, she reminded herself. As much as she had pined for Aidan and envied Cat, Gwenna had never wished for this. This situation was unthinkable, even amidst the peak of her jealousy. There was no world Gwenna could ever envision without her sister in it.

She stared down at her trembling hands. She hadn't tried to call forth that violet light since the night her grandfather died, and she sat in a dark cell in the dungeon to wait out the storm.

If that power was within her, it was hidden so deep Gwenna couldn't find it. She examined every crevice of her soul to draw it out again. Calling and calling to that light, that power. But there was no answer.

Only deafening silence.

Straightening, Gwenna stared out over the kingdom. Over *her* kingdom. Her eyes settled on the empty field where she had last seen the Shifter, and she remembered him beckoning for her. It seemed like a lifetime ago.

She hadn't returned to the Hall of Records but didn't need to. Those stories, those illustrations, were seared into her memory. The Fairies lived with the Shifters. The Fairies had been the ones to curse her, and now her kingdom was cursed.

Gwenna needed to follow the Shifter.

That decision had been easy before. Catriona would see to the kingdom, be heir to the throne, and be beloved by the people. But now Cat was gone.

Gwenna was Queen, regardless of any stupid coronation rules. These were her people, her responsibility. Could she really just abandon them?

She sat up on the parapet, lost in thought. If there was any other way, she would take it. But following the Shifter was the easiest way to get answers. If she *didn't* go, she would have no kingdom, no people.

Glancing back at the courtyard, she saw Kellen exit the Keep. Yawning, he moved into the shadowed corner between the armory and the stables, glancing over his shoulders to make sure no one was around.

Gwenna leaned over the restraining wall, curiosity piqued.

Once sure he was alone, Kellen pulled his floppy hat off his head and held it between his knees. Flipping his head over, he ran his fingers through his curls and scratched at his scalp.

Gwenna stared, not understanding why he acted so suspiciously just to scratch his head.

But when he straightened back up, she saw it.

Kellen had very pointy ears. Very distinct, very inhuman, pointed ears.

CHAPTER 17

Gwenna ran down the steps and into the armory, praying he wouldn't disappear. She grabbed the closest weapon she could see, a heavy dagger the length of her forearm, and ran out the door.

Pressing herself against the wall, she didn't want to give her position away or spook Kellen. She waited for a moment, and he came strolling out of his hiding place, hat crammed back on his head and whistling like there wasn't a care in the world.

She leapt forward. Gwenna grabbed him by the back of his shirt and pressed the dagger's tip into his back until he yelped.

"Wha– *Gwenna*?" He craned his neck, trying to see who held a blade to him.

"You can answer my questions privately, or I'll rip that hat off your head and march you into the middle of the ballroom," Gwenna threatened. "Maybe the council will question you, but I'm betting they separate your pointy-eared head from your lying, traitorous neck without a second thought."

"I'm not a traitor," he breathed. "Ask your questions. I'll tell you anything you want to know."

Gwenna dragged him backward, about to drag him into the privacy of the armory before she thought better of it. He had been friendly thus far, but trapping a monster in an enclosed room full of weapons didn't sound wise.

Instead, she forced him over to the stables. She checked to make sure they were alone before shoving him into an empty horse stall, blocking the exit with her body.

Kellen held up his hands in surrender. "I promise, I mean you no harm."

"What good are your promises?" she hissed, still pointing the dagger at him. "You've been lying to everyone the whole time. Does Aidan know what you are?"

He shook his head, sliding down to the straw-covered floor and burying his head in his hands. "No one does. Ma moved us south right after I was born. We lived on a farm there until she died, and I got a job working for Aidan. He had no reason to ask my background past that."

"What are you?" Gwenna asked. "Are you a monster too?"

Kellen raised his head, voice bitter. "I'm a Shifter, yes. But I'm not a monster. Not like the wolf."

"You know him? The wolf?" Her hand holding the dagger shook, despite herself. "Are you working with him?"

"He's the Alpha; that's all I know. He's the reason my Ma ran away," he replied.

A million questions surged through Gwenna's mind, one after another in such quick succession she wasn't sure where to start.

"You can Shift?" she asked, and he nodded. "Show me."

Kellen hesitated for a moment before slowly climbing to his feet. He held his arms up, away from his body, to indicate he still wasn't a threat to her.

Light flashed before her eyes, temporarily blinding her.

Blinking to clear her vision, Gwenna saw a massive black bear standing on his hind legs across the stall from her. She swore, leaping away. Her back hit the stall door as she brandished the dagger warily. It was the same bear she had seen from her window a few nights back and the one frightening the villagers.

The bear lowered to all fours slowly before sitting back on his haunches. His eyes were the same golden brown, oddly cognisant for a wild animal.

"Can you... understand me?" Gwenna whispered.

The bear, Kellen, nodded his shaggy head.

She stared at his dark fur and curved snout, somehow predatory but distinctively... *not*. He almost looked docile and sweet. For a moment, Gwenna thought about reaching out to touch his soft fur.

"Please, Shift back. I've seen enough," she said softly, unable to look away from how human his eyes were. They were nothing like the wolf's eyes.

Another flash of light and Kellen sat in the straw again, fully dressed, thankfully.

"Any other tricks you'd like me to perform?" He grinned wryly. "I haven't quite learned how to juggle with my paws, but I'd be happy to show you how well I can dance."

"That... won't be necessary," Gwenna said slowly, trying to clear the image of a waltzing bear from her mind.

"Then, would you please put the knife down?" Kellen sighed. "If I wanted to hurt you, don't you think I'd have done it by now?"

The thought made her wince, but he had a point. He had successfully infiltrated the royal Keep. He could have Shifted at any point and gone on a rampage. But he hadn't.

"Swear to me you're not working with the wolf," Gwenna said, still aiming the dagger at him.

"I swear to you, on The Deep and all of Her goodness, that I am not working with the Alpha," Kellen said solemnly, eyes staring at hers the whole time.

She hesitated, the hand holding the knife starting to waver. "How do I know you're telling the truth?"

He chuckled wryly. "You really don't know anything about us."

"What does that mean?"

"We can't lie, Gwenna," Kellen said shortly. "Yes, The Deep has bestowed some of her gifts on my people. But there are conditions. One is a compulsion to tell the truth at all times. I physically can't lie to you."

She believed him. She didn't know why, but she did. Sighing, she dropped the dagger to the floor with a clatter.

"Start talking." Gwenna sank to the stable floor, crossing her legs beneath her.

"What do you want to know?"

"Everything."

Kellen grinned. "We're going to be here for a while."

"I know. That's why I sat down."

CHAPTER 18

"**M**a was a powerful Mage. All of our women are. Well, most." Kellen added as almost an afterthought. "Typically, the women are Mages while the men Shift. Not always, but typically. Anyways, my Ma was a Mage. She could create fantastic Weavings, but she was known for her ability to sense the future."

"Sense the future? Like... have visions?" Gwenna asked.

He shook his head, brow furrowed as he tried to find the words. "More like she just... got these feelings, sometimes. They'd happen randomly, but she always knew they were correct. When I was born, she had her strongest one yet. She never told me what she sensed, but that's why we left our people and went south."

"Where were you living before that?" Gwenna asked, imagining the lake-side dwelling she had seen in the storybooks.

"Thornvale Village, though I don't remember it. We left when I was a few weeks old," Kellen explained.

Gwenna shook her head adamantly. "Absolutely not. Shifters and Mages haven't been seen in Bannon for centuries, and certainly not in Thornvale."

"I don't know who told you that... but Thornvale used to be full of my people. They lived right alongside yours," Kellen said slowly.

Gwenna reflected back on every history book, every ledger she had searched. She had gone through decades worth of records, and there was nothing to corroborate his story. If what Kellen was saying was true, his people had lived down the road less than twenty years ago. Why would they have left? And why wouldn't there be any record of them?

"Keep going." Gwenna waved him on. She couldn't dwell on that now. "What else did your Ma say?"

"Only to be wary of the wolf. She never named him or indicated that he was the Alpha. But at the lake... I knew. Even before he Shifted, I knew," Kellen said hollowly, eyes staring past her into nothingness.

"What does that mean?" Gwenna asked.

"I don't know how Alphas are chosen, only that there's one at a time, and they're typically the strongest of their generation. Mages can do as they please, but other Shifters... well, they're drawn to the Alpha's will. Whatever he commands, they do," Kellen explained. "I've never been around one before. But the minute I saw him, something in me screamed to submit to him. He hadn't Shifted; I had no idea who he was– you have to believe me. But something in me, more primal than my bear, recognized who he was and wanted to yield."

"I believe you." Gwenna nodded slowly as she considered. "Does he know who *you* are?"

Kellen shook his head. "Alphas can't sense anyone who hasn't joined his pack. My bear wanted to, but I kept far enough away that I could overcome it. If I saw him again, though..."

Gwenna nodded, understanding the sentiment. "Do you... think you could find him again? The Alpha?"

Kellen sat bolt upright, gaping at her. "Why would anyone want to do something like that?"

"I need to talk to him," she said quietly.

He scrambled across the floor to her, shaking his head. "Absolutely not. It's too dangerous, Gwenna. You know that he—"

"I know what he did." Wolf tracks, and bloodstains haunted her every time she closed her eyes. "But I need to find him. He's the only one that can help me."

"I smelled him at the ravine where we found your mother and sister," Kellen said quietly, so close their knees almost touched. "Maybe it was a coincidence. *Maybe*. But whatever his reasoning, you can't go after him. I know you want revenge. I would too. But not like this."

"It's not about revenge." Gwenna shook her head. He didn't understand what she was saying. "I need him to break the curse."

"What curse?" His long nose crinkled with confusion. "What are you talking about?"

"My curse," Gwenna sighed, hands over her heart. "Whatever is wrong with me, now it's affecting the kingdom. Whatever that storm was, it had something to do with me."

"That's ridiculous, Gwenna. You didn't cause that."

"You weren't there. You didn't see——"

"I heard Aidan talking about your glowing hands," he interrupted, eyes searching her face. "I still don't believe it was anything to do with you."

Gwenna's heart thudded against her rib cage. His eyes were so warm, so friendly. She wanted to believe him.

"Maybe you were just at the wrong place, at the wrong time," Kellen suggested. "Maybe it had nothing to do with you. Did your grandfather ever…?"

She shook her head quickly. "It wasn't him."

"You don't know that, Gwenna."

"Either way, I have to try."

"And what does the Alpha have to do with this?" Kellen snapped. "Don't tell me you think he's your true love, and one kiss will—"

"No, it's nothing like that." Gwenna interrupted, shuddering at the thought. "Shifters, they live near the Fairies, don't they?"

He jerked back in surprise, blinking slowly. "Yes... I think so...."

"That's who I really need to find. Whatever happened at my Blessing, it started with the Fairies. If they did this to me, maybe they would know how to reverse it. And if I reverse my curse, maybe it will rain again," Gwenna explained. "I need to follow the wolf to the Fairies."

Kellen stared at her for a long moment. She felt the weight of her words hanging between them, and she desperately wanted to snatch them back and laugh them away. It felt stupid saying it aloud.

"That might actually work...." Kellen said so quietly that, at first, Gwenna thought she misheard.

"Really?" she gasped, lungs fully expanding with air. "You think so?"

"You have to know this is dangerous. He could kill you," Kellen said.

Like your mother and sister.

He didn't say the words, but she felt them either way.

"I don't think he will," Gwenna said, straightening her shoulders. "He tried to get me to follow him once before, after the storm."

"You saw him again?" Kellen's jaw dropped. "Why didn't you say anything?"

"That's not important." She waved the question away. "The point is: I think he thinks he can help me. He said as much to Cat."

"She talked to–?"

"Again, that's not important right now," she interrupted. "He's all but invited both of us, separately, to follow him for answers. I think I need to take him up on it."

Kellen sat back, setting his jaw. "Have you thought about the fact that you both are princesses, and he very well might be after the throne?"

"I have," Gwenna admitted. "But I can handle myself. As long as he thinks there's a chance I'll give him a throne, he won't hurt me."

"As long as he thinks there's a chance?" Kellen repeated. "You're not really going to lead him on? Do you know how unbelievably stupid that is?"

Gwenna tossed her head. "Look, I'm the poor, unlovable princess. Don't argue; that's how they see me. If he thinks he will win me over with a few kind words, and I pretend to go along with it... I need to buy enough time to find the Fairies and get some answers."

"And then what?" Kellen rolled his eyes. "You tell the wolf, 'Oh, never mind, no throne for you,' and just stroll back to your castle like nothing ever happened?"

She hesitated, his words hitting home. All of her time and focus had been spent trying to mentally prepare to walk into the wolf's trap. Gwenna hadn't considered anything past finding the Fairies. Kellen had a point: she had no escape plan.

"Maybe marrying a wolf wouldn't be so bad." She smiled weakly, attempting a lousy joke. "Considering my current betrothed hates me."

"Aidan's an idiot, but he's not a murderous psychopath," Kellen pointed out.

Gwenna nodded, conceding the point. She buried her head in her hands, trying to think of some way to escape the wolf's clutches, alive and unmarried.

"I'll give you two weeks," Kellen sighed.

She jerked her head up. "What?"

"You have two weeks to find these Fairies, and then I'm sending Aidan after you," Kellen said. "It'll be a dream come true for Aidan. He'll get to play the hero and rescue the princess."

"Nobody knows where the Shifters are," Gwenna pointed out. "He'll have no idea how to get to me."

Kellen grinned, pointing to his nose. "This isn't just for my dashingly good looks. Your trackers have never had me with them. I'll find your trail, don't you worry. You need to stay alive for two weeks and get your answers before your rescuer arrives."

Gwenna stared at him, offering his assistance. He not only believed in her ability to pull this off but was actually offering his support. Kellen was going to help her.

"Two weeks?" she repeated, extending her hand to shake on it.

"Two weeks," he confirmed. "Now we just need to get you properly kidnapped."

CHAPTER 19

MORNING, FIVE DAYS AFTER

Dressing for her kidnapping was proving to be more difficult than Gwenna had scheduled time for. She needed to appear unsuspecting but also reinforce her status as the future queen. This was no farm girl about to be taken by the wolf. He needed to see her and be reminded of how much she stood to offer him.

Finally, Gwenna settled on a satin turquoise gown. The boning in the bodice was strong enough that she didn't need a proper corset beneath, which was a perk if this was what she would have to wear for the next two weeks. She didn't know what clothing options the wolf had available, but she wasn't counting on much. Her gown had a lace-trimmed sweetheart neckline that suggested her ample bosom without being crude.

Since the storm and subsequent heat wave, Gwenna had refused to wear any extra layers, including petticoats. But today, she put on her fullest set, loving the regal swish it added to her full skirts. She resisted pulling her hair back into a braid, instead allowing it to fall delicately over her shoulders to the small of her back. It was as coquettish as she could possibly look. She felt ridiculous getting this dressed up to walk down to the village. Still, nobody she passed in the Keep's hallways even glanced in her direction.

Gwenna knew that he would refuse if she invited Aidan to join her in walking down to the village. So she didn't ask him.

She just conspicuously left without saying anything.

"What kind of idiot are you?" a furious voice shouted behind her before she even made it to the road.

Fighting back a smile, Gwenna turned around to see Aidan jogging across the long, marble bridge. Kellen was hurrying after him and he winked at Gwenna when he saw her.

"Pardon me?" Gwenna asked Aidan, the picture of innocence.

Aidan looked over his shoulder, noting a dozen guards on the Keep's walls watching and listening to this interaction.

"What do you think you're doing out here alone?" Aidan dropped his voice as he drew up alongside her. "Do you know how bad it makes me look that my future bride is alone out here?"

"I-I didn't think. I'm sorry. I wanted to visit the town," Gwenna said simply, biting her bottom lip to appear regretful. "I know we've been sending rations down to the people. But... I don't know. I thought I needed to see them for myself, to see if I can do anything to help."

Aidan glanced past her at the road, hesitating before he responded.

Kellen had casually mentioned the night before how much it could strengthen Aidan's position if he were seen giving aid in the village. If Aidan won over the people, the council couldn't use him like a puppet.

Blowing out a heavy sigh, Aidan ran his fingers through his tousled black hair and shrugged half-heartedly. "Lead on."

"You mean you'll join me?" Gwenna's jaw dropped in fake shock.

"It's not the stupidest idea you've had," Aidan grumbled, pushing past her and striding confidently down the road. "Let's go. We'll need to be back before the mid-afternoon meal. The council wants to meet again"

Gwenna met Kellen's eyes for a fraction of a second, sharing a look of triumph before turning to follow Aidan, completely expressionless.

Everything, from this point on, was out of her control. She could conspicuously separate herself from the others, but there was no guarantee the wolf would appear. And even if he did, she needed him to appear at the right time. Aidan needed to *see* her get taken. This whole thing would be pointless if no one watched her get kidnapped and assumed she'd run away.

The trio walked in silence down the dirt road into the village. Gwenna was certain Aidan would be able to hear how fast her heart was beating, but he didn't even look in her direction. She couldn't afford to even glance at Kellen in case Aidan saw and got suspicious. So she focused on not tripping in her ridiculously impractical yet perfect damsel in distress heels.

The village butcher came out to meet them on the road, extending his hand to Aidan and clapping him on the back. Apparently, he was concerned about the rations for the remaining livestock. Aidan left without a backward glance, already deep in discussion with the middle-aged man.

"The wolf is close," Kellen muttered, tapping his nose casually and speaking out of the corner of his mouth. "I'd tell you to be careful, but... well, don't."

"You'll make sure Aidan sees the kidnapping?" Gwenna asked him, eyes scanning the horizon of bare tree trunks.

"Just as we planned," Kellen nodded.

He glanced in her direction, and Gwenna's pulse spiked. The insanity of what she was about to do was making her jumpy. Kellen's chocolate eyes were warm as she looked over at him. He opened his mouth to say something, but she cut him off. The way he looked at her made her feel extra fluttery in her stomach, and she couldn't afford to dwell on why that was.

"Two weeks from today, right?" she asked.

He nodded solemnly, swallowing down whatever else he had been about to say. "See you in two weeks."

Kellen jogged after Aidan, long legs closing the distance quickly, leaving Gwenna standing alone on the outskirts of the village. She thought about calling him back, instantly regretting how she had dismissed him. There might never be another chance to hear from him again.

Gwenna squared her shoulders and marched onward, instantly shoving that thought away. She decided to walk up and down each cobblestoned street if that's what it took. The wolf couldn't be far if Kellen could sense him. She just needed to give him the right opportunity, and he would take it.

She hadn't passed three squat hovels before she saw him lurking in the shadows of an alleyway on the opposite side of the street, silver eyes watching her closely. These houses on the outskirts of town were recently abandoned, too damaged in the storm, and not worth the time to repair. Faintly, Gwenna could hear Aidan's laughter drifting back to her on a light breeze. But the butcher's shop was several streets over, closer to the center of the town.

She and the wolf were completely alone.

His white hair was tied back, offset by his dark, thick scruff around his chiseled jawline. He wore the same dirty clothes from the lake. Even from the opposite side of the street, Gwenna could feel the confidence radiating off of him. It turned her stomach. Her people were suffering in this heat, almost starving, and he seemed to be thriving.

Steeling herself, she slowly crossed the street to where he waited.

"If I scream, you'll be surrounded." Gwenna stepped over an oddly large clump of dried brush separating the alleyway from the street but drew to a halt several paces away.

He smirked. "Good afternoon to you too, your Highness."

"What do you want?"

"To begin with, some courtesy. Don't they teach manners in that castle of yours?" A dark eyebrow arched as he studied her.

Standing this close, his eyes were far too vibrant. Too alive. Everyone else she saw, even the courtiers, had a haunted look in their eyes. But not him.

He crossed his thick arms over his chest, unlaced blue tunic revealing a muscled physique. No, the wolf was doing *very* well for himself.

Gwenna quickly looked back up to meet his eyes, face warming. He smirked openly at her, noting her stare.

"Good afternoon, Shifter," she said quietly.

"I thought you said you knew where she was! Why did you let her out of your sight?" Aidan's frustration was unmistakable, and he was quickly approaching. "Gwenna! Where are you?"

Turning quickly, she opened her mouth to respond.

Aidan strode around the nearest corner, Kellen on his heels. The future king's eyes flicked from Gwenna to the Shifter behind her, his hand going to the hilt of his sword.

"You again?" Aidan fell back a step in surprise.

"Now!"

As the words left the Shifter's mouth, a flaming arrow shot from an adjacent rooftop and ignited the dry brush at the mouth of the alleyway. Once lit, the flames immediately spread to the hovels on either side. Everything was kindling.

It was an effective trap, preventing Aidan from getting to Gwenna or the wolf.

Gwenna's jaw dropped, shocked at how quickly this plan had come together.

"Say goodbye to your princeling," the Shifter murmured directly in her ear, coming up behind her.

The low gravelly pitch of his voice made goosebumps erupt over her flesh. There was something very, *very* wrong with him. Her resolve flooded out of her, and she darted towards the flames, scrambling for survival.

Thick arms encircled her waist, and she was dragged backward, deeper into the network of alleyways running around the hovels.

Gwenna screamed, thrashing and trying to break the Shifter's grip. She had made a terrible mistake. "Aidan! Kellen! Help me!"

She heard shouting on the other side of the wall of flames but couldn't make out anything specific over the loud crackles and pops as the wooden homes burned. The Shifter towed her through the alleyways like she was a small child. Her struggle proved no resistance for him.

"Please, don't do this," she begged. "Please, don't hurt me."

The Shifter clamped a rough hand over her mouth, silencing her. "Stay quiet, and no harm will come to you."

They rounded a corner, and the palest boy Gwenna had ever seen stood waiting for them. He was a head shorter than Gwenna, and several years younger. With a bow slung across his back, he saluted the wolf on sight.

"The other fires were a success," the archer reported. "They're cut off."

Gwenna swore under her breath. This had been too well-planned on the wolf's part. She was not in control here. Not in the slightest.

"Mist her," the wolf snapped. "Now."

The boy reached into a small pouch belted at his waist, drawing out a heaping handful of something he kept carefully concealed in his fist. He approached, and Gwenna instinctively shrank away, but the wolf held her firmly in place. The archer, whose skin was so pale he was almost translucent, gave her a mournful look before blowing a dark powder in her face.

Navy blue powder suddenly flew into her eyes. She gasped, accidentally inhaling a mouthful. It coated her throat, and she coughed, trying to get it out, terrified it would smother her.

But the world pitched beneath her feet, throwing her off balance, and her knees crumbled. Only the wolf's rough hands kept her upright. Vision cleared; she blinked rapidly and tried to get the world to stop spinning around her.

A bright light flashed.

The boy was gone. A gleaming white stallion stood in the alley in his place, tossing his mane anxiously.

Gwenna was lifted off of her feet, an arm going under her knees and one cradling her against a muscled chest. The wolf was oddly gentle with her, lifting her onto the back of the horse and balancing her.

There was something wrong with her head. It was so heavy. Gwenna slumped forward against the stallion's withers. Someone mounted the horse behind her, propping her against his broad chest.

Gwenna opened her mouth to protest. Something was wrong. She wasn't supposed to be here with him. Or… was she? It all seemed a little hazy, too far out of reach now.

"Sleep now." The Shifter's low voice sounded like it echoed down a long, abandoned hallway.

Her eyes fluttered closed obediently, her chest rising and falling with the heavy breathing of sleep. She felt her body slump against him, unable to remain conscious anymore, even as her mind struggled to stay aware.

The wolf spurred the horse onward, and the rocking motion of the gallops was oddly soothing.

That voice deep within her hollered, screaming with the last ounce of consciousness to be deceived by the wolf. There was nothing right about him, nothing safe. He would kill her, like he had killed Catriona.

And now she was firmly in his clutches.

PART 2

CHAPTER 20

FOURTEEN DAYS UNTIL RESCUE

E very stone in the cell was stained with blood. Torchlight filtered through the iron bars in the door frame. Rust-colored spatter marks coated each wall. Huddled in the corner directly facing the door, Gwenna kept her knees drawn to her chest and tried not to focus on the ominously large stain in the center of the floor.

Her hands refused to stop trembling, and it had nothing to do with the abnormal chill in the air. After days of unrelenting heat, the cold was almost a relief.

Almost.

Gwenna didn't know how long she'd been unconscious or how long she'd been awake. There was no window to show any trace of sunlight. She could have been awake for hours or a full day. Time didn't exist in this place.

She pushed the fear down, reminding herself that she had *wanted* this. There was a purpose for being here. This was how she could save her people.

Find the Fairies. Break the curse.

Gwenna mentally rehearsed what she would say to the wolf and exactly how she would say it. She would be timid and demure, a helpless damsel in distress. There was no reason to keep her locked in this hell. But the more time that crept by, she felt that persona slipping farther away as fear and hunger slowly took root.

A sudden eerie howl echoed down the hallway. Gwenna nearly jumped out of her skin. The flames of the torch hanging opposite her cell door flickered wildly as a sudden rush of fresh air came down the hall. Gwenna pushed slowly up to her feet, prepared to meet whatever came.

There was no sound to announce his arrival. He merely appeared like a phantom in front of her cell.

"You're awake." It was not a question.

His low voice was rougher than before, a blade scraped against stone. Pale as ever, his white hair neatly pulled back in a knot was a stark contrast to the dark scruff along his pointed jawline. There was scarcely any color in those thin lips twisted in a sneer.

An unlaced baggy white cotton tunic hung from his broad shoulders, with a slate gray vest belted overtop. Tattered sleeves were rolled up above the elbow, revealing meaty forearms crisscrossed with ominous scars. Dark patched trousers came to just below his knee, hems fraying, and he wore no shoes.

In another story, the princess might be distracted by the Shifter's handsome face and rippling muscles. Some beautiful things masquerade as deadly and dangerous out of self-preservation. But that kind of thinking may have gotten Catriona slaughtered. Gwenna would not make the same mistake.

She hurried to the cell door, pressing her face against the bars as tears filled her eyes. "Please. You have to release me."

Her voice was higher pitched than usual and more breathy. Men liked to see women desperate, didn't they? That's what the romances she read seemed to imply, anyways.

The Shifter smirked, shaking his head slowly. "That will not be possible."

He reeked of condescension, but she ignored it.

"Please, you don't understand. You've made a terrible mistake," Gwenna whispered. "I'm Queen of Bannon. Please, I don't want any harm to come to you, but this will not go unanswered!"

He yawned, clearly unimpressed. Smiling, he waited for her to try again.

"Did you kill them?" she asked, switching tactics.

"Kill who?" he shrugged. "I'm afraid you'll have to be more specific. I've killed many people, and I can't be expected to remember all of them."

Gwenna resisted the urge to squirm. "My mother and my sister." Again, he didn't answer. "I know you did. I saw the tracks."

"Tracks?"

"Wolf tracks."

He grinned. "Am I supposed to apologize for every wolf in the area? Surely you can't be that naive."

Gwenna faltered. She'd been so convinced, so sure of his motives. There had never been a moment when she had considered any other explanation. Mother and Cat were dead, found near wolf tracks. The guards with them were slaughtered by some kind of animal.

It had to be this Shifter. Didn't it?

Inhaling slowly, Gwenna forced herself to straighten, her innocent persona wholly forgotten. She didn't believe his innocence in the murders, but she also couldn't let it distract her immediately. There would be time to bring justice to her family once she left this cell.

Drawn up to full height, spine strong as steel, she tilted her head defiantly to meet his gaze again.

"I said: release me," she hissed through gritted teeth.

Amusement sparked in his cold eyes. "Well, well, well, *now* I hear a queen. Thank you for joining us, Highness." His cold eyes roamed over her body, leisurely taking their time. "Though you certainly don't look very queenlike."

Gwenna wanted to peel her skin off; his wandering gaze made her feel unclean.

"What do you want?" The words bolted off her tongue impetuously, and the wicked look he gave made her instantly regret it.

He grinned, revealing a mouth full of impossibly sharp teeth.

"Within a month, your palace will be full of corpses. They will sit in their pathetic castle and starve to death. And that's assuming water rations hold out that long. It's a very dire circumstance in your kingdom right now, *princess*. Your people have no time or energy to even conceive of warfare, let alone mount a rescue mission," he said flatly. "No one is coming for you."

Gwenna braced for the words, but the blow still landed. She tried to shake it off and remain confident. "My betrothed will come for me."

"The fool with the sword?" The Shifter smirked, resting his arms casually on the crossbar of the cell door. "Your idiot prince will not risk his precious royal neck in search of you. Even if he attempted to do the manly thing for once in his life, he would never be able to find you."

"He will come for me," Gwenna insisted, doubling down on the lie. "Aidan will always come for me."

The Shifter raised a skeptical eyebrow but didn't press the issue. He shoved away from the bars, looking like he would disappear into the darkness and leave her again.

"Wait!" Gwenna called frantically. He turned back slowly. "Please... What is your name?"

"My name is Marrock. And yours?" He grinned, and for once, there didn't seem to be any threat harbored behind his sharp-toothed grin. He smiled as though they were two friends meeting in the marketplace, not a murderer and his prey.

"You know my name."

"I don't, actually." His eerie smile deepened. "Somehow, I have never been able to catch the name of the fair princess who now claims to be queen."

She smiled softly, trying to appear more palatable and mild. "My name is Gwenna Lorne, High Princess of Bannon and heir to the throne."

"Princess Gwenna." He emphasized every sound like he was experimenting with how her name felt in his mouth.

Something like a smile twisted his features.

Gwenna hated that her word choice had been so immediately effective. Queens came with politics and alliances. But princesses? They were pawns on a chessboard and easily manipulated. Marrock needed to believe she was a princess to escape this cell. She needed to remember she was the queen if she wanted to survive.

He reached through the bars as though to caress her face, and she flinched back, immediately grateful for the iron separating her from the animal. The cruelty instantly reappeared in his smile when he saw the tiny flicker of fear within her.

"Why do you need a princess, Marrock?" Gwenna asked quietly, trying to find that soft-spoken charade to hide behind.

He may not have admitted to murdering Cat, but he didn't know how much Gwenna knew about his relationship with Cat. Marrock had tried to get both Cat and Gwenna to this place. The question was why.

He arched a pale eyebrow. "Perhaps I'm lonely…."

"There are plenty of farm girls with no knights surrounding them," she pointed out, inwardly cringing as soon as the words left her mouth. If he genuinely had an appetite for women, hoping he'd prey on another was cowardly.

"We have a common goal, you and I… " he began.

"We have nothing in common," Gwenna said quickly. Too quickly. He arched an eyebrow again at the bite in her tone.

"You don't wish for Bannon to prosper?"

The arguments she had been preparing shriveled up in her mouth. She gaped at him, speechless.

"You want Bannon to prosper?" she repeated, mind reeling to recall everything she had ever read about Shifters. Everything had presented them as her enemy, completely opposed to humans on every account.

"I do. Do you?" Marrock asked, smiling with something that could have been construed as innocence.

"Of course I do."

"Then it seems to me we are allies." A smile stretched across his face but didn't quite reach his eyes.

Gwenna gestured to the limestone cell surrounding her. "Strange way to treat your allies."

"You don't trust me?"

"No."

"You're smart for a girl," he smirked. "As it happens, I don't trust you either."

"Good. You're smart for a dog," she snapped. "I'll skin you the first chance I get."

"That's no way to treat your ally." Marrock tutted, echoing her words. He was not cowed by her in the slightest. In fact, that manic gleam in his eye made it seem like her threats almost excited him. "You really don't believe I want Bannon to prosper?

"That depends," she said slowly.

"On what?"

"On your definition of prosperity." Gwenna returned the empty smile, folding her arms across her chest.

He threw back his head with a laugh. She could suddenly very clearly visualize the shaggy wolf inside of him, throwing back his head to howl at the night sky. Exactly how far beneath the surface were those primal instincts?

"I would like to be returned to my home. To Thornvale Keep," Gwenna repeated the request calmly, ignoring how he wiped tears of laughter from his eyes. "Once I am home, I can bring prosperity to my people."

"How?"

"What?"

"How would your return to Thornvale change anything?" He phrased it as a question, but his tone was challenging.

Her mouth fell openly stupidly as she considered. She racked her brain for something– anything– to say in response.

"We need supplies from our allies, and then–" Gwenna tried to find any justification as to why she was needed in Thornvale. But she couldn't help them there. She could only help her people if she stayed here. If she found the Fairies.

But Marrock couldn't know that, or it would all be over. She had to act like she *needed* to go home. He couldn't just call her bluff.

That arrogant smirk spread slowly across his pale face like melted butter on warm bread. He could sense the despair rising within her, and it thrilled him. Like a cat playing with a mouse before it devours it whole.

"There is nothing you can do for your people. At least, not on your own…" He trailed off dramatically, leaving the unasked question hanging in the air between them.

Gwenna swallowed down her frustration, inhaling sharply. This was all a game to him. He had clearly rehearsed his lines, and things were going just according to the script he had created for this moment.

The only thing she could do to foil him was simply refuse to say her lines.

Silence lingered. Gwenna met his gaze but kept her mouth firmly shut, refusing to be the one to speak first. The longer they stood there, glaring at each other, the more his confident veneer began to crumble.

At first, it was the way he narrowed his eyes. He saw through her ruse. And he was certainly not pleased by it. The corner of

Gwenna's mouth quirked up in a smirk of her own. Silence was an old friend of hers. It didn't make her uncomfortable the way it did with others. She would not break.

Gwenna positioned herself at the entrance to her cell, so close that he would definitely reach her if he reached through the bars again, and prepared to wait him out for however long it took.

A vein pulsed in his clenched jaw as he realized she would not play his game. He needed her to ask how he could help her. No, Marrock wanted to watch her *beg* for his help to save her kingdom. But he quickly realized he could not make her.

Gwenna watched him closely, reading each thought that crossed his face with ease. Lips thin, his hands began to shake, and he gripped two cell bars with a white-knuckled grip.

Soft footsteps padded up the hallway.

"I brought a dinner tray, my lord, as you asked," a meek voice murmured.

Marrock pivoted, back-handing a tiny servant girl across the face with enough force to send her sprawling to the floor.

"Do not speak." Unbridled rage laced his words.

Gwenna shrank away from the door, grateful his back was to her.

The redheaded servant girl pushed to her feet, abandoning the tray and scrambling back up the corridor the way she came. There was just enough torchlight for Gwenna to see where the servant's contribution of blood spatter now marked the hallway wall.

The Shifter ignored the tray on the floor and slowly turned back to Gwenna, anger broiling off him. He grasped the bars on her door once more, and for a moment, she feared he would bend them like reeds in the wind.

"You are a pathetic child with no idea what her kingdom needs. *I* do. I am the only saving grace you have. Accept my hand in marriage, or watch your people die." Marrock spat, a chilling wildness in his eyes as he pressed his face against the bars.

"What?" Gwenna breathed.

There was no acting this time. The fear, and the confusion, were all genuine. She stared at Marrock, sure this had to be a trick. She had gotten herself put into this cell on the gamble that the Shifter was operating under a 'give me a throne, and I'll save your kingdom' premise. Was it really going to be this simple?

"You have the night to think on it," Marrock snapped. "Marry me, and this can all be over."

Apparently, it was that simple.

Gwenna kept her eyes wide, mouth agape, and refused to let any of the glee she felt show. This was going to be easier than she thought.

"If you refuse me, know that I will personally ensure your death is not quick," Marrock continued smoothly. "But first, you will watch the complete destruction and ruin of your kingdom so that the last thought you have before the pain overtakes you is that you alone caused the downfall of Bannon."

He turned and stalked out of sight.

Gwenna sank to her knees, tears of relief streaming down her grime-covered face. This asinine plan could actually work.

She conjured up noisy sobs to sell her story as a desperate princess. Marrock was probably still in earshot and probably could hear her wails. Good, they were for him.

Let him believe he had won.

She let the Shifter hear her cry so he could delight in her pain. It was far too easy to get under his skin. The simmering violence barely contained beneath his surface was a concern. But Gwenna had never expected it to be so simple to get him to propose marriage to her. Now the real trick would be postponing the wedding for two weeks.

"Aidan!" she sobbed loudly. "Please, Aidan!"

Her chest burned like she couldn't get enough air, and her sobs turned to pants. The room felt stifling hot, and beads of sweat rolled down the back of her neck.

A buzzing, tingling sensation began in the tips of her fingers. Shaking out her hands, Gwenna tried to massage the feeling back into her extremities, but it was like they had fallen asleep. The tingling was powerful: not quite painful, but certainly uncomfortable. It radiated up the length of her arms to her shoulders, spreading through her chest.

"What's happening?" Gwenna tried to rub the sensation out of her hands even as it spread farther over her body. "What's happening to me?"

The tingling slowly spread down her legs, shooting down her shins to her toes. She jumped up, hoping to restore feeling, but the tingling only increased. It felt like her entire body was vibrating, ready to shatter into a million pieces.

She screamed the Shifter's name, ready to do whatever it took for him to remove this spell.

Marrock suddenly reappeared in front of her cell, eyebrows knit together as he stared at her wordlessly. She moved towards him but faltered. Her legs weren't working right.

Marrock, the cell door, and the cell around her grew steadily taller. She was shrinking fast.

"What did you do to me?"

Gwenna spat the question, tongue somehow too big for her mouth. Her teeth receded into her gums.

She screamed, but all that came out was a terrible screech.

CHAPTER 21

THIRTEEN DAYS UNTIL RESCUE

I mages flashed through her mind. Sensations. Too quickly. Gwenna couldn't make sense of what she was seeing. Dark, webbed feet.

A cricket crawling over a log. Diving for it. Catching it in her mouth. But teeth... no, no teeth. And arms... no arms. Swallowing the grub whole.

Diving into dark water. Somehow able to see the bottom. Swimming.

Down.

Down.

Down. The delicious moss at the bottom.

Surfacing. Tucking her feet underneath. Floating but sitting up. Could she always do that? This felt different... wrong... Tingling in her feet.

That sensation... *That* she remembered.

Stretching. Growing taller, yet her head coming to settle closer to her chest. Sensation flooded back through her legs and feet.

Looking down, Gwenna caught a glimpse of white feathers with black tips fading away to reveal freckled arms and thick fingers. She ran her hands over her stomach and thighs to ensure she was fully there. Nothing changed; nothing altered. It was when she looked down at her feet that she screamed.

Gwenna stood on the middle of a lagoon; the water somehow solidified under her feet. She didn't want to look down but couldn't help herself. The water was so clear she could see the mossy bottom of the lagoon fifty feet down. This was no frozen lake in midwinter: she was standing on water!

She wanted to run, but where would she go? If she moved at all, she would break whatever magic kept her suspended and sink like a rock. She still wore the turquoise satin gown she had chosen specifically for her kidnapping, with the many layers of petticoats. All of that fabric would pull her straight to the bottom. She'd never be able to swim.

"Let's go," a harsh voice snapped.

Gwenna's head snapped up, searching for Marrock.

She stood in an enormous round limestone cavern. It was open to the sky above but with steep cliffs on all sides. A massive lagoon of rich blue water filled the expanse of the cavern, with Gwenna somehow standing on it. The cenote would have been breathtaking if there had been no fear of imminent drowning.

A few paces away, stone-carved steps led from the water's edge to a trail circling the perimeter of the cavern, about halfway up between the surface of the lake and the sky above. They reminded her of the steps carved into the wall of Thornvale's cistern, intended to allow the people to easily draw water. Marrock stood at the top of the stairs, thick arms crossed over his chest and a furious scowl on his face.

"What do I do?" Gwenna called. "Help me! Please!"

He rolled his eyes. "Walk out."

"What?"

"Walk to the stairs already. You won't sink. Her power won't allow Her more aquatically-inclined children to sink after a Shift." He dared to sound bored.

Arms still outstretched to keep her balance, she fell into a half-crouch as though that would keep her from sinking. Her heart pounded in her ears, but Gwenna took one step. The still rippling water held her like she was standing on a paved road. Unable to believe her luck, she took another step.

And then another.

With each step, she was certain whatever spell this was would shatter, and she would plummet into the depths. But it held her, forming a solid path beneath her feet that led from the middle of the cenote to the steps on the side.

Gwenna was so focused on her feet that she wasn't ready for Marrock's rough hand to grab her forearm and wrench her up the steps. She stumbled after him, trying to get her bearings while also marveling that no water was on her. Her gown and shoes were both completely dry.

Looking up, her jaw dropped at seeing a massive fortress carved into the side of the limestone cliff directly opposite the steps. Columns and turrets reached the surface far above, while a terrace stretched out to overlook the water. Arching windows revealed the telltale flickers of candles and glimpses of warm hearths. The gravel trail weaved its way directly beneath the fortress, where carved steps leading up to the terrace before the trail continued its way around the perimeter of the still water.

Glancing straight up, Gwenna saw that twilight was gathering. Her stomach lurched. How many days had passed since she had been taken? How long was she unconscious in that dungeon? And how long had she been… in whatever condition left her floating in a cenote covered in feathers? She needed to figure out how many days she had left before Kellen sent Aidan after her.

Finally, up the steps, her slippered feet skidded across the gravel as Marrock whirled around quickly to face her.

"What are you?" he hissed, nostrils flaring. He wore the same thing as the last time she had laid eyes on him, white hair unbound and falling freely to his shoulders.

Gwenna shook her head quickly, not understanding the question. "I-I'm Princess Gwenna Lorne."

His fist flew through the air, and she ducked, pushing away from him. His fist connected with the limestone wall of the cenote as though that had been his intention all along.

"Don't lie to me!"

"I'm not lying!" she cried, gesturing towards the middle of the cenote. "I have no idea what is going on. What happened to me?"

Marrock produced a folded piece of parchment he had tucked in the waistband of his trousers and thrust it towards her. "One of the village children drew a portrait of you."

Hesitantly, she accepted it and unfolded it slowly.

It was a charcoal sketch of a large bird. The underbelly was bright white, with a long black neck and a white face. A band of black feathers stretched from the beak to the eyes, making it look mask-like. Strong wings held the bird in the air as it hovered over what appeared to be water.

Gwenna stared at the feathers on the wings: white feathers fading to black at the tips. Her heart knocked against her ribs, and she glanced from the child's drawing to her trembling hand holding the parchment.

It was as though she could still sense the feathers just below the surface of her skin.

Glaring, she shoved the parchment back at Marrock. "Very clever. Release me from this spell."

"Spell?" he repeated, eyes widening.

"By The Deep, you turned me into a bird!" Gwenna snapped. "Remove the spell! You've had your fun by turning me into a swan!"

"I believe you were a goose, if you want to be specific," Marrock smirked but held both hands up in mock surrender. "But your fight is not with me, Gwenna. Whatever happened, I didn't do it."

"What are you saying?" she faltered, eyes studying his face carefully.

"You Shifted, as you humans call it. And that had nothing to do with me," he said.

"That's impossible. I'm no Shifter," she said flatly, moving her hair back and running her fingers over the smooth, curved edge of the shell of her ear. "I'm human."

He shrugged, trying to appear casual. "Personally, I would have wagered that a princess would be something more like a swan. Apparently, your essence is Welded to a goose."

"Remove the spell."

"Just because I can Shift doesn't mean I can force others to."

She hesitated.

"I'm no Shifter," Gwenna repeated, talking more to herself than to him. She glanced down at her hands, almost sure they would glow with faint purple light. "I-I would have known...."

A quiet voice in the back of her mind began to whisper about her curse. Her denied Blessing, her glowing hands, and now Shifting... None of this could be a coincidence. She was no closer to finding any answers, but her list of questions for Fairy Maeve kept growing. She hid her hands behind her back, not wanting to pique his interest.

When Gwenna looked up at him, she realized it was far too late for that. Curiosity shone from his silver eyes. It was clear that whatever this was– whatever *she* was– he hadn't anticipated it. This was something he hadn't planned for. But thankfully, he didn't seem angry about it but rather... surprised.

"Am I one of you?" she asked softly, trying to find some angle that would endear her to him. She couldn't go back into that bloodstained cell after standing in this open, fresh air.

His eyes darted to her mundane, curved, human ear. "No."

"What am I?" Gwenna asked. "A... half-Shifter?"

"Those don't exist," he said brusquely. "We would never demean ourselves like that."

She let the insult roll off her back. "A spell, then?"

"No spell can initiate a Shift. It is a gift given by The Deep to Her children, and no magic can replicate it," Marrock explained absently, eyes glazing over as he turned away from her and stared out across the cenote.

Looking down at the turquoise water, she remembered Aymer's recollection of how his mother had described The Deep as a real place, not just a philosophical theory. She had dismissed this belief before. But now... it resonated within her.

This place was something otherworldly. Divine.

"*This* is The Deep?" Gwenna breathed. "It's real?"

"Of course it's real," Marrock scoffed. "Your understanding of The Deep is a bastardization of what She really is. There was once a sacred name for Her in my people's tongue, but that has long been forgotten. But make no mistake– She belongs to Her children."

He turned to fix an icy stare on her. "And besides, the hypocrisy is disgusting. How can you claim to worship Her in one breath while vilifying us, Her children, in the next?"

"Her children?" Gwenna stared at him. "The Deep is what allows you to Shift?"

Once again, he smirked. It seemed to be his only expression. "Where else would such power originate? Yes, we Shifters, as you call us, are Her children. So are the Mages and the Fairies. All children of magic, and therefore Her children."

Gwenna turned away quickly, hoping he would interpret it as shock. Her pulse quickened at the mention of the Fairies, and she could only pray Marrock didn't notice. She hardly dared to breathe.

"I had no idea..." Her eyes traced the gravel path as it wound its way around to the other side of the cenote.

There appeared to be a village carved into the cliffside over there. Dozens of individual homes, with staircases branching off in all directions to connect the town. In the growing darkness, lights were beginning to be lit in these homes, flickering through the bare windows. Something about the sight of candles in windows felt comforting. The village was much too far away to see anyone, but to know there was other life here– that she wasn't alone with the wolf– eased her fears.

"Irrywellium," Marrock's hot breath hit the back of her neck, and she jerked away, twisting around to keep eyes on him. He ignored her scowl, eyes focused on the village or the cenote; she couldn't tell which.

"Irrywellium is the name of this place as a whole?" Gwenna asked. "Or of the village?"

"Through the years in hiding, Irrywellium has grown to encompass all this." He gestured to the expansive lagoon and the limestone walls stretching overhead with one wide sweeping motion.

"Why are you in hiding?" Gwenna asked gently, unable to take her eyes off his moonlit face. The princess persona was quickly within reach, and she cloaked herself in it. Soft, graceful, and naive.

He glared at her. "Don't ask questions you already know the answer to."

She flinched. "But I don't–"

"Though you must be telling the truth about not knowing your goose form. Otherwise, your benevolent king would have had you slaughtered in your sleep," Marrock said darkly.

Gwenna's jaw dropped.

"But there will be time to unravel that particular mystery after we are wed, my dear. And, I will admit, I much prefer a bride with an animal beneath her skin. I doubt your sword-wielding idiot would say the same," he smirked.

Her mind was spinning with everything he had just said about her grandfather, The Deep, and this place. She couldn't make heads or tails of any of it, let alone string something coherent to say.

So instead, she fell onto her knees and buried her face in her hands.

"Aidan." Her voice was barely audible, a tiny whimper.

Marrock barked out a laugh. "You can't really be crying out for that clod-headed fool."

"Please," She forced a quivering note of emotion into her voice. "Please, I-I cannot stay here–"

"I have told you the terms," he said sharply. He wrenched her to her feet and pulled her in close, so close she was pressed against his broad chest. "Marry me, or watch your kingdom die."

"How will marriage save my people?" she whispered, shaking her head in disbelief.

"Look at this place. We've been in hiding for seventeen years. Our food stores are vast, and our water supplies are even more lush. We have plenty to see Bannon through their crisis," Marrock explained. "All of that can be yours if you accept me as your lord husband."

Eyes full of tears, Gwenna stared up at him with a quivering lip.

"But sir," she began voice trembling. "I do not love you."

Marrock rolled his eyes. "That boy does not love you! He will not come for you."

Gwenna shook her head mournfully. "You are kind, sir. Too kind. Your offer is generous. But if I were to accept you, and then he arrived, I would never be able to forgive myself."

She buried her face in her hands, hiding from Marrock's sharp gaze. Thoughts of Cat's broken body brought tears streaming down her cheeks instantly. She felt sick even pretending to consider his proposal. But right now, it was the only move she could think to make. Head bowed, Gwenna prayed to The Deep and pleaded that Marrock would believe her.

"You think he will ride here on a white horse and rescue you?" Marrock asked snidely. "That's why you want to delay?"

Apparently, her prayers worked.

Sniffling, Gwenna raised her head to look up at him once more. "It is out of consideration for Lord Aidan that I cannot accept an engagement now. Surely, you must understand. If the circumstances were reversed…"

"I would not allow something of mine to be so easily taken," Marrock scoffed, rolling his eyes.

She bristled at how he made her sound like an object but forced herself to swallow it down.

"Of course," she agreed quickly, keeping her voice as meek as possible. "You are so kind and generous to want to help my people. I am so grateful. But with my betrothed… I don't know if it would be appropriate—"

"Will one week be sufficient time to wait?" He blew out a sigh of resignation.

Gwenna's jaw dropped, both shocked that he bought her love-struck fool act and horrified that his deadline was so soon.

"So soon? But my lord, he is from the south! He is unfamiliar with the terrain! Surely it will take him longer than—"

"I am to be your husband, Gwenna. Please, call me Marrock," he said softly, reaching out to tuck a stray hair behind her ear and caress her cheek.

She stood her ground, not cringing away from his touch. Not when she was so close to getting him to accept her terms.

The moonlight glinted off his sharp cheekbones, and she was transfixed by his beauty despite herself for a moment. These were the moments she loved reading about. His sudden intimacy and gentleness in his voice should have been enough to steal her breath away.

183

But she kept breathing just fine. He was beautiful, but there was something... off.

This wasn't how it was supposed to feel.

"Please, Marrock..." His name felt clumsy on her tongue, heat rising from her cheeks from how closely he looked at her. She wanted to move away and put distance between them, but she didn't budge.

"You really think he's coming, don't you?" Marrock marveled, tilting her chin up to meet his gaze.

"Of course." She breathed the lie so gently that it was almost a prayer.

He had to feel her pulse pounding in her throat. Hopefully, he thought it was infatuation rather than everything in her screaming at her to get his hands off of her.

"You know this place is Warded, don't you? Against your kind?" Marrock asked, and a chill ran through her. "How else do you think we've been able to stay hidden all this time?"

She tucked that morsel of information away to unpack later. Wardings wouldn't be needed if this place were far from Thornvale.

"True love can overcome anything," Gwenna mumbled.

Marrock's eyebrows shot up his forehead, something almost like joy washing over his features, and she instantly regretted it.

"True love?" Marrock pounced on the phrase. "Surely you don't think... *He's* your true love?"

Face hot, Gwenna didn't say anything.

Somewhere inside was that little girl who felt so much for the Kaldonna boy who taught her chess. Aidan as a grown man, was such a disappointment. But Gwenna still couldn't let go of that friend she once had. He was the only one she had ever felt for, but he was also not what she thought he was. But if Aidan wasn't her true love... who was?

"We're getting sidetracked." Gwenna cleared her throat and met his gaze once more. "I ask for one month. One month out of consideration for Lord Aidan and his… claim to me." She inwardly cringed at the phrasing but pressed on. "After such a time, I can consider your marriage proposal."

"Consider?" Marrock arched an eyebrow. "I will not wait a month for you to *consider* the proposal. Your people certainly cannot wait a month."

"That's my second condition," Gwenna said quickly, trying to adopt her grandfather's calm and confident manners when deliberating in council meetings.

"I'm listening…." Marrock kept that one skeptical eyebrow raised.

"My people cannot last the month. Not while we politicians hammer out the details of an alliance. My second condition is that you keep them well-fed during my absence." Gwenna's voice was steady. A glimpse into the leader she hoped was hiding somewhere inside of her. "If you truly have the power to save Bannon from its fate, consider this a sign of good faith."

Marrock rubbed his chin, contemplating her offer.

Gwenna turned away, feigning a sneeze as a cover to invoke the sign of the Deep. If She had any power, Gwenna needed her aid and protection more than ever.

"I will arrange for supplies to be left in the village weekly. But I will not be held responsible for your people distributing them evenly," Marrock said finally.

Tears pricked at her eyes as she turned back to him. "I understand."

"I have some conditions of my own…" he said. Gwenna nodded for him to continue. "We will have a Mage create a Weave to indicate your willingness to wed, should your precious savior never show up. Consider it an act of good faith on your part."

Gwenna chewed her lip but didn't say anything.

"We will wait one month for your ridiculous prince to disappoint you one final time," he continued smoothly. She thought about correcting him– Aidan wasn't technically a prince. "In the meantime, I will arrange weekly supplies delivered to your village, and you will agree to the Weave."

Marrock extended his hand for her to shake on the arrangement.

"Will I be trapped here?" she asked suspiciously, keeping her hands firmly at her sides. "I will not be confined to a cell. Or to a house." She nodded towards the ornate manor looming overhead.

"You are my bride, not my prisoner," he said.

"That wasn't an answer." Gwenna narrowed her eyes. "Will this Weave trap me here?"

"The Weave does not operate on something as simple as geography." Marrock sighed. "However, I would advise against you trying to escape from Irrywellium. As a fledgling Shifter, you must stay in Her presence to complete the Shift. If you fly away during the day, you will remain a goose forevermore. And if you try to run at night, the pain of an unfulfilled Shift will have you ending your own life within the week. I am not trying to trap you here, Gwenna. But you will stay."

"I'm going to be a goose *every day*?"

He grinned. "Your Shift will be tied to the sun until you can master it."

"How long will that take?"

"It depends on the individual. How stubborn are you?"

"It won't be a problem then. I'll have it mastered before our… wedding." Her voice cracked on the word, and Marrock grinned. "I can't exactly rule Bannon nocturnally."

"Any other conditions, or do we have an agreement?" Marrock asked, holding his hand out again.

"What if Aidan *does* come for me?" she asked cautiously, watching his eyes closely for any hint of the beast beneath his skin.

"I'll still help your precious kingdom, if that's what you're concerned about." Marrock grinned. Gwenna breathed a sigh of relief. "Just as soon as Aidan proves he is your true love."

CHAPTER 22

E very foul word Gwenna had ever heard ran through her mind as she stared at the gloating Shifter.

"Aidan has to *prove* he's my true love?" she repeated. "How in the five kingdoms is he supposed to do that?"

"Through the Weave. Now, Mages are powerful, but they are limited. It is the Fairies that are truly one with The Deep: it is their magic that can never be broken. Weaves can always be broken by a true love's kiss," Marrock explained calmly.

"A true love's kiss…." Gwenna repeated faintly, remembering how Aidan's face had twisted in disgust in the ballroom.

"Of course." Marrock grinned. "Just one chaste little kiss. If our Weave dissolves, well, who am I to stand in the way of true love? I will step aside and allow you two lovebirds, pardon the pun, sweet goose, to ride off into the sunset together. Though I will ensure that Bannon remains well-fed and watered during the remainder of your drought."

"I-I need to sit down…." Gwenna muttered, massaging her temples.

"You also need to eat. Your first Shift can be quite taxing on the body. Come along, my bride; I had the staff prepare a meal for you." Marrock swept his arm out with a flourish, sinking into the role of dutiful host. "We can continue to discuss the arrangements over some libations."

Gwenna quickly followed after the Shifter as he strode to the steps leading up to his manor's terrace, lost in a trance. Her supposed love and faith in her betrothed had earned her time to delay the marriage. She could not afford to let her facade slip. Not now.

Aromas of fatty meats and freshly baked bread hit her halfway up the steps to the manor. Gwenna's knees buckled. The smell alone brought tears to her eyes.

The wide terrace of Marrock's manor allowed for beautiful views of the cenote. Still, the sight of an entire banquet table had her completely transfixed. Tall paned-glass doors were thrown open to invite them inside what once must have been a ballroom.

A hearth large enough to stand in comfortably held a raging fire. One plush armchair sat directly in front of the fireplace, with a small end table beside it. Gwenna assumed the closed double doors led to other passages inside the manor. In contrast, the small arched doorway tucked in the corner of the room must have led to the servant's passages. The far wall opposite the terrace displayed a faded fresco, and the stone floor glistened in the torchlight. But the true beauty was the long stone table laden with roasted turkey, boiled potatoes, hard cheeses with grapes, and candied plums.

Marrock's pace seemed so slow in the presence of a feast. It took all of her willpower not to push past him and run to dish up a plate.

No.

Her legs stiffened, slowing her pace. Gwenna could not, and would not, lose herself. Silently repeating Catriona's name, she breathed through her mouth to avoid smelling the turkey.

She would not crumble at the first good meal this beast offered her.

Straightening her spine, Gwenna forced herself to appear impassive and unimpressed.

Marrock glanced over his shoulder at her, smirking more openly now.

She moved slower and even more casually, eyes drifting around the room as though she was admiring the decor. Place settings were arranged to allow the two to be seated at opposite ends of the long table, the banquet serving as a barrier between them.

But the moment Gwenna sank woodenly into her seat, the Shifter moved his chair to be seated on her right-hand side. Even with keeping her gaze focused straight ahead, she could feel his proximity as though he were an open flame directly next to her. Dropping her gaze to her lap, she feigned interest in delicately arranging the linen napkin to distract her from the intimate way he watched her.

Feeling his eyes roam over her made her skin crawl.

"Shall I dish you a plate?" he asked in a rough voice. When she refused to answer, he took it upon himself to pile food on her plate. "I apologize for my rough manners. I haven't dined with royalty before."

The moment the first bite of turkey touched her tongue, Gwenna knew she was done for. She could not pretend to be unaffected by this meal after the last few days of grisled rations in Thornvale. But she had nothing to lose by filling her stomach, so long as she kept her emotions in check.

At least, that was the justification that ran through her mind as she ate with unabashed pleasure. Marrock could have grown another head, and she would not have noticed. Not with this feast on the table. A governess would have shuddered at her appalling table manners, but she couldn't bring herself to care.

"How long was I... gone?" Gwenna asked, breaking the silence. Her memories of the day were strained and foggy.

"One day. From the first ray of sunlight on the water to the last," Marrock explained. "I monitored you closely to ensure you were safe."

She bristled at being *watched* while not in control of herself. It felt painfully intrusive.

"Is it just you here?" she asked, desperate for any conversation to break the oppressive silence.

"A handful of staff," he said coolly. "Why? Is there something you need?"

"N-no. I assumed …."

He set down his fork, swiveling in his seat to look directly at her. "Tell me."

"I imagined Shifters living as part of a pack."

A smile slowly spread across his face, instantly sending her back to that moment in the devastated field outside Thornvale when the same devilish look had appeared on the face of a large black wolf.

"What else have you imagined about me, my bride?" He winked suggestively.

Gwenna's stomach threatened to empty itself at his lewd laughter. She breathed deeply to combat the nausea.

"Do all of you Shift into creatures in daylight?" She finally broke the silence, taking a sip from her goblet. It was some kind of sweetened juice, but refreshing nonetheless. She never cared for wine anyways.

"At first, yes. As children. It's a sign of maturation when you're able to master your Shift and Shift at will," he answered, eyes full of surprise that she continued to initiate conversation. "It seems you'll spend your days as a goose and your nights here with me in the manor."

"I will do no such thing," she said through gritted teeth, face burning at the thought.

He arched an eyebrow. "Excuse me?"

"I will not *spend the night* with anyone," Gwenna said quietly, eyes focused on the grapes on her plate. "If that's what you presume–"

Marrock laughed aloud, cutting her off. He poured himself another goblet of something that appeared far darker than juice.

"I'm no beast, milady. No harm will come to you in Irrywellium. You have my word on that." He drank from his goblet, lips stained a dark red as he looked over the brim at her. When he met her eyes, crimson liquid dripping from his sharpened teeth, he grinned. "Though I cannot promise you will not throw yourself at me. Some time away from that human idiot, and you may realize you crave a man after all...."

"You're a pig," Gwenna muttered, cheeks flaming.

"Wolf, actually," He grinned as he wiggled his eyebrows suggestively. "We may be primitive to your royal tastes, but we revere Her too much to commit violence in Her presence. You are far safer here than in your precious palace."

"Is that why you slaughtered my mother and sister in the mountains near Thornvale? Didn't want to pollute this place with their spilled blood, so you left their corpses for the animals?" she demanded, knuckles whitening as she skewered a potato on her fork. Her hand shook so violently that she abandoned her cutlery, hiding her hands in her lap instead.

"I am the only one who can help save you and your beloved kingdom. It is in your best interest to not push me further." Marrock said tightly. His canine teeth caught the torchlight, glinting as they subtly lengthened.

Gwenna shrank back in her chair, palms sweating slightly.

Marrock stood abruptly, shoving away from the table and striding to the doors out to the terrace. He looked out at the growing darkness, hands clasped behind his back.

Gwenna remained in her seat, frozen in place.

"I should not have lost my temper." His voice was low, restrained, and quiet. "But I will not have my wife speak to me that way. Do not do it again."

"I'm sorry," Gwenna lied.

He turned back to face her but kept his distance.

"As I was saying, the ability to control a Shift is a sign of maturity, but stress can interfere as well," he explained with a shrug. "As much as your kind would loathe the idea, we're not that different from you. Sometimes, our limbs rearrange into a new form when we stretch a certain way."

She couldn't focus on what he was saying. By mentioning Cat and her mother, she had re-opened the floodgates of her mind. The food turned to ash in her mouth. Tears pricked her eyes, and she blinked quickly to clear them away. To accept even something as simple as a meal from him felt complicit.

"My bride?" A note of irritation strained his voice.

Gwenna looked up quickly, realizing he was waiting for a response to some question she hadn't even heard him voice. "My lord?"

"I asked you to call me Marrock."

"My apologies. Marrock."

"Join me."

It wasn't a question.

The heavy chair scraped against the floor as she pushed away from the table, abandoning a plate still half full of food. Gwenna approached where he stood on the terrace, bathed in moonlight once more.

They stood there facing each other for a moment.

"You never Shifted before last night?" he asked.

"No."

Callused fingers grabbed her chin, wrenching her head upwards so those silver eyes could stare into hers.

"Do not lie to me."

"I'm not," Gwenna said softly, chin quivering despite herself. "Please... You're hurting me." He tightened his grip for a moment, eyes narrowing.

Then the moment was over, and he released her.

Gwenna instinctively fell back a few steps, resisting the urge to massage her chin.

"You have had ample time to consider my offer. I have fed you. And now I am awaiting an answer," Marrock said. "What will it be?"

Gwenna took a deep breath, reflecting on all of his terms. He would feed her people and wait a month before claiming her as his bride. Yes, he intended to put some spell on her that only a true love's kiss could break. As much as she loved Aidan, he probably wouldn't ever want to kiss her.

But that was a problem to be solved later on. Right now, she needed to keep her people alive and buy herself time to find Fairy Maeve. Once whatever curse was on Bannon was lifted, then she could worry about the Shifter and his Weave.

"I agree to the terms," Gwenna mumbled.

He tilted her chin upwards again, though his fingers were light as a feather this time. His eyes almost sparkled, and a hint of his smile quirked at the corner of his mouth.

"Say it, Gwenna."

"Say what, Marrock?"

"Say you'll marry me," the Wolf whispered, eyes studying every inch of her face.

It wasn't love in his eyes. But it wasn't disgust or fear either. And for a moment, it almost felt like that was enough.

"I will marry you."

CHAPTER 23

Inside the manor, the quiet clattering of porcelain dishes collected after a meal caught Gwenna's and Marrock's attention.

Gwenna immediately recognized the slight frame of the redheaded serving girl who had attempted to deliver a tray of food to her dungeon cell. The girl was busy clearing the table, eyes determinedly downcast and not daring to glance toward the terrace. Her pointed ears poked out of the kerchief binding her hair back, and the right corner of her lip was split.

"Joanya!" Marrock barked, and the girl almost leaped out of her skin before dropping into a trembling curtsy.

"Yes, milord?"

Gwenna couldn't focus on the girl's face. Her attention was snagged on a yellowing but still distinct bruising pattern around the girl's neck. Like an enormous hand had grabbed her by the throat and squeezed.

"I require a Weaving." Marrock inspected the dirt under his nails as he ordered her around. "For my bride and myself."

The girl, Joanya, finally looked up and, for a moment, met Gwenna's eyes. She looked several years younger than Gwenna, barely old enough to be sent away for finishing school if she lived in Thornvale. Fearful brown eyes stared at Gwenna for a heartbeat before the girl collected the dishes in her arms and hurried out of the room down the servant's passageway.

It stung, seeing the servant girl so afraid of her. But Gwenna couldn't blame her, either. If she was in Joanya's shoes, she'd be terrified of any woman who agreed to marry a monster like Marrock.

"She's a Mage?" Gwenna asked, turning back to Marrock.

He grunted in confirmation, still focused on cleaning the dirt from his nails.

"Can all Mages do spellwork?" She glanced over her shoulder towards the glowing lights of the village of Irrywellium.

"The Deep has given her children two abilities: Welding and Weaving. Welders are born with their blood and essence infused with that of a beast and, eventually, can adopt the other form at will. Your kind calls them Shifters. You– whatever you are– seem to have some Welding abilities," Marrock explained gruffly. "Weavers are what you call Mages. Their Weavings can appear like spells to outsiders."

"What's the difference between a Weaving and a spell?" Gwenna rubbed her arms, unused to the chill in the night air.

Marrock noticed her shivering and nodded for them to go back inside. She followed behind him, grateful for the crackling fire in the enormous stone hearth. He settled himself in the armchair facing the fire without a backward glance at her. She hesitated for a moment before settling herself at his feet. If this was some kind of silent power struggle, she'd just as soon defer to him and stroke his ego.

"Spells imply some use of otherworldly forces. Weavings don't require anything other than Her power and the individual Weaver's energy," Marrock finished.

Gwenna sat for a moment, considering. For every answer he gave, he introduced a hundred more questions she hadn't thought to ask.

A sudden ear-splitting scream rang through the manor, shattering the silence.

Gwenna leaped to her feet, looking around and fearing the worse for poor Joanya. But when she turned to Marrock, he was glancing upwards at the ceiling with an amused expression. Gwenna followed his gaze, and as she looked up, something boomed overhead like a hefty piece of furniture was toppled.

Marrock snorted and rolled his eyes, unbothered but amused.

"Should we go see if the staff is alright?" Gwenna asked, glancing upwards again nervously.

He shook his head. "Don't you worry your head about that, my bride. It's none of your concern. Please, make yourself comfortable. That pathetic girl should be back soon enough."

Reluctantly, Gwenna sank back down and tucked her legs beneath her.

Silence stretched between them, and Gwenna waited to hear any more from upstairs. Whoever had screamed had sounded like they were in serious pain...

"How old are you?" Marrock asked suddenly.

She looked up at him in surprise. "Seventeen."

He nodded slowly but didn't say anything and instead went back to staring into the flames. Panic seized her. Was that too young for him? Should she have lied and made herself sound older and more mature?

"How old are you?" she asked hesitantly.

"Nineteen."

Numbers ran through her head. He was younger than Aidan and probably Kellen, but the same age as Catriona. His answer surprised her. Being in his presence and watching how he conducted himself, something about him seemed so much older. Like his hard flinty exterior was the result of him aging prematurely. It couldn't be healthy to have so much rage constantly simmering inside you for so long.

Joanya came hurrying back, mumbling apologies. She had shed her apron and kerchief, her hair now pulled back in a tight braid. Pausing at the edge of the carpet, she dipped into a respectful curtsy. Her freckled collarbones caught the light beneath her wide-necked black gown. For a girl serving and likely preparing this much food, she wasn't eating any of it.

"I am prepared to Weave, Milord," she said quietly.

"Let's get on with it then." Marrock rolled his eyes and shoved himself out of his chair with a heavy sigh.

"Please, drink. Just one sip will do." Joanya produced a small flask from the pocket of her dress and nervously approached, offering it to Gwenna.

Gwenna's eyes darted from the girl to Marrock and back again, but she did as commanded. The liquid was flavorless but so cold that she felt it blazing a path of ice down her throat and coiling in the pit of her stomach. Joanya took the flask back and then handed it to Marrock, who drank as well.

"What is that?" Gwenna asked, voice cracking. Her throat felt frozen shut.

"The Deep provides," Joanya said softly.

Glancing out towards the terrace, Gwenna wasn't sure if she spoke literally or not.

Gently, Joanya took Gwenna by the hand and helped her to her feet. She positioned Gwenna with her back facing the hearth, Marrock at her side.

"Take each other's hand," Joanya instructed, slowly falling to her knees at their feet. Gwenna glanced at Marrock, but he was stone-faced as they complied. "No... Fingers intertwined."

Silently, they obeyed. Gwenna hoped Marrock couldn't feel her trembling. The intimacy of his long, callused fingers wrapped around her was startling.

She was struck, again, by how romantic this moment should be. No one had ever taken her hand before unless it was a footman handing her up or down from a carriage. That was completely different. This was intentional and personal. It should have been meaningful and full of emotion.

But it wasn't. It was forced and cold.

Gwenna pushed the thought away, forcing herself not to commit this moment to memory. She would get out of this place, out of this engagement, and have a life far beyond this. Someone, somewhere, would take her hand because he wanted to. It would be real, and she was determined to not let this farce rob her of that future joy. Heart pounding, Gwenna redirected her attention to where Joanya knelt.

Joanya's eyes were closed, her mouth moving silently as a constant stream of words noiselessly escaped her lips. The flames crackled and popped in the hearth behind Gwenna, and Marrock's hand tightened around hers.

More color rushed to Joanya's cheeks, and her lips moved faster. Sweat beaded on her forehead, but she didn't seem to notice. Her fists shook in her lap as she screwed up her face in concentration.

Gwenna glanced up at Marrock as fear began to curdle in her stomach. He appeared unaffected, staring at the opposite wall as though bored. Was this normal? The mage looked like she was in severe pain.

Joanya's breaths came in great gasps, chest rising and falling rapidly, but her eyes remained closed. She silently continued her chantings. Her face was even more scarlet than her hair. Nimble fingers clenched into a white-knuckled fist as her arms slowly raised above her head. Sweat poured off of her, fat droplets plinking against the stone floor.

Gwenna opened her mouth to say something to the servant girl to stop this when Gwenna gasped in pain. Her whole hand felt like it had been plunged into an ice bath, freezing and burning all at once.

Joanya's eyes burst open, bloodshot eyes staring at the matching silver rings Marrock and Gwenna now wore.

Joanya panted, eyes flickering up to Marrock for approval. "It has been Woven, as requested."

Marrock gripped Gwenna's hand tightly, lifting it to his thin lips and planting a small kiss on her finger right above the incriminating piece of jewelry.

"Thank you, my bride."

She burned where his lips touched, as though branded like a broodmare, but she didn't dare flinch away.

"Show my bride to her chambers." Marrock dropped Gwenna's hand unceremoniously. He strode away without a backward glance, calling to her. "You'll be able to get a few hours of sleep before you Shift at dawn."

CHAPTER 24

TWELVE DAYS UNTIL RESCUE

Gwenna dreamt of glowing purple light. Her grandfather yelled. She ran towards his voice, but then Catriona screamed somewhere behind her. It was dark. Too dark. She tripped over her feet, the only light coming from the light streaming from her two hands.

Gwenna's hands burned.

But not with pain...

A buzzing, vibrating, tingling sensation that spread over her limbs.

She sat bolt upright, unable to remember where she was. The bed was far too large, the chamber too cold, to be in Thornvale Keep. She couldn't remember anything, couldn't think straight. Not with her body pulsing so unnaturally.

"It's almost daylight. Would you like to be outside again?" a low familiar voice asked from the darkest corner of her chamber.

Adrenaline surged through her. She would remember that voice until the end of her days. The wolf had allowed her to sleep in a bed chamber rather than a dungeon, but she had locked the door immediately.

She remembered finding the wardrobe in the corner, filled with gowns tailored to her measurements. Grateful for a nightgown, she hadn't questioned the magic and just changed into the comfortable shift immediately. The last thing she remembered was opening the large window next to the bed to get some airflow, and then climbing into the soft bed.

How had Marrock gotten in? And how long had he been here?

"Marrock?" Gwenna grabbed the thick quilt and pulled it up to her chin, anything to shield herself from him. "What is–"

"Calm yourself, my bride." The mattress sagged as he sank onto it, one pale hand reaching towards her from the darkness. "Don't fight the Shift."

Every muscle in her body tensed, beads of sweat rolling down her forehead as tremors wracked her frame. Flames of pain licked her joints. She heard Marrock's words but couldn't let her guard down. Everything about this was *wrong*. Monstrously wrong.

A cold hand cupped her face. Large, callused fingers.

"Relax."

Gwenna tried to pull away from him, but he held her chin tightly. No pain could distract her from how her stomach turned at his touch. Her pulse pounded in her ears.

The door to her chambers flew open, but Gwenna couldn't see anything. Everything was out of focus. Her eyes...

Something was wrong with her vision.

"Kill the little priss and be done with her." A new voice. Feminine. High-pitched but cold. Angry.

"Get out before I tear your arms from your body." He wasn't addressing Gwenna, but his voice had a new level of cruelty.

Something burst within Gwenna all at once. Her eyes wouldn't open. She couldn't feel anything anymore. Just that same awful screeching sound... and then darkness.

Diving. Down, down. Arch the neck. Then up and up.

Push now. Wings out. Dripping feet but soaring up. Higher. Bright sun. So warm on her head. Stretch the muscles and tendons. Float on the breeze.

Blue sky. Fluffy clouds.

Heart pounding. Need... something? Not hungry. Not tired. No need to mate. Look at the sky. Need.

Need.

Go farther. Fly. Over trees. Go. And go farther.

Down. Down is home. Down is water. Deep and quiet.

The Deep. Ours.

Down is sleep. Soft feathers. Sleep.

Not going farther. Must go down.

Needing nothing out there. Up there.

Home is down.

Air immediately rushed into Gwenna's chest, the painful buzzing faint in her extremities. She stretched her newly returned human limbs, looking closely for any sign of black and white feathers. Nothing but freckles remained.

Glancing up to the mouth of the cenote, Gwenna stared at the quickly darkening sky. Had she really been up there? In the air?

The memories were fragmented, barely coherent images in her mind. But a sense of familiarity wrapped around her heart as she stared at the limestone rocks kissing the open air.

"If you fly away as a goose, don't expect to ever be able to Shift back," a high-pitched voice said, breaking her from her reverie.

Flinching, Gwenna turned to see a petite woman glaring down at her from the top of the stone staircase. Familiar pangs of inadequacy ran through her. Living alongside a Beauty like Catriona had never been comfortable, but standing in this woman's presence was a new sensation. As though beautiful was too mild a word. Pointed ears were clearly visible beneath the cascading waves of her glossy black hair.

Tendrils of pure power were practically visible, steaming off of her figure. She wore her allure like armor. Her blue silk gown was like a second skin, clinging to hourglass curves and displaying ample cleavage. Onyx skin glimmered in the fading light, and claw-like nails tapped impatiently upon her hips.

"I-I beg your pardon?" Gwenna stammered, rooted to the spot in the middle of the cenote. Risking a quick glance away from the woman, she looked for some sign of Marrock up near his manor but couldn't see him anywhere.

The woman's large amber eyes narrowed, and Gwenna's knees suddenly felt unsteady. Standing before this woman, alone, was the last place she wanted to be. She glanced down at herself, realizing she was only wearing the thin white shift she had worn to bed the night before. Wrapping her arms around herself, Gwenna walked across the water and up the steps.

The woman stepped in front of her, blocking her way, and glared down at her with a scorching hatred. She was short, barely five feet maybe, but radiating a wave of anger that left Gwenna feeling minuscule in her presence.

"Fernella!"

Marrock's roar echoed off the cenote's walls as he stormed down his manor's stairs and toward where they stood.

Gwenna sucked in a breath of relief. He was dangerous, but she knew how to avoid his anger. This woman was a new threat that Gwenna instinctively wanted to avoid.

"What are you saying to my bride?" Marrock demanded.

As the woman, Fernella, swiveled to face him, her mannerisms' flinty edge dissolved to nothingness. She gently traced a line from his shoulder down to the palm of his hands, a subtle sway in her hips.

"I was beginning to worry about you, lamb." Fernella tucked a strand of Marrock's hair behind his ear with the confident grace of familiar intimacy.

"What did you say to my bride?" He repeated, lips bared ever so slightly to reveal the hint of predatory teeth beneath. "I told you I wanted to be here when she Shifted in case something went wrong."

"Look at her stupid face," Fernella giggled cruelly. "Obviously, *something* went wrong with that Shift. Would you like me to fix her for you?"

"That's just how she looks," Marrock said wearily, resigned to the fact.

Pain lanced through Gwenna's heart. She didn't want to be attractive to either of these people. But the callousness in the conversation stung. Insulting her like she wasn't even there was demeaning.

Marrock's cold eyes tore away from Fernella's sultry pout to look Gwenna over. Seeing no apparent damage to his property, he extended an arm to Fernella to escort her back to the manor without a backward glance.

Gwenna reluctantly followed after them. She could hear Fernella's high-pitched crooning all the way up the stairs to the manor but couldn't make out anything she said. Marrock was fully engrossed in the conversation, however. A smile twitched at the corner of her lips. Perhaps Fernella's presence was a gift from The Deep. The longer that woman could keep Marrock occupied, the better for Gwenna. Maybe she could start looking for the Fairies this evening.

The large banquet table was laden with food as Gwenna stepped inside the manor, dishes steaming in the early twilight. She sat at the far end, allowing the table length to separate her from the happy couple. She bit into an apple, heart soaring with the prospect of a silent meal free of Marrock's cold scrutiny.

Fernella, however, seemed to object to her mere presence.

"I thought I heard she was a princess, lambkin. The grub must have lied to you. Look at the way she eats! Look at how she parades herself around in nothing but a shift! My first guess would be she's a lady of the night at some poor village inn, but I can't imagine she'd ever be able to make a living that way. Not looking like *that*!" Fernella cackled.

"Fernella…" Marrock chuckled darkly, sounding like a weary parent attempting to reign in their toddler but not truly caring. He sprawled in his seat, eyes never leaving Gwenna's face as he drank from his goblet.

"Come now, you know I'm just having a bit of fun." Fernella sat on the edge of her chair, leaning so far forward her breasts threatened to spill out of her dangerously low neckline and onto the table beside the cheese platter. It would be a terrible degradation of delicious cheese. "You used to like having fun too…"

Cheeks slightly flushed from the wine, Marrock finally settled his attention on Fernella as if realizing she was there. He slowly drank in the sight of her.

"I still like fun." There was a huskiness in his voice that Gwenna had not heard before.

Her chair screeched loudly against the stone floor as Gwenna stood, and two pairs of eyes rounded on her freezing her in place.

"I'm going to retire to my chambers," Gwenna announced, voice a little louder than she intended. Her face felt hot. Whatever was about to happen was nothing she wanted to witness.

Marrock slammed his fist into the table, knocking all the goblets over and cracking the veneer of the polished mahogany wood.

Gwenna instantly sat down hard in her chair.

"Eat." The wolf commanded, silver eyes still locked hard on Gwenna's.

"I'm not hungry, Marrock." She didn't flinch.

Fernella stood slowly, moving even closer to wrap her arms around Marrock's thick neck. He stared over her shoulder at Gwenna, using one strong arm to push Fernella away as though she were a small child.

"My bride must not go hungry." Marrock ignored Fernella, even as she leaned forward and began to kiss up his scruffy jawline towards his ear, fingers tangling in his pale hair.

"I'm not hungry."

Gwenna slipped the knife from her place at the table and slipped into the folds of her shift. Each time he called her his bride, the noose around her neck tightened ever so slightly. It had been less than two days, but she felt dangerously close to losing air. It was no term of endearment but a declaration of ownership.

Gwenna Lorne didn't exist to him. Just an object he was impatiently waiting to take ownership of and wield however he liked.

"I said: eat."

"And I said no," Gwenna spoke calmly, but her leg bounced frantically beneath the table.

A vein throbbed in Marrock's forehead, a spark in his eyes that had nothing to do with how Fernella passionately kissed his neck.

"Ignore the grub, lamb." Fernella's breathy voice was barely audible. "I know you've missed me–"

Marrock never broke eye contact with Gwenna, shoving Fernella away again.

"I'm going to retire for the evening," Gwenna repeated.

"My bride will not defy me." Marrock's voice had a flinty edge to it.

Gwenna pushed to her feet and turned away from the table, still clutching the knife in the folds of her skirt.

"My name is Gwenna," she called over her shoulder, heading for her chambers. "Not 'your bride.'"

A loud screech of chair legs against the stone floor echoed as Marrock shoved to his feet.

"You will heed me."

Gwenna whirled around to face him, adrenaline coursing through her veins.

"Ignore her, lam–" Fernella clutched his arm to try and pull him back to her.

"Release me!" Marrock whipped around, seizing Fernella by the hair and yanking her off him. She shrieked in pain, clawing at his wrists, but he did not release his grip. "Embarrass yourself elsewhere! How do you dare be as impossibly stupid as you are ugly? Can you not tell that you are not wanted?"

He threw Fernella to the floor, and her head cracked against the stone floor.

Gwenna froze, waiting to see if the woman would rise again. Her fingers tightened around the knife hilt in case the wolf came for her next.

A pitiful whining sound emanated from Fernella. She looked impossibly tiny with Marrock looming over.

"Lamb…" she moaned, looking up at him with glassy eyes. Blood trickled down her forehead.

The air around Fernella, right around her face, appeared almost hazy. Gwenna blinked, trying to clear her vision, but the haze remained. The woman looked almost blurred from view.

Fernella had Woven a glamor around herself, and her grip on it was slipping.

"Remove yourself from my presence," Marrock said coldly, landing a kick to Fernella's ribs.

Gwenna did not wait for him to turn to her. She fled to her chambers before he could stop her. This time she didn't stop at locking the door. She dragged her large vanity table over to barricade anyone from entering.

Even then, she couldn't close her eyes. Gwenna sat up the whole night, facing the door, knife clutched in her trembling hands until the first ray of sunlight hit the cenote, and she Shifted once again.

CHAPTER 25

ELEVEN DAYS UNTIL RESCUE

When Gwenna Shifted back at sunset the following evening, Marrock stood at the top of the stairs with a cold smirk. Every muscle in her body tense, she climbed out of the lagoon to meet him. She waited for him to berate her and vowed not to give him the satisfaction of a response.

"Ladies first," he said snidely, inclining his head before gesturing for her to lead the way up to the manor.

That was the only thing he said all evening.

He wouldn't let her out of sight but wouldn't speak either. Drinking heavily, he watched her.

If Gwenna was waiting for any kind of apology for Marrock's behavior with Fernella, it never came. He never mentioned the Mage's name or referred to the way Gwenna had defied him. Marrock still referred to Gwenna as his bride, with a new gleam in his eye as though silently challenging her to say something about it.

The image of blood trailing down Fernella's face was enough reason to hold her tongue.

She retired early to her chambers to get some privacy. Laying awake, she tried to envision any scheme that would get her to the village on the other side of the cenote. Mages and other Shifters had to live there. If Fairies lived near The Deep, they would have to be in the village too.

Laying on her bed, she rolled to face the floor-to-ceiling window that looked out over the water. She counted every light in the village, imagining the people that must live there. Marrock may have let her out of her cell, but it was somehow more torturous to see where she needed to go and not be able to get there.

Too many days had passed. Gwenna had to get to the Fairies.

Ten days until rescue

"Every night that you refuse to marry me is another night that the curse over your land could have been broken," Marrock sighed dramatically as he swirled the wine in his goblet casually.

Bile leaped into Gwenna's throat, but she forced her face to remain neutral and to finish her bite of roast pheasant.

The phrasing was too specific, too pointed. She had consciously tried never to mention a curse in front of him. Marrock had acted as though it was bad weather affecting Thornvale, not something much darker. Gwenna had played along, knowing that the Fairies would have the answers, not the wolf.

What did Marrock know about a curse?

"Curse? What curse?" she asked innocently.

He looked up at her, eyes flashing, but didn't take the bait. "The first food drop to your village was made this morning."

That made her sit up straight.

"What happened?" Gwenna demanded.

"Nothing. The food was there when the sun arose. My men ensured it was discovered before returning and reporting." He yawned.

Their table settings were placed next to each other once more: Marrock at the head of the table and Gwenna on his right-hand side. He sprawled in his chair, invading her space so much that her legs were tucked uncomfortably out of the way to avoid touching him. But at this moment, when he was being so talkative, she was grateful for the proximity. She could observe him better.

"Who found the food?" she asked.

Images of Aldessa, her maid, flooded her mind. She hadn't thought of her or her little brother Aymer in days. In their last conversation, Aldessa mentioned that their sister was sick. Surely they could use some nourishment.

And Kellen. Kellen, who was far too noble to work beneath someone like Aidan. He deserved a hot meal if anyone did. Though he would probably be the last one to eat, knowing him.

The thought almost made her smile, but she held it back.

Marrock scoffed. "How would I know that? My men were instructed to remain close by and ensure that it was found. That's what they did."

"Was Aidan there?" Gwenna asked, forcing a note of breathlessness into her voice.

"They didn't say." The Shifter rolled his eyes, refilling his goblet.

"Do you worry he'll track your men here?" Gwenna cocked her head to one side, watching closely for his response.

Marrock threw back his head in a laugh, white hair falling off his shoulders and hanging down his back. It was unbound tonight, the dark scruff around his jawline longer than she had ever seen.

"You esteem him far too highly," he laughed, leaning back in his chair and resting one dirty foot on the table as he crossed his legs.

"Why does he bother you so much?" Gwenna asked, watching every tick of the muscle in his jaw. "You hate all of my kind, on principle, I know. But he seems to particularly bring out your hate…."

"Because he's a pitiful excuse for a man, let alone a king." Marrock sipped his wine coolly.

Gwenna rolled her eyes but let the insult go. She could only defend Aidan's honor so many times.

"Tell your herd that for the next drop–"

"Don't call us a herd," he said sharply, bringing his fist down on the table with aggressive force.

Gwenna flinched, falling silent at once.

Nostrils flared, he took another long drink of wine.

She sat motionless as he drained the goblet and yelled at Joanya for another.

"We are a pack, not a herd," he said curtly. "You may think there's no difference and that it doesn't matter. But to us, it matters. Don't call us a herd."

Gwenna looked down. "I'm sorry, my lord. I didn't mean to offend. My people, we don't know–"

"Yes, they do."

"No, I've sat in meetings where they've used–"

"It's intentional," he said flatly, meeting her gaze as understanding dawned on her. "They know exactly what they're doing. Yes, even that beloved grandfather of yours. Especially him."

Gwenna froze, trying to reconcile this new information with what she already knew. Her grandfather was the most loving man. He had never had an unkind word about anyone, especially their enemies. King Domhnall had been dignified, a good leader.

Could you still be a good leader if you knowingly hurt people?

"I'm sorry," Gwenna repeated, sincerely this time. "It will not happen again. When I return to Bannon-"

"When *we* return to Bannon, you mean?" He grinned, the moment of tension suddenly gone from the room. He reached to grab her hand, and she casually pulled it away and laid it in her lap. "When *we* return as husband and wife, king and queen, we will ensure it never happens again."

"Of course," Gwenna muttered, cheeks reddening.

He threw back his head and laughed.

"You never answered my question about the curse," she muttered, reaching for her goblet.

"I'm aware," he replied lightly, raising his goblet in a mock toast.

Eight days until rescue

Slowly but surely, Gwenna was able to remain more conscious during her time as a goose. Her senses were still foggy, but she felt she could control herself a little.

The first thing she did was make herself a nest high up on the walls of the cenote on a little ledge and curl up for a nap. She knew that the more she slept during the day as a goose, the more she would be useful at night to find the necessary answers.

One week until rescue

"Did you make another food drop to my people?" Gwenna asked softly, wanting to moan at the cream-based soup she couldn't get enough of.

"Yes, yes. It was delivered yesterday morning," Marrock said carelessly.

"It's such a shame to ask your staff to go to all that work…." Gwenna began, but he cut her off.

"My bride cannot accompany my men on the next drop. How improper! Though it is so selfless of you to offer," Marrock said, eyes sparkling maliciously.

"I was merely going to offer to assist in the kitchens to prepare the food." She kept her eyes downcast, avoiding looking at him. "I would never dream of trying to leave Irrywellium, Marrock."

"Oh no, you wouldn't dream of it." He rolled his eyes as he took a sip of wine. "Just as I'm sure you wouldn't try to slip a note pleading for rescue among the grapes. If your prince needs hints to find you, he doesn't deserve you."

She rolled her eyes and kept eating. At best, it had been a long shot, but she had to try. This week had gone by so quickly, and Marrock was not letting her out of his sight. She needed more time.

According to the reports, no one in Thornvale was the least bit curious about where the mysterious food baskets came from. Aidan praised The Deep each time he arrived on the scene, but that was it. Shouldn't he be at least a little suspicious? She would be hard-pressed not to throttle him the next time she saw him.

If she saw him again.

"Dreaming of your true love?" Marrock mocked.

Gwenna looked up quickly, flashing an apologetic smile. "Am I that transparent?"

"All women are. Transparent, predictable, and simple-minded," he rattled off the list coolly.

She ground her teeth together and reached for another serving of the soup.

"Anyways, there's a festival tomorrow evening in the village. Joanya and the other staff members will have the evening off. Would you be interested in joining them?" Marrock asked casually.

Gwenna's spoon hit the table with a hollow thunk.

He smirked, watching her dab the splatter off the front of her gown before continuing as though nothing had happened.

"Yes, there will be two evenings of merrymaking and carrying on in the village. I have business to attend to elsewhere, so I will not join. But I will tell Joanya to attend to you and ensure you have a good time," he said, crossing his arms over his broad chest.

Gwenna wanted to shriek with joy at the prospect of leaving the manor for any reason, let alone going to the village. But at the same time, it was impossible to ignore how cryptically he had mentioned he would be absent. That was nothing if not suspicious.

She had to maneuver this very carefully.

"I would be thrilled!" she cried, grinning broadly. The corners of her lips cracked. It had been too long since she last smiled. "Thank you so much, my lord!"

"That would make you happy, my bride?" He reached forward to take her hand, and she didn't pull away.

"The happiest." It wasn't a lie, but she didn't believe for a moment that he was doing this out of the kindness of his heart.

"Consider it done! I'll arrange everything," he announced grandly. If he ever managed to get himself on a throne, he would have all the pomp needed.

"Will you be alright?" Gwenna forced a note of nervousness into her voice, making her eyes widen.

"Me?" He stood, stretching his arms over his head. His tunic rose, and she saw the muscled cut of his abdomen. There was strength to him, even if he wanted her to forget that.

Power beyond that of a man.

"I haven't known you to have business outside these walls during my entire stay here. Is everything alright?" Gwenna softened her voice.

No schemes or tricks. She was merely a concerned but simple-minded woman. A dutiful wife.

He patted the top of her head as he passed to the armchair before the hearth.

"Nothing to concern yourself with, my bride. I am a powerful man. Much of my business takes place beyond these walls. I cannot tend to everything while you are feathered and flying beneath the golden sun. There are things I must see to before we return to Bannon and are wed." His voice dripped with condescension.

Gwenna's throat felt raw with all the rage she swallowed, but she dragged herself up to follow him.

"I've always wondered what you do during the day," Gwenna said gently, taking her place sitting at his feet before the hearth. Eyes downcast, she arranged her skirts delicately. "What exactly is your business?"

He looked down at her from his plush armchair. "As I said, do not concern yourself with my business."

"I am not concerned." Unruffled, she met his gaze. "I merely need certain assurances."

"Assurances?" His eyebrows shot up his forehead.

"Swear to me that you are not going to harm Bannon or its people," she said coolly.

"You think I am occupying you with the festival while I turn around and slaughter your people?" His voice had a dangerous edge, teeth flashing in the firelight.

Goosebumps trickled over her skin, but she couldn't back down now. "Are you?"

"No."

Silence. His chest heaved with repressed anger, hers with fear. She noted how his fingers dug into the arm of his chair, but she kept going.

"You will not attack Thornvale?" she pressed.

"My business has nothing to do with you or your people," he said flatly. "How many more ways do I need to phrase it before you believe me?"

Gwenna wasn't sure how many more ways it could be phrased. He seemed to have mastered the art of half-truths. She hadn't yet caught him deceiving her yet, but it was only a matter of time. Whatever information he wanted to withhold, he would find a way to do it.

"I don't trust you," she said flatly in a moment of unbelievably stupid honesty. "I don't think you've told me the truth. About a lot of different things."

The pit in her stomach roiled, sure she had just made a mistake. She hadn't brought up the subject of Cat's death in days. It made sense that he would want to avoid the issue. Getting a girl to marry you would be considerably more difficult after you admitted to slaughtering her family.

"You're smart not to trust me," he said, equally candid.

Gwenna hesitated a moment, scanning his face for any emotion other than anger or condescension. There was none. She searched his eyes, seeing only darkness and fury. If there was even the tiniest hint of goodness to be seen in him, she was determined to find it. So far it didn't seem to exist.

"*But* believe me now when I tell you that nothing will befall you or your people during my absence," Marrock said, meeting her gaze calmly. "I thought you would enjoy the festival. Fernella requires my assistance outside of Irrywellium as it is the full moon. I will be gone for two nights, but I hope you will dine with me again on the third day."

Gwenna's stomach lurched at Fernella's name, but she kept her face impassive. A kernel of doubt swelled within her, but she bobbed her head.

"Thank you, Marrock." It was all she could say. She may not get another chance to visit the village.

"Enjoy the festival, Gwenna."

CHAPTER 26

SIX DAYS UNTIL RESCUE

The beginning hours of each day were lost. From the tingling in her feet to a flash of light into darkness. For hours. But slowly, *slowly*, Gwenna's mind was able to awaken inside her feathered body.

The sun was so high in the sky. Too high. Mid-afternoon, at least.

Gwenna, the goose, was floating in the middle of the cenote, feet idly paddling beneath the surface of the cool water. When she flinched, her head jerked violently and almost made her dizzy.

Long neck.

That would take some getting used to.

Gwenna looked around the cenote cautiously, unsure what to do with her consciousness in this new body. It was surprisingly comfortable how her limbs naturally adapted to this unique anatomy. Her head so far from her chest was odd but not awkward. She had to keep her movements small until she adjusted.

Inhaling to calm herself, she glanced up at the sunlight streaming through the opening of the limestone walls high above. It warmed her from the inside to see pure light and not the moon's reflection. She hadn't seen the sun in days.

Raising her arms– or wings– she flapped tentatively. Water streamed off her feathers, and instantly, she rose through the air.

Gwenna gasped, a honk that echoed off the limestone walls. She glanced down to see how high she had gotten with just a few strokes of her mighty wings and honked again, this time out of terror. The water was so far below now.

Human panic began to overwhelm what her body was naturally doing, and she faltered. Her vague memories over the past few days told her that she had flown as a goose before, but this was her first time consciously doing so at this height.

She pushed the fear away and focused only on her wings. Craning her neck up, she stared at the fluffy white clouds as she rushed to meet them. This is what she was born to do. Instinctively, primally, she knew exactly what needed to be done.

It was merely a matter of trusting herself.

Gwenna soared through the cenote's roof with no trouble, up into the open air miles above the water's surface. It should have been crisper and cleaner up so high; more refreshing. But it wasn't. The air hurt her throat and felt *wrong*. She banked left, circling to see if she could spot Thornvale somewhere on the horizon.

A honk tore from her throat. Thornvale Keep, her home, was not far off in the distance. It was less than a day's ride from the cenote. Granted, it would be a harrowing ride through the mountains with no actual trail to follow. But still: she was *so close*.

She dove towards the castle, the wind growing hotter and hotter as she descended. Gwenna had to pull out of the dive for fear of overheating, soaring back up again into slightly cooler temperatures.

Fernella's words echoed in her mind. If she left Irrywellium now, she wouldn't have the power to Shift back. And there was no denying the heat and lack of water in the air. It had only been a week since she'd been kidnapped. Still, the cool humidity of Irrywellium had somehow made it so easy to forget what Bannon was plagued with.

The sand dunes in the sea sparkled beneath the punishing sun. Each glint was a sharp reminder of how much heat was broiling off its surface. Looking up, the cool blue of the sky and the fluffy clouds looked peaceful and comforting. But the cracked dirt and empty pyres told a different story.

Funeral pyres.

Over a dozen were erected in the village of Thornvale, smoke still wafting from the funerals the night before. Gwenna's heart twisted in a distinctly human way.

Those were her people. Her responsibility. And while she was spending the day paddling around the water, they were dying.

Gwenna banked right, turning in a full arc to head back towards the cenote and Irrywellium. The peaks of the Marshora Mountains loomed before her, but her goose instinctively knew how to get home.

Flying towards the tallest peak, the Mother, Gwenna watched as the granite shimmered in the sunlight as though translucent. She soared towards it, watching an unnatural golden haze cover the mountain. As she flew through the Wardings, the glamor of The Mother disappeared, revealing a mountain peak that was tall... but not as tall as it appeared to the humans in Thornvale. Once the glamor was broken, Gwenna could clearly see the top of the cenote and Irrywellium's hiding place.

She pulled her wings close to her body and began to dive. Plummeting through the air, through the opening of the cenote, back to Irrywellium, and down to the water. She threw her wings out at the very last moment to slow her descent. Air buffeted against the underside of her wings, and she made a graceful, feet-first landing in the water.

Paddling for a few moments, she let the adrenaline rush subside before mentally turning to the task at hand. There had to be a way to break out of this form without waiting for the moon.

Throwing back her head, she closed her eyes and let the rays of the sun warm her face. It was a pleasant warmth, this far removed.

Gwenna inhaled sharply and tried to conjure up those pinpricks in the tips of her wings or between her webbed toes.

Nothing.

Again and again, she tried to spark something in her extremities, but nothing worked. There was no flash of light or sudden expansion in her limbs as her feathers disappeared.

Slowly, the sun arced across the sky high overhead, and long shadows began to fall in the cenote. Frustrated and dejected, Gwenna finally tucked her head beneath her wings and surrendered to the fact that she remained a slave to her goose.

Time was flowing through her fingers like water through a sieve. If she couldn't master her Shift, her days would remain useless. Closing her eyes, she floated into a restless sleep for a few hours as she waited for night to fall and release her again.

CHAPTER 27

SIX DAYS UNTIL RESCUE

Joanya stood at the steps to the water, completely unphased as Gwenna stepped back into her body. The Mage's fiery hair spilled freely over her shoulders, and she wore a simple gown the color of bluebells. Her face was scrubbed clean, with no bruises or split lips. Just an ordinary girl, ready to attend a festival in her village for a night of fun.

Other than her round, haunted eyes.

The Mage picked at the ends of her hair as the human princess exited the water completely dry.

"Good evening," Gwenna greeted with a soft smile. "Thank you for letting me join you. I'm sorry if we're late."

Joanya stared at her, unblinking, before she bobbed a curtsy as an afterthought. "It's my pleasure, milady."

"Please, call me Gwenna." She spoke as gently as possible, sensing that this girl was as skittish as a newborn deer. "You're Joanya, right?"

She nodded but didn't speak. The girl was maybe fourteen and seemed to shrivel in on herself, unused to taking up space or having someone speak kindly toward her.

"It's lovely to see you again." Gwenna pressed on. "Have you been working for—" She paused, unsure what to call Marrock. "Have you been working in the manor long?"

"As soon as I became a Weaver," Joanya said quietly. "Nearly a year now."

But she said nothing more on the subject, and Gwenna didn't push.

"Is there anyone else coming?" Gwenna looked up towards the manor, but all the windows appeared dark.

"The Alpha left hours ago. I was to wait for you and accompany you to the village," Joanya explained quietly, still not looking up.

"I'm grateful for you," Gwenna said, and the girl's head shot up in surprise. "You're the only one I've met from this place. Other than the master. But he's...."

"He's the Alpha," Joanya said. There was a finality to her voice, as though everything Marrock was, every dark impulse inside of him, could be summed up by his title.

Gwenna nodded. "He is. But I'd like a friend or two while I'm here. I don't know much about this place, and I was hoping you could teach me."

Joanya froze, eyes studying the princess closely to try and find the trap in her words. Gwenna waited patiently for the girl to take stock of her.

She had purposefully dressed simply in a violet day gown that would fit nicely in a Thornvale festival. It was fitted and ruched through the bodice with a rounded neckline and skirts billowing out above the hips. Fitted sleeves came to the forearm, and she had left her hair free of a braid.

Gwenna was surprised there was no weight to Joanya's gaze. It was innocent and uncalculating. She had no idea what the girl knew about her or her reason for being in Irrywellium. But at that moment, standing and letting the Mage pass judgment, she felt more confident than she ever had in court.

And it had nothing to do with Gwenna but everything to do with Joanya.

"I would like a friend," Joanya said shyly. "I haven't had a friend in a very long time."

"Me either," Gwenna confided.

"You are beautiful," the girl said simply. "I wish I had curls in my hair."

"Oh…" Gwenna tucked her hair behind her ear self-consciously, instinctively deflecting. "It's really just bushy and raggedy."

"No, it's lovely," Joanya insisted. "You should feel proud that your ancestors passed on such a gift. They gave you all that you are. You should be proud to have received it."

The Mage turned on her heel and began striding confidently down the trail towards the mysterious village on the other side of the water. Everything in her mannerisms communicated that the conversation was over. Gwenna was left reeling. There was so much to unpack in that philosophy. But she finally had someone from Irrywellium willing to talk to her. She couldn't waste this opportunity. Her kingdom couldn't wait any longer.

"Can I ask you a few questions?" Gwenna asked nervously as she fell into step beside the Mage. She glanced around to see if they would be overheard, but there was nothing but the trail beneath their feet and the limestone wall to their left.

Joanya chewed her lip, considering for a moment. "As long as it's not about something the Alpha has forbidden me to speak of… Yes, I suppose that would be alright."

"He's forbidden you to speak of things?" Gwenna blurted out. But the girl kept her lips firmly sealed, silently making a point. "Sorry. You're the first Mage I've ever met. That means you can… Weave, right?"

"Yes. I am a Weaver. Your people refer to us as Mages."

"And the others in your village are Shifters?" Gwenna prompted. "The boys?"

Joanya nodded. "The boys are Welded to another form. But times are changing."

"Joanya, you know I can Shift or... am Welded?"

"Of course," the girl giggled. "I saw your goose just now on the water."

"But I am not a man...." Gwenna trailed off, waiting for the girl to understand the implicit question. But Joanya stared expectantly until Gwenna had to finish the thought. "How can I Shift if I am a woman?"

"You're not one of us." Joanya shrugged simply as though that was all the needed answer.

"But if I'm not one of you, what am I?"

The question came out as a bellow of frustration that echoed off the stone surrounding them. Gwenna wanted to take the girl by the shoulders and shake her like a rag doll to get answers. But her frustration didn't lie with the Mage.

Denied by the Fairies. A curse upon her kingdom. Her grandfather's murderer. And now a goose?

It was too many titles for one girl. None of that had been anything she had ever *chosen* to be. She had never decided to draw this power out of her, and she had no idea what awful thing she was capable of next.

Gwena had come to this place and allowed herself to be kidnapped by her family's murderer to break the curse on her kingdom. But now, she was gathering more questions and mysteries than she could unravel.

She came here, Gwenna, the Queen of Bannon. But now she wasn't even sure if that was true anymore. Her damsel in distress act was blurring the lines of reality. Was she scared by Marrock? Did she hate him? Would she really allow herself to marry him?

Not to even mention Aidan. It was becoming frighteningly easy to completely forget everything cruel he had ever said or done. The longer she cried for him and pined for him, for Marrock's sake, the more she could feel the roots of that childhood crush sinking deeper and deeper into her heart. She had weeded that out and was determined not to let anything sprout again for a long time. But these feelings for Aidan were comfortable and familiar. That was their home. He had a home in her heart, even as much as she wanted to deny it.

Gwenna wanted to sit down in the middle of the trail and sob. Nothing made sense anymore. She was exhausted and stressed, and unsure of anything. Least of all, herself.

Even if she somehow could break Bannon's curse, what would that mean for her? The more she searched for answers, the more she began to feel the curse snaking around her, coiling tighter and tighter like a constricting snake.

This was not a foreign, external thing. Maybe once, she had been naive enough to believe that. But now, she knew this curse was *her* curse. She was the curse. How did you break something that was woven into the very core of your being?

Stories made it sound like curses could be easily broken. They were binding and tangible things that a simple kiss or countercurse could easily remedy.

But the storybooks had been wrong before. This was no curse that would be thwarted by true love. Even if Aidan swept in here on horseback and declared his undying and true love for her, it wouldn't be enough to break this.

Whatever this curse was, whatever *she* was, they were interconnected. Both were twisted around and around each other like a ball of knotted twine, almost impossible to untangle. The curse began and ended with Gwenna.

The mystery of who she was: the denied beauty, the luminous hands, the heat threatening to collapse her kingdom, and now her ability to Shift. All of it was connected, one leading to the next and to the next.

It wasn't enough to just find the Fairies now. Gwenna had imagined finding them and pleading with them to restore her kingdom, which they would do with a wave of their little magic wands or whatever they had. The Fairies would be the ones to lift this curse.

More and more, that was ringing hollow in Gwenna's ears. This was not something that the Fairies could simply "undo." This was something that she was going to have to break. And Gwenna was starting to get the feeling it would mean breaking herself.

Inhaling sharply, she continued with her next question. "How am I Welded?"

Joanya glanced around awkwardly as if there was someone around to overhear. "*You* should call it Shifting."

"Is it different than... the other word?" Gwenna asked delicately.

"No, it means the same thing. But... Welding is *our* word for it. And you are not one of us. You are something else," Joanya explained, oddly defensive over just a word.

"But what am I, Joanya?" Gwenna cried frustration back with full force now.

"I don't know," Joanya said bluntly, turning to resume her walk to the village. "Perhaps you should ask The Sisters."

Something in the way she enunciated the words piqued Gwenna's interest.

"The Sisters?" Gwenna jogged a few steps to catch up. "Are they Mages as well? Leaders in your village?"

The Mage giggled, and, once again, Gwenna had the mental image of shaking some sense into the girl. Joanya wasn't unkind, but she wasn't exactly helpful either.

"The Sisters aren't Mages. We can't fly." Joanya giggled, walking on the balls of her feet in an odd bouncing motion.

Gwenna's breath caught as she realized what the girl meant.

"Joanya!" She grabbed the Mage by the arm, pulling her back to meet her gaze. Glancing around, Gwenna kept her voice low. "The Sisters... are they Fairies?"

They appeared alone, but Gwenna couldn't afford to be overheard. Marrock had claimed he had left Irrywellium and left the cenote altogether, but she had no idea if that was the truth. The last thing she needed was for the wolf to get wind of what she was searching for.

"Yes, I think that's what your kind call them," Joanya said absently, a dreamy look on her face as she stared out over the water.

"Do they live in the village? Are they going to be at the festival this evening?" Gwenna couldn't keep the urgency from her voice, but she relaxed her grip on Joanya's arm.

"No." Joanya giggled, somehow innocent and patronizing all at once. "They don't come to festivals."

Gwenna bit back a groan of frustration and tried to remain patient with the girl. It was like talking with a small child: Joanya would answer the specific question but nothing else.

"Joanya, do you know where I can find The Sisters?" Gwenna asked sweetly, and the sudden change in tone left the Mage eying her suspiciously. "I've always been interested in them. My Mother used to tell me stories about them, and I'd very much like to meet them."

"My Ma told me stories about *your* kind," Joanya said, her voice dropping to a whisper as her eyes widened. "You like to steal baby boys from their beds and run away with them!"

Gwenna jerked back in surprise. "What? No, we don't!"

"Yes, you do."

"Joanya, how would we do that? My people don't even know where this place is!" Gwenna massaged the spot between her eyebrows.

"That's why we must stay here," Joanya continued hushedly. "To protect our little ones from the bandits. But our Wardings are failing... Your people keep coming.... The babies are taken...."

She shuddered before turning and hurrying along the path with increased urgency.

Gwenna let the girl put some distance between them, suddenly understanding the source of the Mage's anxiety.

"Joanya, I would never hurt your people." She spoke softly but emphatically, eyes boring a hole in the Mage's spine.

The girl glanced over her shoulder, a small smile on her face. "Yes. *You* are a kind one."

"Thank you," Gwenna smiled. "Do you know who I am?"

"The master's guest..." Joanya shrugged. "His new wife...."

"I'm a princess, Joanya. That means that I rule over my kind. And I give you my word that we will not hurt your people. Ever." Gwenna closed the distance between them and looked directly into her eyes. "And if someone has been hurting them, I didn't know about it. And that's no excuse. But I am sorry. I know now. And it will stop."

The apples of Joanya's freckled cheeks turned pink. Her brown eyes looked a little glossy in the moonlight.

"I believe you," she said softly. "You are good. And kind."

"I would like to be your friend," Gwenna said shyly. "I don't have many friends here."

Her face lit up. "I would like that too." She took Gwenna's arm, and they began walking up the path toward the village together.

They didn't make it a dozen steps before Joanya halted.

"If you are my friend, you should know..." Joanya took a deep breath as though steadying herself. "Do not let the Alpha know you are hurting. He enjoys seeing women in pain." Her hand drifted almost unconsciously to her cheek.

It felt like a boulder crashed into Gwenna's chest, knocking the air from her lungs. Marrock and Joanya both had strongly implied that the staff was forbidden– perhaps magically– from speaking out against the wolf. This was an outright accusation and a warning.

In an instant, Joanya was grinning again, and the solemn moment was over.

She squeezed Gwenna's bicep gently. "Come! It's time for the festival!"

CHAPTER 28

The village didn't look far from the manor, but the girls had to walk quickly for nearly an hour before reaching it. The houses jutting out of the cliff face looked much larger up close, and there were dozens more than had seemed from across the cenote.

Cookfire smoke wafted towards them on a gentle breeze. Joanya led them up a few flights of narrow steps carved into the side of the limestone walls, past several homes. Narrow corridors branched off in every direction leading to more walkways and homes.

"Joanya... what happens at the festival?" Gwenna asked nervously as they approached the echoes of a crowd.

"Tonight, we commemorate those we have lost. Those that were slain by–" Joanya paused on the stairwell and glanced hesitantly over her shoulder direction. "Those that were slain by our enemies. We eat. And we tell their stories."

Gwenna winced, sensing who these 'enemies' were.

"It sounds beautiful, but I don't want to intrude. Perhaps I should go...." Gwenna took a step back.

Walking into a festival of magical beings as the only human was already daunting. To have to sit and witness those people telling stories of their families murdered at the hands of humans didn't sound very wise.

"Why would you be intruding?" Joanya asked innocently, cocking her head to one side.

"I wouldn't want to make anyone feel uncomfortable with my presence. As you said, I am not one of you," Gwenna explained.

"No, you're not," she agreed. "But you're not one of them either."

Joanya wrapped her hand around Gwenna's wrist and towed her up another short flight of steps before leading her through a maze of corridors. Rounding a corner, the scene opened into an expansive town square hollowed beneath a rocky overhang. Stripes of color ran through the rocks: rusty reds and cool swirls of blue and gray.

The square was packed with bodies of every shape and color. The diversity was shocking but beautiful. Gwenna had pictured everyone in the village of the same make, but no. These people were as varied as different kinds of flowers in a meadow, all different hues mingling and laughing together.

Long trestle tables were laid end to end to bear the weight of the communal feast. Children darted through the crowd and between legs in a made-up game. Mothers stood together, rocking infants and gossiping quietly. The men tended to the fires, arms crossed over chests as they surveyed their work.

Tears pricked Gwenna's eyes at the amount of *life* packed into the square. Families and friends gathered to laugh and support one another. When was the last time her people had a cause to celebrate? They had been so serious even before her curse that dried up the land. The court had parties and balls, but the village had nothing like this. And the court events were stuffy and political, more stressful than any kind of celebration. Those were events to flaunt your standing or begin a subtle campaign to scramble further up the ladder. Gwenna was all too familiar with the seedy underbelly of royal events; she had capitalized on it on more than one occasion.

But there was none of that here. No one casually kept watch on rivals while pretending to be thrilled by dancing. These people were here to celebrate. Even if tonight was to mourn their losses, the joy in the square was palpable.

"Joanya! You made it!" A familiar-looking pale youth came bounding through the crowd. "And you brought the human!"

"Gwenna, this is Epon," Joanya murmured, cheeks suddenly much pinker than they had been a moment before. "Epon, this is my friend Gwenna."

Gwenna stared at him a moment too long.

"I was the horse," Epon hinted.

She flinched as the memory of being magically drugged and thrown onto the bare back of a white stallion flooded over her. It was odd to look him in the eye and know he had aided and abetted in her kidnapping. He didn't seem to feel any of her discomfort, and she wanted to say something snide.

"The Alpha commanded him," Joanya whispered. "He had no choice."

Heat rushed to Gwenna's face. Kellen had mentioned something about Shifters being unable to defy the Alpha. Anything she felt towards Epon was misplaced.

Her anger was with Marrock.

"Nice to see you again." Gwenna inclined her head respectfully, unsure what to say to a horse she had ridden. Epon flashed her a polite smile.

"Your brother saved a seat with us over there," Epon told Joanya, pointing to the far side of the square. "I'll bring you both plates. You made it just in time for the tales!"

Epon hurried towards the food. Joanya's cheeks burned so scarlet Gwenna thought they might actually catch fire.

"He seems very sweet," Gwenna teased gently, bumping the Mage in the ribs with her elbow.

Joanya tossed her hair. "You can dance with anyone in the village that you wish. But *not* Epon. Otherwise, we cannot be friends."

"I understand," Gwenna assured her.

Satisfied, the Mage led the way through the crowd in the general direction that Epon had indicated.

No one spared Gwenna a second glance, but she felt woefully out of place with these people. The weight of a million sets of eyes would crush her into the dust, even if she logically knew that no one even noticed her. Still, she kept her hair over her ears so no one would see how round they were.

Once on the far side of the square, Joanya headed towards a boy with hair the same shockingly red shade as his sister's. He was tawny, and his ears protruded farther from his head than anyone Gwenna had ever seen. She forced herself not to stare at his ears and instead lock eyes with him as he stood to greet her.

"This is my older brother," Joanya explained.

"Orrin. Welcome to Irrywellium," he said with a piercingly white smile.

"Thank you. I'm Gwenna. It's a pleasure to meet you." She returned the smile, and Orrin turned, gesturing to the seats on the floor he had saved.

The three sat with backs against the stone wall of the cave, facing the center of the square where a space had been cleared for the speaker. Epon quickly reappeared with two plates piled high with food. Gwenna slid over so he could take the spot beside Joanya, who was beaming ear to ear at him, but he didn't seem to notice.

Irrywellium's festival food would not have been out of place at her grandfather's high table. It was even more delicious than the nightly meals she shared with Marrock. The rack of ribs on her plate was so tender that the meat fell off the bone, smothered in a peppery sauce with just the right amount of spice. Gwenna did her best to eat like a lady, but it was easily the best meal she had ever had.

"There's a whole other table of sweets when you're ready," Orrin whispered, sitting on her right side. Gwenna could only manage a grin in response, but he seemed to understand. "May I ask you a question?"

"Of course!" she cried, wiping her mouth with the back of her hand.

"Wh-what is your essence?" he asked carefully. "Joanya has said you're Welded. But she doesn't say much about it...."

"A goose," Gwenna admitted, cheeks burning with the embarrassment of it.

Orrin's face lit up. "How fantastic! Are you really able to fly?"

"Oh." She shrugged modestly. "I'm still working on mastering it, but yes."

"That's really incredible... I have to admit, I'm jealous. Drew, one of the boys in town, has the essence of a hawk. Says there's nothing like being able to fly," he confided, leaning in as though it were a secret.

"Oh... what's your essence?" Gwenna asked before looking around in paranoia. "Wait, it's not supposed to be some kind of sacred secret, right?"

"Nah, there's no hiding anything in Irrywellium," Orrin chortled. "I have the essence of a moose. Bet you couldn't have guessed it by my ears." He tugged on his earlobe bashfully.

"I never would have suspected," Gwenna said quickly, and he beamed. "You must be quite tall after you Shift."

"Mighty tall." He gave her a knowing grin. "Ma wouldn't let me in the house while I was mastering it. Said my antlers would punch a hole clean through the roof."

Gwenna smiled in return. "I must admit: you're the only Shifter I've had a chance to talk to about it. We don't have them where I come from...."

"Of course not! The humans aren't worthy of such a thing!" He snorted. Gwenna hesitated to respond, and his eyes widened. "Oh, I'm so sorry. I didn't mean–"

"It's ok," she assured him quickly. He still looked embarrassed, so she quickly changed the subject. "Can you tell me more about the essences? Each Shifter is born with one essence?"

"Yes. Each boy is born with the one animal whose essence you're Welded to. There's no way of knowing your essence until that essence comes upon you for the first time. It's just a mystery 'til you're grown," he explained.

"Until you're grown?" she repeated.

"Well, until you're mature. I don't know much about humans, but I imagine you undergo bodily changes in your youth…?" he asked awkwardly. She understood where he was going and nodded quickly. "It's the same with us. Except, well, your body changes a little more."

Gwenna nodded, musing over everything that he had said. It made a lot of sense. And confirmed everything that Marrock had said.

"Are there any girls in the village that can Shift?" she asked.

Orrin quickly shook his head, shaggy hair falling in his eyes. "Of course not. Girls are the Weavers." He gave her another apologetic grin. "Whoops. I mean–"

"I know what you mean," Gwenna said with a tight smile, bringing her knees to her chest and wrapping her arms around them.

The sensation of feeling like she didn't fit in wasn't a new one. She was just… different. A little bit too much, or perhaps a little bit not enough. Whatever the sum of her parts, it didn't come out the same as it did for everyone else. That feeling, loneliness with a tinge of self-consciousness and a dash of humiliation, was all too familiar.

But to feel that familiar sensation here, in a new place with new people, was unexpected.

"Are there any children born who can do both?" Gwenna wondered aloud, bringing Orrin's head up. "Children who can…." She hesitated, not wanting to say something blasphemous in front of new friends. "Children who are both Shifters and Mages."

"No, no, of course not," Orrin said in a hushed voice. "That would be an abomination to Her. She is benevolent in gracing us with power. It would be monstrous to even think about taking more. No creature needs that much power."

Gwenna nodded. "I understand. Thank you, Orrin, for answering my questions."

"You seem sad," he observed.

"I feel a little sad," she admitted, surprised by her honesty.

"You wish to be one of us?" Orrin asked somberly.

"No... and yes." Gwenna sighed. "I was hoping to understand more. I'm not one of you. But also not one of the humans. I thought I was. But now... I don't know."

"Maybe it's time She created something new," he said simply, and that brought her head up in surprise. "Maybe you're supposed to be the first one. But if there's one, there has to be more. You just haven't found them yet."

Gwenna smiled at the thought. Perhaps her people were out there after all, and waiting for her to find them.

CHAPTER 29

A hush fell over the crowd as a man, probably as old or even older than the late king, approached the makeshift stage at the center of the village square. The four new friends were seated behind him. The crowd formed one large ring around him, and for a moment, Gwenna worried that he was too feeble to preside over a large group.

"That's Laisren. He's the eldest," Orrin whispered as anyone left standing began to find their seats.

Gwenna looked up at the man, skin as leathery as an old tortoise in the sun, yet with a full head of pure white hair. A sharp pain resonated in her chest as she thought of Grandfather. She buried her hands, her traitorous hands, in the folds of her gown.

"Eighteen years ago, our people were attacked. Butchered. Murdered in their homes." Laisren's booming voice rang through the square, echoing off the walls. His hands shook, but his voice was steady. "Tonight, we gather to remember those we lost. Those who were taken from us."

"Tomorrow, we will celebrate our strength. Our resolve. Our home along Her shore. The way She has provided for us these past years. But tonight, we mourn. We allow ourselves to feel that pain that we otherwise would push away. To wonder what might have been. To wonder who they may have grown to be. Many of our numbers do not know them. Do not remember that time. And there will be a time that our people will gather, and none were there that fateful day. None will see those images each time they close their eyes. They will not remember the screams. That day is coming, and it is coming quickly.

That is why tonight is important. Because while I know we all are grateful that our children do not bear those scars, we cannot allow them to grow up blind. They must know. As long as they know, they can be protected." Laisren slowly turned in a circle as he spoke to lay eyes on everyone in the crowd.

Gwenna felt his gaze fall upon her, and her breath caught in her throat. Part of her expected him to scream, yell, and demand that she be removed from his presence. His eyes locked with hers, and she could see it in his eyes: he knew she was not one of his people. He knew she came from the enemy.

And yet, he continued speaking, continued rotating so that he could see others in the crowd.

"Since the dawn of Bannon, our people co-existed happily alongside the humans. They were our neighbors. Our friends. Our children played together. We accepted the King's rule. We honored him. Loved him. Many of us worked inside his palace. And not only as servants and maids and stablehands. No, we advised him. The young prince was my closest friend in the world. My father sat on his father's council. We played together as boys. I stood beside him at his wedding, I was present when The Sisters presented a Blessing upon his daughter, and I was the first to bow before him at his coronation," Laisren recounted. "King Domhnall of Bannon, they announced. He was sure to be the greatest king yet."

Gwenna was grateful that his back was turned so he couldn't see her jaw drop as he mentioned her grandfather's name.

She had never heard of Shifters and Mages living in Bannon, let alone Thornvale. It was impossible. Up until a month ago, she thought they were just storybook creatures.

But her grandfather knew them. He had worked with them and grown up alongside them.

So much had changed in Bannon during her grandfather's rule. A growing sense of dread told Gwenna that she didn't want to hear the end of Laisren's story.

"We all mourned when Queen Treasa was killed. That loss ran deep, through the whole kingdom. She was beloved. Domhnall was my friend. I believed him to be a good man, a fair man. But that loss changed him. And changed our lives forever."

Laisren was a phenomenal storyteller, able to remain ominous and aloof in his narration. But as much as he seemed to have a flair for the dramatic, Gwenna could not shake the feeling that he spoke honestly. She wanted to bury her face in her hands as Laisren resumed speaking, but she resisted. Sitting up straighter, she set her jaw, determined to sit through this. She couldn't hide. She couldn't run.

Whatever happened to these people, whatever had happened during her grandfather's reign, that was her legacy. As the queen, Gwenna had to know the truth.

"I will never understand what caused the king to blame us. I will never know what made him forsake years of shared history and friendship. But he was deceived. He was told that Queen Treasa's blood was on our hands, and he would not believe otherwise. He would not listen to reason. I will never be able to forget the things he said that day. The things he accused me of. But even with as much vile as he spewed, I never thought he would be capable…." Laisren's voice broke with a sudden onslaught of emotion.

Bile churned in Gwenna's stomach as pieces fell into place before her eyes. She hated how much it made sense. Laisren was a Shifter, unable to lie.

"I returned to my home. To my wife. To our baby boy." Laisren was facing her directly now, and she could not look away. Tears ran freely down the old man's face. "Domhnall and his guards came that night. They spared no one and nothing. Homes burned. There was so much screaming. Those who could, ran. We had nowhere to go, but we knew we could not stay. Ennis, my beautiful baby boy, was ripped from my arms by the king himself. Domhnall beheaded him in front of me."

The silence was smothering. No one in the crowd made a noise. No fussing babies. No coughs or the rustle of stones against the stone floor as someone adjusted their footing. The oppressive absence of noise felt wrong.

It felt like death. Like mass graves..

Laisren didn't turn away from Gwenna, nor did she from him. There were several rows of people between them, but it felt like she was the only one in the room.

He may have recounted this tale every year.

But tonight, he spoke directly to her.

"Tomorrow, we will celebrate the Rolfe's family generosity by extending their ancestral home to us," Laisren said. "But tonight is for their memory. Tonight, I honor Ennis. Those who feel so inclined may come up and tell us their tale of that night so that we may remember. The King was deceived. And the King exterminated our families. We cannot forget that."

CHAPTER 30

G wenna lied.

She escaped to her chambers at the manor when Laisren finished speaking, claiming she couldn't keep her eyes open. Joanya had accompanied her without hesitation. Gwenna did everything she could to protest, but the Mage was committed to attending to her. It wasn't until Gwenna noticed how Joanya kept running her fingers, almost unconsciously, over her recently healed split lip that Gwenna finally stopped arguing.

Joanya's company was less about Gwenna than fear of the wolf. The last thing Gwenna wanted to do was put the girl in harm's way.

The walk back to the manor was silent. Both girls were lost in their thoughts, and Gwenna could not have been more grateful. She wanted time to herself.

She *needed* time to process everything.

Guilt pressed down upon her, shaming her for walking away from the very people who would know about Fairies. This was her first night without Marrock's supervision, and she was crawling into her bed rather than getting the answers her people needed to survive. It was a wasted opportunity.

The girls parted ways in the empty dining room. Joanya assured Gwenna she would be available if she needed anything but hurried off to the servant's quarters without further discussion.

Gwenna collapsed on the ornately carved four-poster bed in her chambers, staring up at the velvet hangings. It was criminal how little time she had to enjoy the soft mattress, forcing herself to sleep during her goose hours and becoming nocturnal. Her body was heavy with exhaustion, but sleep would not come. Not with the old man's words echoing through her mind.

The nausea in her stomach had nothing to do with the food in her stomach. Gwenna had planned and schemed to protect her grandfather's legacy from lesser men. She and Cat had both been willing to marry for an alliance rather than love, because of their love for their family legacy.

Bannon's throne, the seat Gwenna now stood to inherit, was stained with the blood of innocent people.

She had never heard her grandfather raise his voice, let alone his hand. He could be commanding and decisive but never cruel or angry. King Domhnall was known by his subjects to be loving and mild-mannered, a kind and devoted king. The kingdom mourned his death because his people loved and respected him.

It should have been impossible for Gwenna to reconcile the king she knew with Laisren's tale of a man who unapologetically committed genocide.

But it wasn't.

Something inside her resonated with Laisen's words, feeling and sensing the truth more than consciously understanding. Time spent with Marrock had taught her that just because Shifters were incapable of lying didn't mean that they were consistently truthful either. She should have been finding holes in Laisren's story. Her mind didn't want to accept it, but her heart could not deny it.

She felt pinned to the earth flat on her back as the world spun around her. Time melted away as her view of her world shattered and slowly began piecing itself together. Frozen, she felt and watched her thoughts and emotions swirl around her like tangible objects. She wasn't even inside of her body anymore.

Gwenna was a foreigner. Other. Somewhere far away from this shell, sequestered and hiding away until things made more sense.

Gradually, she became aware of the sharp pain in her chest. She felt cracked down to her core and split through. There were no tears. Just pain.

Memories washed over her. Slowly at first, like a trickle of a stream running over small pebbles. The king reading fairy tales to his granddaughters. Picnics as a family. Laughter. Hugs.

Love.

A kernel of anger sprouted in her chest. All of it felt like a lie now. No one who committed such acts of violence could be capable of love. He had fooled them all.

Any bit of love within him must have died with his wife. He had never spoken of her. The only stories Gwenna knew of her grandmother came from her mother. The late Queen Treasa had died a few months before Gwenna was born. The ruby fever claimed her grandmother and her father the same night.

On the one hand, she could almost understand how the king could lose himself in his grief. After all, Gwenna had lost her entire family in only twenty-four hours. She knew all too well how closely crippling grief could blend into a rage.

But Gwenna hadn't turned to violence. That was where she and her grandfather differed. She had thrown herself into breaking the curse on her kingdom. It had given her a problem to solve and something to occupy her. In no way had it healed her. Grief lurked like a monster in the shadows, waiting for any quiet moment to sink its teeth into her and drag her down into the depths. She was not rid of it and worried that she never would be.

Had it been the same for her grandfather?

He may have been mild and soft-spoken, but the stories he told his granddaughters were not. They were full of fear and danger. Death lurked around every corner. He had embellished every tale he told them, heightening the risk and adding in his own advice. The girls should mind their elders. They shouldn't stray. Bannon was strong. The kingdom and the crown could not be wrong.

Who were you trying to convince, Grandfather?

Perhaps both versions of her grandfather were correct. A human soul was a complex thing. It could hold all the love and tenderness of a grandparent, while still leaving space for atrocities. Soldiers were asked, sometimes daily, to kill another person without remorse, but then return home unphased.

King Domhnall had done great things for his people. The kingdom had flourished and alliances between the five kingdoms were stronger than ever. That was the legacy Gwenna thought she was inheriting. But while he was a benevolent leader, he was cruel to his enemies. Both facts could stand, independent of each other. Both versions of Domhnall were true. She didn't need to choose one or the other. Gwenna could be proud of the things he accomplished, and determined to make up for his mistakes. Right now, it felt like there were two versions of her grandfather. She would work for the rest of her life to not only merge those two people into one, and become comfortable acknowledging that level of ambiguity.

It would dawn in an hour.

There was no indication of this, no visible lightening of the sky outside her window. But again, she felt the truth of it. Perhaps the proximity to the Deep or her newfound ability to Shift had given her this ability to feel the truth of things.

It would be time to Shift soon, and tonight, after she shed her goose, she would head back to the village with Joanya for the second day of the festival. There wouldn't be time to prepare later, so she had to do it now.

Gwenna dragged herself into the attached bathing chamber for a quick bath. Once scrubbed clean, she pulled on a mustard colored gown in the same style as the one she wore the night before. She pulled back half her curls with a matching ribbon, leaving a few tendrils to frame her face.

The cracked oval mirror over the washbasin showed the same reflection she had seen in all of the gilded mirrors in Thornvale. Her face didn't show it, but she certainly *felt* different. She wasn't the same girl that left Thornvale barely a week ago. Straightening up, her gaze fell on her silhouette, and she sucked in her stomach out of habit. Her hands moved to smooth the pleats in her gown as if she could simply brush away the extra padding on her wide hips.

A quiet knock on the door indicated Joanya's arrival with a breakfast tray, as promised.

"You look prettier than a pheasant all trussed for dinner!" Joanya beamed as Gwenna let her inside. Was the bird reference intentional, or just a saying in her village?

"Thank you. I wasn't sure what to wear for the festival…" Gwenna shrugged, absently trying to smooth out her hips again.

"We like you no matter what you wear." Joanya giggled as she set the breakfast tray on the trunk at the end of the bed. She had changed out of her day gown and back into the simple gray dress that seemed her uniform at the manor. Her scarlet hair was braided in a thick rope down her back.

"If only it were that simple everywhere," Gwena muttered, helping herself to a piece of buttered bread.

"What do you mean?" Joanya plopped down on the end of Gwenna's bed.

Gwenna's first instinct was to flinch at the girl's casualness in her chambers. But as she took in Joanya's big eyes that were impossibly genuine and interested in what Gwenna would say, she realized she was grateful for her company. It felt right having Joanya sit down and speak as equals. After all, the Mage had taken her into the village and introduced Gwenna to her people. Why should things be different between them in the manor?

"Things aren't that simple at my home," Gwenna explained before hastily adding, "At the palace. Where there are royals and balls and things."

"What you wear affects how people treat you?" Joanya scrunched up her nose at the thought.

"They pretend to be above such things, but yes. Suppose you wear the wrong style or look a certain way. In that case, it can... affect things," Gwenna said carefully, instantly remembering the withering look Aidan had given her his first night at Thornvale.

A pang of residual pain reverberated through her. That slight felt so long ago and not remotely important anymore. But the hurt remained, tucked away inside of her.

"That's the stupidest thing I've ever heard," Joanya snorted. "Even for a bunch of savage humans."

"Well, you treat Epon differently from the other boys, don't you?" Gwenna asked, adding some apple butter to the next piece of toast and ignoring her description of humans. Given what Laisren had experienced, savage seemed to be appropriate.

"What does Epon have to do with this?" Joanya asked hotly, cheeks flushing.

"You like how he looks, so you treat him differently. That's all I'm saying," Gwenna said, raising a hand in surrender.

The Mage stared. "I don't care how he looks."

"What? But you said I couldn't dance with him!"

"And you better not!"

"I won't!" Gwenna assured her quickly. "But I thought you fancied him!"

"Well, of course, I fancy him! But what does the way he looks have to do with anything?" Joanya snapped, arms folded tightly across her chest as she scowled

"What do you like about Epon?" Gwenna asked patiently.

"He's kind! He makes me feel heard," Joanya faltered, the tips of her pointed ears turning pink in the low firelight. "He takes time out of his day to speak to me, and he really listens. I just... feel important around him."

Something burned in the pit of Gwenna's stomach, and she looked away quickly. "That's lovely, Joanya."

"You fancy boys based on how they look?" The genuine astonishment in Joanya's voice made Gwenna smile.

"Maybe it's a human thing," she shrugged. "You don't?"

"I can Weave up a glamor to change my eyes or hair, be taller or shorter. Once they master their essence, the men can Weld themselves to walk around as an animal. The Alpha can even Shift himself to look like whoever he wants. So why put any stock in something so fleeting?" Joanya shrugged. "A yolk is a yolk, no matter the color of the shell."

That brought Gwenna's head up quickly. "What?"

With a roll of her eyes, Joanya repeated it more slowly this time, as though Gwenna was a naughty child who hadn't listened when her mother spoke.

"What?" Gwenna repeated.

"I-I don't know. It's something silly the old women say-" Joanya's face flushed, and she pushed to her feet, heading for the door.

"No, wait!" Gwenna called her back. "I'm not making fun of you. I just... I've never heard that before. I don't know what it means."

"Oh..." She turned around bashfully. "I don't know where it came from originally, but it's something you grow up hearing when you're surrounded by boys who boast about what magnificent beast they'll Warp to one day. Every little boy wants to be something large and mighty– a stallion, a mountain cat, or even an eagle. But not everyone is. Kelden was devastated to be Welded to a snowy white rabbit. So the mothers and the grandmothers in the village, whenever they hear the boys wishing for a specific kind of Weld, they say that."

"A yolk is a yolk…." Gwenna repeated slowly, faltering and looking for help when she couldn't remember the rest of the phrase.

"No matter the color of the shell," Joanya finished with a smile. "The important part of the egg is unchanged."

Joanya's words echoed as Gwenna strode down the steps to the water's edge. A familiar tingling sensation began in her toes. Taking a breath, she tipped her head back, allowing her face to rise to meet the first rays of sunlight.

Her neck began to lengthen.

In that fleeting moment between woman and bird, Gwenna flung her arms out wide to take in the power and majesty of her ebony wings. A laugh bubbled out of her lips in that last second.

Pride.

Power.

This yolk was unchanged.

CHAPTER 31

FIVE DAYS UNTIL RESCUE

Where the village square had been solemn yesterday, it was full of glee tonight. Epon and Orrin met the girls the moment they entered the square. Lanterns dangled from every eave to bathe the yard in light, a wide open space in the middle of the square full of couples dancing. The dais had been pushed to the far wall bearing the weight of three men with fiddles and another two clapping their hands and stomping their feet to provide the percussion.

"Oh, I love this one!" Joanya squealed as the band began a new tune.

"Come on then!" Epon grabbed her by the hands and pulled her over to join the dancing. She shot Gwenna a beaming look over her shoulder, cheeks already pink from Epon's hand in hers.

Orrin turned to Gwenna, grinning ear to ear. "Come on, Gwenna!"

"Oh, I don't know this one..." she said apologetically.

"It's probably best if you don't know what they're saying," Orrin said with a cheeky wink. "Come along; I'll teach you the steps."

Orrin was lighter on his feet than any man in Thornvale, and he made it very easy for her to keep up. These were not the refined, small steps of a waltz. The jig was quick, the steps frantic hops to keep up. They whirled around and around the dance floor as onlookers kept time by pounding their fists or banging their tankards against the tables. The tune was jaunty, and the few words Gwenna could hear made her want to blush. But nobody else seemed to mind, many small children singing loudly.

After two songs in a row with Orrin, Gwenna was completely out of breath from the fast steps. He bowed low, kissing her hand, and thanked her for giving him the honor of dancing with royalty.

"You're the best partner I've ever had." Gwenna laughed, bobbing a curtsy. "I may need you to come teach some dukes a thing or two about how to lead a dance!"

"Find me a duke, and I'm there." Orrin grinned.

They stood on the edge of the dance floor, and already Gwenna could see more than one village girl slowly picking their way towards them, eyes fixed hungrily on their prey of a worthy dance partner.

"It seems you're quite popular with the ladies," Gwenna teased quietly.

Orrin flushed, refusing to make eye contact with his predators. "Is there any chance for escape, or am I surrounded?"

"Surrounded," Gwenna confirmed, and he groaned. "I'm surprised. Most men I know would be thrilled to have their choice of dance partners."

"The moment I dance with any of them, they become convinced I've changed my mind on the subject of marriage." Orrin rolled his eyes. "And not just the girls, but their mothers as well."

"You don't wish to be married?" Gwenna asked before she could stop herself.

She wanted the privilege of choosing a husband rather than being assigned one. But deciding never to marry? It was unheard of.

"Not to a woman," Orrin said with a conspiratorial wink. "And unfortunately, no other men in the village have the same attitude."

Gwenna grinned. "You really will have to come to Thornvale then. I know several dukes I could introduce to you too."

"I'll hold you to that." Orrin bumped her with his elbow. Spotting someone standing behind Gwenna, his eyes lit up suddenly. "Lidiya! I need a dance with you!"

Gwenna laughed as she turned to watch him scoop up a young girl no older than eight out to the dance floor. Lidiya was dwarfed by Orrin, but she took the dance very seriously and rose up on her tiptoes to place her hand on his shoulder. Gwenna hid a giggle behind her hand as she saw those marrying-age young women slink away dejectedly now that Orrin had found a partner.

The song's tempo increased gradually, and Orrin began showing off for the crowd. He incorporated several impressively timed lifts and spins into their dance, Lidiya being a good sport as he threw her and spun her. Eventually, all of the other couples stopped dancing to watch the show.

Gwenna spotted Joanya standing on the opposite side of the square, hollering loudly to cheer on her brother. Epon had an arm slung casually around her shoulders, nestling her against him. Something deep inside Gwenna stirred at the gesture of confident intimacy, an arm around her neck, her leaning against him.

What would being that comfortable in someone else's presence feel like? To seek out that kind of connection and not be spurned. Where no one was ashamed of you or ashamed to be seen with you. Epon was entirely at ease, eyes focused on Orrin's dancing. He wasn't clutching Joanya possessively, trying to make a statement to bystanders. He wanted to be close to her and wasn't embarrassed for others to know.

Suddenly, all Gwenna could see in the square were the couples and families clustered together. Arms around one another. Mothers holding their children's hands. Heads on a partner's shoulder. A group of girls near Lidiya's age sat clustered near the refreshment table, all in a line to braid one another's hair. Boys pushed and jostled, wrestling playfully with one another. Several couples stood on the outskirts or sequestered in corners, completely intertwined around one another and unaware of anyone else's existence.

Irrywellium is beautiful.

It had nothing to do with stripes of color bleeding through the rocks and everything to do with the palpable warmth in the square. Houses carved out of stone and stalagmites hanging from the stone roof above somehow felt far grander than Thornvale ever had.

At first glance, there had been no sign of life in the cenote. There was no greenery except small lichen-covered stones jutting from the lagoon's edge. It was only the blue of the water and the pale rock. Marrock's manor had felt skeletal in the best of times.

But somehow, standing amid that village square, Gwenna could feel the vibrance of the place thrumming within her. These people were not squeaking out a barely passable existence. They were thriving in a way completely unmatched by anything she had ever seen before.

This was joy at its highest level, and it was a privilege to be part of it.

A voice within her whispered again: these were not her people. This was a place entirely untouched by man. This was someplace else. Perhaps that was the secret: her people *could not* live like this. It was their absence that allowed Irrywellium to thrive.

Magic thrived here; there was no doubt about it. Its potency was palpable not just in The Deep but in the people. This site, these people, this was the definition of something sacred.

Loneliness pierced her like an icicle straight to the heart.

She was surrounded by everything she wanted but was still unable to access. It felt like the cruelest form of torture. Maybe that was Marrock's purpose all along...

Eyes suddenly wet, Gwenna navigated through the crowd towards the carved trail leading her back to the lagoon as Orrin's song ended. This square was so full of love, of happiness. It was not a place for her.

She was not made for love or happiness. Gwenna was made to be a queen and save her people.

"Gwenna!" Joanya's sweet voice called from behind.

Wiping her eyes quickly, Gwenna turned back around to greet her with a smile. "You and Epon... fit nicely together. I'm happy for you."

It felt odd to say. Gwenna's first thought had been to tell Joanya that she and Epon looked beautiful together. But she wasn't sure how the Mage would take a compliment that seemed to be based on appearances.

Joanya's face lit up, and Gwenna felt confident that she had said the right thing for once.

"You should come with Epon and me!" Joanya grasped her by the hand, grinning so big Gwenna almost worried her face would split.

"I don't want to intrude," Gwenna said lightly.

"It's a full moon!" the Mage whispered conspiratorially.

Gwenna paused, waiting for her to continue. But she didn't. "Joanya... I don't know what that means..."

"Oh! Of course, your kind doesn't believe in the old magic." Joanya giggled, rolling her eyes. "There's an old tale that if lovers kiss beneath a full moon, their love will be eternally Blessed."

Gwenna nodded slowly, not wanting to take away from her joy but also confident she was physically unable to bear being around any lovestruck couples.

"Again, I'm happy for you and Epon...but I really don't want to intrude..." she said weakly.

"I thought you wanted to find them!" Joanya stamped her foot, hands on her hips as she glared.

"By The Deep, what are you talking about?" Gwenna groaned, rolling her eyes and scrubbing her hand over her face.

"A kiss, beneath a full moon, in front of the Sisters!" Joanya said slowly, as though it were obvious. "I thought you wanted to see the Sisters!"

Gwenna gaped at her. "You're going to find the Sisters? Right now?"

Joanya nodded a mischievous gleam in her eye. "Aye. Are you coming or not?"

CHAPTER 32

*O*nly the Fairies can lift the curse.

    Gwenna repeated the thought a dozen times as she followed Epon and Joanya into the tiny fissure of stone that Orrin called a slot canyon. Joanya and Orrin believed this path was the way to the Fairies. Epon, on the other hand, was far more skeptical. He followed the girl he loved into the dark because he loved her, but not because he believed in old superstitions.

Either way, clinging to a frayed rope and squeezing between, beneath, and over outcroppings of stone in the pitch black was the best option Gwenna had. Her cheek stung from where she had scraped it against the rock, and her hands trembled.

"Keep breathing," Orrin said quietly. He had volunteered to take the rear, and she was grateful for his presence.

They had to sidestep and scuttle between the rock walls because it wasn't wide enough to walk through. It was too dark to see, but Gwenna was convinced she was on a narrow ledge, and any misstep would send her plunging down to her death. Orrin said the trail was flat; it was just the walls that narrowed without warning. Either way, she felt like the walls were about to collapse in on her.

Ahead, Joanya sang loudly as she and Epon scampered through this slot canyon like mountain goats.

"Should she keep it down? We don't want to wake up anything living here…" Gwenna muttered under her breath, hands clammy as she gripped the guide rope for dear life.

"There's nothing in here. It's your mind playing tricks on you," Orrin said.

"Up until recently, I thought Shifters and Mages were just myths. Who's to say what other creatures of the dark are real?" Gwenna whispered.

"We made it!" Joanya sang loudly from somewhere far ahead.

One step. Then another. Gwenna had to consciously force her feet to keep moving, fighting through every instinct that told her to stop. Step apart, and then step together. Over and over again until she rounded the last bend and saw a crack of light up ahead. The canyon narrowed impossibly small, and she pressed herself against the stone to squeeze out. Still, eventually, she stepped out into the moonlight.

The canyon widened to reveal a much smaller cenote than they had left in Irrywellium: the tunnel leading up to the open air was much more narrow, and the pool much more shallow. Joanya and Epon stood waiting in the pool, water coming to their knees.

"The next bit is some swimming," Orrin explained. "Hold your breath and follow the tunnel. It's not far at all."

With no warning, Joanya dove into the water and disappeared through a narrow tunnel burrowed into the stone on the far wall.

Gwenna turned back to Orrin, eyes wide. "There is not a chance I'm doing that."

Two rhythmic thumps sounded against the stone wall on the far side of the pool. Epon took a deep breath before diving under and disappearing.

"That's the signal," Orrin explained calmly. "You make it through, knock twice, and then the next person goes. If you don't knock, we'll come get you."

Right on schedule, two more thumps indicated Epon had made it to the other side. Orrin stepped into the water, reaching back to offer her a hand. Shaking like a leaf, Gwenna took it.

The water ballooned her skirts up, and she nervously patted them down to cling to her legs.

"If I don't knock, you'll come find me? What if I bang my head on a rock down there?" Gwenna asked nervously, glancing at the narrow tunnel. She was wider than both Epon and Joanya. There was no guarantee she'd fit.

"If you don't knock, I'll come," Orrin assured her. "Don't think too hard about it. Take a deep breath and go."

This was her only choice if she wanted to break the curse. She could now turn and walk away, but her people would die.

Emblazoning those words on her heart, Gwenna sucked in a breath before diving under the water and propelling herself into the underground tunnel.

Forcing her eyes open even though it was too dark to see anything, she felt the water current push her through the tunnel easily. She broke the water's surface on the other side with two strokes of her arms.

Gwenna sputtered in surprise at how quick of a swim it had been while Epon grabbed her and hauled her out of the water. Joanya, perched on a jutting stone, thumped the stone wall to signal Orrin of Gwenna's safe arrival.

Gravel crunched beneath Gwenna's feet as she hit the rocky beach and stumbled forward, landing in something smooth and cool to the touch. Looking down in shock, she was lying in the softest grass. A willow tree towered overhead in the middle of this canyon. Dewy grass covered the canyon floor, except for the narrow stretch of gravelly beach behind her. The pool the friends emerged from trickled down to a babbling brook, playfully splashing its way to the base of the grand tree. Moonlight bathed the canyon in white light. But it was the willow tree Gwenna couldn't look away from.

Orbs of every color decorated the drooping branches, each glowing vibrantly. Gwenna climbed to her feet, eyes prickling with tears. A warmth ignited in her chest as she stared at those lights, warming her from the inside out. She hardly dared blink, sure that the lights would vanish in the fraction of a second that she took her eyes off the tree.

The Fairies would vanish. Again.

She couldn't afford to let them out of her sight.

"The Sisters." Joanya appeared beside her, awe painted across her face too. "Orrin, can we meet them?"

Gwenna turned to see him nod. Given how confident he was on the journey, it shouldn't have been surprising that he had been here before. But it still was startling.

Her people desperately waited for the Fairies to return, and Orrin knew right where they were. Clearly, Irrywellium's Sisters weren't hiding from everyone.

Epon took Joanya by the hand, smiling shyly at her. She returned the look, and, hand in hand, they made their way towards the tree. Gwenna hung back, suddenly unsure.

These creatures had spurned her as a baby, leaving her people to struggle and now die. What if they wanted nothing to do with her? If they wouldn't help her, what then?

Orrin's gentle voice broke her from her paralysis. "Would you like to meet them?"

"Yes, I-I have to." Gwenna breathed. "I need them… I need their help."

"This way." Orrin led the way to the tree without any further questions.

Gwenna followed, grateful for his discretion but at a loss for words. The grass whisked against her wet skirt.

Joanya and Epon stood at the edge of the tree's branches, a halo of glowing orbs hovering over their heads. Epon spoke to the Fairies, and she nodded in agreement. Gwenna held the image in her mind, studying the way the glow of the Fairies shone in Joanya's round eyes and reflected off Epon's pale cheeks. She couldn't remember the last time she had the time to paint, but this was one moment she wanted to replicate later.

She and Orrin gave the couple a wide berth, approaching the willow tree from a different angle to allow them privacy. As they approached, an emerald orb no bigger than Gwenna's fist zoomed down from the hanging branches to hover in front of their noses.

"Hello!" a tiny but undoubtedly female voice chirped.

Gwenna couldn't hold back a smile, the reality of the moment finally sinking in. She couldn't control what happened from here. But she had done what she had set out to do.

The Fairy glowed so brightly it was impossible to see more than the faint outline of her tiny body at the center of the orb. She was slender, with sharp angles, but Gwenna couldn't see any distinguishing features.

"Hello, dear Sister," Orrin said softly, grinning from ear to ear. He extended his palm, and she landed gently on it. "May I know your name?"

The Fairy let out a small giggle. "I am called Reilusia."

"Hello, Reilusia." He spoke with gentle reverence. "I am called Orrin. My friend is called Gwenna, and she has searched most desperately to find you."

"To find me?" the Fairy squealed with delight, fluttering from Orrin's palm to land on Gwenna's nose.

The touch was so gentle that she barely felt it when the Fairy gasped suddenly. "You have been Blessed! Never before have I met one Blessed by a Sister!"

"It is a pleasure to meet you, Reilusia," Gwenna whispered, entranced by the tiny creature's beauty. "I wonder if you might help me find the Fairy who gave me the Blessing. I believe her name was Maeve?"

Without a word, Reilusia leaped into the air and flew up into the highest branches of the willow tree before disappearing around the far side.

Gwenna's heart turned to stone. She gaped at Orrin, thunderstruck.

"What did I do wrong?" she cried.

He shook his head in wonder as he stared at the tree, scratching at his large ears. "I've never seen that happen before…" Orrin turned to look at her more closely. "Have you really been Blessed by a Fairy?"

"As a baby," Gwenna admitted, hoping he didn't press further.

"Wow…" he trailed off, pointing at the tree in surprise. "Look! She's coming back!"

Indeed, Reilusia's signature emerald glow flew faster than Gwenna thought possible before coming to a clean stop just in front of her face.

"The Mother will see you," Reilusia announced solemnly. "In the heart of the tree."

Fairy Maeve was the Mother of the Fairies? She had no expectations of the Fairies, but this was a surprise. It could be really good news, a Fairy endowed with the power and authority to help her. Or really, really bad news…

Mouth dry, she followed Reilusia around to the far side of the tree. Sweeping the branches aside, Gwenna stepped through their green curtain to see the earth carved away from the tree's roots. A darkened tunnel led into the earth, where the faintest hint of blue glowed.

"In there?" Gwenna asked Reilusia hesitantly.

She bobbed up and down, the Fairy equivalent of a nod.

"I'll wait for you here," Orrin called from behind. "Take your time. I hope… I hope you find exactly what you're looking for."

Gwenna flashed what she hoped was a confident smile. Reminding herself once more that there was no other way, Gwenna dropped to her hands and knees in the dirt. Gown still wet from the swim, mud instantly caked her skirts, but there was nothing to be done about it now.

Ducking her head, she crawled forward beneath the roots and up into the Heart of the tree to meet Fairy Maeve, the creature that had cursed her.

CHAPTER 33

I f purity could be reduced to a single odor, it would be damp soil after a rainstorm. Crawling into the earthen tunnel, Gwenna inhaled deeply. Perhaps that cleanliness could scour her from the inside out and break her curse.

The tunnel was short: four paces on her hands and knees. Gwenna straightened, sitting up on her knees in the Heart of the hollowed-out willow tree. It was a vast cavern for the Fairies, but the space would not have allowed another person to join her.

Fairy lights glowed from small windows carved out of the bark, and Gwenna sensed the weight of hundreds of tiny faces staring at her. A million little bells seemed to jingle as the Fairies called to one another, as though she was surrounded on all sides by a concert of wind chimes. Parallels between the town of Irrywellium and the Heart of the Tree were not lost on her as she stared at the rings of homes lining the inside of the tree.

Which came first: the Sisters' home or the Shifters?

"It is a wonder to see you here." A voice over her head caught her attention. Still inherently feminine, Fairy Maeve's voice was lower than Gwenna expected, an alto amidst a chorus of soprano voices.

Glancing straight up, the sapphire blue orb seemed to be contracting smaller and smaller as it slowly descended. The light pulled in on itself until, as Fairy Maeve drew level with her, there was no glow surrounding her at all. Gwenna could look directly at her.

Half the size of Gwenna's tallest finger, Maeve hovered in the air in front of Gwenna as though standing upon solid ground. She seemed to share the same basic anatomy of a human, but each limb was impossibly sharp and angular like shards of glass. At first, Gwenna assumed her skin was sapphire blue. But it slowly occurred to her that perhaps Maeve was translucent; her humanoid shape was like a lantern to hold the radiating sapphire light within her. The Fairy wore a simple shift of the same shade as her skin. Blue hair was swept up atop her head, tiny gems twinkling throughout. Diamond-shaped eyes held discerning black pupils as she studied the human before her.

"You know me?" Gwenna asked, goosebumps prickling her arms. The recognition was unexpected. It felt like coming home.

"I do not forget a Blessed," Fairy Maeve said with the warmth of a grandparent. "Though I suspect you do not know yourself, and that is why you have sought me."

"I do not come for myself," Gwenna said quickly. "It is my people, the people of Bannon. We are suffering and–"

"You do not come to absolve yourself of the guilt you feel?" There was nothing unkind in her voice, but Gwenna flinched as though she had backed into something sharp.

Ashamed, Gwenna bowed her head and looked away.

"Hear me when I speak, child: you are carrying a burden that was never yours to bear. Set it down, and walk away. It was never yours to begin with."

Gwenna's head snapped up, heart pounding in her ears. Her mouth opened and closed before opening again. The question on her lips refused to be pushed away.

"Then who brought the curse on my people?"

"King Domhnall," Fairy Maeve said calmly. "Your grandfather."

A tidal wave of emotion slammed into Gweena, shattering the chains of guilt and shame. Clean air rushed into her lungs for the first time in weeks.

Every time she closed her eyes she could see herself leaning over her grandfather's body. Gwenna could still feel the terror clawing up her throat, knowing her grandfather was dying beneath her hands and she couldn't stop whatever it was she was doing to him.

His last word to her: cursed.

He wasn't sentencing Gwenna, but admitting his own guilt.

"I didn't hurt my people?" Her voice was barely audible. "I didn't kill Grandfather?"

"No, Gwenna. It was his time to rejoin The Deep, and he had not fulfilled his responsibility to Her. You did not bring the curse." Always gentle, Maeve seemed to speak even more delicately now. "You are not a curse. You have *never* been a curse."

Something deep within Gwenna's chest resonated with the words. It was as if her soul was pulled as taut as a lute string, with a calm, divine hand strumming it and causing her to vibrate with pure truth.

It was similar to the way she knew it close to dawn, or that Laisren's tale about her grandfather was true. But this was even stronger and more undeniable.

Fairy Maeve knew who Gwenna was, and what she was. The Fairy spoke true.

A sob bubbled up from her throat, and Gwenna clapped a hand over her mouth to soften the noise. Her shoulders shook violently as a lifetime's worth of grief surfaced all at once. Tinkling sounds echoed as curious Fairies, who had come to investigate the large stranger, dove for cover from Gwenna's tears.

Gwenna sat in the presence of the Mother of the Fairies, bawling like a child. She tried to collect herself several times, but the tears kept coming. Fairy Maeve showed no sign of impatience. She watched, and she waited.

With a tiny sentence, Gwenna's entire worldview had shattered for the second time in less than a day. But this time, she did not mourn. This was pure relief.

Gwenna's life had orbited around one singular fear: she was a curse not even the Fairies could break. Even if she tried to pretend it didn't affect her, that thought was always simmering in the background. And now... it was gone.

What was her place in this new world? This was a world where she was not a burden or a curse on her family or her people. The corners of the map had just expanded, leaving an endless world of possibility for her future. She carried no secret and uncontrollable darkness.

As Gwenna regained composure, Fairy Maeve began speaking again.

"Your Grandfather asked for a specific Blessing for you," Fairy Maeve said. "You knew this?"

"Yes. He asked that I be Blessed with Beauty, like my sister was," Gwenna said, wiping her face with the hem of her skirt. Wet mud smeared across her cheeks, but she couldn't bring herself to care. Fairy Maeve certainly didn't. Gwenna felt more alive and confident in her presence than she had felt with hardly anyone else.

"It is a common and traditional Blessing for royalty," Fairy Maeve said lightly. "Humans are not very forward-thinking when considering their women."

Gwenna's cheeks warmed, but she couldn't bring herself to say anything in defense of her people. Maeve was not incorrect.

"Why did you refuse my grandfather's Blessing?" Gwenna's throat burned as she voiced the question she had waited her entire life to ask.

Women were worth more than their beauty. To arrange marriages as though it was nothing more than playing chess was dehumanizing, to say the least. But as much as Gwenna hated it, she could not deny how much easier life would have been if Fairy Maeve had granted her grandfather's request.

How many sleepless nights would have been spared? Tears would not have been spilled. Friendships could have been forged. She could have fallen in love. Real, authentic, and *reciprocated* love. The ache in her chest throbbed even more sharply as she considered Aidan. What might have been if she had only been Blessed like Catriona had?

"It was not a choice, Gwenna. Your blood would not accept a Blessing of Beauty," Fairy Maeve chimed.

Gwenna jerked awake out of her own self-pitying daydreams. "What do you mean?"

"Your blood–"

"Catriona was Blessed!" Gwenna cried, surprised by the anger bubbling up. "Why was she made beautiful and not me?"

"As I approached to bestow the traditional Blessing, something in you barred the path. It would not allow you to be altered. I had never felt resistance to a Blessing before. My sisters and I had to return to the Heart to seek understanding," Fairy Maeve explained softly. "The King's Blessing was impossible to grant. But it opened the way for me to provide the Blessing that she requested."

"She?"

"Your mother." Fairy Maeve's eyes seemed suddenly softer. "She asked for Clarity and Strength. Things she knew would benefit a princess far more than beauty ever would."

With a rush, Gwenna finally understood. All of those moments she *felt* the truth had come from her Blessing of Clarity. It was real, and something her mother knew she would need.

"Thank you, Fairy Maeve, for granting her request. The understanding you have given me this evening means more than you will ever know," Gwenna said softly, marveling at the warmth radiating through her from the inside out.

"No one ever truly understands the love of a parent," Fairy Maeve slowly descended to stand on Gwenna's knee. "And it is imperative you remember this as I continue to speak."

"My mother's love?"

"Your family's."

Something about the careful word choice made the hair on the back of Gwenna's neck stand up. She took a breath and nodded, indicating she was ready for the Fairy to continue.

"King Domhnall and Queen Treasa had one daughter named Orlaith," Fairy Maeve began.

Gwenna nodded. "I am Orlaith's daughter."

"Princess Orlaith married a man named Curran. Curran produced one heir before he fell ill with ruby fever and died," the Fairy recounted.

"Two heirs," Gwenna corrected. "Catriona and myself."

"That is what you have been told."

CHAPTER 34

G wenna shook her head.

"There was only my father," she insisted. "Father was the love of Mother's life. She had many offers of marriage after he died so young, but she refused. She chose to abstain from ever being queen rather than marry another."

"Your mother was deceived." Fairy Maeve's voice rang with sorrow. "She was violated in the cruelest ways but went to her grave without knowing the truth. She firmly believed Curran was your father."

"What are you talking about?" Gwenna asked softly.

"Curran had been in his sickbed for over a month. Your mother knew The Deep would claim him soon. Imagine her surprise and joy when he came to her bed in the late hours of the night. The love of her life was restored!"

As the Fairy spoke, Gwenna could see the tale play out before her eyes like illustrations from a storybook hovering in the air.

Gwenna had never met her father but recognized him from the portrait in her mother's chambers. He was tall with a narrow chin and long nose, all traits Gwenna had gotten from him. Catriona had his fair hair, but Gwenna's facial shape looked so much like her father's.

He stood over the bed where a woman, his wife, slept. Orlaith looked impossibly young but was clearly overjoyed when she woke up to see him standing there.

Fairy Maeve continued her tale.

"He shared her bed once more. It would be nearly two months before your mother realized a child was conceived that night. In the early morning, he arose and crept from the chamber. As The Deep would have it, your grandfather approached your mother's chamber at that exact moment. Curran, your mother's husband, had finally been claimed by The Deep, and his body lay cold. Your Grandfather saw a man bearing Curran's face slip from your mother's chambers before donning a new face– the Shifter's *true* face. A Shifter your Grandfather recognized as one of the members of his trusted council."

Moonlight streaming through the arched windows illuminated the sneer carved on Curran's face. Grandfather rounded the corner, coming into view of Father when Curran pulled Mother's door closed with one hand, the other still fumbling with the buckle of his breeches.

White light flashed. A strange man stood frozen where Curran had been a moment before. The stranger stared at King Domhnall. Significantly older than Orlaith but not so old as the king, the man was devastatingly handsome. He was tanned, with crisply parted golden hair and a dark birthmark on his chin.

There was no sound in the image Fairy Maeve conjured to hover in the air. Gwenna couldn't hear the way her grandfather roared at this stranger. But the rage on the King's face was unmistakable. The edges of the Fairy's vision grew fuzzy as Gwenna's grandfather knocked the stranger to the floor. The heel of his boot collided with the man's face repeatedly as the vision finally dissolved in on itself.

It was only Gwenna and Fairy Maeve in the Heart of the Tree again.

"Your mother did not lie to you," the Fairy said gently, seeing her paralysis. "And your grandfather… he did what he thought was best."

"That's why he attacked the Shifters…." Gwenna said faintly, understanding how cleanly this fit into the narrative Laisren had shared the night before.

"Yes."

One act of violence sparked another. It did not absolve her grandfather. His hands were still coated in the blood of innocents. Yet… there was context.

King Domhnall knew what had happened to his daughter. His friend, a man he trusted, had deceived and violated her. It sparked a rage in Domhnall that was not satiated until his kingdom was purged of the Shifters. What began in the hallway of the Keep was finished on the streets of Thornvale as the King purged his kingdom of the Shifters.

It was not forgivable. But it could be understood.

"Where is…?" Gwenna faltered.

"The Shifter who sired you is dead." Fairy Maeve said firmly. "I will not speak his name. Violent men do not deserve a place in history. It is the innocent that die because of their cruelty that deserves remembering. That man knowingly instigated a war between the two peoples of Bannon. Make no mistake, Gwenna: his actions were purposeful. He knew exactly what he was doing. Do not pity him for a moment. He was killed by your grandfather the following day during the raid on the Shifters."

Gwenna's mouth felt dry.

"But why attack all of them? What this man did was horrible, but why would Grandfather hold the entire community responsible?" She shook her head in disbelief.

"Not all of Bannon was happy about their neighbors having more power than they. Things may have been peaceful between the humans and the Shifters, but do not imagine they were always friendly. Rumors of Shifters and Mages trying to overthrow the monarchy had lasted for centuries, Gwenna," Fairy Maeve understood. "This one atrocity against the King's own family was all the rationale he needed to wage war. It confirmed all of his deepest fears and prejudices that he had nurtured with care over the years."

"That man who found my mother… how was he able to do that– to look like Curran? I thought Shifters had one animal whose essence they were Welded to." Gwenna's mind was reeling.

"It's a power reserved for the Alpha alone. Never before has it been used for something so heinous as this," the Fairy explained. "But the abilities of the Alpha are not well known among your people. I suspect your grandfather had no idea this level of shape-shifting was even possible until that moment. He assumed this ability was available to all Shifters, and therefore posed a huge threat to the kingdom."

Gwenna nodded, falling silent to soak in these revelations. She was a child of assault, a child of violence and deception. A Shifter had fathered her. And not just any Shifter, but an Alpha. Gwenna's mind flickered to the Shifters and the people of Irrywellium that she had met. The connection she felt to them may have deeper roots than she had realized…

"Did he have a family?"

"No," Fairy Maeve said firmly. "My Sisters and I worked endlessly to answer that question with confidence. You are the only one. The only half-child in Bannon."

Half-child.

"That's why I can Shift." The pieces were beginning to fit together in her mind. "I have Shifter blood, but it was so diluted that I had to be in the presence of The Deep before I could Shift…."

Fairy Maeve bobbed her tiny head. "Precisely."

"But if he was the last Alpha…." Gwenna pictured Marrock's face and shuddered. Perhaps there was an outcome worse than being the last of her family still alive.

"The Alpha is not passed down by bloodline like your monarchy is. When the previous Alpha dies, the next strongest essence in the pack is selected by The Deep. Marrock Rolfe had no relation to the previous Alpha and, therefore, no relation to you," Fairy Maeve assured her. "The Rolfe boy was a child when he was chosen by The

Deep. His family had been the ancestral caretakers of this place, and his father led their people to safety here after the raid."

Gwenna nodded. She had wondered why Marrock had such a sizable and ornate home so far from the village.

"To be chosen as the Alpha is a great honor. But the Rolfe family history is stained by violence a hundred times over. The current Alpha has done terrible and inexcusable things. But such a level of cruelty is not something a soul is born with, but something beaten into them," Fairy Maeve counseled.

"He killed my mother and sister, didn't he?" Gwenna whispered.

Fairy Maeve landed lightly on Gwenna's knee, more gently than a butterfly. Her tiny face radiated so much love and pity that Gwenna knew before the Fairy spoke.

"He did."

It was the answer she had waited weeks for. She had prepared for and anticipated it. Yet it still hurt so much more than she expected.

She had thought she had cried all of her tears, but more bubbled to the surface. The stupid silver ring on her finger seemed to burn with incrimination. Everything Gwenna did was to her people and honor her family. Yet staying in Marrock's house, eating his food, and even pretending to consider marriage felt like the deepest betrayal.

Tears fell as she silently prayed for forgiveness. Maybe it was blasphemous, but these prayers weren't for The Deep. They were for Cat and Mother. She wanted them to know how sorry she was.

"I know the heart of every child that I Bless. You have done nothing to shame yourself or your family." Fairy Maeve's words were like a warm hug. Gwenna could almost feel her mother's presence beside her. "There is nothing to apologize for. Your family is so proud of you."

It took several long moments before Gwenna could collect herself. Fairy Maeve, again, waited patiently. Once calm, Gwenna began to sort through the answers she had received versus the questions she still had.

"It was my Shifter blood you could sense at my Blessing, wasn't it?" Gwenna spoke aloud to make tracing her train of thought easier as everything slid into focus. "It prevented you from altering my shape. But Cat... Cat was only human. She could be Blessed with Beauty."

"And you have Clarity," the Fairy reminded gently.

Gwenna leaned her head against the tree bark, closing her eyes so she could process everything Fairy Maeve had said. A half-child. Not a curse, but merely the first recorded of her kind.

"When Grandfather died...." Gwenna began, opening her eyes to gaze down at her fingers.

"You saw a light."

"But I didn't harm him?"

"Had you ever conjured magic before that point?" the Fairy asked. Gwenna straightened, shaking her head quickly. "I thought not. And have you conjured anything since that day?"

"No."

"Then why are you so certain you caused that light?" Fairy Maeve said, not unkindly. "You are Stronger than you realize, Gwenna. But you have no such ability. Our Mother, The Deep, carefully ensures no one contains too much of her power. It is blasphemous for any of her Children to try to assume more power. Those that attempt to lose themselves, falling farther and farther from themselves until all that remains is monstrous."

"Monstrous?" The words chilled her.

"Welding– that's what her Children call the ability to change their form. Weavers, however, can call upon Her to change the physical realm." Fairy Maeve explained. "Weaving must be done delicately, respecting the balance The Deep provides. A Weaver draws from her body to replenish what she borrows from The Deep,"

Gwenna recalled how flushed and sweaty Joanya had been while creating the Weaving for Marrock.

"Sometimes," Fairy Maeve continued. "A Weaver goes too far. They take more than they can ever repay. Ambition outweighs ability."

"What happens?"

Joanya's face had seemed far too red. Sweat poured off of her petite frame. It was an eerie experience, watching the girl Weave, and one that Gwenna had almost stopped because it seemed too painful. But for a Weaver to knowingly push farther…

"It is called a Warping. If a Mage draws more from The Deep than she can replenish, it is drawn from her mind. A body is strong, but the mind is… more pliable," Fairy Maeve said darkly.

"They lose themselves?" Gwenna breathed.

"Eventually. It might begin with a loss of emotional control. Each creature holds the capacity for both morality and depravity. A Warped soul loses the ability to distinguish between the two," Fairy Maeve said quietly. "The Deep has established balance, Gwenna. To upset that balance for any reason leads to chaos. It is why your Grandfather was cursed."

Grandfather instigated a genocide against half of Bannon's people. The curse was his. Not Gwenna's.

Of course.

"The Deep requires balance. The streets ran red with Her children's blood. It was all at your grandfather's hands," Fairy Maeve continued. "My predecessor, Fairy Liatira, warned him. But he refused to listen. His legacy, he insisted, was the most important thing to him. And so a curse was placed upon his head: if he did not restore balance in Bannon, his legacy would never come to fruition. His family and his kingdom would follow him to the grave."

Gwenna stared at her fingers, remembering the violet light pouring through them. The light that never glowed from her hands but from her grandfather's heart.

She had a sudden need to find Kellen and hug him. Hadn't he suggested she was innocent, sitting in the horse stall? At the time, it had seemed too far-fetched. But he had believed in her and in her innocence all along.

"Fairy Liatira... Was she purple in color?" Gwenna asked quietly.

Maeve bobbed in agreement.

"As part of the curse, Fairy Liatira caused the whole kingdom to forget, didn't she?" All of the missing histories from the ledgers suddenly made sense. "No one remembers that we used to have these neighbors. They don't remember what we've lost."

"Only your grandfather remembered," Fairy Maeve confirmed. "His men returned to their homes after following his orders and slaughtering their neighbors but had no memory of what they'd done. That entire section of the town disappeared overnight. Businesses, homes, and farms were all gone, leaving no evidence of what your grandfather did. He was the only one to remember. It was his burden to bear."

"I don't think he ever felt very burdened...." Gwenna muttered.

"Nevertheless, Bannon is dying, Gwenna. Your kingdom has pushed Her children away, rejecting and scorning them, but never realizing that you were pushing away the very thing your land desperately needed. The longer you withhold the same magic that the earth is gasping for in its dying breath, the faster you bring about the complete destruction of your kingdom. Bannon will be nothing more than a wasteland– an example for centuries to come of what occurs when the balance is not respected," Fairy Maeve said.

"Magic is welcome in Bannon!" Gwenna cried, a desperate note of pleading entering her voice. "Tell the others: the Fairies, the Mages, and whoever else! Bannon welcomes them with open arms!" Marrock's sneer appeared in her mind's eye. "It's only the Shifters—"

"That's what you humans still have not learned," Fairy Maeve interrupted. "You cannot pick and choose the parts of magic you accept. We are one, or we are not at all."

"Then bring the Shifters. I will speak to Marrock. He wants to rejoin Bannon; I'm sure we can find a solution where everyone is welcome," Gwenna insisted.

"The current Alpha wishes to rule, not to join. You know that."

Gwenna hesitated. That was a problem she hadn't figured out how to overcome yet.

"Even so, it is not enough," Fairy Maeve continued simply.

"Then what do I do?" Gwenna cried. "Grandfather is dead. Is there any way to break the curse now? Is there any hope for my people?"

"Balance. That is the answer. I cannot say more because Liatira herself would not speak about it." Fairy Maeve fluttered upwards, brushing Gwenna's forehead with what could only be described as the lightest kiss. "But there is always hope, Gwenna. Always."

CHAPTER 35

After the quick swim through the tunnel, Joanya Weaved a drying spell so the group wouldn't be sneaking back into Irrywellium dripping wet. Every muscle in Gwenna's body tensed as the Mage worked, terrified that Joanya would push herself too far. But Orrin and Epon didn't even bat an eye.

The dancing continued as they crept back into the village square. Crowds had thinned, smaller children taken home to bed by anxious mothers, but the remaining group did not notice the late hour.

Two hours until sunrise. Gwenna could feel it.

Epon swept Joanya onto the dance floor immediately, pulling her closer than ever before. They had kissed before the Fairies, pledging their love. Orrin had explained that it wasn't an official wedding or even a promise to wed, but it was meaningful to the two of them.

Everything Fairy Maeve had divulged in the Heart of the Tree had left Gwenna exhausted. She wanted to climb into her feather bed in the manor until sunrise, but Orrin coaxed her into one more dance to end the night.

This dance was rowdier, with more hollering and a louder percussion line. Orrin twirled her faster each time until he lifted her clean off her feet and swept her over his head in a great arc. Gwenna couldn't stop laughing, feeling completely graceful and weightless.

Levity filled her chest. Nothing was the same as it had been when the night began. But it also didn't matter.

These *were* her people. She belonged to them. They seemed to have always known it and never doubted it. To her, it meant so much more than she could ever say.

Gwenna wanted to bottle up the joy, the feeling of belonging, and pour it into a tiny vial to wear around her neck for the rest of her life.

But the song ended. Another one began immediately after, and she knew that was her cue to leave. Orrin graced her hand with a kiss, and Epon waved. Joanya opened her mouth to offer to return to the manor with her, but Epon wrapped his arms around her and pulled her against his chest. She melted into him, forgetting Gwenna completely. As she should have.

Heart lighter than it had been in years, Gwenna practically floated along the gravel path back around the lagoon to the manor.

Lights were lit in the windows, though Marrock was not due home for another day. She didn't question it; there were other servants besides Joanya, and not all had attended the festival.

A scream echoed off the stone as Gwenna stepped through the terrace doors and into the dining room. The joy she felt evaporated, snuffed out like a flame.

Another scream.

It was a man.

Grabbing a fire poker from near the hearth, Gwenna held her breath and waited to see if the scream came again. When it did, she dashed towards the sound, down the one hallway that led to the dungeons. Cells in Thornvale were kept below ground, but here in Irrywellium, they were the rooms deepest in the manor. Surrounded by the most stone, with only one entrance and very little light.

The screams kept coming. A predictable pattern to them. The man was being beaten, she realized. Probably whipped.

Gwenna quickened her pace.

Hesitating outside the heavy iron door leading to the dungeon cells, she waited until the man screamed again to open the door. Hopefully, the man's pain would cover the sound of the rusty hinges screeching.

She was plunged into near-total darkness when the door swung shut. Torches were few and far between the cells, and there were no windows this deep into the stone. An eerie orange glow pulsed from the farthest dungeon cell. Gripping the poker tighter, Gwenna crept towards it.

The crack of the whip set the tempo for the symphony of pain: a sharp staccato rhythm with a melody of screams bleeding into whimpers.

"You will break long before I will. That, I promise you." Gravelly threats swept down the hall, and the whipping ceased momentarily.

Marrock was back.

Something almost like relief flooded through her as she recognized the voice. Marrock was not the one in pain. Gwenna sagged against an icy wall, forcing herself to breathe.

She didn't trust Marrock or particularly like him. But he was the enemy she knew. She hadn't been prepared for someone else to grapple with.

This was the Marrock she knew, the villain who had murdered her family.

He had never hidden who he was. It was clearly spelled out in the stains on these dungeon walls. Whatever happened in that far cell should have been no surprise to her. The relief withered away in an instant.

Marrock was what he always had been. A violent, brutal monster.

Gwenna pushed herself onwards. Closer to that end cell. Her intuition regarding Marrock was clear, but she still didn't trust herself with him. He was too charming, too quick to make her forget. She needed to see him in the act to remind herself who he truly was.

The whip cracked again, followed by a wet thud as skin slammed against skin. When Marrock had hit Joanya that first night, it sounded like that. It could very well be a woman he was beating in that cell.

Standing outside the cell, out of sight of the brutality, Gwenna hesitated. She adjusted her grip on the poker, shifting her feet nervously as she summoned all of the Strength Fairy Maeve said she possessed.

Gwenna stepped into the light, the sharp edge of the poker aimed right at Marrock's throat as he raised the whip once more.

"Stop."

A shirtless Marrock stood, bathed in orange torchlight. Muscle rippled across his broad shoulders, bicep bulging as he froze with the whip in the air. His white hair was pulled back in a low knot. His dark trousers and boots were spattered with blood. A sneer was still pasted on his pale face as his eyes darted to her in surprise.

His chest heaved as he stared her down. Gwenna did not move an inch, keeping the tip of the poker aimed right at his jugular. Rage, unlike anything she had ever seen before, burned behind those silver eyes. But she would not stand down.

"Marrock." She spoke softly but firmly, forcing herself not to grimace as she said the words she knew he wanted to hear. "My husband. Enough of this."

"Gwenna?"

She turned her head a fraction of an inch, looking at the strung-up prisoner for the first time.

Heavy manacles clasped his wrists, hanging him from the ceiling with his back to her and Marrock. He wore only tight-fitting breeches to the knee, leaving most of his body unprotected from Marrock's wrath. Scarlet lines crisscrossed almost every inch of the exposed flesh of his back, many torn open and bleeding heavily. The scars continued down his legs. One of his knees looked swollen, and she could see the kneecap was facing the wrong way.

Her gut twisted. The beating must have been going on for hours before she interrupted. The prisoner's breaths had come in hard pants since she arrived, but now there was a ragged sound. Tearing her eyes away from the flayed skin of his back, she glanced up to see that he was twisting himself around to stare at her.

Blood-matted hair clung to his face, and his nose looked broken, but she lost all feeling as she stared into those oddly familiar soft eyes.

"Kellen?"

PART 3

CHAPTER 36

For a moment, time stood still in that dark and bloodstained cell. The only sound was that of three chests heaving. Marrock looked like he would burst a blood vessel if the vein in his forehead throbbed any harder.

But it was Kellen that Gwenna couldn't take her eyes off of.

Sweet, *stupid* Kellen. She wanted to laugh and cry and scream all at the same time. *What was he doing here?*

His presence threatened everything she had accomplished and had yet to do. She was supposed to have four more days until Aidan came to rescue her.

Gwenna could feel the weight of Marrock's calculating glare as he searched for cracks in her armor; the expensive porcelain doll he intended to purchase was useless if it was broken.

My husband.

That's what she had called Marrock. And Kellen heard.

"Where have you been?" she asked Marrock frostily, focusing on him.

"You know this man?" The wolf chuckled darkly, sharpened teeth flashing dangerously.

"Answer my question." Gwenna pressed the poker tip into Marrock's neck with a steady hand. He clenched his jaw, eyes darting to the iron at his throat and back to her.

"I had business to take care of," he said stiffly. "I told you."

"*This* is your business?" she snapped, jerking her head toward the man strewn up from the ceiling. "You swore to me you would not hurt my people."

"My business had nothing to do with your pathetic humans. I did not lie. He--" Marrock's eyes darted in Kellen's direction, but he didn't dare move his head. "- tried to *hunt* me." The last words came out as a snarl. "Pathetic fool turned from predator to prey before he could loose an arrow."

Her eyes flicked to where the servant boy hung, despair pooling in the pit of her stomach. Why would he jeopardize everything?

Jaw set, Kellen stared at her with an intensity she had never seen before. His eyes were like molten steel, his lips never moved, and not even a muscle ticked on his face. But the words were written clearly in his gaze: this was no accident.

That truth burned within her, the consequence of her Blessing of Clarity.

Kellen was precisely where he planned on being.

Her breath hitched, and Gwenna looked away, fearful of giving anything away to the wolf.

"He's just a farm boy," she said wearily, dropping the poker with a clatter. "From my village. Let him go. He's harmless. You've sent your message."

"A farm boy?" Marrock repeated coolly. "He was very well-armed. And a humble farmer on a first-name basis with the future queen? That's quite the tale indeed…."

"Enough of this," She rolled her eyes, turning away. "It's almost sunrise, and I'm exhausted. Would you care for something to eat?"

Long fingers dug into her collarbone, causing her knees to almost buckle as she twisted back around. Marrock loomed over her, one hand grasping her hair at the roots to hold her in place.

"I don't take kindly to liars either, my bride," he snarled. "Who is he? Where is he from?"

"Let go of her!" Kellen hissed. "She has nothing to do with this!"

The pain was excruciating. With one hand, Marrock's nails dug into her shoulder and forced her almost to her knees, but with the other, he gripped her hair so tightly he threatened to yank it from her scalp. Tears brimmed in her eyes, knees quaked.

"H-He's a servant," she whispered, breaths coming shallowly from the pain in her head. "Please–"

"Say my name."

"Marrock, please," Gwenna begged, eyes watering uncontrollably now. "He's a servant from Bannon."

He threw her to the ground, knees banging against the stone floor as her hands flew out to catch her. She landed at Kellen's feet, close enough to smell the iron scent of blood dripping off him. Pushing herself up to sit, she twisted around to face Marrock. Her fingers were stained scarlet, and she could feel the dampness soaking through the seat of her gown, but she refused to turn her back to the wolf.

"Thank you for honoring me with the truth, my bride," Marrock said in a dangerously calm voice. "I will not abide a deceitful woman."

Gwenna shuddered at the implication.

"Bride?" Kellen coughed, but it felt like a knife twisting into her heart.

Marrock's eyes gleamed as he looked at the princess, crumpled on the floor at another man's feet. A man whom he had beaten nearly to death.

"It's a shame your prince was not man enough to come to fight for your honor. And he wouldn't even spare a knight. Just a poor farm boy," Marrock sighed with mock sympathy.

"Aidan will still come for me!" Gwenna cried, channeling anger into pseudo-passion as she stood. "If this simpleton can, a prince can!"

She tensed as the words left her mouth, a gnawing feeling growing until she felt almost hollow. Her heart battered against her ribs, begging to glance back at the prisoner.

Many things were forgivable in the wolf's presence, but an unkind word about Kellen felt like the most profound betrayal.

Marrock said something unkind about Aidan, utterly unaware of how much her pain stemmed from Kellen and not at all from her fiance, but she missed it.

Desperate, she tried again. "Marrock, my husband, *please* let the boy go. I know how fiercely you desire to protect this place from your enemies. But this is a simple misunderstanding. He does not deserve this."

"My bride." With a slight smile, Marrock reached to cup her face with his large, pale hand.

She didn't move away from his touch. "Yes?"

"Your ugliness sometimes makes me forget that you bear a woman's heart. But then you speak and prove you are as stupid as all the rest." His fingers tightened around her jaw. "Had you not interfered, perhaps I would have released him. But now he has seen your face due to your insufferable nature and insistence on poking your nose into my business. And I cannot allow anyone, not even a stupid farmer, to return home knowing the location of the bride I kidnapped. He can rot down here, or I can slit his throat– the choice is yours. But he will never leave here alive."

He pulled her in roughly, planted a kiss on her forehead, and then strode away.

Tears burned as Gwenna massaged her jaw and listened to his footsteps echo up the corridor. His people didn't believe in beauty or ugliness; Marrock was just cruel on every level.

The iron door to the manor squealed open and then loudly slammed shut.

A choking cry wrenched from her throat as she dashed to Kellen's side.

Ducking under his chained arms, she moved to face him head-on. "What are you doing here?"

She stood apart from him momentarily, not wanting to upset any of his wounds. But he leaned forward, pressing his body against hers in an approximation of a hug, and she wrapped her arms around him in return. His forehead came down to rest against her neck as she clung to him.

"I let him catch me. It wasn't an accident," he mumbled into her curls. "Don't feel pity me."

"I know," Gwenna said softly. "But you shouldn't have come. A few more days and this would all be over...."

He straightened, pulling away to look at her straight-on. One of his eyes was swollen shut and purple. Red surrounded his other iris, but he stared at her steadily.

"And let you take on a Shifter by yourself? Where's the fun in that?" He attempted a joke, wincing as the smile cracked the scab at the edge of his mouth.

Kellen straightened, and before she could say anything, white light flashed. His large black bear stood there on its hind legs. His front paws were still manacled to the ceiling. With a grunt, he pulled against the chains and broke them with little resistance. Sinking back down to all fours, he Shifted back into his human form.

"Finally. I've been waiting for him to leave so I could do that," Kellen grunted, slipping the broken cuffs off and massaging his red wrists. Just from Shifting back and forth, the open wounds on his back had already scabbed over. He swayed, not entirely steady on his feet, and Gwenna put her hands up to brace him.

"How did he not sense you?" Gwenna asked quietly, brushing his shoulder-length curls away. His ear, usually pointed as all Shifters and Weavers were, was round, smooth, and human. "What is this?"

He grinned. "I've been working on it since you left. I've heard some Shifters not only Shift into animals but can also alter their appearance. Ma always said it was incredibly difficult, and she wasn't lying. I exhausted myself so much that I think Aidan thought I was on my deathbed for a few days. I couldn't get out of bed. But eventually, I mastered it. Look!" He wiggled his ears proudly and pulled her in for an even tighter hug. "I look totally human!"

"That's incredible," Gwenna breathed, sinking into the embrace. "And Marrock didn't question it or sense you?"

"Not at all. The Alpha has no idea what I am," Kellen assured her.

"Good."

She was the only thing holding up right, but he held her in his arms like nothing had happened. Gwenna kept her face pressed against his chest, grateful to hear another person's heartbeat. The manor felt more like a mausoleum most evenings. Marrock was some semblance of a living creature, but so cruel Gwenna questioned whether he had a heart within that cavern of a chest. Gwenna had never needed physical contact, and her family hadn't ever been close like that. They primarily expressed themselves through words, which had always been enough for her.

But here, in Kellen's arms, she felt pieces of herself begin to reassemble themselves. The healing had begun before this moment, culminating in everything Fairy Maeve taught her about herself. That conversation seemed like a lifetime ago, even though it had only been an hour or two at most. But ever since, her heart had begun to mend. Kellen's touch was like a hot iron, melting away the imperfections and finalizing that seal. She wanted to stay in this moment forever.

"Did you marry him?" Kellen asked a raw note in his voice.

She shook her head, trying to find her voice. "No. He tried. But no. I told him I was waiting for Aidan."

Kellen's body tensed for a moment before he released her from his embrace and stepped away.

Gwenna opened her mouth to explain, but a familiar tingling began in the tips of her fingers, and the sun was beginning to climb somewhere, far outside the stone walls.

"I have to go. I'm so sorry," she choked out.

"Go?" Kellen repeated, eyebrows shooting up his forehead.

"I'll be back tonight. I'll explain everything. I won't let Marrock hurt you. I'll get you out of here."

"Tonight?" Kellen's eyes widened in fear for a fraction of a second, the first glimpse that he wasn't as confident and self-assured as he seemed.

"I'm sorry," Gwenna said again, every limb vibrating. Her neck began to lengthen, and Kellen's jaw dropped. "I'll explain everything tonight!"

She sprinted up the darkened corridor, pain spiking as she fought against the Shift. Sweat beaded along her forehead. It was one act of depravity to chain a human being away in here. Still, something primal within her raged at the thought of an animal being trapped in this windowless hell hole. She was no danger to Kellen in her other skin, and he would never hurt her. That was not the fear.

The fear was the cage of these stone walls.

Gwenna collapsed against the iron door as pain pierced every nerve ending in her arms. Stiffly, she forced her elbow to bend and her fingers to close around the iron handle. Harnessing every bit of strength she had left, Gwenna pulled against the door to open it.

It creaked open a fraction of an inch, letting the tiniest breeze of fresh air inside. She gasped, lungs expanding with the taste of freedom and fresh air.

The handle was wrenched out of her hands as the door slammed shut. Someone on the other side of the door slid the lock into place with a distinctive click.

Bile rose in her mouth.

"Take some time to think of your loyalties," Marock's cold voice said through the door.

Gwenna stood, rooted to the spot in complete shock. That split second with a loss of concentration was all it took; the Shift took hold, pain immediately yielding to the tingling sensation that ripped over her with new force.

Reaching out to try the door again, nothing but feathers brushed uselessly against the handle. A shriek of frustration melted into a honk as she tried, again and again, to pry the door open.

Marrock was not a dog that learned to bite after being kicked one too many times. He did not yearn for a master to bring him to heel or a soft hand to roll over and show his belly to. No, Marrock was the rabid animal that lured small children in with his big eyes and soft, shiny coat. He waited until the silence and the dark when trust solidified; he ripped out their throats and dragged their corpses into his den.

Marrock's essence wasn't merely Welded to a wolf. He had allowed himself to become a beast.

CHAPTER 37

ONE DAY SINCE KELLEN'S RESCUE

H unger pains wracked her body as she stepped back into her skin.

It felt wrong. Too dark, and the air stagnant and hot. Gwenna's mind whirled, unable to make sense of anything.

Her knees threatened to buckle as memories of the past twenty-four hours swept over her like an avalanche. From Fairy Maeve and everything she divulged… The beauty of Irrywellium and that one tantalizing taste of *joy*…

To this.

She turned to see Kellen, unchained and slumped against the far wall of his cell. One eye still swollen shut, he was staring openly and fearlessly at her.

"You're a…."

"A goose," Gwenna finished, dropping to her knees before him. "How are you feeling?"

"Well enough, all things considered. My back is feeling much better, but my eye and knee will take a little more time," he admitted. "Shifting can hurry up the healing process for minor things. I've Shifted a few times today just to help the process along, but your husband worked me over pretty well."

"He's not my husband." The words came out hard and bitter.

"That's not what he said when he came here to gloat."

"He wants the throne," Gwenna sighed wearily. "He wants Bannon. I've held him off by making him think I'm waiting for Aidan, but I'm running out of time."

Silence fell as Kellen studied her, that one bloodshot eye flicking back and forth across her face. His lips were split at the corner and pulled into a thin line. Angry, swollen, and red, his nose was clearly broken, blood staining the unshaven beginnings of a mustache.

"I believed you last night," he said quietly. "I didn't understand, but I knew you were too tough to give in to that bully."

Gwenna dropped her gaze so he didn't see her eyes glossed with tears. "Thank you."

"So why didn't you tell me you were a goose?" He yawned and started to stretch but winced and clutched at his ribs.

"It's not what you think," she said quickly. "I'm not a Shifter."

"I know. You're pretty and remarkable, but you're still just a human," Kellen said with a grin.

Gwenna's cheeks burned, but she wouldn't let herself get distracted.

"It's more complicated than we realized. I don't know why your mother took you away from here, but I've met your people, Kellen. And they're incredible," Gwenna said softly, sitting back on her heels. "You would love them. Don't judge all of them on *him*."

Kellen smiled softly, reaching over and placing one of his rough, callused hands on hers. "You sound like a queen with a plan. How can I help you?"

For the second time in the brief conversation, Gwenna's eyes burned with tears. He spoke simply, but the sincerity was overwhelming. After weeks of measuring out every word she said, being in the presence of someone so accepting and genuine felt like safety in a way Gwenna would never be able to describe.

"I still need you to bring me Aidan," Gwenna said quietly.

Something flashed behind Kellen's eyes, too quick for her to recognize it. He stared at her for a beat, at a loss for words.

"Aidan?" he repeated, almost sounding skeptical.

Gwenna shifted uncomfortably. "I'm cursed and–"

"You're *not* a curse, Gwenna," he said sharply, hand gripping hers a little harder.

Cheeks warming yet again, she had to look away from his impossibly sincere brown eyes. Her stomach pitched in a new and odd way.

"You have a fever," she whispered, staring at his hand on hers.

"Probably." Kellen shrugged. "Nothing that time with a royal woman won't fix, I'm sure."

"You need to get out of this cell," she muttered, glancing towards the door.

Kellen caught her other hand in his.

"Gwenna, listen to me," he said lowly, pulling her in a little closer. He paused suddenly, looking down as his finger ran along the smooth silver ring she wore. "What's this?"

"A Mage did a Weaving." Gwenna was almost whispering, shame settling over her shoulders at the look of hurt in Kellen's eyes. "It's a spell. A curse. And Marrock created it so that only Aidan can help me break it."

"And what, exactly, does he have to do to break the spell?" Kellen's eyes burned into hers.

Down the hall, the heavy iron door slammed shut. Shuffling sounds of bare feet on stone echoed down the darkened hallway.

Gwenna jumped up, moving to meet Marrock at the doorway to the cell. She had never been so grateful for the wolf as she was at that moment. Behind her, Kellen slowly pushed to his feet, wincing at every movement.

"Welcome back, my bride." The Shifter's hulking frame emerged from the blackness, silver eyes glinting.

"You dare to speak to me of marriage?" she cried. "You locked me away in here!"

He smirked but said nothing, reeking of arrogance.

"I'm taking the farm boy out of here. He will eat his fill, and Joanya will tend to his wounds afterward. He will sleep in a proper bed, and when his strength is recovered, he will be allowed to walk out of here," Gwenna said coldly. "These are my terms."

Marrock arched an eyebrow, thick arms folded across his chest. "And if I refuse your terms?"

"This is not a negotiation. I am a queen, Marrock, and I will always do what is best for my people." She folded her arms across her chest, trying to mask how her heart was racing. "If you hope to see a throne, you will let us pass. You promised not to hurt my people, and you clearly have violated that oath."

"He cannot leave this place," Marrock hissed. "He cannot be allowed to return home."

"You will not stop him."

Kellen drew level with her, a united front. Gwenna wrapped an arm around his waist to stabilize him, slinging his arm across her shoulders. Her skin blazed where Kellen touched her. It was probably his fever.

Jaw clenched, Marrock's eyes threw daggers at the girl standing before him. But nevertheless, he took a step back and allowed her to pass out of the cell along with her wounded farm boy. Kellen limped, leaning heavily on her, but they made their way down the dark hall to the heavy door leading to the rest of the manor.

"You forfeit your right to wait for your betrothed," Marrock called after her.

Kellen tensed, bicep flexed against the back of her neck.

"I forfeit nothing. You chose this path when you imprisoned one of my subjects. If you ever hope to see a throne, you will not defy me again," she said coldly.

Her stomach twisted with fear as the words came out of her mouth, but she didn't stop moving. If she played the role of the confident monarch long enough, perhaps one day she would actually feel worthy of the part.

Gwenna could feel the questions steaming off of both men, grateful for the dark to hide her face from view.

CHAPTER 38

TWO DAYS SINCE KELLEN'S RESCUE ATTEMPT

K ellen slept for two days.

By the time he awoke, the swelling in his eye was almost gone. Faint white scars criss crossing his body were all that remained of the damage inflicted with the whip. His knee had been reset, though Joanya admitted it would always twinge when it rained.

"Up the trail, through the cave," Joanya said quietly as Gwenna donned the cloak she was lending her.

Gwenna forced a confident smile as Kellen joined the girls on the terrace.

Joanya had brought him a tray of food to eat before he set off on their journey, and judging by the broad smile on his face, he had eaten every crumb. A healthy color flushed in his cheeks now, the fever gone. He wore his own boots, but every other scrap of clothing was cast-off from Joanya's brother. Kellen had a much narrower frame than Orrin, so the tunic hung almost to his knees.

"It's better than a loincloth." Kellen grinned as Joanya asked him about it. "And that's all the option I had without you or your brother. But I feel naked without a sword. If you have one of those…"

Beet red at the mention of a loincloth, Joanya shook her head quickly.

"We found you this." Gwenna handed him a shepherd's crook, and he took it with a scowl. "You're supposed to be a farm boy, remember?"

"I didn't forget," he grumbled, rolling the staff in his palm.

"The master left early this morning and has yet to return," Joanya said softly. "You must leave. Now. He's been in a temper...."

Gwenna had avoided him since she had moved Kellen into her chambers the night before. She spent her day on the water and sitting at Kellen's bedside for the first part of this evening. Getting Kellen to safety before Marrock changed his mind about letting him go was her only priority.

She would deal with the wolf later.

"Thank you for your assistance," Kellen said, reaching for Joanya's hand.

It was an innocent gesture in Bannon, but Joanya looked scandalized. Clutching her apron, she fled back into the manor without another word.

Standing alone on the terrace, Gwenna asked the same question she had asked him several times since he woke up. "You understand that I can't come with you?"

He inhaled sharply, turning to look out at the moonlight on the lagoon, leaning against the staff. "Just swear to me that it's because of this ring and its curse."

"Why else would I stay?" Gwenna demanded, grabbing his arm and pulling him around to look her in the eye. "If you have something to say to me, say it."

"A princess trapped alone in a secluded castle with a hulking man? I've heard that tale before, Gwenna." He arched one eyebrow skeptically. "She chooses to stay behind, but it's not because of any spell."

"Is that what you think of me?" Gwenna asked, flinching as if he'd slapped her. "You've seen what he's like, and you'd really think so little of me?"

"You really need Aidan to come for you?" Kellen asked, his voice rough as he closed the distance between them. She inhaled sharply, but didn't move away. She didn't want to. "I'm here. Right here. I knowingly followed that monster into this place. But you want me to go all the way home and fetch Aidan? Even though I'm standing right here and chose to come for you?"

His brown eyes flicked from her eyes to her lips and back again. Something in her chest tightened. Gwenna opened her mouth to respond, to explain herself. But she couldn't find the words. She licked her lips and stared up at him, somehow blooming and wilting under his gaze all at once.

"Forget I said anything." Kellen turned away, not waiting for a response. "You need a prince, not a farm boy."

He pulled the hood of his cloak up and took the terrace steps two at a time.

Shame pooled in the pit of her stomach, but Gwenna followed after him.

Side by side, they walked in complete silence. Emotions swirled through her, each more convoluted than the next. The gravel path pitched steeply upwards. As Joanya had said, the path led to a tunnel high up in the limestone cliff face.

Gwenna was doing the right thing: freeing Kellen and sending him home. Marrock would've *killed* him. She was saving his life. If the man couldn't recognize that…

"Thank you for getting me out of there." Kellen broke the silence as they stepped inside the darkness of the cave.

She flinched at the sound of his voice. It sounded impossibly loud, echoing off the rock walls surrounding them. In response, Gwenna opened her mouth to say something biting, something witty.

Without the echo, she wouldn't have been able to make out what Kellen said next. "I really thought I was going to die down there…"

A chill ran through her, and she immediately swallowed her angry retort. She had been so wrapped up in herself that she had hardly considered what Kellen experienced. Not truly. It stung when he questioned her motives, but perhaps that constant suspicion of others kept him alive.

The cave was a straight shot through the mountain. Gwenna could see the tiny pinprick of light ahead and moved towards it, first at a cautious walk through the cave's pitch black. But her feet pulled her onward, faster and faster. The light at the end of the tunnel brought freedom and life. It drew her in like leaves upon a fast-moving stream.

"How long were you there before I found you?" she asked, breaking the silence.

"Just a few hours, I think," he hesitated. "I don't really remember it clearly...."

"Thank The Deep."

"I thank *you* for your bravery, Gwenna," Kellen said solemnly.

There it was. The gratitude that she deserved. But now that it was here, it felt wrong. Kellen spoke far too highly of her. Yes, she helped him. But anyone would've done what she did. He didn't need to grovel at her feet. Who was she to expect that?

"It was nothing," Gwenna mumbled. "Anyone would've done it. I couldn't have left you there."

There was a moment of silence between the two, and her heart sank. Had she offended him? She tried to imagine how they had sounded to him. She didn't mean to imply any kind of weakness on his part; he was no maiden in need of rescue.

Face burning with regret, Gwenna opened her mouth to apologize. "Kellen, I'm–"

"I couldn't leave you either. That's why I came. I couldn't bear the thought of you here and waiting... It was too much. I couldn't leave you."

"---sorry." Her breath hitched in her throat, a strange levity in her chest. "I... *sorry?*"

She whipped her head in his direction, but the cadence of his footsteps changed. Kellen took off into a dead run, sprinting away from her with all his might.

Her jaw dropped. She pulled her cloak even tighter, a piercing chill in her core at his sudden absence.

Kellen appeared silhouetted in the moonlight, several paces ahead as he ran towards the mouth of the cave ahead, arm holding his shepherd's crook high.

"Who's there?" he shouted.

Only then did Gwenna see a shadowy figure standing silhouetted by moonlight at the end of the tunnel.

She didn't realize she had screamed Kellen's name until the rocks echoed it back as she ran after him. Her stomach was in her throat. If that was Marrock, and he had changed his mind about letting Kellen go, Kellen was running to his own death.

But Kellen didn't hesitate in tackling the stranger to the ground, the two rolling out of sight.

Gwenna pushed herself faster, listening to grunts as the two struggled and wrestled. Raising a hand to shield her eyes from the sudden light of the full moon, blinding after the tunnel's darkness, Gwenna barrelled out of the cave. Heat slammed into her as she passed the magical barrier hiding Irrywellium from Bannon and its drought.

Gwenna picked up Kellen's discarded crook.

Kellen lay flat on his back with a dagger aimed at his throat, a dark-haired man straddling him.

"Yield!" the attacker barked.

Gwenna whipped the staff through the air, aiming right for the back of the dark-haired man's head. The sudden movement caught Kellen's attention, and his eyes widened, darting from her to the man hovering above him.

"Move!" Kellen barked.

The attacker swiveled to face her.

Gwenna had just enough time to register beautifully handsome features as she brought the staff down across the chiseled face of her betrothed, Aidan.

CHAPTER 39

A crack echoed through the still night air as the wooden staff connected with Aidan's skull. His head jerked back from the impact, and he stumbled back a few steps in shock.

"I'm so sorry!" Gwenna gasped, immediately dropping the staff to the ground as though it burned her.

He slowly turned to face her as one hand held the top of his head where a giant goose egg was forming. The string of swear words trickled away to stunned silence as he stared at her. Gwenna gaped through her fingers at the emerald eyes that had enchanted her for so long. For once, they didn't look angry or disgusted.

"*Gwenna?* Is it really you?"

Woodenly, he moved towards her. His fingers dug into her doughy arms, and the touch confirmed that he was real.

Aidan stood before her in the mountain glen.

His eyes were bloodshot. Unkempt dark hair stuck up at odd angles, and his usually unblemished face was covered by a sheen of dirt and sweat. He still wore the ensemble of a nobleman: a white flowing shirt beneath a form-fitting maroon doublet with dark trousers. But now those trousers were ripped at the knee, and the neckline of his shirt was torn open almost to his shoulder.

"What happened to you?" Gwenna asked, panic spiking. "Were you attacked?"

Marrock thought Kellen was a simple peasant. There was no telling what he would do if he found Gwenna's actual fiance.

"Attacked? No, I haven't seen anyone all day! I've been out here trying to find my valet." Aidan grinned.

Looking around, Aidan clapped his valet on the back and began regaling Kellen with the tale of his past six hours in the mountains. Both men grinned as though they had conquered this harsh wilderness like true manly champions.

Ignored and wholly forgotten, Gwenna stood there, gaping at them. Realization hit her over the head much harder than she had struck Aidan.

Aidan had been scouring the woods to find Kellen.

Kellen.

He had been missing for less than three days, whereas she had been gone for almost two weeks.

Before that moment, Gwenna thought emotions were somewhat orderly. They took their time, didn't push in line, and there was little overlap between them. But at that moment, she was overrun and utterly overwhelmed.

Fury. Hatred. Disgust. Disappointment. Betrayal. Heartbreak.

All at once. All clamoring and rising and pounding and thrumming and screaming to be released.

Any guilt she may have felt about smacking Aidan in the head evaporated. It was good that the staff was out of sight in the bushes somewhere, or she may have tried to club him again. This was the man she was supposed to be waiting to save her, and he currently had his valet in a headlock out of some kind of masculine joy that he was alive.

Kellen, meanwhile, had actually shown up for her. He'd allowed himself to be taken. But the Weaving would only be broken if it was Aidan…

Gwenna turned away, walking away from the pair without another word. All she had intended to do was see Kellen to safety. It was clear that Aidan would see to that. Her job was finished.

The entrance to the tunnel back to Irrywellium was nowhere to be seen. Just a rocky outcropping jutting up into the sky. She pressed her hands to the cool stone, tracing her fingers along the grooves, trying to find the entrance. Something at her core nudged her in the right direction, instinctively responding to the power of The Deep.

"Gwenna, what are you looking for? We have to return to Thornvale immediately. There's no time for girlish games," Aidan called.

"I'm not going to Thornvale." She didn't look back at him, continuing to run her hands over the rocks to find the way back. It definitely was getting closer, just Warded and magicked out of sight.

"What?"

"There's a curse," Kellen explained quietly. "She's connected to that beast. She can't leave."

Gwenna was ready to argue with him when she realized he had summed up the situation correctly. Kellen was right. But at that moment, she wasn't returning to Irrywellium because of the Weaving and the magic ring on her hand; she was walking away from Aidan. The Weaving was irrelevant.

Goosebumps spread over her arms, Kellen's accusation ringing in her ears about choosing to stay.

"Lead me to the beast, and I'll slay him!" Aidan said pompously. "I'll slay all of them! It's been far too long since I've been in a good battle."

Gwenna whirled around and stalked towards him, stabbing him in the chest with her finger. "You need to leave this place. Immediately. There is nothing for you here, and you will not harm a single soul."

Aidan already had his hand on the hilt of his sword, but he faltered.

"I thought you wanted me to–" Kellen's brow furrowed, eyes darting toward Aidan. Gwenna shook her head sharply, silently praying he wouldn't say anything. "You can't marry him, Gwenna! That's not a solution."

Aidan jolted in surprise, looking from her to Kellen and back again.

"Married? Who is getting married?" Aidan asked. "We are still betrothed if that's what you're saying."

"No one is getting married." Gwenna rolled her eyes. "Please, go. If you're found here, it will only make things worse."

"Thornvale is running out of water. They need us to restore order together." Aidan said quietly, moving to take her hands. "If you were to return with me, I'm sure it would raise everyone's spirits."

"If there's no water, it won't matter where everyone's spirits are," she said bitterly, pulling her hands out of his grip. "I know you've been getting the food I've been sending. Keep everyone fed. I just need a little more time, and I' 'll break the curse. Everything will be alright. But you need to go. Now."

"You sent the food?" Aidan's jaw dropped.

"How are you going to break the curse?" Kellen pressed, moving to stand at Aidan's shoulder. He glared at her. "Less than an hour ago, you needed *him*–"

"Who is this 'him'?" Aidan demanded, hands on his hips. "Is this the monster that Kellen told me of? Is he trying to convince you to marry him? Has he laid a finger on you? Has he defiled you? You are supposed to be my bride, and I will not have–"

"I don't need anyone!"

Both men froze at her sudden outburst. Gwenna planted one hand on each of their chests and pushed them back a step towards the treeline.

A hair-raising howl suddenly rang out from the direction of Irrywellium. Gwenna spun back towards the sound, heart in her throat. Whatever glamor was in place over the tunnel held firm: all she saw was the rock.

"You need to go."

But another monstrous howl sounded, and she knew no Warding would hold back the beast coming for them.

"You have to go. You both have to go right now!" Gwenna yelled over her shoulder, planting her feet and trying to shield both men from view as best she could.

Marrock wouldn't hurt her, not badly. He couldn't. Not when he still needed her.

"She's right, sir." Kellen's voice was sharp and tense.

"I am on a rescue mission! I can't very well leave her here un-rescued!" Aidan cried stubbornly, grabbing Gwenna's arm and trying to pull her into the undergrowth with him.

"I don't need rescuing! But you'll need someone to rescue *you* in a moment! Get out of here!" she snapped, prying her arm out of his grip.

The seemingly solid rock outcropping shimmered in the moonlight and became translucent. Behind her, Kellen inhaled sharply.

A wolf howled again, growing louder as it barreled toward her. Gwenna could see dark shadows churning inside the tunnel.

She heard the distinct scraping sound of Aidan unsheathing his sword.

"Move, and I'll end this once and for all," he chuckled darkly, moving out in front of her before she could stop him.

A snarling black wolf with white hair on his head bounded out of the tunnel. He jumped, powerful back legs launching him clear across the glen and sending him flying directly at Aidan.

Gwenna leaped, colliding with the mass of fur and muscle in midair and tackling him to the ground. They hit hard, and she rolled a few feet away. Scrambling up, she leaped again, locking her arms around Marrock's neck and trying to hold him back.

"Go!" Gwenna screamed, voice muffled against the dark fur.

Aidan stood dumbfounded, sword drooped uselessly at his side as he watched her. Kellen darted from the undergrowth to grab Aidan and shove him toward the trees. But even the steward faltered, turning back to stare at Gwenna wrestling with a wolf. And winning.

The mass of fur beneath Gwenna tensed. White light flashed, and Gwenna had her arms locked around Marrock's sinewy neck, legs around his core. All fur and snout were immediately gone. He suddenly grunted, shifting his weight, and had her on her back in the dirt, pinning her down with his hips as he loomed over.

"You continue to surprise me," Marrock panted, tucking a loose strand of white blonde hair behind his ear. For once, his eyes burned with something other than rage.

It almost looked like amusement.

"I'll admit– that one surprised me too," Gwenna admitted, out of breath. Her lungs burned. She could feel the heat of Marrock's body pressing against hers, and she lay there, pinned beneath him and gazing into his silver eyes.

"Don't touch her!" Kellen shouted.

Marrock tore his gaze off of her and looked up at the sound.

Lifting her head a fraction of an inch, Gwenna saw Kellen still trying to drag the prince away through the trees. Her eyes met Kellen's, and his grip on Aidan slackened enough for the future king to pull away. Everything in the steward seemed poised to run and put as much distance as possible between him and the wolf. But he hesitated, seeing Gwenna pinned beneath the man. Kellen adjusted his grip on the shepherd's crook in his hand, gaze darting to Marrock before back to Gwenna. She knew Kellen would not hesitate to leap in and use that club to defend her if Marrock didn't release her.

"Get off of her!" Aidan roared, drawing not only his sword but everyone's attention.

Gwenna could only see the scruff along the bottom of Marrock's chin but could practically hear him rolling his eyes. The Shifter jumped to his feet in one swift motion, chuckling darkly.

She clambered to her feet, eager to end whatever this quickly escalated into.

"Aidan, *don't*." There was a note of pleading in her voice now. Softer, more feminine. It was the same voice she always used on Marrock when she needed him to feel his strength and masculinity validated without resorting to violence.

Aidan's eyes flicked to hers for a moment before darting back to Marrock. Apparently, it worked on him too. It was almost infuriating. None of these men ever listened. But they paid slightly more attention if she was sweet and honeyed her words.

Inhaling sharply, she shoved the fury away and tried to channel more of a damsel in distress. More docile, less aggressive. Not nearly as confident, just scared and trembling.

Gwenna grabbed Marrock's arm, trying to hold him back as he prowled toward Aidan. He stopped moving forward but planted his feet defiantly and placed himself directly between her and Aidan. Marrock was now holding Gwenna back more than she was restraining him.

"The lady has asked you to leave," Marrock said coolly. "The farm boy already owes her for his life, and now she's saved your pathetic skin. Respect her wishes and be gone."

"Pathetic?" Aidan repeated, brandishing his sword.

"Of course, that's what you took from that," Marrock chuckled, voicing Gwenna's thoughts exactly.

"I've come for the princess, and I'll not be leaving empty-handed," Aidan said haughtily. Gwenna knew it was a blatant lie, but at least it sounded noble. And it was precisely what she needed Marrock to believe if she would keep her charade up.

"She will not be leaving."

"She's not your property, pup," Aidan sneered.

"Oh, I'm fairly confident that I treat her less like property than you or your kind ever did," Marrock said smoothly, glancing over his shoulder at her. "Care to weigh in here, my bride?"

Gwenna felt the eyes of all three men on her, Marrock's sweetened words echoing in her ears. Not only echoing but etching into her mind. Into her core. He was right, and she hated him for it.

"Aidan, I told you there's a curse. Please... *go.*" Her voice broke on the last word, not entirely intentionally. "You need to go now."

It felt like a knife twisting deeper into her chest. Kellen's eyes were so full of pity, she couldn't look at him.

She stood before two men who wished to marry her but would never love her and wouldn't claim otherwise. Gwenna closed her eyes momentarily, letting herself imagine a world free of either of them.

It wasn't enough to wish that either Marrock or Aidan loved her. Her fate would still be shackled to a man, even though she was the heir to the throne. Marriage to Aidan would be happier than marrying the man who slaughtered her family. But it was a sadly narrow margin. It was still a means to an end. *She* was still a means to an end.

And that wasn't enough for her anymore. She deserved to rule because of who she was, not who she married. Bannon deserved that much. That was the world she intended to create.

But to see that world, she had to fight for it.

And that meant ensuring that Marrock believed she was a dutiful princess waiting for her true love, Aidan. At least for now.

Let the wolf think she was conflicted. Let him think there was a possibility for him to win the throne. Let him believe whatever he needed to. Once Bannon was fed, watered, and thriving once more, there would be time to rid herself of either nauseating marriage proposals.

Bannon needed balance if her grandfather's curse was going to be lifted. And while she still didn't know what that looked like, more bloodshed between the humans and the Shifters would not tip the scales in the right direction.

A tear trickled down her cheek. That part wasn't part of her act. But Gwenna softened her gaze to look past Marrock to Aidan with as much love and devotion as possible. Both men needed to walk away without bloodshed.

Gwenna could solve the rest. She could find some kind of balance.

There was no other choice.

She looked deep into those emerald eyes she once loved and silently pleaded for him to listen for once. Aidan appeared to soften under her gaze.

But then his eyes flicked towards Marrock and narrowed, a sneer marring his handsome face. Dread clawed up Gwenna's throat.

"Yes, I heard about the curse. Why in the world would a princess ever marry you?" Aidan asked cruelly. "As I see it, I cut your head off… and then there's no more curse. Seems like a simple fix to me." He stepped forward, brandishing his sword.

"Aidan, don't," Gwenna said in a low, warning voice. He never listened when she screamed. Gwenna had to speak reasonably.

"Sir–" Kellen's eyes widened as the wolf stepped forward.

Marrock snorted. "I wouldn't try it if I were you, little prince."

"Let the girl go," Aidan demanded.

"I cannot." Marrock shrugged casually.

Aidan dropped into a fighting stance, sword raised, and knees bent.

The Shifter stood, feet shoulder-width apart, chest puffed forward, and arms clasped behind his back. With one hand, he swept Gwenna out from behind him so she stood off to the side. His chiseled chest was clearly visible with the laces of Marrock's grimy shirt undone. With a clear and unguarded shot at his heart, Marrock couldn't look like more of an easy target.

It was a trap.

Gwenna screamed Aidan's name to warn him. But the noise was drowned out as Aidan tipped his head back and let out a mighty battle cry. Sword held high, Aidan dashed forward with the tip of his blade aimed right at Marrock's exposed chest.

Gwenna looked from the sharpened gleaming blade to Marrock's steely eyes. He stood perfectly still, unblinking. Not even his jaw clenched.

"NO!"

Leaping forward, Gwenna threw herself in front of Marrock.

Aidan's eyes widened. He tried to slow his momentum but was still moving too fast. Arms wrapped around Aidan's waist, as Kellen hauled him backward. But it was too late.

Paralyzed, Gwenna could only watch as the sword plunged toward her.

The blade nicked the top of her breast, arcing up and leaving a shallow gash up her collarbone towards her neck before flying overhead and landing with a clatter in the bushes. Aidan collapsed onto the ground, Kellen's arms still locked around his waist.

Stunned, Gwenna gasped for air, and fingers flew to her wound.

Kellen leaped to his feet and lunged for her. "Gwenna!"

But cold, white fingers grasped her and spun her around before Kellen could reach her. Marrock gripped her tightly, eyes searching hers.

"What did you do?" His voice was low and tense.

Gwenna pulled her hand away to show him her wound, fingers barely stained. It was shallow, likely not even to scar.

"It is time for the bloodshed to end." Gwenna pulled herself out of his grasp and turned to look at Aidan's stunned face as well. Her voice carried through the glen, nothing wavering. That Blessing of Clarity burned inside of her as she spoke. "I am Queen of Bannon, and I am telling you that it is over. The Shifters and Mages– the people of Irrywellium– are my people too. They will be safe in Bannon."

Thunder crashed so close it shook the trees, emphasizing her words. Gwenna glanced up to see violet light radiating through the night sky, bathing everything in its glow.

A chill ran down her spine. It was the same light she had seen in her grandfather's bed chambers: a hallmark of Fairy Liratira's curse upon King Domhnall.

Gwenna held up her ordinary and pale hands. They were purple-tinged, but that was from the light shining down on them and not because of anything glowing inside them. She hadn't doubted Fairy Maeve, but still…

She glanced over at Aidan and saw him staring from her face to her hands and up to the sky. He shook his head in awe as he stared straight up.

The violet light pulsed once more before it disappeared, leaving the night noticeably darker than it had been before.

Thunder boomed again. A flash of lightning illuminated a sky full of dark, heavy clouds that hadn't been there moments before.

Then the rains fell.

CHAPTER 40

THE NIGHT THE CURSE WAS BROKEN

B ig, fat raindrops full of life plummeted to the earth. Face tilting skyward, Gwenna closed her eyes to listen to the soft pitter-patter melody. It was the most beautiful thing she had ever heard.

The first drops were tentative, as though nervous about how they would be received. She raised her arms above her head to welcome each and every one of them, praying they would never leave again. Cool, blessed water ran down her face, intermingling with tears. Gwenna could almost hear every living thing drinking their fill, full of relief and restored to health. This was more than a random summer storm. That purple light in the sky was a sign: the curse King Domhnall brought upon them was broken.

Balance was restored.

Within minutes, the heavens unleashed all its moisture in a torrential downpour. Gwenna was vaguely aware that her hair that had come loose from its braid was now plastered to the side of her face, and the skirts of her gown were clinging to her thighs. But she couldn't find the energy to care or hide from the glorious rain. She needed to soak it in.

Bannon was saved because of her.

Joy. Relief, of course. But the immeasurable pride coursing through her veins left her speechless. She did not have to carry around the worry and fear on behalf of her people anymore.

She was not Gwenna the Cursed. She was Gwenna the Cursebreaker.

Opening her eyes, she watched both Aidan and Kellen stomping their feet through the quickly-forming puddles like giddy children. They whooped and hollered, spinning in circles in the rain.

Marrock, however, was oddly silent.

Gwenna looked through the torrent to find the Shifter on his knees in the middle of the glen. His head was bowed as though he sat in silent prayer.

Cautiously, she approached him.

He opened his eyes and looked up as she sank into a deceptively deep puddle beside him.

"You did this." He looked up at her, face empty of any emotion.

"I did," she said calmly.

Slowly, he rose to his feet, eyes never wavering from hers. "You jumped in front of his blade. You saved my life."

"I know," Gwenna said. "And I meant what I said, Marrock: the bloodshed between our people *must* end. There have been atrocities committed on both sides. How long will both sides suffer because of inherited pain? We can end this. The people of Irrywellium should return to Bannon."

"I am not interested in bowing to another man."

"I know who you are," she responded, thinking of the scars Kellen would bear for the rest of his life. "But we do not have to be enemies."

Aidan let out a particularly loud holler at that moment, and it seemed to break Marrock from his reflective trance. His eyes narrowed at the sight, the hardened mask reappearing over his features.

"I will not speak of these things here," he said gruffly. "Bid your would-be prince farewell."

"You gave until tomorrow to be rescued by him. He came for me," Gwenna pointed out, crossing her arms over her chest.

Marrock arched an eyebrow. "He came for you yet did not sweep you off your feet and kiss you. Interesting…"

He didn't come right out and call her a liar, but the implication was clear. Gwenna couldn't even blame him: she had painted a detailed picture of their devotion to each other. Aidan was playing in the mud like a toddler and not paying her any attention.

"He came," she said simply.

Marrock glanced in Aidan's direction and rolled his eyes. "We will discuss things. But not here."

"I would like to uphold our alliance without a marriage." Gwenna stepped before him, not letting him turn away from her. "Your people will need you in this transition. *I* will need you."

"You need me more than you know. Though I'm afraid, you'll be married to that fool long before you realize how much you need a man like me in your bed." Marrock winked lewdly. "Let me take you home, and we can discuss things."

Gwenna rolled her eyes, stepping away as he tried to pull her to him.

"Wait, you're going with him?" Kellen called from behind, causing both Gwenna and Marrock to turn around. "But the curse is broken!"

He and Aidan looked like dumbfounded drowned rats, both soaked to the bone. Gwenna knew she didn't look any better.

"My grandfather's curse is broken, yes." Gwenna tucked a lock of hair behind her ear, conspicuously flashing the incriminating silver ring. Kellen's eyes widened as she saw it, understanding dawning on him. "There are negotiations to be had, and I must return to Irrywellium to have them. Return to Thornvale and take care of the people. Part of this curse was that my people had forgotten the people of Irrywellium, their neighbors. There's sure to be a lot of confusion. Navigate it as best you can, and I'll return soon with answers."

"What do you have to negotiate?" Aidan demanded. "The alliance between our houses was established well before that monster came into the picture. I forbid you from marrying him and turning your back on our alliance!"

Gwenna's hands clenched into fists at her side.

"You will forbid me from nothing," she said coldly. "I am Queen of Bannon, and you would do well to remember that. I will see to my own negotiations. Our ally here has made it quite clear that he has no interest in discussing things with you."

Aidan grinned, looking past Gwenna to where Marrock stood. "Intimidated, eh?"

"Enough of this! You are a visiting noble with no true authority other than what I bestow upon you, Aidan Kaldonna. Don't you dare forget your place. I command you to return to Thornvale immediately," Gwenna barked. "Now go."

"What about–?" Kellen asked hesitantly, eyes darting to Aidan and back to Gwenna.

It had been a long night. One curse was broken, but she was no closer to returning to her people unwed without this Weaving than when it started. But she didn't have the energy to explain all that now, and she certainly didn't want Aidan hanging around.

"I will return as soon as I can," Gwenna snapped with an air of finality.

Turning on her heel, she walked away without looking back, and Marrock, smirking, followed her back to Irrywellium.

CHAPTER 41

ONE DAY SINCE THE CURSE WAS BROKEN

Negotiations were delayed because of Gwenna's goose. She Shifted halfway back to the manor and spent the day on the water, as usual.

When she stepped back into her body, rain poured through the open-air ceiling of the cenote. The little sky she could see was cloudy and gray.

Marrock did not bother meeting her at the water's edge. Instead, he sat at the large dining table, waiting with a predatory grin.

"It rained all day," he informed her as she stepped through the terrace doors. "My men tell me that already the hills of Bannon are green once more."

Gwenna's jaw dropped. "That's impossible. Overnight?"

He rolled his eyes, using one foot to kick the chair on his right side away from the table so she could sit. "Some might think your naivete is endearing. I, however, find it incredibly dull. How much magic must you see before you stop gaping at everything like a child?"

"I didn't think it was magic. Just rain…" Gwenna mumbled, cheeks burning as she sank into the chair.

"Does normal rain always heal your wounds?" he sneered.

"My wounds?"

Huffing in irritation, Marrock grabbed the neck of his shirt and pulled it to the side to reveal a thin scar running above his heart to his collarbone. It looked identical to the wound she had received from Aidan's sword.

Breath froze in her lungs, and her hand flew to her chest. She knew from watching Kellen's healing that Shifting could make the healing process go faster. But it still should have been red and puffy. Instead, it was completely scarred over with a thin white scar, barely indicating what had happened.

"How is this possible?" she whispered.

"Magic rain," Marrock spoke slowly like he was talking to an idiot.

"The sword pierced me. Not you." Gwenna narrowed her eyes. "I took that blade for you. So why, then, do you bear an identical wound?"

Silver eyes gleamed wickedly. He steepled his thin fingers and leaned forward in his chair towards her, one eyebrow raised.

"Oh, dear... Did I somehow forget to mention this? With our Weaving, we are connected. *Joined.* Whatever wound one of us sustains, the other sustains as well." He spoke impossibly softly, but his words landed like a blow to the heart.

The blood drained from Gwenna's face, and Marrock smiled eerily.

"But that means...." Her mind whirled.

"That means that should there be an attempt made on my life, your life would be in jeopardy as well," Marrock cooed. "It was so noble of your beloved prince to think it would be as simple as killing me. Little did he know, his blow would've severed your royal head like mine."

"That's why you didn't fight back." The realization snapped into place.

"I certainly wasn't going to let the idiot land a lethal blow. Have no fear, my bride: your life was not at risk last night. But can you imagine the look on his chiseled face when he realizes that drawing my blood also draws that of his beloved?" He leaned back in his chair once more, satisfaction simmering off of him.

Gwenna turned away from him, busying herself by dishing up a plate.

"He is your beloved, isn't he?" he asked lightly.

"Of course," she responded automatically. "Would you like some potatoes?"

"I'm surprised there was no true love's kiss last night."

Keeping her focus on her plate, Gwenna began to eat politely. Not every question deserves a response, after all. And a lady would never speak on such things.

"Could it be that the princess is doubting her true love after all this time? Perhaps her eyes are finally opened to the fact that he is a pitiful excuse for a man, let alone a future king," Marrock mused.

Gwenna continued to eat, carrying herself as unbothered as possible. Inwardly, she scrambled to find some kind of response. The only thing that delayed her marriage to Marrock was the claim that she could not betray Aidan.

Except now, Aidan had entered the picture, and here she was, still without a true love's kiss and trapped with a villain.

If she agreed with the wolf's claims and spoke truthfully about how far the prince had fallen from grace, Marrock could call for a marriage that evening. Just because she had spared Marrock from the sword did not mean she for one moment entertained the thought of marrying him.

He had murdered Catriona. She could tolerate his presence as a necessary evil to bring balance to her kingdom. But she could never forgive him for what he'd done.

In breaking her grandfather's curse, she saved her people. Was it possible she also doomed herself? Bannon was free, but she could not hand herself over to Marrock.

"Perhaps you and your prince are waiting for a more romantic setting for your kiss, is that it?" Marrock mocked.

Gwenna's head came up quickly. "Of course. Everyone knows that a true love's kiss can't just happen anywhere."

"No, of course not." He propped his chin on his fist as he watched her. "You would need the perfect ambiance. A royal ball or something, perhaps?"

"Oh, everyone knows that balls are the most romantic of places," Gwenna swooned dreamily, forcing herself to think of the balls from the books rather than those she'd actually attended. "All the best examples of true love's kiss happen at a ball."

Too late, she saw the triumphant gleam in Marrock's eye. She had walked right into the trap he had laid.

"That certainly would explain why your prince is inviting us to a ball then," he grinned.

Gwenna dropped her spoon with a loud clatter. "He did *what*?"

Marrock produced an envelope and handed it over. The wax seal was broken, but she saw the crimson Kaldonnian crest staring back at her. Of course, Aidan already had his own stationery.

Gwenna had to read through the invitation three times before the implications truly began to set in. Aidan was throwing a ball to celebrate the end of the drought. He invited 'the Dog King and his ambassadors' to join him in establishing peace talks. Even though she had insisted that she had everything under control.

Gwenna quickly returned the parchment to Marrock before she crushed it in her fist. How was it possible for one man to be so insufferably ignorant? She had asked Aidan for one thing– just one! He needed to look after her people to see they were recovering well and leave the peace talks to her. Of course, he couldn't stay out of things.

Gwenna buried her face in her hands, breathing deeply to try and control herself before she erupted in rage.

"It seems odd that your kingdom has been brought back from the edge of annihilation for less than a day, and he's already planning lavish parties...." Marrock said lightly.

A humorless chuckle escaped her throat.

"Do humans frequently choose to insult their guests while trying to extend an invitation?" the wolf continued, not holding back the amusement in his voice now. "I know he doesn't know my name, but certainly, he could do better than The Dog King."

Shoulders slumped, Gwenna wearily looked up at him. "Please allow me to extend my apologies."

"I guess we'll have to ask him ourselves," Marrock grinned.

"You can't actually think of attending!" she cried.

"Why not? He went to all this trouble to personally write us an invitation. It would be rude to ignore it," Marrock said.

"What if it's a trap?"

"Oh, I'm counting on it." He grinned wickedly.

"Please- ignore this." For perhaps the first time in her stay in Irrywellium, the pleading note in her voice was genuine. "He has no idea what he's doing. He means well, but...."

"So you agree: your betrothed is an idiot?" Marrock pounced on the idea.

Gwenna dropped eye contact, ashamed to be playing right into his hands. Again.

"If I do, will you burn this note and never speak of it again? You won't attend this ball?" she asked quietly.

"I'll certainly consider it," he said loftily. "Though I'm afraid I can't commit to anything. This provides me and my people, as a whole, with an opening we've been waiting many years for. We are not often invited to sit down with royalty."

"You and I have dined together almost every evening," Gwenna said. "I am Queen of this land. He has no power here. You and I can negotiate everything we need without his interference or any stupid ball."

He pretended to consider the idea for a moment.

"Oh, my bride, how could I be so cruel? You said so yourself: no setting is more romantic than a royal ball. What better place to receive your true love's kiss?" He spoke so softly it was almost a purr.

Goosebumps swept over her skin, and dread coiled in the pit of her stomach.

"What?"

"I think this ball provides the perfect opportunity for you to see this prince for who he truly is. Not just him– but those humans as a whole. They are *not* your people. Let's allow them to prove it to you," Marrock said, a smile slowly spreading across his face.

"What are you talking about?" she asked again.

"I'll send for Fernella at once. A Weaving of this size will take many hours to prepare."

CHAPTER 42

F
ernella appeared startlingly quickly.

She didn't arrive from the terrace but instead through the doors leading to the interior of Marrock's manor. Rain still poured outside, but Fernella was completely dry without a hair out of place. It was as though she had been in the bowels of the manor all along. Gwenna looked to Marrock for clarification or explanation, but he said nothing.

Gwenna remembered the scream and crash of furniture she had heard one of her first nights in the manor. Had Fernella been locked away in here the whole time?

The tiny Mage sashayed across the room wearing a clingy scarlet gown. Her sheer cape around her shoulders fanned out dramatically behind her. She ignored Gwenna completely, crossing directly to where Marrock lounged in his armchair before the hearth and splayed across his lap, pressing her chest against his. The two shared a passionate kiss. Gwenna looked away in discomfort, studying the rain outside the terrace doors with renewed interest. But there was no escaping the sounds they made.

Gwenna realized she hadn't seen Fernella since that unfortunate dinner encounter where Marrock had beaten her until she struggled to maintain her glamor. But he had talked about her— she was the one he had business with outside Irrywellium.

What were the two of them involved in?

Marrock suddenly cleared his throat, and Gwenna realized the wet lips smacking had finally ceased.

"I need your help with something." His voice was low and raw, which he never used when speaking to Gwenna, thankfully. "I have a chance to change our lives forever… but I can only do it with you by my side."

Gwenna couldn't suppress the shudder rolling down her spine, but neither one seemed to even remember she was in the room.

"Of course." Fernella's voice was breathy, a slight purr to her words. "You know I am yours to do with as you please. I am yours to command from the first day you claimed me. What can I Weave for you, my lover?"

"I am attending a ball with the humans. My bride will need a new face for the event, and I'll need someone to wear her face. Someone I can have complete control over, you understand. We'll be walking into enemy territory." Marrock was no longer sultry and smoldering but all business.

Fernella let out a disbelieving chuckle, gaping wide-eyed at him.

"My lamb, what you are asking for is no simple Weaving…." She began, shaking her head slowly. "The last time you asked something of this magnitude—"

"You recovered, didn't you?" Marrock grinned frostily. One finger trailed down her cheek with almost tenderness before he gripped her chin between his fingers with enough force to break her jaw. "You *will* do this for me, no matter the cost."

This was not a request; it was a command.

Gwenna froze in place, hearing Fairy Maeve's warning about Weavers that pushed their abilities too far.

Something glimmered in Fernella's large eyes, and Gwenna could see her trembling even from across the room.

Nevertheless, the Mage nodded. "I am yours to command, as always."

Ice ran down Gwenna's spine.

"Don't speak such blasphemy in my presence," Marrock said coldly, standing up abruptly and causing Fernella to tumble to the marble floor. "I have no patience for weaklings in my presence. You are not the Mage you claimed to be when I found you in the gutter. Be grateful I don't return you from whence you came."

Fernella's eyes met Gwenna's momentarily, fear radiating from her. Gwenna opened her mouth to say something, anything, but Fernella shot her a nasty look and pushed to her feet. Turning her back to Gwenna, she turned to Marrock again with a simpering smile.

"When is the ball, my lamb?" she cooed.

Marrock stood at the long table, downing a cup of wine in one gulp. "Two days. Who do you want to bind first?"

CHAPTER 43

TWO DAYS SINCE THE CURSE WAS BROKEN

Gwenna was spared by her goose once again. Marrock summoned Joanya and forced her into a hard-backed chair before Fernella when Gwenna Shifted. But when she returned to the manor at dusk, it didn't look like anyone had moved all day.

Joanya sat in the wooden dining chair, fingernails digging into the armrests. Fernella stood over the servant girl and stripped her of her own mind. Marrock sat in his plush armchair, rotated to get the best view, arms folded across his chest as he supervised.

"Hello, my bride," Marrock greeted cheerily, leaping to his feet to meet her at the terrace doors. "Don't fret about the kitchen girl– she's entranced and fully under my control. No harm will come to her. Your Weaving won't take nearly as long, don't worry. You'll keep full control of your mind. This ball will be one I want you to remember for the rest of your life."

Gwenna shuddered at his ominous words, staring at Joanya's white face. Marrock claimed she was not in pain, but every muscle in her body was strained, back arched away from the chair.

"I can't watch this," Gwenna mumbled, turning away. "I think I'm going to be sick."

"Oh, you're not going anywhere," Marrock said coldly, one hand clamping down in a vice-like grip on her shoulder. "I am doing this for you."

"This has nothing to do with me. You're getting pleasure out of this." She spat, trying to pull her arm away. His fingers tightened, and

Gwenna cried out softly, causing his eyes to flicker with something like amusement.

"You're not wrong," he admitted, leaning in and licking his pale lips. "But no, we are attending this ball for *you*. All of this is for you, my bride. So you will sit here and watch every moment."

Both hands on her shoulders, he steered her to his armchair and shoved her roughly into it. He hovered beside her, delighting in the scene like a child at a festival.

Fernella knelt before Joanya's unconscious body, wearing the same scarlet gown as the night before. Dozens of ruby scratch marks crisscrossed up and down her arms, where she had torn at her own skin. Clumps of what appeared to be black fur surrounded her. Her chignon had come loose, unbound hair around her shoulders.

As Gwenna watched, Fernella began shaking back and forth, lips moving in a silent chant. When she turned, several huge bald spots on her scalp were evident that hadn't been there the night before. It wasn't fur surrounding her, but tufts of her hair that she had pulled out by the root.

Joanya had looked uncomfortable when she had Woven for Marrock. But this was torture. Gwenna heard Fairy Maeve's words, warning about the dangers that lurked when Weavings were taken too far.

Warping.

"Is this safe?" Gwenna breathed, staring at Fernella.

"The kitchen girl will be fine. She'll have no memory of our time with the humans. The binding only lasts three days, but she'll make a full recovery in about a week," Marrock said dismissively.

Suddenly Fernella arched backward so violently that Gwenna was certain her spine was sure to snap. A piercing scream tore from her throat as her hands moved to her face. Her claw-like nails pierced the skin below her eyes and tore down, ripping gouges in her face.

"And Fernella?" Gwenna clarified, stomach roiling. "Will she recover?"

Marrock didn't say anything. She peered at him from the corner of her eye. The wolf stared almost hungrily as blood trailed down Fernella's face.

"She did last time," Marrock shrugged. "Mostly, anyways."

Gwenna swallowed the bile down. Forced to witness a broken mind try to subdue a healthy one, she sat in the chair but retreated as far inside herself as she could. Her eyes remained open, but she stopped watching what was going on. Instead, she counted the stones on the floor, the fall wall, and the ceiling. She recited every single sonnet she knew and told herself the fairytales from her childhood. Anything that would take her far, far away from this room.

Fernella was torturing herself, *killing* herself, for Marrock's sake. And he didn't have a shred of sympathy or remorse. He was almost... aroused.

Hours later, silence fell.

The motion of Fernella rising to her feet snapped Gwenna back to reality. On wobbly legs, the Mage crossed to Marrock and stood before him.

"The girl has been broken." Her voice was ragged and hoarse, more like an old beggar woman than a powerful sorceress. "You control her mind for three days. No more, no less."

She dropped a heavy metal ring into Marrock's open palm. Glinting in the firelight, the faint outline of a doe was etched upon it.

When Marrock slipped it upon his first finger, Joanya stood from her chair. Eyes open but unseeing, she crossed to stand in front of Marrock, eyes unfocused.

"What else can I do for you, my love?" Fernella croaked.

She seemed unaware of her patchy scalp or the weeping scratches running down her smooth cheeks. Within a day, she had aged a century. The remaining hair she had was graying and limp.

Whatever glamor she had once held was long gone. Gwenna felt like she was intruding to see Fernella so vulnerable. This once majestic woman who radiated power was a shell of herself. The healthy glow to her skin was gone. Her gown hung limply from her skeletal frame, no curves left to be seen.

"Where are the glamor charms?" he asked coldly, eyes not leaving Joanya's blank face.

Gwenna vowed to never leave her friend's side when she was in this state. Marrock was violent even when Joanya could fight back. She would not leave Joanya alone and defenseless with him.

"They have been boiling all day and should be complete. All that is left is a hair from each." Fernella breathed raggedly, hobbling towards the hearth.

"Excellent. Get the charms," Marrock instructed, moving to the empty dining table. He ran a finger along the smooth silver of his ring, and Joanya followed behind him like a dog on a leash.

When Fernella straightened, she held an iron cookpot in her hands. The handle was bright red with heat, smoking against her palm, but she didn't notice. Instead, Fernella limped to join the Alpha at the table. She upturned the pot, and two red-hot lockets fell onto the table with a hollow clunk.

"My bride, come." Marrock didn't even look over his shoulder at her.

Numb, Gwenna obeyed.

Fernella yanked hairs from first Gwenna's and then Joanya's head. Gwenna rubbed her scalp, observing as Fernella held up the hairs to the light, examining them closely.

"What are you doing?" Gwenna asked, but Marrock laid a hand over her mouth.

"It's rude to distract someone while they're working," he said quietly.

"Why did she need my hair? What is she doing?" Gwenna demanded, shoving his hand away and rolling up on tiptoes to see better.

"I have to take off the Weaving the kitchen wench made," Fernella said hoarsely, back still turned. "I can leave your energies conjoined so that no harm comes to either of you."

"Do it," Marrock commanded.

"I would very much like to un-conjoin our energies," Gwenna hissed.

"After our wedding, my bride." Marrock grabbed her hand and placed a cold, rough kiss on it.

Gwenna didn't hide her disgust as she snatched her hand away, and Marrock chuckled.

Fernella turned and came prowling over, foggy eyes fixed upon Gwenna. Instinctively, Gwenna hid her hand behind her back.

Marrock scoffed, grabbing Gwenna's arm and twisting it roughly from behind her back to hold her wrist out for Fernella. In the witch's hand was a small glass vial containing a liquid of the purest black.

"Is this going to hurt?" Gwenna asked nervously, watching Fernella unstopper the bottle and hold it out over the thin silver band encircling her ring finger.

The witch tipped the bottle, never answering Gwenna's question. One, two, and then three drops spilled from the vial. Gwenna winced as the drops hit her finger, expecting a sizzling pain, but she didn't feel a thing.

The ring began smoking and hissing. It folded in on itself, shriveling and turning a stunning bright red color, before crumbling into ash on the stone floor. Marrock released his grip on her arm and stepped back.

Gwenna stared at the ash, expecting to feel suddenly lighter. But she felt the same.

Fernella suddenly lunged at her, and Gwenna fell back a few steps in surprise. The witch thrust something around her neck, and Gwenna was too off-guard to defend herself. The deed was done: a heavy locket hung around the Queen's neck.

An all-too-familiar tingling sensation started in Gwenna's feet. She wheeled around, sure there was no way it was already daylight and time to fly to the water. But no, pure moonlight shone down on the cenote.

A bright white light enveloped her, and she suddenly felt much shorter. Still human, just... petite.

"What-?"

Another flash of light, this time behind her.

Gwenna turned around to see *herself* staring back at her.

Joanya was gone, but this Other Gwenna wore the Mage's clothes.

Marrock laughed loudly, standing next to the imposter and gesturing to her proudly.

"Gwenna, meet the Other Gwenna," he said. "Let's see how noble and true this alliance is when simple vanity can shift so much."

Gwenna turned to the far wall, now covered in mirrored glass panels Marrock seemed to have put out for this moment. Hurrying towards it, she saw a redheaded young woman with ample freckles in her reflection. The ballroom, a place she had spent almost every evening in, looked odd from several inches lower. Her brown eyes were perfectly round, with long thick lashes, and she now had a cute button nose. Her hips had no curve, and her chest was flat as a board. She looked younger and more innocent.

Gwenna wrapped new gangly arms around herself, all at once realizing how much less space she took up. There was less of her.

It was eerie.

Turning back, Marrock and Fernella both stood inspecting this Other Gwenna. As the true Gwenna approached, she could hear Marrock commenting on features that needed changing.

Fernella spoke to herself, mumbling quietly, touching different features to adjust them.

Orlaith's curls were the first to go. The corkscrews were softened, lengthened, and stretched into glossy waves. The hair was made shinier, the color richer and glossier. Curran's nose was minimized, refined, and upturned.

Gwenna stood, rooted to the spot, watching as her body was altered and edited in front of her eyes.

Perfected.

She had always assumed that, with a Blessing of Beauty, she would resemble Catriona or even her mother. But nothing like this. The features that connected her to her family, the ones she recognized in the paintings of her ancestors, were the first to go.

Looking at this new imitation of herself, Gwenna realized her heritage was gone. The Other Gwenna was a stranger, familiar... yet totally different.

First, magic had deprived her of a life with her family. Now it seemed hellbent on stamping out any reminders of where she came from.

If this was the cost of beauty, maybe she didn't want it.

A lifetime of wishing– secretly wishing, even if she told herself she didn't– to be beautiful, and now that it was here... it was wrong.

Fernella collapsed into a chair, chest heaving and a high-pitched whistling noise sounding every time she sucked in a breath.

"I won't have much time to get a gown together by tomorrow night, but I'm sure I'll find something suitable," the witch wheezed.

Marrock poured himself a goblet of wine, dismissing Joanya– the Other Gwenna– to lay down in the corner of the room and sleep. "You're not going."

Fernella's jaw dropped. "I just assumed… We've always talked about attending a human ball *together*…."

"I'm trying to elevate my status in this world. I certainly can't do that with a common whore on my arm," he said off-handedly. He didn't see how Fernella recoiled as though slapped, but Gwenna did.

"I was your bride once…." Fernella whispered, with pain in her scratchy voice.

Marrock pointed, lips stained purple with wine, at the unconscious Other Gwenna lying flat as a board against the wall.

"*This* is the only bride for me. Do not dare to ever place yourself as her equal. You cannot compare to royalty, and I will only take the very best," Marrock said coldly. "My bride is quite ugly, but even she is not as pathetic and disgusting as you. And, as you've proven, whatever displeases me about her looks can be fixed to my liking."

Gwenna opened her mouth to speak but saw the storm brewing in Fernella's eyes and instead backed up against the wall. This conversation may be about her, but it didn't include her.

"*I am what you made me,*" Fernella hissed, rising to her feet shakily. "How dare you suck the life from my bones and throw me away like something from your chamberpot?"

"We were never married," Marrock smirked. "Not formally. Your old superstitions do not count, witch. You convinced yourself of our marriage to placate yourself. I will not allow the ramblings of a delusional witch to confuse my true bride."

"You cannot deny our marriage when it becomes inconvenient to you. When *I* become inconvenient to you. You forced me to destroy my mind once before, and then locked me away in a windowless room at the top of the manor, only to drag me out when you want something more from me." Wind whipped at Fernella's clothes and hair, an unseen force raging only around her. Something white-hot glowed behind her eyes. "You knew that another Weaving of this size would destroy my ability to maintain my glamor. You called on me on purpose, knowing that in shattering me, I would not be able to stop you...."

Marrock smiled cruelly, settling himself on the edge of the banquet table. "I hoped it'd kill you. I could show your body to the village and prove I was eligible to take another wife. With their support, the humans would not stand a chance against me as their future king."

"I am stronger than you thought," Fernella hissed.

"You're as weak and pathetic as I knew you to be," the wolf sneered. "If anything, the servant girl's mind was too weak."

"Don't forget, lamb, that I know what you've hidden deep within the mountains. I could ruin you," Fernella whispered, pushing herself against him.

"I'd like to see you try, witch."

"You'd be nothing without me," Fernella cooed, grasping his tunic in her gnarled hands. The edges of the fabric began smoldering immediately, but neither seemed to notice. "And you'll *be* nothing without me when you try to take the humans alone. You need me– you've always needed me. I'll laugh when the humans skin you like the beast you are. And I'll keep laughing all the way to *my* throne."

The back of Marrock's hand collided with her face with a sickening thud.

Fernella straightened up, face stoic, as she spit blood and phlegm right into his face.

"You made a mistake not killing me when you could, lamb." Fernella backed away, eyes never leaving Marrock. "It's unfortunate you'll be dead before you see just how big of a mistake it was."

She threw her hands out to the side, and lightning erupted from her palms, striking the floor-length curtains and the linen tablecloth on the banquet table. Flames roared, the fabric immediately going up in flames.

Gwenna threw a hand over her eyes, barely able to see Fernella's silhouette disappear into the rain.

CHAPTER 44

THREE DAYS SINCE THE CURSE WAS BROKEN

Hoods of their cloaks drawn, the trio stood shoulder to shoulder at the edge of the white stone bridge leading to Thornvale Keep. The rain had finally stopped, but the mist and low-hanging fog kept a chill in the air.

An armored rider in Bannonite colors had galloped up to the castle as the three figures arrived at the edge of the village before traveling up to the Keep. From the number of curious heads peering down from the parapets above, it was clear they had garnered attention.

Still, they waited.

Other Gwenna, the perfected and beautiful intruder, stood centered. Still wearing Joanya's freckled face, the true Gwenna was on her right, and Marrock on her left.

Gwenna Lorne stood, heart pounding, looking at the home she fought to protect from the monster she was about to follow inside its walls.

Sloping mountain hillsides were covered in evergreen trees once more. The water level of the fjord was lower than she had ever seen before. But, considering it had been an ocean of sand dunes three days ago, Gwenna was not concerned. Leaves sprouted on trees overnight, lush and full. The crops in the field were thriving.

Simultaneously comforting and eerie, it looked as though nothing had ever happened.

The sun had set behind the tall mountain peaks behind them, night coming on quickly. Gwenna marveled at the gorgeous colors of the fading twilight sky. The Marshora Mountains stood sentinel. Her human eyes couldn't see the glamor on the tallest peak that hid Irrywellium from view. But her goose could still sense its pull.

Other Gwenna, the perfect imposter, wore a beautiful turquoise gown. The corseted bodice was studded with tiny silver beads, giving the illusion of water shimmering in the moonlight. One layer of tulle fell to just below the knees, flaring dramatically, while the other trailed out several feet behind in a gorgeous train. Delicate white silk flowers were embroidered along the soft sweetheart neckline, which connected to wide, slitted sleeves that were long enough to touch the ground while still showing off pale arms. Her gorgeous curls were unbound, offset nicely with a simple silver diadem.

Queen Gwenna, however, was much less extravagantly dressed. Still wearing Joanya's body, her gown was a forest green and her red hair was braided in an elegant crown. Puffed sleeves came to just above the elbow. The dress was laced tightly, but there were no curves to display. It was a simple design, with a square neckline and a skirt that flared from the waist. She wouldn't look out of place at a royal ball, but she also wouldn't turn heads either. It was appropriate for the ladies' maid she was supposed to be acting as.

"Here they come…" Marrock spoke calmly as the portcullis was raised.

He had used the shapeshifting ability only the Alpha possessed to disguise himself in the body of an overly busty blonde woman. The pink gown was inappropriately low cut for a noblewoman and scandalously tight through the hips.

Marrock's feminine voice jolted Gwenna to reality: nothing about this was right. She stood on the right side of a girl wearing her face, forced to pretend to be a stranger in her own home. Marrock had yet to fully reveal his plan for this ball, but Gwenna already knew he was not planning to merely be an innocent guest.

Please, let the sun rise again with no blood having been spilled.

Aidan strode out of the gates, grinning ear to ear as he crossed the bridge to meet his guests. He looked completely different than the man Gwenna had found in the woods. Hair coiffed and swept back, he wore absurdly form-fitting pants and tunic, with freshly polished boots that came over his knee. Rather than a cape, he wore a maroon tailcoat. The cuffs, shoulder, and collar were trimmed in golden thread. It was cut in a way to emphasize his form and hung down past his thighs.

"I'm so glad you all could make it!" he called halfway across the bridge.

Other Gwenna smiled at him. It wasn't a genuine smile– it never reached her slightly vacant eyes– yet Queen Gwenna also knew that she had never smiled as beautifully as the imposter with her face did.

Aidan jogged the last dozen paces to close the distance.

"So, who do we have here?" he sighed.

As if on cue, Other Gwenna's dainty hands pulled back the hood of her cloak, releasing her thick glossy hair to cascade down her back.

Aidan fell back a step, jaw dropping open as he drank in the sight of his perfected princess.

Other Gwenna's skin had a healthy glow, with plump lips and a cute upturned nose. Her dark eyes were proportional and sparkling. It wasn't only her gown that was gorgeous.

"Aren't you going to at least say hello, Aidan?" Other Gwenna teased good-naturedly, extending her hand to his.

Stunned, he moved forward to take it but stumbled over his own feet. Face pink, he quickly recovered and kissed her hand gently.

Face burning, Queen Gwenna stared at her feet. She had been here before, standing to the side and watching Aidan's face light up at the sight of a beautiful woman. Once again, she was not on the receiving end of his delight. When would it stop hurting so much?

"I thought you couldn't leave that place," he said, awestruck.

"No spell could keep me away," Other Gwenna said softly. "It's over. I told you I would handle it, and I did. I got away and came as quickly as I could."

"I-I can't believe it's you!" he stammered, almost unable to take his eyes off her. "Who are your companions?"

The question was abrupt, like he had just realized there were other people around.

"Ambassadors. You did say to bring them," Other Gwenna said gently.

He nodded, accepting this immediately, and his eyes returned to her, fixating on this new polished face.

"Did something happen? You look... different..."

"A little Fairy magic." Other Gwenna touched her dimpled cheek self-consciously. "I haven't looked in a mirror..."

"You look *wonderful*." He looked into those sparkling eyes and watched her smile a little brighter at the words. "Truly, Gwenna. You're beautiful."

"Thank you, Aidan," Other Gwenna murmured, not taking her eyes off him.

"Did you walk all the way here? You must be exhausted!" Aidan cried, breaking the silence. "Please, come rest. The ball doesn't begin for another hour, and I still have some preparations. I have your chambers arranged for you. There will be plenty of time to talk after."

Arm in arm, Aidan and Other Gwenna led the procession across the stone bridge and into Thornvale Keep. The real Gwenna, Queen Gwenna, kept her eyes downcast, knowing Marrock was watching her closely. If she looked up and saw anyone she knew, Queen Gwenna wasn't sure she could play the role of Joanya convincingly enough.

These were the people that raised her. The courtiers were never people she sought out, but the staff had believed any part of her being cursed. That was a superstition only for the elite. The staff at Thornvale Keep were the only family she had left, in a very literal sense. It was better to not see their faces than to pretend not to recognize them.

But she didn't think she could bear seeing their reactions to the beautiful Other Gwenna. It was one thing for Aidan and strangers to be impacted by beauty. But it would hurt too much for the people she loved and trusted to change how they treated her because she was more beautiful.

Blissfully, Aidan was true to his word and immediately led the group to Gwenna's chambers to rest before the ball.

Other Gwenna and Marrock sailed right through the doorway. Queen Gwenna's knees wanted to lock at the blatant intrusion, but she forced herself to continue into the private sitting room she had decorated with Catriona.

Memories of her sister were everywhere in this room. Gwenna's old writing desk in the corner was full of letters to Aidan that she had never sent, drawers crammed full of sketches of him. Two doors sat opposite one another, one leading to Cat's bedroom and the other to Gwenna's.

Queen Gwenna sank into her familiar armchair by the bookcase, ignoring decorum altogether. Since she was pretending to be Joanya, she should have waited for Other Gwenna, the princess, to seat herself. But this was her room, after all. Other Gwenna and Aidan were too busy discussing the ball to even notice her.

When the door to the sitting room closed, and the trio was left alone, the blonde woman's face melted away to reveal Marrock's snide sneer.

"Lock the door," he instructed Other Gwenna, running a finger along the silver ring he used to control the mindless Mage. "Then retire to your chambers. The real princess and I need to speak alone."

Still wearing the bright pink gown of the Shifter woman he was impersonating, Marrock laid down on the settee, hands behind his head as he looked up at the gilded ceiling. Other Gwenna obediently glided out of the room to Cat's chambers, closing the door firmly behind her.

"It's rather cozy here, isn't it?" Marrock kicked off the heeled slippers beneath his gown, putting his filthy bare feet on the furniture. "I have to say, that was a much happier reunion than I could have anticipated. Did you see the way he looked at you? Well, no. It wasn't *you*, was it?"

Gwenna folded her arms, stone-faced.

It was the happiest Aidan had ever been to see Gwenna. And the real Gwenna had the perfect view of the look of surprise and awe when he saw the new face. The transformed and beautified face.

Marrock had planned it all perfectly.

"Why are you doing this?" Gwenna asked him quietly. "He wanted to meet with you. Talk with *you*. You could be having peace talks right now, but instead, you're dancing around in this ridiculous charade. Why? What do you have to prove?"

"I need you to see who you're really aligning with," Marrock snapped, sitting up and letting his feet swing to the floor. He leaned forward, elbows on his knees in a truly unladylike position. If he had been in disguise, Gwenna would have been able to see nothing but his heaving breasts. "You're so blinded by this dream you've concocted in your head that it's blinded you to reality. He will *never* be what you want him to be. You'd rather live a lie instead of waking up and realizing that I'm right here offering you something that he could never!"

"I don't love you!"

"I certainly don't love you either!" Marrock threw up his hands, forehead wrinkled in disgust at the idea. "But you really think that that idiot loves you? Come now, Gwenna, you give him far too much credit. Watch him tonight. Watch how differently this Gwenna is treated when she's beautiful. Watch how *everyone* treats her now."

"He'll never believe it," Gwenna said nobly, folding her arms across her chest. "There's no way Joanya will be able to convince him. She doesn't know me well enough. She'll spoil your whole plot."

"The servant girl doesn't have to convince him of anything. He sees what he wants to see, and he'll believe what he wants to believe," Marrock said darkly. "She can act *nothing* like you, and it won't matter. He's so dimwitted he'll believe anything now that he has a pretty face to look at."

"It won't work," she said stubbornly.

"I thought you'd say that," the Shifter said coyly. "So let's make a little wager…"

Her adrenaline spiked. "What are the terms?"

"If my imposter can deceive your 'true love,' you will forget him forever. You and I will wed. Immediately. Then we can focus on strengthening *our* people together," he said smoothly.

"And what if you're wrong?" Queen Gwenna pressed. "What if Aidan doesn't fall for it?"

"If he is unaffected by beauty, then perhaps he is your true love after all. Your glamor will dissolve at dawn, and you are free to seek out that true love's kiss," Marrock said simply.

Gwenna leaned back in her chair, falling silent as she considered.

Marriage.

Everything had come down to this. She had tried to fight against it and run away from it, but it always found her. After all, what good was a woman with a crown if she didn't immediately hand the throne over to a man? It didn't matter that she was only seventeen years old; a queen needed a husband.

Her grandfather's last request was to see his throne passed down to a worthy male successor. Aidan had been chosen. Would it betray her grandfather's final wishes if Gwenna didn't give Aidan the crown?

Although, it hadn't truly been Aidan that was selected for the alliance. They hosted that ball, hoping to align with Tristan, the elder brother. It could be argued that perhaps Aidan had no actual claim to the throne at all…

But if she didn't choose Aidan, the other option was Marrock. And that was a non-starter.

"What choice do you have, Gwenna? If the boy is your true love, wonderful. But if not, you will marry me and stop wasting time," Marrock said flatly. "There's nothing to decide here."

"It's just that simple?" she asked bitterly.

"Yes."

"If you and I wed, you will swear to not raise a finger against Aidan?"

"Already doubting your true love?" he smirked.

She ignored his jibe. "I want you to swear to the safety of Aidan and his household. You've already sworn to the safety of my people, and I will hold you to that. There will be no ill will. As *you* said, you will focus on strengthening our lands."

"Of course," he nodded.

"And the kiss….?" Gwenna faltered, heat rising in her face at the thought.

A smile spread across his face as he noticed her blush.

"I sometimes forget you're still such a child. Yes, yes, 'the kiss,'" he repeated, rolling his eyes. "As I've said before, who am I to stand in the way of true love?"

"*If* Aidan and I kiss, the curse is broken? The Weave joining you and I will dissolve?" she asked.

"As with all Mage spells," he agreed. "A true love's kiss will break it."

"And you'll leave us be?" Gwenna pushed further. "If that is my choice, you will not make a claim to the throne? You will support peace in Bannon and the unity of our people even if you are not the king?"

"If there is a kiss— not just *any* kiss, but the all-important spell-breaking kiss of true love– I, Marrock, will honor it."

She ignored his skepticism. The emotions and the love were something for her to figure out later. This was the time for political conversations. "You will meet with me, Queen of Bannon, as an emissary for your people so that we may work together to establish balance and restore our lands to what they once were?"

"Of course." He smiled wickedly. "The Queen of Bannon can end the night with an idiot high lord. *Or*, she can end the night with a far more handsome and powerful husband-to-be, and together they can work to raise the kingdom to new heights."

"It seems like this will be a very big night for the Queen of Bannon," Gwenna said quietly. "It's good she is resting."

"Aye, it is," Marrock agreed, flopping back on the settee. "Now, I've never secured a wife before, but I assume it to be very tiresome work. I would like to rest before the night unfolds. You're welcome to come over here and rest in my arms if you would like. It might be your last chance before your idiot wins you back. Or it may just be the start of the rest of your life."

Anxiety pooled in the pit of her stomach, but she didn't bother to answer him. Gwenna was an animal caught in a snare. Suddenly she understood the primal urge to gnaw off a limb if it meant to escape.

She would gladly gnaw off multiple limbs if there was a way out of this.

CHAPTER 45

Three days since the curse was broken

Q ueen Gwenna stood, wearing another girl's body, as she watched herself glide down a grand staircase straight into the arms of the man she had spent her entire life swooning over.

Onlookers applauded. She tasted bile.

Other Gwenna extended her hand, and Aidan skimmed the faintest of kisses upon it, staring up into her gorgeous eyes. Aidan raised a hand to signal the orchestra, and as the first few notes rang through the ballroom, he swept the perfected Gwenna into his arms and began to waltz.

Queen Gwenna wanted to scream, suffocated by the press of bodies watching two beautiful people fall in love before their eyes. Fernella had removed the physical ring from her finger but Gwenna could almost feel it tightening with every rotation the happy couple made around the ballroom.

"What a beautiful couple!" Someone near her murmured. "Prince Aidan looks so happy!"

"He's not even a prince," Gwenna muttered under her breath.

"He certainly does look happy. In love, I'd say," the blonde woman Marrock was posing as whispered for only the true Gwenna to hear. Queen Gwenna plastered a smile on her face and drove her heel into the top of his foot.

Marrock yelped, the canine sound bringing several heads around to look at him in surprise. He flipped open his fan, fluttering it before his heart-shaped face.

"Oh, I do believe I require some refreshment. Pardon me," Marrock murmured in a woman's voice before disappearing through the crowd.

Gwenna didn't trust him alone for a moment, yet simultaneously appreciated the break from his watchful gaze. Needing to compose herself without the wolf breathing down her neck, she retreated to the edge of the ballroom to take refuge behind her column.

"Excuse me," a voice at her elbow murmured. A short, balding man leered up at her. "Would you like to take a turn about the gardens?"

"Oh, no, thank you," Gwenna murmured, bobbing a curtsy to be polite.

His fleshy hand grasped her spindly arm tightly in his fist. "I don't think I've seen you at court before. I would so dearly like to get to know you…"

"Here you are! I'm so sorry I was delayed, my love!" A figure with dark curly hair slid through the crowd, arms held up so as not to bump anyone. Kellen flashed a smile at her as he slid to her side. "I'm so pleased you promised me your first dance!"

He shot a meaningful glare at the plump man, who grumbled under his breath but released his grip on Gwenna and waddled away.

"Thank you, Kellen," she breathed a sigh of relief.

"Consider it repayment for saving my life," he muttered quietly. "I've been looking to speak with you, actually. Is Gwenna… I mean, is she alright? Whatever curse she was under sounded pretty serious, but then she shows up here and says everything is solved?"

Queen Gwenna nodded quickly, forcing a smile. "She handled it."

"She is… *different*, isn't she?" He looked back at the dancing princess in the middle of the floor, a curious look in his eye. "I guess, well… I don't know… It seems like she's changed."

"Well… I suppose the whole ordeal would change anyone," Other Gwenna said slowly, following his gaze to the floor. "And yes, there was some magic involved…."

"But that's not what I mean," Kellen sighed, rubbing his hands through his curly hair. "I guess… Well, I don't even know what I mean. Of course, she's been through a lot. I can't even imagine. But there's something *different* about her. And it's only been a few days. I can't help but feel like that monster did something…."

"I–" Gwenna's throat constricted suddenly as she tried to answer his question.

Her hand flew up to her throat, worried she was being strangled by some invisible force. But she could breathe. Gwenna inhaled, filling her lungs with air, and blew it back out again. Breathing wasn't an issue. But something was preventing her from speaking too candidly about Other Gwenna or Marrock.

"Are you alright?" Kellen's eyes were round with concern.

She nodded mutely.

"Do you need something to drink?" He asked, looking around for one of the servants carrying refreshments.

"My darling!" A voice sang loudly. Marrock, still the busty woman, pushed his way back through the crowd, holding a glass high. "You didn't lose your voice again? Here! Drink!"

He thrust the goblet into Gwenna's hand, and gratefully, she sipped and tried to clear whatever was lodged in her throat.

"Losing her voice?" Kellen repeated dubiously, looking skeptically at Marrock, who giggled and tossed his long wavy hair over his shoulder.

"It happens sometimes. Almost seems like *magic*, doesn't it?" The wolf's eyes flashed in Gwenna's direction. "Ooh, who is your new friend?"

The blonde woman's face showed no sign, but Gwenna could feel the wolf beneath the tanned skin staring skeptically at Kellen. She had told Marrock that his prisoner had just been a simple farmer, but now that farmer was at a royal ball?

Kellen still wore his floppy hat. Memories had been returned to the kingdom, and there was a thrill in the room due to the pointed ears on the bodies Marrock and Queen Gwenna wore. But Kellen apparently was not ready to announce his heritage, and Gwenna couldn't entirely blame him. He wore a tailored coat similar to Aidan's, but less embroidered and in a simpler fabric. He could pass easily as a lower noble but certainly not a farmer.

"This is Kellen. He works with Lord Kaldonna," Gwenna said lightly, careful to not contradict anything she had already said.

Her insides twisted as Marrock batted his eyes and giggled at Kellen. Aidan being mixed up in this madness was one thing. But not Kellen. He deserved so much better.

"Oh, you're so handsome!" Marrock giggled into his hand.

Kellen offered a tight, uncomfortable smile but turned back to Gwenna.

"Are you sure you're well?" he asked, and she nodded.

"Are you taken for the first waltz?" Marrock fanned himself, staring hungrily at Kellen.

Gwenna looked between Marrock and Kellen, heart in her throat. If either one realized they stood in front of a Shifter, there would be no way to resolve this peacefully. Marrock was suspicious that Kellen wasn't a farm boy, but hadn't seemed to pick up on the bear beneath his skin yet. Kellen, on the other hand, seemed completely oblivious that he was standing in front of the Alpha. Apparently Marrock's shape-shifting could mask that part of himself from even his kind.

"He just asked me, actually," Gwenna piped up, boldly linking her arm with Kellen's and leading him to the dance floor as another waltz was called for. Anything to get the two away from each other.

"Thank you," he murmured, placing his hand on her lower back, "She's a little... intense, huh?"

"Oh, you have no idea," Gwenna said darkly as the music started playing. "Actually, may I ask you a question?"

"Of course," Kellen said quickly, peeling his eyes off Other Gwenna to focus on her.

"Do you know how Aidan was able to find you?" she asked before dropping her voice. "I mean, the princess explained how you found our home: you're one of us. But how did Aidan do it?"

Kellen grinned sheepishly. "I wasn't particularly stealthy on my hike through the mountains. That's how the wolf was able to find me. I didn't plan for Aidan to follow me, but a child could have found my trail and stumbled right to the Wardings to your home. I'm sorry I wasn't more discreet."

She shook her head quickly. "No need to apologize. I was just curious."

The waltz was quick, and then Kellen muttered some apologies before retreating into the crowd again. She couldn't fault him: she had not been a gracious dance partner. Her attention was split between Marrock prowling around the room's edges and Aidan and Other Gwenna making eyes at each other. Kellen had tried several times to make conversation, but it was apparent she was distracted.

As soon as Kellen was gone, Marrock reappeared at Gwenna's side.

Another man did a double take of Marrock's busty blonde disguise.

"Your neckline is inappropriate for a lady," Gwenna muttered.

"Good thing I'm no lady." Marrock elbowed her conspiratorially as he boldly winked at the man who was now craning his neck to better look at the ample cleavage on display.

Aidan led Other Gwenna off the floor and towards the dais.

"They're on the move," Queen Gwenna muttered. "Are you coming?"

"No, I think I've found something much more interesting to do. You go along without me," Marrock said, allowing himself to be whisked onto the dance floor by the leering man.

Queen Gwenna wasted no time making her way through the crowd towards Aidan and Other Gwenna, anxious to keep as close an eye as possible on them.

"I'm not tired!" Other Gwenna was saying, looking over her shoulder at the dance floor as the musicians struck up another song.

"Come, have a glass of wine and sit for a moment," Aidan said.

Queen Gwenna seamlessly fell into step behind them, picking up Other Gwenna's trailing hem and playing the role of handmaiden. Neither of them noticed her presence.

Two thrones sat upon the dais. Aidan settled himself into the larger one without hesitation. Gwenna's blood boiled seeing him sit on her grandfather's throne like he already owned it. Other Gwenna settled in Orlaith's empty throne.

Queen Gwenna had to look away quickly. She took her place off to the side of the dais, inconspicuous to any of the ball's guests yet close enough to still hear everything that transpired between Aidan and the imposter wearing her face.

In this bizarre night of disguises and false identities, it felt oddly right for Gwenna to be in this position. Here she was, once again positioning herself to eavesdrop and gain needed information from guests. So much had changed, but maybe she hadn't changed as much as she thought.

Aidan flashed his dazzling smile, and both Queen and Other Gwenna's cheeks flushed at the sight. Despite everything that transpired, that smile still held such power over her. He gestured for a servant to bring goblets of wine, handing one to Other Gwenna, who took a deep sip.

"You look lovely, Princess Gwenna." Jeyne Byrne bobbed a curtsy as she passed in front of the dais. She smiled broadly at Gwenna, something she had never done to the real Gwenna before. "It's so good to have you back. I was so worried! All that mountain air has done wonderful things for your complexion. You'll have to come for tea one afternoon and tell me your secret."

Queen Gwenna's nails dug into her palms, but Jeyne Byrne glided away from the dais and toward her.

"Wait, are you a Mage?" Jeyne's brown eyes lit up as she laid eyes on the pointed ears of Gwenna's new body.

"Oh, um..."

"It's so lovely to have you here!" Jeyne squealed, throwing her arms around Queen Gwenna. "My name is Jeyne Byrne. I'm so happy you're here at court! Have you been introduced? Let's see, how old are you?"

"Uh..."

"No matter. Have you met Roshelle Martine? She must be about your age," Jeyne turned, searching the crowd. "I'll go find her!"

Jeyne scurried away, and Gwenna was so grateful for the solitude. Watching courtiers acting so sickeningly sweet to Other Gwenna was infuriating. Jeyne pretended to be friendly with Catriona, but never to Gwenna. They had never been friends. Only when this imposter Gwenna showed up looking beautiful.

"The friends you brought with you seem to be settling in," Aidan commented after draining the cup. He nodded to where busty blonde Marrock was leading one of the noblemen around the floor. Marrock hadn't gotten the message that women should let men lead.

"Yes, I suppose so," Other Gwenna said absently, taking another long sip of wine. "That's your man standing over there, isn't it?"

Queen Gwenna followed the imposter's line of sight to see Kellen leaning against a column on the opposite side of the dais, also clearly watching the couple on the thrones.

Aidan cleared his throat. "Who, Kellen?"

"Kellen?" Other Gwenna giggled, rolling the name around on her tongue like she had never heard it before. "Kellen…. Hmm… Perhaps. This wine is delicious! I don't remember the last time I had wine!"

"Yes, *Kellen*. My steward and valet." Aidan reached over and casually plucked the empty goblet from her hand. "Surely you remember him…"

Queen Gwenna was moving towards the dais before realizing she had decided to intervene.

"My apologies, your Majesty. She's a little worn out from our travels." Queen Gwenna curtsied, waiting for permission to approach. Heart hammering, she stared up at Aidan, silently pleading for him to spare a glance in her direction.

In a moment, she was transported back to another night in this very ballroom as she stared longingly at Aidan and silently pleaded for him to see her. The night he proposed to Catriona.

The night before the world shattered.

So much had happened in barely a month. In so many ways, Gwenna was not that same girl. She had mourned the deaths of her grandfather, mother, and sister. She had watched her kingdom crumble beneath her feet.

But she was also the girl who found the Fairies. She was a cursebreaker. Queen Gwenna was the reason these people were celebrating. She had saved their lives.

And yet, here she was once again. Gwenna was standing in front of Aidan and hoping he could be her true love. Silently, she pleaded for him to notice her.

She could wrestle a wolf and break a curse, but it seemed she was destined to always end up here.

Aidan's eyes flicked to her momentarily, waving Queen Gwenna forward before he looked away again to survey his ball. There was no emotion on his face. She was invisible to him.

No matter what face she wore, he would not see her. Not really.

Because as much as she had changed, Aidan had not. Aidan was who he always had been. She just was finally seeing *him* clearly.

Aidan had never been the man she wanted him to be. Her love was for someone that didn't exist, a phantom she had created out of hopes of romance that only existed in her mind. Aidan, the true Aidan, was not that man. She couldn't expect him to be.

He was not her true love.

She pushed the thought away as soon as it came. Her Blessing of Clarity told her it was true, but she couldn't dwell on it. Not now, not here, in the middle of a ball. The consequences were too steep.

Pushing away the tears threatening to overwhelm her, Queen Gwenna knelt before the Other Gwenna and tried to capture her attention. The beautiful imposter swayed slightly in her seat, eyes unfocused.

"My lady?" Queen Gwenna whispered.

"With your majesty's permission, perhaps I should assist the lady to her chambers?" Marrock suddenly appeared at Queen Gwenna's shoulder, closely inspecting the Other Gwenna.

Queen Gwenna looked up at Aidan, waiting for him to give the word on what he wanted to be done with his 'beloved,' and saw his gaze focused directly on Marrock's chest.

"Of course," Aidan nodded absently. "Shall I send for a court physician?"

"That's really not necessary. Some sleep will do the princess well. I tried to get her to rest this afternoon, but she was too worked up. Her nerves, you see? The ball was so exciting for her; I think she wore herself out. She has been through so much lately, the poor girl." Marrock gently pulled Other Gwenna to her feet. He wrapped an arm around her waist, and began helping her down the dais' steps.

"Well, the least I can do is see her back to her chambers," Aidan protested, finally returning to his senses now that there wasn't cleavage in his face.

"No, don't! Please, your majesty! She wouldn't want you to see her in such a state. I'm sure we can manage," Marrock said sternly. "Enjoy yourself! Tonight truly is a night for celebration."

Leaving the ballroom was fine. The real issue arose in getting a very drunk Other Gwenna up the large marble staircase. Progress was slow, considering the fake princess's inability to stay steady on her feet.

"Step up!" Marrock's voice slipped from the husky tone of the woman he was dressed as and instead indicated the growl of his regular cadence. "If we weren't in a palace right now, I'd throw her over my shoulder like a bushel of grain…."

He tried to pull Other Gwenna up the stairs.

She swayed on her feet, giggling incessantly, and placed her foot on the next step but put no weight on it.

"What's wrong with her?" Queen Gwenna asked, slinging the girl's other arm over her shoulder again.

"The wine went straight to her head," Marrock grumbled as they towed her up the steps together.

"How much did she have?" Queen Gwenna gasped.

"Just one goblet of wine. But my people can't stomach fermented drinks," Marrock explained as they reached the landing. "I suppose we have to have *some* weakness."

"You drink wine at every meal," Gwenna pointed out.

"Perks of being an Alpha," Marrock snorted.

"Gwenna!" a voice behind called in alarm. "Is she injured?"

Together, Marrock and the Queen turned to see Kellen bounding up the steps with Aidan on his heels.

"I told you– it's the wine," Aidan called after his steward before turning apologetically to Marrock. "We're sorry to disturb you, ladies. I told him, but he wanted to see for himself."

Kellen looked at Other Gwenna with wide-eyed concern as she hung almost limply between her friends. Aidan was, once again, still trying a bit too hard not to glance at Marrock's breasts that were almost spilling out of her bodice.

"How much did she have to drink?" Kellen asked in a low voice.

"Just one goblet," Aidan shrugged.

"She can't stomach the stuff," Marrock explained quickly, all feminine wiles now. "She told me so. Never you mind, she'll sleep it off quickly. She always does."

"Always?" Kellen repeated, bringing his head up at that. "This has happened before?"

"What else do you think she did in the mountains with nothing but that monster for company?" Aidan chuckled, clapping his hand on Kellen's shoulder. "I'd drink myself into a stupor too. Please, ladies, allow us to see you to your chambers for the evening."

He stepped forward and lifted Other Gwenna into his arms with no hesitation. The real Gwenna watched as Aidan cradled the girl in his arms gently.

"Oh, what a gentleman!" Marrock cooed, following on Aidan's heels towards the chambers they were staying in.

Kellen stalked after them, watching Marrock suspiciously. "Have you noticed anything different about the princess tonight?"

"Me?" Marrock turned, hand lightly falling on his chest. "I'm sure I don't know what you mean."

"He's convinced there's something different about Gwenna," Aidan sighed, pausing in front of the wooden door to their chambers.

"And what about you, milord?" Queen Gwenna asked, jumping on the opportunity. "Do you find anything amiss?"

Aidan looked at her, surprised a servant would speak in his presence. For the briefest moment, their eyes met. The real Gwenna stared into those emerald eyes and silently pleaded for recognition. He may not recognize her with this face and this body. She could forgive him if he didn't recognize her when she was disguised as Joanya.

But he *had* to see there was something different behind this beautiful face. Gwenna Lorne had to be more than just a face to him. She was more than a crown and a means to an end.

That wasn't too much to ask. Was it?

Aidan's eyes slowly left hers, and he looked down at the perfected Gwenna, snoring softly against his chest.

It was only a moment, but the weight of that one instant in time pressed on each person in that hallway.

"Nothing amiss at all," Aidan said quietly, eyes softening as he stared down at the Other Gwenna. "She's *perfect.*"

Queen Gwenna's fumbling hand found the latch to the door, and she leaned back against it, opening the door for Aidan to sweep past with the girl he thought he loved in his arms.

Pain wracked her chest. She was only vaguely aware of Marrock leading Aidan to lay the princess in her bed. Kellen stood near the door, suspiciously watching Marrock's every move.

The real Gwenna could only lean against the door and try to bring air into her lungs even as her chest felt like it was caving in on itself. Words were exchanged. Somewhere she could hear Aidan's low laugh at something Marrock had said.

And then suddenly, through the haze, she heard Marrock speaking very clearly.

"Thank you, your Majesty. I do not have the words to properly thank you for what you have done this evening." Marrock smiled at the would-be king, but his eyes flicked past Aidan to land on Gwenna.

Further pleasantries were exchanged, and Aidan and Kellen left the room to rejoin the ball. Marrock closed the heavy door behind them. Gwenna numbly slid down the wall to collapse onto the floor.

Marrock shed his feminine disguise between heartbeats and loomed over Queen Gwenna, his regular angular features appearing out of place in the woman's dress. He crouched in front of her and gently cupped her chin, bringing her head up to gaze into his eyes.

"Please don't," she said hoarsely. "Don't say anything."

He nodded slowly, rising back to his feet.

"Mourn your losses. At dawn, we wed."

CHAPTER 46

FOUR DAYS SINCE THE CURSE WAS BROKEN

Sleep evaded her.

Numb, Gwenna sat curled in a ball on the cushioned window seat of her sitting room, gazing out at the darkened shadows of Braewood Forest. She still wore Joanya's body and would until dawn.

When Marrock would claim her as his bride.

Her disappointment in Aidan was for more than breaking her heart. She would get over that. But he was abandoning her to a monster without even realizing it. Yes, she wanted him to love her. But right now, she needed him to save her.

And whether it was a matter of being unable or unwilling, he would not be her rescuer no matter how badly she wanted him to be.

Leaning her head against the cool windowpane, she forced her mind to go over every conversation she and Marrock had ever had. Again. There had to be something she was overlooking. Some clue that would free her from these shackles.

Killing him was out of the question. They still were Woven together. Merely breaking the agreement and denying him would lead to outright war.

How did she get out of this marriage?

Gwenna closed her eyes and prayed to The Deep with all she had.

"You look pale, my bride," Marrock's voice broke her from her reverie. One milky finger traced her jawline, and she turned her head away. "Why do you look so conflicted? Broken-hearted over your one true love's betrayal?"

"Please, just leave me alone," Gwenna said bitterly. "You've won. Do you need to gloat about it?"

"I brought you something to eat. I'll leave you now," Marrock said softly.

He handed her a small bowl of stew before retreating to the small antechamber intended for a lady's maid. Gwenna wondered vaguely where Aldessa had been moved to. She'd have to find out in the morning.

Looking down at the stew, her resolve cracked. It was a kind gesture, maybe a gesture of goodwill.

Lifting the spoon, Gwenna took a bite. Her last meal as an unwedded woman.

The stew turned to ash in her mouth. Flaky and crumbling, it coated her tongue. She tried to spit it out, but it was too late.

"What did you do to me?"

She leaped to her feet, the clay bowl shattering upon the stone floor. Her lips were already turning numb, pulse thudding in her ears.

Vision spotty and blurring rapidly, she saw Marrock smirking as he crossed his way back to her. Gently, he guided her to the settee and laid her down upon it.

"I have a few things to take care of before I become king. I will not have any man rivaling my right to you or my throne. But I wouldn't want you interfering. You understand, of course?" he whispered, smoothing hair off of her forehead. "Sleep tight."

The last thing she heard before she fell unconscious was Marrock closing the door behind him as he stepped out of her chambers and into the corridor.

A wolf was loose inside her castle, and she had let it in the front door.

CHAPTER 47

The poison was heavy in her system, but Gwenna kept her eyes open out of sheer spite. She could not sleep, not now.

She needed to follow Marrock. It sounded like he would go after Aidan, and she couldn't let that happen. Aidan was an idiot, but he didn't deserve to die because Gwenna had imagined him to be someone he couldn't be.

Marrock didn't know how much Gwenna had embellished about Aidan or their relationship. He just saw Aidan as a threat.

A threat he needed to eliminate.

Gwenna inhaled sharply, trying to think of anything she could do. She didn't know what had caused this in her body, whether it was magic or poison, but she needed to heal quickly.

Shiftings can accelerate healing.

She remembered Kellen's words from that cell. He had Shifted to get himself out of his chains, but it had also almost entirely healed his back. His eye and knee weren't healed without Joanya's Weaving, but at least it was a start.

Gwenna needed to master her Shift. Now.

Marrock had described it as simply stretching and taking on a new form. It couldn't be that difficult, right?

She relaxed, closed her eyes, and inhaled deeply, filling her lungs as much as possible. She straightened, aligning every inch of her spine as she lay on her back.

Exhaling slowly, Gwenna visualized her gorgeous feathers and elegant neck. No, she was no majestic eagle or graceful swan. But there was nothing embarrassing about being a goose. Gwenna imagined herself racing out and embracing her goose. It was no more of a curse than anything else she thought she had been plagued with.

Gwenna thought back on flying high over the cenote. The wind in her face and the exhilaration it was to be so free. She held tight to that memory and willed her muscles to relax and drop their form.

A ripple started on the crown of her head. For once, Gwenna didn't flinch away or try to fight it.

Slowly it cascaded over her whole body. Gwenna shivered as a comfortable warmth enveloped her in a hug.

Her mind was her own. She was in complete control and aware of everything around her. But her body felt different.

Alive.

Opening her eyes, the sitting room she knew so well was filled with vibrant colors. Feathered wings skimmed against her rounded sides. Flinging them outward, she saw how her wingtips formed a natural gradient from the purest white to the darkest black.

Gwenna released a cry of surprise and joy from her bill as a soft honk.

Was this what mastering a Shift meant? A new form that she loved and that she was in complete control of.

Power radiated through her limbs, and as she turned her slender neck to look out the window, she felt an overwhelming urge to leap into the rapidly lightening sky. To soar upon wind currents over Braewood Forest, seeing those colors through these new eyes.

Aidan needs you.

It reverberated in her mind, piercing her core and silencing anything else. Thoughts of food or sleep, floating or flying, none of that mattered.

Marrock was in this castle, and a goose would be useless against him. But Gwenna, the cursebreaker, was anything but useless.

Trying to remember exactly how she surrendered to the Shift, she raised her wings far above her head and brought them down again.

This time, she focused on everything she loved about her human form. Shooting arrows with incredible accuracy or swimming in the lake with her sister. She had a powerful body that kept her alive and safe, even while living with a monster. She thought of Irrywellium and the joy she had felt there. She pictured Joanya, Epon, and Orrin smiling. She thought of Kellen, and the way he made her laugh.

The ripple came again, but this time it was followed by a strange cold.

Shivering slightly, Gwenna opened her eyes and saw she was back in her own body. No longer Joanya, no longer a goose. The teal gown that Other Gwenna had been wearing the night before was now magically altered to fit her perfectly, including the delicate diadem on her head.

She was Gwenna Lorne, with a slightly asymmetrical face and thicker limbs. She was Blessed with Strength and Clarity. She was Queen of Bannon and no man's means to an end.

The sun was rising over the forest, but she felt no compulsion to Shift.

She was the master of her Shift. She was Gwenna Lorne, imperfect and powerful.

CHAPTER 48

THE MORNING AFTER THE BALL

The Keep was eerily silent. No screams and no bloodstains. Not yet.

Either way, Gwenna was grateful she had a quiver of arrows on her hip and a bow firmly in hand as she searched for the wolf.

"Where is he?" Her shouts echoed off the entrance hall as she ran down the grand staircase, one hand holding up the layers of tulle of her gown so she didn't trip. "Where is Aidan?"

The guards at the doors looked at each other in confusion.

"He took his morning meal in his study," Aldessa, the maid, said as she stepped out of the banquet hall. She smiled as she saw Gwenna and nodded respectfully. "Good to see you again, milady."

"Is he alone?" Gwenna asked, out of breath.

Aldessa shook her head. "One of your friends from the mountains has been with him. Your friend wanted to see our water reserves, and I believe they're down in the cistern now."

Swearing under her breath, Gwenna dashed down the stairs.

She threw open the door to the cistern, racing down the spiral stairs and praying not to see Aidan's corpse floating in the water.

Much like the water in the fjord outside, the water levels in the cistern were lower than Gwenna had ever seen. But still significantly improved from where they had been during the curse.

Aidan stood, hands on his hips, with his back to the door. He looked over his shoulder, eyes widening in shock and confusion as Gwenna stood, panting, in the doorway. Standing beside Aidan, back also to the door, was a blonde feminine silhouette Gwenna instantly recognized.

"Gwenna...?" The smile started to fade from Aidan's face as he took in the princess's unperfected face and fluffy ball gown.

A feral snarl tore through the blonde woman, and her elbow connected with Aidan's temple in one swift movement. Aidan stumbled forward, allowing the Shifter to get behind him, grab the dagger hidden in her pink skirt, and have it pressed to Aidan's neck before he could catch himself.

Marrock tsked, his blonde woman's face twisted into a horrible sneer. "We were enjoying a nice conversation before being rudely interrupted."

Gwenna watched the vein throbbing on his forehead.

"What is going on?" Aidan whispered. "Gwenna? You look..."

"Different?" Marrock sneered. "Funny thing about that, princeling."

"Leave him alone, Marrock," Gwenna said coldly. "You don't have to do this."

"There's no such thing as too much royal blood spilled," the wolf jeered, licking his lips slowly. "Once you have the taste, the craving becomes unimaginable."

Her knuckles were white as she gripped the bow tighter in her hand, already nauseous at his implication.

"He has no royal blood, so there's no need for that," she said steadily. "Let him go."

"This was supposed to be a clean and simple kill before you got here. I certainly can't let him go now; he knows too much," Marrock sneered. "And you, my bride, must be taught what happens when you disobey me. I think I'll take my time with this one and make you watch every moment of it."

"What is going on?" Aidan whispered, eyes wide.

"Your Mother looked especially delicious. If only her horse weren't so easily spooked… I never got the chance to taste and test that theory," Marrock sighed dramatically. "Thankfully, your sister was more than enough to compensate for the loss. I've never tasted anything like her… So sweet. So fresh…"

"Wh-What is this?" Aidan went a little paler at the mention of Catriona's name.

"He's a Shifter, Aidan," Gwenna said shortly, focusing on Marrock's cold, dead eyes and not the filth he was spewing. "The wolf from the woods."

"He?"

With a laugh, Marrock transformed back into his own shape. His ample cleavage was gone, and his large biceps were now locked around Aidan's throat.

"Surprise," he cooed, breathing softly on Aidan's ear.

Aidan flinched, trying to distance them, but only pressed more into the blade at his neck. A single red drop blossomed on his throat, and Aidan froze.

"Careful now," Marrock sang. "Wouldn't want you to hurt yourself." Teeth sharp, he nibbled on Aidan's ear, maintaining direct eye contact with Gwenna. "That's my job."

Aidan cringed but couldn't move away.

"Don't touch him," Gwenna whispered, slowly drawing an arrow from the quiver at her back. "Odd. I feel we've been here before, you and I."

"You couldn't shoot me then and certainly won't shoot me now," Marrock said coolly.

"I wouldn't count on that."

"You'd risk your lover boy's life?"

"I'm a pretty good shot," Gwenna hissed.

"I'll call that bluff." Marrock's thin lips twisted up into a cruel smile. "You may not wear my ring, but we're still Woven together, darling. If I die, so do you. And you may love this spineless idiot for reasons that I cannot fathom, but you certainly don't love him enough to die for him."

"No one has to die," she said through gritted teeth. Her grip tightened on the bowstring, trying to calm her breathing despite her pulse hammering in her ears.

"This boy would *never* do this for you." Marrock lifted one thin eyebrow. "You know that, don't you?"

Aidan flinched, guiltily dropping his gaze from Gwenna's as his cheeks reddened.

She waited for the pain and the grief. That wound whose scab was torn open again and again was sure to open again. And yet… it didn't. Gwenna marveled at it for a moment. Aidan had hurt her for the last time.

"Why are you here?" Gwenna asked wearily, seeing the feral look in the Shifter's eye. "You got what you wanted. You knew I would marry you: there was no way to avoid it. A few more hours and you would have gotten your alliance and your crown and your throne, with no bloodshed. Why do this? Why go after him?"

"Do you want the noble reason?" he smirked.

"I want the truth."

"Would it ease the pain to hear that I wanted him dead to avenge your honor? I saw how he hurt you and swore it would not stand? That an offense to you was now an offense to me?" Marrock asked softly. "Would that make this easier? More palatable, my bride?"

"Tell me the truth," she repeated, steeling herself.

"Or, perhaps, I knew that as long as this miserable excuse of a man still lived, there was still a chance for you to choose him over me." Marrock continued, eyes gleaming. "That I could see it in your eyes: that you *still* loved him. Despite me *proving* to you that he wasn't worthy. Perhaps I knew that if I simply eliminated him as a choice, it would make my life easier and my alliance more secure."

Aidan's handsome face paled.

"Don't pretend this is about me," Gwenna said coldly. "You didn't have to do this, Marrock. I meant it when I said I wanted peace. By The Deep, I saved your life! I spared you from *him*! Why would you do this?"

"What would you like to hear, princess? That I really have built up an affinity for royal blood? Fine." He grinned maliciously. "I ran your mother off a cliff. Your sister hit her head on a rock but didn't go over the edge. She may have been unconscious, but her heart was still beating, and her blood was still warm when I ripped her throat out and feasted. Then I dumped her with your mother and left her for the true animals. My hands have been clean for far too long in order to appease you, but enough is enough. A man has needs."

Gwenna's chin quivered, but her hand on the bow was steady. She refused to visualize the scene where she found Cat.

"Stop," Aidan croaked, watching Gwenna carefully now. "Enough of this. Leave her alone. Do what you want to me, but leave her and her family out of this."

"And you, dear, sweet, foolish Gwenna. Believe me, I wanted to finish you off, just like the rest of your miserable and pathetic family. But no, I *needed* you. I needed you to trust me. To give me what I wanted, what I needed, what I *deserved*. And it was almost too easy. I overcame everything. I murdered your entire family, and you were *still* willing to admit I would make a better husband and king than him." He grabbed a fistful of Aidan's hair, yanking his head back further.

Now it was Gwenna's turn to feel guilty. Tears crept down her cheeks.

"I never said that," Gwenna whispered fiercely, eyes locking onto Aidan's.

"You may as well have," Marrock crowed. "But you want a reason? Maybe I'm here because I couldn't get that royal smell out of my nose. It drove me mad. I knew I shouldn't. I won. I got what I wanted. The alliance was secure: Bannon was *mine*. But when the thrill of victory had faded, that craving was stronger than ever. So here I am. You let me have this," He gestured to Aidan's pale exposed throat. "And I will never spill a drop of blood in Bannon ever again. Consider it my wedding present to you, my bride."

There was a madness in Marrock's eye that Gwenna had never seen before. He had always been cruel, but there was a crazed, feral air about him.

Perhaps Fernella wasn't the only creature who had become Warped.

"Release him, or I will shoot."

"I have plans you don't even realize," Marrock said softly. "Call my bluff. Shoot me down. You'll die right alongside me, and you will doom your people. Fernella knows everything and will move in for the kill without mercy. You heard her, how she thinks she'll become what I never could. Don't you understand? You've lost, Gwenna. This is happening. Now would be the time if you'd like to avert your eyes."

"You're not going to hurt him," Gwena said calmly, steadying her bow arm.

"Gwenna... keep your people safe," Aidan breathed, eyes closed as he resigned himself to his fate.

"He's not going to hurt you!"

There was a loud commotion at the door at the top of the stairwell, and Marrock glanced towards the doorway.

Gwenna could see the frustration in his eyes. What was supposed to be a quiet regicide was becoming more complicated.

"Check the door. Get rid of them." Marrock hissed. "And not a word from you, princeling."

The door at the top of the stairwell squeaked open.

Gwenna backed up but kept her bow trained on the wolf.

"Who is it?" she called up the stairs.

"Kellen. I'm coming down."

"Get rid of him!" Marrock hissed, pulling Aidan's head back even further.

"It'll arouse suspicion!" Gwenna warned, playing for time. "He doesn't go anywhere without Aidan."

"Fine." Marrock snapped. "I'll kill him too."

Hands raised, Kellen rounded the final curve of the spiral staircase and stepped through the doorway.

He froze, taking in the scene: Aidan with a dagger to the throat, the silver-haired Alpha almost strangling him as he threatened him with the knife, and Gwenna, with a bow aimed at the Shifter.

"Not a word," Marrock snarled. "We're in the middle of something."

Kellen kept his hands up in surrender, eyes flickering over to her. "Gwenna?"

"Nice to see you again," she said calmly, eyes on Marrock. "You're just in time."

Before she could reconsider, Gwenna fired once, shooting an arrow directly into the top of Marrock's hand that gripped Aidan by the scalp.

The Shifter roared, dropping the dagger at Aidan's throat in the cistern's water and grabbing his injured hand.

Blood from the hole in Gwenna's hand splattered onto the floor.

But was already restringing another arrow and firing again.

This arrow hit Marrock right in the chest.

Gwenna fell to her knees, the pain in her own heart confirming her aim was true.

CHAPTER 49

AFTER

Marrock and Gwenna collapsed in unison.

In a blur of motion Aidan caught the Queen before she hit the ground. A loud splash sounded as Marrock fell into the water.

Gwenna tried to breathe through the pain, but it came out as a wheezing sound.

Her eyes fluttered.

"Gwenna! Open your eyes!" Aidan yelled, cradling her head. "Look at me! Guards! Someone get the physician!"

"Is she breathing?" Kellen was on her left, kneeling over her. "What's happening to her?"

"There was a Weaving?" Aidan's voice shook. "What does that even mean?"

"It's old magic. A Mage's spell. If he dies, so will she," Kellen said softly.

"She knew… She knew, and she did it anyway…" For perhaps the first time since he arrived in Thornvale, Aidan's eyes were focused solely on Gwenna.

"You have to kiss her!" Kellen said suddenly. "Aidan, it's the only way. She helped me escape that monster, and I was supposed to bring you back to her, but she wouldn't tell me why. But a true love's kiss is the only thing that can break a Mage's spell. You have to do it now!"

"But I…" Aidan faltered.

Gwenna heard the hesitation in his voice and knew exactly what he was trying not to say. She already knew. Once upon a time, Aidan may have been her true love. But she wasn't his.

"It doesn't matter! You have to try!"

Aidan made a sputtering noise, eyes wide with panic.

"Damn it man, you have to do something for once in your life!" Kellen's voice broke on the last word.

Gwenna's pulse rang in her ears, growing noticeably slower.

Aidan looked down at her, and there were tears in those green eyes she had once loved so much. She had dreamt of him weeping for her, but not like this...

She opened her mouth to say something, to reassure him, but nothing came out. Her mind had been made up when she let that arrow fly. This was her choice. Gwenna already knew how he felt.

She knew he wouldn't be able to save her.

But he would be a good king. He would be good to the people. This last thing, this last sacrifice, was something she could do for the kingdom. She could spare them from a monster.

And this way, she would maybe get to see Cat and her mother again. And her grandfather. Maybe even meet her grandmother.

That would be enough. It had to be.

Aidan began to lean down to her, eyes slowly closing. Each moment seemed to last for a hundred. He pulled her in, cradling her like a delicate maiden. It was everything she had once wanted, and yet terribly wrong.

He didn't believe in this. Aidan knew this wasn't going to work. But at least, when The Deep claimed her, Aidan would have kissed her just once.

Gwenna's mouth curved into a weak smile as Aidan leaned in.

Long fingers wrapped around her cold, trembling hands, trying to rub warmth back into them.

She tore her eyes away from Aidan and saw Kellen sitting there, holding her hand and smiling down at her.

"You're going to be ok."

She couldn't hear the words but saw his lips form them.

Warmth spread through her chest.

Gwenna lunged at Kellen, wrapping her arms around his scrawny neck, pulling him down, and kissing him with all the Strength she had left.

Then everything went black.

CHAPTER 50

KELLEN

She was trembling, but so was he.

Her lips were soft, and she smelled faintly of strawberries. Kellen held his Queen tightly, praying it would be enough. He kissed her lips, forehead, round cheeks, and even the tip of her nose.

"Please," he whispered, pulling her limp body close to his chest. "Come on, Gwenna."

There was an agonizing moment of silence, and he closed his eyes against the tears. He tried to save her once before, and she had refused. Now… It was too late.

"Kellen…" Aidan said softly.

Gwenna suddenly burst up from his arms, taking the loudest and most glorious breath he had ever heard.

Kellen stared at her, hands still supporting her as she resurfaced from wherever she had gone. The color was already rushing back to her face, and she was breathing regularly now. Her eyes were bright and full of life.

"Gwenna?" Aidan asked distantly.

But when she looked up, it wasn't at the nobleman but right at the steward himself. Her round eyes focused on him like she had never seen him before, and, for a moment, the rest of the room faded away for him.

"Is that what they mean when they talk about kisses that take your breath away?"

CHAPTER 51

No one spoke.

Three hearts pounded, adrenaline pumping and minds whirling. But no one had any idea what to say or do next.

Kellen blushed, releasing Gwenna and sinking back onto his knees. He watched her carefully, but didn't dare reach out and touch her again.

Gwenna remained slightly out of breath, face also pink from embarrassment. She hugged her knees to her chest, staring at the velvet slippers poking out beneath the tulle.

Bewildered, her fingers gingerly explored the hole in her chest that was just large enough for an arrow to pierce. The bleeding had stopped and her heart beat rhythmically once more. But her skin had not fully healed. The hole in the back of her left hand was the same: not bleeding, but not fully healed either. A Shift or two would fix that. Dry, crusted blood ran down the side of her hand, but she paid it no mind.

Aidan scooted back, sitting down hard on his backside and staring from Gwenna to Kellen and back again. He cleared his throat and fidgeted uncomfortably.

"I don't want to marry you," Gwenna said, breaking the silence and staring straight at Aidan. He flushed and opened his mouth, but she cut him off. "We will maintain our alliance, but the marriage is off."

"I owe you an apology," Aidan mumbled.

"For what?"

"For…" He waved his head vaguely in her direction, blush deepening. How to phrase an apology for not loving someone enough to magically kiss them back to life? "You saved my skin, multiple times, and then I couldn't…"

"I forgive you," Gwenna said softly. That brought his head up, eyes wide with shock. "I'd like for us to find a way to be friends again. If you're open to that…"

He grinned, and for the first time since he arrived at Thornvale, it appeared genuine. It was a tiny glimpse of that chess-playing boy she had once known.

"I would really like that."

Gwenna extended her hand to him. "To friends and allies?"

"Friends and allies," he agreed, shaking on it. "What are you going to do about a King? Are you and Kellen going t–?"

"For the sake of our newly restored friendship, I beg you not to say another word," Gwenna mumbled, burying her head in her hands.

There was so much that needed to be said to Kellen, and so much that she needed to sort out in her own head. They had shared a few looks, and left so many things unspoken.

Kellen was her true love.

She didn't hate the idea. It made her feel fluttery and nervous in a good way. But it was something Gwenna had never allowed herself to even think about until that final moment…

It was a lot to process. And nothing she wanted Aidan muddling about in or teasing her and Kellen about.

Anxious, she snuck a peek over at Kellen. His tanned cheeks were stained pink and he looked lost in thought as well. When he noticed her looking, he winked.

Heart racing, she glanced away again.

"Wait, how did you know that the woman in the pink dress was the wolf?" Aidan asked, drawing Gwenna's attention away. The southern lord looked absolutely dazed. "Why was she– or he– so mad at me? And why did you look different last night?"

"There's a lot we need to talk about," Gwenna sighed, massaging her temples. Her hair, still styled from the ball, was still unbound but the glossy curls were gone. It just felt frizzy and she desperately wanted to braid it as soon as possible. "The Shifters... It's complicated, but we have time. I can explain it."

Kellen cocked his head to the side. "Only a few hours, actually. A group of Shifters are heading this way." Aidan and Gwenna both flinched, faces paling. "No, no! They mean well. They're peaceful."

"More Shifters?" Aidan asked in awe. "How do you possibly know they're peaceful?"

Kellen's jaw dropped, and he ducked his chin as he tried to think. "I... don't know."

Gwenna stared at the Alpha's body floating in the water, Clarity thrumming within her.

"Kellen!" She gasped, grabbing his hand. "You're the new Alpha! You can sense the members of your pack!"

He stared at her hand in his, unable to process what she was saying. He curled his hand around hers instinctively, not allowing her to pull away in embarrassment.

"The Alpha?" Kellen repeated hoarsely, still staring at Gwenna's pale hand.

"That's why your Ma fled after you were born," Gwenna said softly, confident in the knowledge. "She could sense who you would become, and she wanted to hide you from the wolf."

He mumbled something under his breath, eyes growing misty.

"What's an Alpha?" Aidan piped up, reminding the two that he was still sitting there. "What are you talking about?"

Kellen finally looked up, meeting Aidan's confusion with a sheepish grin.

"While we're confessing and apologizing, I might as well speak up." He pulled his floppy hat off, revealing his pointed ears.

Aidan swore, scrambling backwards in alarm. "What are you?"

"A Shifter," Kellen admitted. Aidan glanced over his shoulder at the body of the last Shifter he'd met, still floating face down in the water. "Not like him."

"You're a *good* Shifter?" Aidan asked nervously, and Kellen nodded. "What do you... Shift into?"

"He's a bear," Gwenna said, a note of pride in her voice. Her cheeks flamed and she had to pretend not to notice how Kellen was grinning at her. "A black bear. I believe he may have been scaring some of the villagers."

"You knew?" Aidan demanded. "Wait, how long have you two been togeth–?"

Kellen shook his head quickly.

"Never," Gwenna insisted.

"Not like that," Kellen agreed. "She found out my secret before she surrendered to the wolf."

"Wait, *surrendered*?"

Gwenna nodded guiltily. "I needed to find the Fairies."

"Wait, Fairies are involved now?" Aidan buried his head in his hands. "What is happening?"

"A lot has changed in the last few days," Gwenna admitted.

"My valet is a bear. And an Alpha bear, whatever that means," Aidan muttered, shaking his head in disbelief. "This same bear is also my betrothed's true lov–"

Gwenna kicked his out-stretched boot to silence him.

"Ow!" Aidan grabbed at his foot. "You haven't kicked me since we were children... And you always manage to get my little toe."

"Stop acting like a child then," she scolded.

"Wait... what *are* you going to do about the throne? Who is going to be king if we aren't getting married?" Aidan asked.

She hesitated, suddenly gnawing on her fingertips. "About that…"

"Gwenna should be Queen," Kellen said calmly, and the pair looked over at him. "She broke the curse, and killed the Alpha."

Her heart beat a little faster, and she couldn't hold back the smile that flooded her face.

Aidan ran his fingers through his dark hair, considering. He nodded, still lost in thought, but his face twisted in a grimace.

"Let's get some breakfast and talk about everything: the Shifters, Alpha, Fairies, Mages, curses, *everything*," Gwenna suggested diplomatically. "Nothing has to be decided today. But if Kellen is right, we'll have guests in just a few hours."

"Breakfast sounds good," Aidan agreed weakly.

"Just because we aren't betrothed doesn't mean there isn't a place for you at court, Aidan," she said, bringing his head up again in surprise. "You are a good leader, and the people love you. I'm going to need your help."

"That's kind of you to say," he said, meeting her gaze. "I know I haven't been particularly kind since I arrived. And, I'm sorry about that too. There were a lot of things happening at home before I left, but that's no excuse and I shouldn't have been so rude to you. I'm sorry."

Gwenna smiled softly. "Thank you, Aidan."

Aidan pushed to his feet, stretching his arms overhead as he looked around the cistern.

"I'm going to go find some knights to fish that monster out of the lake." He realized what he said and shot Kellen a guilty look. "Oh, I'm sorry. I didn't mean–"

Kellen waved him off. "Monster is a good title for what he was."

Embarrassed, Aidan nodded. "Anyways… we should get the dead body out of our drinking water sooner rather than later."

"He won't contaminate anything," Gwenna said off-handedly. "The Deep is protecting us."

Aidan and Kellen both stared, but the Queen didn't offer any explanation for why she spoke with such certainty. She just mentally added her gift of Clarity to the list of things she needed to explain over breakfast.

"Ok..." Aidan said slowly, eyes darting between the two of them in confusion. "I'm going to go. And you two should probably figure out whatever is happening between the two of you. There's no way anyone at court will take you seriously if you keep blushing like a fool everytime Kellen speaks."

It was Kellen who kicked this time, missing Aidan's boot and connecting with his shin instead.

Aidan cursed, rubbing his shin indignantly. "I'm going to go before I get kicked again."

"You know you deserve that and much more," Gwenna called as he hobbled through the doorway and started up the spiral staircase.

Aidan's laugh echoed down the stairs, but he didn't disagree with the statement either.

Gwenna and Kellen stared at each other in silence, listening to Aidan's footsteps up the spiral staircase. The door leading to the entrance hall opened and closed with a thud.

"So..." she began.

"How are you feeling?" Kellen asked, warm eyes searching her face carefully.

She swallowed roughly. "A little tired. But good, considering..."

"Good."

Kellen closed the distance between them in a heartbeat, pulling Gwenna against him before she knew what was happening. One hand wrapped around her waist, the other buried itself in her curls.

His lips were on hers and he was kissing her. She leaned into him, kissing him back.

This kiss was softer and sweeter than the first, more of an anxious question to see if there really was something between them.

Kellen pulled away too soon, looking down to stare into her eyes.

"I've wanted to do that for a long time," he told her solemnly.

"I think I did too…" Gwenna admitted, surprising herself.

"I'm sorry I waited so long."

"Your timing was perfect," she assured him.

Kellen planted a kiss on her forehead, slowly unwrapping his arms from around her and moving back a respectful distance. "What do we do now?"

"Well… I'm Queen. And you're the Alpha," Gwenna said slowly, trying to wrap her mind around the new world she was in. "The curse is broken. But now I think we have a kingdom to mend. Together."

"Together sounds nice." He grinned.

"I thought so too." She smiled back.

"What about you and I?" Kellen asked, a look of fear in his eyes. "That first kiss meant–"

She held up a finger to his lips.

"We have a lifetime to figure out what the first kiss meant," Gwenna said gently. "Maybe we should start with breakfast."

The End.

EPILOGUE

The residents of Irrywellium poured through the Warding, heading back towards their home in Thornvale.

No one noticed the cloaked figure watching from the trees.

Families passed paces from her, herding their children and carrying everything they owned on their backs. Overnight, their homes in Thornvale had been magically restored to how they had been before King Domhnall's attack. The new Alpha was aligned with the Queen of Bannon. Peace was assured.

They were going home.

No one mentioned the previous Alpha. His reign was a brutal and cruel one. There was no one to mourn him. His manor had succumbed to a mysterious fire the night before the Alpha traveled to the human's ball. No deaths had occurred, but the manor was ruined beyond repair.

The forest quieted as the Mages and Shifters picked their way down the trail towards Thornvale. No one looked behind at what they left.

A gnarled hand emerged from the folds of the black cloak and adjusted the cowl of her cloak.

The witch was not going to Thornvale. Not yet.

Her lamb was dead, slain by the humans like she had warned. He never listened.

No, she had her business in the mountains to look in on first. They would not need her there for long. But she was all they had left.

Then, she would turn to Thornvale. She could already feel her sister's blood calling to her.

But first, the mountains.

* * *

If you enjoyed Cursebreaker, *please take a moment to leave a rating or review—it really makes a difference!*

If you are hoping for more of these characters, don't miss Crownmaker, *a novella exploring the Kaldonna family's background before Aidan takes center stage. Are you ready?*

OTHER BOOKS BY SYDNEY HUNT...

A novella exploring the Kaldonna family before Aidan Kaldonna takes center stage in Crownmaker, book 1.5 in The Chronicles of The Deep.

Bannon and all of its inhabitants will return in book two of The Chronicles of The Deep Book 2 - *Wishmaker*, a dark Cinderella retelling.

ACKNOWLEDGMENTS

I want to thank the readers that made this book a reality. I'm so humbled and grateful by your support and love.

To my ARC and Beta Readers, please know that your comments, feedback, and encouragement were invaluable. I am grateful to each and every one of you who took a chance on me and this book.

I am the luckiest girl in the world to have landed in such an amazing writer's group. Daniela Mera and Elayna Gallea, there's no way Gwenna's story would have ended up in the hands of readers without your feedback and cheerleading. Thank you for being my sounding board, cheerleader, and critic. I'm so grateful for your reassurances that something is working, and your honesty when it isn't. You saw this thing through from baby idea to full book, and I'm so grateful that you were so patient with my little baby author self.

Kourtney Fullmer, my geological queen, thank you for all of your feedback. Science is not my strong suit, but I'm grateful for your ability to apply real world geography to my little fantasy world. The cenote would not have worked without you.

I had no idea what to expect when meeting up with another writer from Facebook, but Heather I'm so glad I did. You make me better and I'm forever grateful.

Gruncle Dave, I promise that when I ask for medical or anatomical insight in the future I will clarify upfront that it's for book research. Your dedication to the dead horse was admirable. Also thanks for setting me up with Dean.

To Kelsey and Britney, I wouldn't be here without you two. Thank you for believing in me.

Mom and Dad, I love you. Thanks for being patient with your bookish daughter.

Dean, thank you for being on my team. Thank you for believing in me more than I did, and for pushing me to go sit and write even when I didn't want to. Thank you for all of the afternoon, evening, and weekends where you were solo parenting without complaint so I could write down the voices in my head. Every love story I'll ever tell really stems from you. I'm a better person because of you. I like you, and I love you.

There's nothing wrong with the fairytales I grew up with, and everybody knows I'm a sucker for a Disney movie. But C and S, I hope you know how strong you are. Not every prince is charming, some bad guys are just bad, and you are absolutely the author of your own story.

S2, this first book baby may have taken all of my attention recently but know that I am so excited to meet you. Thank you for a relatively easy pregnancy. I can't wait to see who you are.

ABOUT THE AUTHOR

Sydney Hunt has loved fantasy since Harry Potter said "troll boogers". She loves board games, planning movie nights with elaborately themed snacks, and Dr Pepper. Should she ever disappear off the grid, you could find her happily living somewhere amongst penguins (but don't go looking for her—she's quite content as a hermit). A resident of Las Vegas, Sydney is living the dream with her dreamboat husband, two fantastic girls, a little boy on the way, and a very chatty golden lab named Ginger. You can find information on her newsletter and upcoming projects here:

linktr.ee/authorsydneyhunt